sisters
under the
RISING
SUN

Born in New Zealand, Heather Morris is an international number-one bestselling author, who is passionate about stories of survival, resilience and hope. In 2003, while working in a large public hospital in Melbourne, Heather was introduced to an elderly gentleman who 'might just have a story worth telling'. The day she met Lale Sokolov changed both their lives. Lale's story formed the basis for *The Tattooist of Auschwitz* and the follow-up novel, *Cilka's Journey*. In 2021, she published the phenomenal conclusion to the Tattooist trilogy, Three Sisters, after being asked to tell the story of three Holocaust survivors who knew Lale from their time in Auschwitz-Birkenau. Together, her novels have sold more than 16 million copies worldwide. In 2020, she published *Stories of Hope*, her account of her journey to writing the story of Lale Sokolov's life. Her fourth novel, *Sisters under the Rising Sun*, tells the story of the women imprisoned by the Japanese army during WWII and of their courage and determination to survive. In 2024, *The Tattooist of Auschwitz*, a major new series based on Heather's book, was released by Sky to great acclaim.

Also by Heather Morris

The Tattooist of Auschwitz trilogy
Cilka's Journey
Three Sisters

Sisters under the Rising Sun

Stories of Hope

sisters
under the
RISING
SUN

HEATHER
MORRIS

ZAFFRE

First published in the UK in 2023 by
ZAFFRE
An imprint of Zaffre Publishing Group
A Bonnier Books UK company
4th Floor, Victoria House, Bloomsbury Square, London, WC1B 4DA
Owned by Bonnier Books
Sveavägen 56, Stockholm, Sweden

This is a work of fiction based loosely on historical events. It is not
intended to be a true and accurate version of the events depicted,
and characters are either entirely fictional or used fictitiously.

A CIP catalogue record for this book is
available from the British Library.

Paperback ISBN: 978-1-78658-225-6

All music and photos of Norah Chambers and family courtesy of Seán Conway
Image YMS 16139 reprinted with the kind permission of the Australian Manuscripts Collection,
State Library Victoria
Photo of Nesta James with husband Alexander Noy: courtesy of Kathleen Davies and
Brenda Pegrum
Images 044480 and P01701.003 reprinted with the kind permission
of the Australian War Memorial

Map illustration by Jake Cook

Every reasonable effort has been made to trace copyright-holders of material
reproduced in this book, but if any have been inadvertently overlooked,
the publishers would be glad to hear from them.

Also available as an ebook and an audiobook

1 3 5 7 9 10 8 6 4 2

Typeset by IDSUK (Data Connection) Ltd
Printed and bound in Great Britain by Clays Ltd, Elcograf S.p.A.

Zaffre is an imprint of Zaffre Publishing Group
A Bonnier Books UK company
www.bonnierbooks.co.uk

To nurses everywhere – past, present and future
You make the world a better place

To Sally and Seán Conway
Thank you for sharing your mother/grandmother's story –
Norah Chambers

To Kathleen Davies, Brenda Pegrum and Debra Davies
Thank you for sharing your cousin's story –
Nesta (James) Noy

In 1942, the Japanese Army entered World War II, conquering the islands of the Pacific, reaching Malaya and the then British colony of Singapore, which fell to the Japanese on 15th February, 1942.

The *Vyner Brooke*, a merchant ship carrying desperate evacuees away from Singapore, was bombarded from the air by the Japanese Air Force. Within a few hours, she lay broken on the seabed.

Many survivors made it to a remote island in Sumatra, Indonesia. They were soon captured by the Japanese, the men and women and children separated and sent to prisoner-of-war camps deep in the jungle, along with hundreds of others rounded up by the invading army. The camps were places of starvation and brutality, where disease ran rampant.

They would remain there, moved from camp to camp, fighting for survival, for over three and a half years.

This is their story . . .

PROLOGUE

Norah Chambers sits on Sally's bed, waiting for her daughter to wake up. The conversation that follows is the most painful of her life. Telling her of the decision she and her husband, John, have made to send Sally away with her aunt Barbara and cousins is received just as she expected. She holds on tight to her distraught little girl, desperate to stay with her mum and dad, crying that she will not leave them, not now, not ever. Even when her two cousins burst into the room full of the news that they are about to embark on an adventure, and sail the seas no less, Sally barely registers their presence.

'Sally, we're going to Australia!' they chant. 'On a big ship!'

Singapore is falling; what choice does Norah have? John is in hospital with typhus. As soon as he is better, they will follow, she promises Sally.

On the car journey to the wharf Sally doesn't stop crying, her face turned away from her mother to the window. Norah's attempts to comfort her are shrugged off. As they walk to the boat, Sally wraps her small arms tight around her mother's waist. It's going to be hard to let go, for either of them.

An explosion nearby only compounds their fear, their terror of what lies ahead, and Sally's cries erupt into petrified screams. Norah is frozen, numbed by the horror of what she is witnessing, the distress she is causing to the most precious person in her life. As the world explodes around them, Barbara swiftly lifts Sally into her arms and runs to the waiting gangplank.

'Daddy and I will be right behind you. Be a good girl, my darling, we'll be with you in a few days, I promise,' Norah screams after her daughter.

Sally continues to sob, her arms reaching for her mother. Norah takes an involuntary step forwards, only to have her younger sister, Ena, grab her arm and pull her away. They watch as Barbara and Sally disappear onto the deck and out of sight. There will be no happy waving from the boat or the dockside, from either mother or daughter.

'Will I ever see her again?' Norah cries.

Part I
The Fall of Singapore

CHAPTER 1

Singapore
February 1942

'I don't want to go! Please. Please don't make us go, Norah.'
Ena Murray's cries are swallowed up by the screams of
women and children, by explosions erupting around them and
the screeching of Japanese warplanes overhead.

'Run! Run!' parents implore their sons and daughters, but it's
too late. Another missile hits its target and the allied ship
harboured in the Singapore wharf flies apart.

As the shrapnel rains down, Norah's husband, John, and Ena's
husband, Ken Murray, crouch beside their wives, shielding them
from the flying debris. But no good will come of staying put. Ken
helps the sisters to their feet, while John, gasping for breath, tries
to stand.

'Ena, we have to get on, we have to go now!' Norah is still
imploring her sister to board HMS *Vyner Brooke*. There is may-
hem all around, a terrible urgency to get as far away as possible
from this chaos, to find sanctuary. Norah takes a brief moment
to wrap her arms around her husband. John should still be in

hospital; he is so weak, and can barely catch his breath, but he would use the last ounce of his strength to protect these women.

'Ena, please listen to your sister,' says Ken. 'You have to leave, my darling. I'm going back to your parents, I promise I will take care of them.'

'They're *our* parents,' Norah replies. 'It's us who should be looking after them.'

'You have a daughter somewhere out there, Norah,' says Ken. 'You and John have to find Sally. And you must look after Ena for me too.' Ken knows he is the only one who can stay in Singapore to take care of his parents-in-law. John is desperately sick and so is the women's father, James – too sick to attempt to leave. Margaret, their mother, has refused to abandon him.

Another bomb erupts close by and everyone ducks. Behind them, Singapore is on fire; ahead, the sea is littered with the burning wrecks of ships, boats, big and small.

'Go! Go while you still can. If the ship doesn't leave now, it won't get out of the harbour, and you need to be on board.' Ken yells to be heard. He kisses Norah, squeezes John's arm and pulls Ena into a tight embrace, kissing his wife one last time before he pushes her towards the ship.

'I love you,' Ena calls out, her voice breaking.

'Get out of this hellhole. Find Sally. Find Barbara and the boys. I won't be far behind you,' Ken shouts to their retreating figures.

Norah, John and Ena are amidst the crowd of passengers now, forced to move along the wharf towards the ship.

'Sally, we have to find Sally,' John mumbles, his legs giving way beneath him. Norah and Ena each take an arm and hurry him along.

Norah has no more words. The cries of her daughter fill her head as she stumbles towards her destiny. '*I don't want to go.*

6

Please let me stay with you, please, Mummy.' Just a few days earlier, she had put eight-year-old Sally on a different ship and sent her away.

'*I know you don't, darling,*' she had cajoled. '*If there was any way we could stay together, we would. I need you to be a strong little girl for me and go with Aunty Barbara and your cousins. Daddy and I will be with you before you know it. Just as soon as he's better.*'

'*But you promised you wouldn't send me away, you promised.*' Sally had been beside herself, the tears flowing freely, her cheeks blotchy.

'*I know I did, but sometimes mummies and daddies have to break their promises to keep their little girls safe. I promise—*'

'*Don't say it – don't say you promise when I know you can't.*'

'*Come on, Sally, can you hold Jimmy's hand?*' Barbara had said. She was Norah and Ena's older sister. She spoke softly to her niece. There was some comfort here for Norah; Sally would be safe with her family.

'She didn't look back once,' Norah whispers to herself as she trudges along. 'She just boarded the ship and was gone.'

Entering the cordoned-off area of the wharf, passengers with the approved paperwork gather. Amongst them are terrified adults and wailing children, each of them struggling under the weight of their most essential possessions.

A group of Australian Army nurses wave their paperwork at the officials and are hurried through the fenced-off area. They stand to one side as civilians file past before another group of women in the same uniform burst through the gates. The reunited nurses embrace, greeting each other like long-lost friends. Amongst the newcomers, a petite woman pushes her way through.

'Vivian, Betty, over here,' she calls.

'Hey, Betty, it's Nesta!'

The three women huddle in a hug. Sisters Nesta James, Betty Jeffrey and Vivian Bullwinkel became firm friends in Malaya, where they were posted to nurse Allied soldiers before it was overrun by the Japanese army. Like everyone else here, they had been forced to flee to Singapore.

'It's so good to see you again,' says Nesta, overjoyed to see her friends. 'I didn't know if you'd left with the others yesterday.'

'Betty was meant to leave yesterday but managed to go AWOL when they were leaving for the ship. We both hoped we wouldn't be sent home, there's just so much to do here,' Vivian says.

'Matron's gone to plead our case one last time. We're not on the ship yet, so maybe High Command will see the benefit of letting us stay here in Singapore with those who are too ill to leave,' Nesta tells them.

'They're boarding the launches now, she'd better hurry,' Betty says, looking at the line of men, women and children climbing into the wildly bobbing boats that will deliver them to the HMS *Vyner Brooke*. Bombs continue to hit their targets, churning the sea into waves and crashing them against the wharf.

Nesta is staring at the launches where the passengers are embarking.

'It looks like someone could do with a hand; I'll be right back.'

'Do you need some help?' Nesta asks Norah and Ena, who are trying to work out how to help John down the steep steps and onto one of the boats. It is now half full of distraught passengers, some weeping, others paralysed with fear. Norah feels a hand on her shoulder.

Norah turns to see the smiling face of a pint-sized woman in a nurse's white uniform. She looks so tiny that Norah wonders how she could possibly help them, given that she, her husband and her sister are taller than the average man or woman.

'I'm Sister Nesta James, a nurse with the Australian Army. I'm stronger than I look, and I've been trained to help patients much bigger than me, so don't worry.'

'I think we'll be fine,' Norah tells her. 'But thank you.'

'Why don't one of you get into the launch while two of us help the gentleman down and you can take over from there?' Nesta is politely insistent. 'Have you been in hospital?' she asks John, taking his arm as Norah lets go.

'Yes,' he says, allowing her to guide him towards the boat. 'Typhus.'

As soon as Norah is safely in the launch, Ena and Nesta help John into her waiting arms.

'Aren't you coming with us?' Ena asks the young nurse.

'I'm with my friends. We'll get the next launch.'

Ena looks around and sees a large group of women dressed in the same uniform.

As the launch pulls away with Norah, John and Ena on board, they hear singing from the wharf. The nurses, arms around each other's shoulders, stand proudly, singing with all their might, loud enough to drown out a nearby petrol tank detonating into a ball of flames.

'Now is the hour when we must say goodbye
Soon you'll be sailing far across the sea
While you're away, oh then remember me
When you return, you'll find me waiting here'
Another bomb goes off on the wharf.

* * *

9

Matron Olive Paschke catches Nesta's eye. 'Matron Drummond made one final plea to the authorities to let us stay here and care for our men, but the lieutenant told her that our request is denied.'

'It was worth one more try, wasn't it? It just doesn't seem right to be abandoning them when they will most likely need us. How did Matron take it?'

'The only way she could, by simply raising her eyebrows at him,' replies Matron Paschke. 'If she'd said what she was thinking, she'd have been in trouble.'

'Which means she doesn't accept it but will begrudgingly go along with it. I wouldn't have expected anything less from her.' Nesta shakes her head.

'Come on, let's get the others. I think we're the last to leave.'

Once on board the HMS *Vyner Brooke*, Sister Vivian Bullwinkel entertains them with her knowledge of the ship.

'She is named after the third rajah of Sarawak and now has HMS in front of her name because the Royal Navy requisitioned her. She's only meant to carry twelve passengers but has a crew of forty-seven.'

'How do you know all this?' Betty asks.

'I had dinner with the rajah, didn't I? Yeah, I know, me – little old Sister Vivian Bullwinkel from Broken Hill – had dinner with a rajah. Not alone, mind you, there were others there.'

'Oh, Bully, only you would add the last bit, the rest of us would leave it at *I had dinner with the rajah*,' Betty says, laughing at her friend.

When the last nurse is on board, the captain gives the order to slip anchor and proceed with caution. He knows British minefields lie ahead and will be as big a threat as the enemy dominating the skies above.

As the sun sets, the passengers watch as Singapore burns, the bombing, shelling and gunfire relentless. Above the noise of the death of a city, Norah, John and Ena turn away from the cacophony to the sweet singing of the Australian nurses on deck. And, just for a moment, that's all they can hear.

CHAPTER 2

HMS *Vyner Brooke*, **Banka Strait**
February 1942

'*You'll come a-waltzing Matilda with me . . .*'
'What a cheery bunch those nurses are. We're lucky to have them on board, given everything.' Norah is struggling to keep her voice light and airy.

The final words of 'Waltzing Matilda' are accompanied by the piercing shriek of air-raid sirens echoing across the harbour towards the slowly departing ship. An oil storage tank explodes, throwing debris into the air. Around them, burning vessels are sucked into seething waves. Only the skills of an accomplished captain will get them through the harbour, past the mines laid by the British Navy to thwart the Japanese Navy, and out to sea.

Norah turns away from the apocalyptic scenes.

'Do you want to see if there's a place downstairs to rest?' John asks as he stares out to sea, but it's obvious to Norah he's trying to conceal his discomfort at needing her help.

'I'm happy to stay on deck; there are mothers with children here and lots of old people. I think they should take the cabins,' Ena suggests.

John looks at Norah. Her response will decide if they venture below deck or not.

'Quite right, Ena, let's find some space up here where we can lie down. We all need a minute.'

Norah can see the relief wash over his face. She knows her husband so well; now they won't have to help him stagger up and down the stairs.

As they shuffle along the deck looking for a space to settle down, they stop for a moment to watch the nurses, gathered around an older nurse as she issues instructions.

'Must be their matron,' Norah offers.

'We'll head down to the saloon where the captain has given us permission to set ourselves up. We have a lot of planning to do, and we must be prepared for anything,' the woman in a matron's uniform tells her nurses. Another matron stands amongst them, beaming, her pride in her nurses evident. She is clearly happy for her younger colleague to take charge.

As the nurses file towards the hatch, Norah, Ena and John claim some space on the upper deck for the first night of their escape. The fires burning along the shore compete with the brilliance of the setting sun over what was once a tropical paradise. Now, it resembles Armageddon.

John slides down the ship's bulkhead, coming to rest on the wooden floor planks. He indicates for Norah and Ena to join him, and they take a seat either side of the sick man, huddling close to him to keep him upright. John wraps an arm around each woman and they watch their world disappear, in silence.

The nurses file into the saloon, chattering amongst themselves. They are excited, terrified and, right now, they need the comfort of their friends and colleagues.

13

'Quiet, girls! We have a lot to do.' Matron Olive Paschke calls them to order. 'We are going to split into four teams. Some of you will be responsible for those below deck and others for those above. I will assign each a senior who will be responsible for the appointed area, along with the discipline and morale of their group. But first I want to make it clear that should the worst happen, and we must abandon ship, you are to assist with the evacuation, and we will be the last to leave.'

Matron watches her nurses take this in. The girls glance at one another, nodding; fully understood.

Nesta, second in command to Matron Paschke, is the first nurse appointed to lead a team. Quickly, efficiently, the nurses divide the medications and bandages between them.

As the nurses assemble, Matron Drummond addresses the entire group.

'First, I want to say how incredibly proud I am of all of you. We'll get through this together. I've been advised by the captain that there are not enough lifeboats on board for everyone if we must abandon ship. Therefore, please always keep your life jackets on. Sleep in them; they could mean the difference between life and death.'

'And,' adds Matron Paschke, 'if you end up in the sea, don't forget to take your shoes off. Girls, I am not going to sugar-coat our voyage. We'll be bombed, there's no doubt about it. I'm sorry, but it's inevitable.' The matron pulls back her shoulders, stands taller, a show of strength for her nurses. 'Now, let's head to our allocated areas and practise evacuation. Matron Drummond and I will come around and check on you. Oh, one more thing, if we are to abandon ship, Matron Drummond will give the order. Understood?'

Nesta leads her group up top and to the port side of the ship. Norah, John and Ena watch them practise the drill of assisting people over the side, identifying where ropes can be used. Nesta tells her nurses they will be dealing with terrified, possibly injured, men, women and children. In gentle tones they rehearse the words of comfort they will use to persuade unwilling passengers to jump into the sea.

'Remember, there will be people who don't know how to swim, including children and even babies. Tell them there will be help at hand once they're in the water. There are portable life rafts which the crew will throw down to us.'

Norah is watching Sister Nesta James, distracted for a moment from their surroundings to admire the young woman's command of the nurses in her charge. Nesta catches her eye and gives her a broad smile. She evidently remembers helping this trio earlier. Her smile is saying, *Nothing to worry about here. All part of the job.* Norah isn't sure she's reassured but she appreciates the gesture, the humour in Nesta's smile as they sail through a war zone.

But, too soon, Norah becomes aware once more of the danger they are in. She buries her face in John's arms, stifling the sobs that threaten to break free, telling herself she can't cry, can't be a baby after having watched the brave nurses show their unwavering commitment to saving those who need their help.

'You're thinking about Sally, aren't you?' John whispers into her hair.

'Did she go through this, John?' Norah weeps. 'Was she thrown overboard by a well-meaning person? If only we knew she'd made it, where she was right now. Tell me she's safe.'

'I would know if she wasn't, I would feel it,' John reassures her, lifting her chin from his shoulder with shaking fingers. 'You would too. You'd feel it here.' He places a hand over Norah's heart. 'Our Sally is safe, my darling, you must believe that. Hold on to that image and we'll be with her very soon.'

Ena leans across John to hug her distraught sister. 'She's safe, Norah. She's waiting for you,' she comforts her.

'Well done, girls!' Matron Drummond says, after observing Nesta at work with her nurses. 'Sister James, finish off what you're doing and take your girls downstairs to rest. Unfortunately, we've heard there are food shortages on board, so Matron Paschke and I have already said we will donate our allocation to the children. I'll see you down there.'

'Excuse me, Sister James, but I can't swim,' one of the nurses announces.

'You're in good company, neither can Matron Paschke,' Nesta tells her.

'Really? D'you know that for a fact?' The nurse brightens.

'I do. We were together in Malacca in Malaya. It had the most wonderful beaches and when we were off duty, we often went there to swim. We couldn't even get Matron to have a paddle, she was terrified of the water.'

Few of the sleeping and exhausted passengers notice when the ship's engine is turned off, or the anchor dropped. The captain has decided not to run the risk of detection in the exposed Banka Strait. But a moment later, he changes his mind.

'We can't stay here,' he tells his crew. 'Let's go full speed ahead towards the Strait. Fast as we can.'

The sun wakes those sleeping on the deck. The oppressive heat wakes those below deck. The nurses set about serving the meagre rations, before heading back to the saloon for further orders.

'Matron and I met with Captain Borton a short while ago,' Matron Drummond tells the assembled group. 'Unfortunately, we're lagging behind where he needs us to be. Rest while you can. Will the leaders please stay, and everyone else go upstairs where it might be a little cooler?'

'Please remind your nurses to always wear their Red Cross armbands,' Matron Paschke tells the group leaders. 'Should the worst happen, they will be identifiable. You never know, maybe the Japanese pilots will see them and spare the ship and its passengers. Captain Borton has told us if the ship's siren sounds short blasts, it means we're under attack. In which case, proceed to your duty stations and await further orders. If the siren sounds a continuous blast, that means abandon ship, and you all know what to do. Go and speak to your girls now; Matron and I will shortly come around and inspect your stations.'

The top deck is busy with the passengers trying to escape the heat and humidity below. Many doze where they can find a little shade. Many don't hear the approaching plane. Those that do, stand transfixed, eyes raised to the skies, watching as the aircraft dips towards the sea and heads straight for them.

'Take cover! Take cover!' booms a voice over the loudspeaker. And then it is bedlam.

Passengers scramble as the machine gun fires on the deck from the air. The bullets strike hard, ricocheting off metal fixings in a second attempt to find their mark.

'Run! Run!' John screams, grabbing the arms of Norah and Ena. But, in the end, it is they who drag him away.

The nurses race to their allotted stations, ready for what the next moments will bring. The attack, however, is over, and the skies are once again clear. A collective sigh of relief is drawn. There are few injuries to the passengers, but the ship's lifeboats have taken the brunt of the attack, rendering many of them useless.

* * *

'We're sitting ducks out here; the bombers will be on their way soon enough. We have to get into the Strait if we're to stand a chance of outrunning what's coming,' Captain Borton tells his crew.

As the ship jerks into action, the captain scans the horizon and spies land ahead. Now, if they can just make it in one piece.

'Sound the all-clear. For now,' he tells an officer.

'Let's stay down here,' John suggests. He looks exhausted and Norah feels his forehead to find his fever has returned. There will only be so many more times he can struggle up those stairs.

The nurses have heard the all-clear and immediately head back to the saloon from their different locations, for further orders. Thankfully, they are all able to report only minor injuries amongst the passengers, mainly from flying pieces of splintered wood where the bullets struck the ship. Now, the engines begin to scream at the task ahead, as the ship heads straight towards the Banka Strait. There will be no more zigzagging to avoid mines.

It isn't long before the sirens sound again and calls of 'Approaching aircraft!' reach the ears of those below deck.

These passengers can't see the planes coming, but they feel the effects of the first bomb exploding in the water all the same, rocking the waves and wildly pitching the ship to and fro.

'One!' someone calls out.

Captain Borton commences evasive manoeuvres as he attempts to avoid the bombs now raining down on them. Word has spread there is land ahead; now is the time to pray for a miracle.

'Two, three . . . Fourteen, fifteen . . . Twenty-six, twenty-seven.' Norah, John and Ena listen as another passenger counts the number of bombs falling around them; miraculously, not one seems to have struck the ship.

'Twenty-eight, twenty-nine . . .'

And now an explosion rips through the ship, throwing passengers into the air, into the walls, into each other. Panic breaks out and everyone below deck scrambles for the passageways to head upstairs.

'Are you all right? Are you injured?' John shouts to Norah and Ena.

'We're fine, but we need to get on deck, it's not safe down here,' Norah yells.

'I agree. You two go on ahead, I'll follow you.'

'Help him up, Ena; he goes where we go,' she says, looking squarely at John. 'That's our pact.'

The women help John to his feet, sandwiching him between them.

Norah leads the way, pushing through the crowd, being pushed by the crowd, everyone now desperate to escape the sinking ship.

'Off you go, girls, we'll see you up top,' Matron tells the nurses still in the saloon.

Nesta and her team head for the nearest staircase, towards the light of day, more than ready to carry out the work they are trained for. As she bursts onto the deck, another plane is approaching, firing madly from its guns, hitting those already wounded, further destroying the lifeboats. Nesta instructs her nurses to stay where they are until the plane is gone.

'Look for injured, for those you can help. Come on!' she shouts.

Norah is heading up too, still hanging on to John. It is a slow climb, made even slower by the girl in front, who is struggling to place one foot in front of the other. Norah gently touches her shoulder.

'You're injured,' she tells her. 'Badly injured. Your back . . .'

'Am I?' the girl says, oblivious of the wounds, her blood-soaked dress.

Finally, the injured girl staggers onto the deck, where she collapses.

'Nurse! I need a nurse over here,' Norah shouts. She sits down beside the girl, gently laying her head in her lap.

Nesta is the first nurse by her side. She feels for the girl's pulse in her neck and checks her eyes. 'She's gone, I'm sorry; there's nothing we can do for her,' she tells Norah.

'We need to leave her, Norah. I'm sorry, my darling, but we have to get off this ship,' John whispers. 'We'll have to swim for land.'

Once again, the two women help John to walk as they are swept up by the crowds trying desperately to reach the lifeboats.

Matrons Paschke and Drummond are still below deck; they will make sure everyone is above or on their way up before they leave. An eerie sense of calm pervades the room as the passengers shuffle out, but then comes a woman's cry.

'Stop! Everybody stand still!'

The world is in chaos, the ship is sinking, the wounded are dying, but everybody freezes at the shrill voice.

'My husband has dropped his glasses,' the woman announces.

As ridiculous as their situation is, both matrons and many of the passengers begin to laugh before pushing on up the stairs.

The drills each nurse has practised now come into play. Nesta's team, less two nurses who never made it on deck, begin to help women and children into the lifeboats. Above the noise, the distress, the cries of *help me* from the injured and terrified, Matron Paschke issues instructions in her clear, patient voice. Lifeboats full, children are using the rope ladders to lower themselves into the sea, their parents behind them.

* * *

20

'I'll go in first,' Ena tells Norah. 'You help John, then join us.'

Ena grabs hold of a rope dangling over the side of the ship. The rope runs through her fingers as she slides down into the water. Immediately, John lands beside her, having taken the quicker route and jumped. His life jacket brings him to the surface and Ena reaches out to grab him. She screams as her hand closes around his arm. Her palms are scraped raw and bloody from the friction of the rope. She waves frantically to Norah, yelling, 'Jump! Norah, jump, don't use the rope.'

Seeing Ena waving, Norah grabs the rope, lowers herself over the side and slides down.

John sees Ena's hands and as Norah hits the water, he frantically tries to swim towards her, knowing she too will be registering the pain of rope burns and torn flesh.

But they don't have time to nurse their wounds, they have to get away from the sinking ship. John rejects their help; he knows he is on his own, and must now find whatever strength remains to him to help them.

With the seamless flow of men, women and children entering either the lifeboats or the water, Nesta registers the dwindling numbers remaining on deck. Nearby, a passenger thrusts a small boy into the arms of one of the crewmen.

'Matron, over here, we have a lifeboat for you both.'

Nesta watches as Matrons Paschke and Drummond are helped into the remaining lifeboat. The ship lurches and they topple over, instantly giggling at their most unladylike positions as they help each other regain their composure. As the lifeboat is lowered over the side of the ship, Matron Drummond calls out.

'Time to go, girls! Abandon ship!' she yells.

'We'll meet on the shore to get teed up,' Matron Paschke adds.

As the lifeboat disappears over the side, Nesta turns to the remaining nurses.

'You heard Matron, it's our turn. You have all done an amazing job, thank you. Now, take off your shoes, hold your life jacket under your chin and jump.'

'What's the use of taking my shoes off, I can't swim, so I might as well drown with my shoes on,' a nurse comments.

Nesta looks around and sees part of a door lying uselessly on the deck.

'No one's drowning,' she tells the defeated nurse. 'Help me with this door. We'll chuck it over the side and after you land, you can hang on to it.'

They launch the broken door overboard. Nesta watches as the nurse jumps, surfaces, and scrambles towards the plank, hanging on tight as her feet paddle away.

Looking around one last time, Nesta pulls up her dress, tugging her stockings down, before kicking them and her shoes away. No longer in proper uniform, she jumps overboard.

All around them in the water are cries for help, cries for loved ones. These pleas combine with the symphony of noise from the creaking and breaking up of the HMS *Vyner Brooke*.

Norah, Ena and John pause for a moment to look back, watching in horror as the ship rolls onto her side. Her stern rises from the water, proudly displaying her propeller, before silently, gracefully, sinking into the depths below.

'There she goes,' John says quietly.

'Oh, no! Over there,' Ena suddenly cries.

Others in the water have also noticed the Japanese aircraft heading straight for the stranded passengers. All around them, the sea begins to churn as bullets strike the water; some finding a target. Too many who have survived this leap into the unknown now float lifeless in the waves, their fight over.

'Mummy! Mummy, where are you?'

Ena and Norah spot a girl of barely school age disappear beneath a wave. Swimming away from John, the pain in their damaged hands forgotten, they move towards the plaintive cries. A wave throws the young girl back to the surface and Ena reaches out and grabs her, pulling her close.

'I've got you. I've got you. You're going to be all right,' she murmurs.

'Hold on to her, Ena. Let's get back to John,' Norah calls.

'Where's my mummy? I can't find her,' the girl wails, taking in water and spluttering it out again.

'We'll find her, I promise,' Ena says. 'Look, just hang on to me and we'll float. What's your name?'

'June. I'm June. My mummy's name is Dorothy. I'm five years old.'

'Nice to meet you, June. My name is Ena and this is my big sister, Norah. We'll look after you until we can find your mummy.'

Ena grasps June around the waist and slowly they paddle over to John, who is swimming towards them. The current is dragging everyone away from the sunken ship, but not fast enough to prevent some from being engulfed in the oil bubbling up from the ship's fractured tanks.

'Can it get any worse?' John laments as they try to brush the oil from their faces. With no clean water, their attempts are futile. 'Let's try to make it to the island.'

'We seem to be moving away from it,' Norah says.

'It's the current, it will keep pushing us out into the Strait. Let's rest a little and gather our strength before we swim hard for land.'

With June clinging to Ena, they bob along, letting the current take them where it will, which isn't where they need to be.

Nesta hits the water hard, sinking far below the waves. She lets go of her life jacket and, using both hands, fights to reach the surface. Bursting free, she gasps for air and is immediately struck by a floating body. Her instinct is to check for signs of life, but she soon realises there is no hope for this poor man.

Hearing cries of 'help', Nesta swims towards the needy. She sees several nurses clinging to a floating plank, but they call out to reassure her they are fine. She kicks her legs, heading for a lifeboat that is moving away from her. As she rises on a wave, she recognises Matrons Drummond and Paschke, along with several nurses, some of whom are injured. One of her colleagues has two small children draped around her neck. Hanging on to the sides of the boat are desperate men and women. Nesta is relieved: her friend Olive Paschke is safe, and Matron Drummond is with her. They are all doing what they're trained to do: care for the vulnerable.

Betty Jeffrey swims towards her. 'Nesta, Nesta, are you OK?' she calls out.

'Betty, yes, I'm fine, you?'

'Uninjured, trying to find others, I don't think we all made it,' Betty says, her voice breaking.

'Over here! Over here!'

The women weave around to see several other nurses treading water together. Without comment, both women swim towards the group.

'Is everyone OK, any injured?' Nesta asks immediately.

A chorus of 'no' comes back to her. But Nesta spies free-flowing blood from Sister Jean Ashton's head.

24

'Jean, I can see the gash on your head; do any of you have injuries I can't see?' Nesta asks of the young nurse.

Jean shakes her head and no one admits to being seriously hurt, other than the knocks and abrasions the salt water is doing its job to heal.

'What do you want us to do?' a nurse asks Nesta, acknowledging her seniority even as they float, shipwrecked, in the sea.

Clutching on to each other in a tight circle, the nurses hold an impromptu meeting to discuss any possible ways of helping the injured and vulnerable. 'Assist where you can, but we need to make getting to safety our priority,' Nesta assures them.

'Let's get ashore and take it from there. Did you see the matrons?'

'I did, they're both in the same lifeboat with some other nurses and civilians,' Betty informs the group.

'I saw them briefly; I don't think they saw me before I was carried away,' Nesta tells her.

'Matron Paschke looked particularly pleased with herself,' Betty says. 'To see her that close to water and not panicking was so strange. Remember, Nesta, how she wouldn't even get her feet wet in Malacca?'

'I remember how we used to make fun of her. She's never going to let us forget how she survived out in the ocean after being shipwrecked.'

'Should we separate and look for others?' Betty asks.

'Yes, try to grab on to one of the planks floating past. I'll see you ashore,' Nesta calls out as she allows the current to take her away.

'Some of them have made it ashore, so if they can, we can,' Norah yells to the others.

Norah, Ena, John and June join several survivors trying to swim to an island which comes into view each time they are lifted by a wave, only to disappear as they drop back into the calm ocean. Thank God the water is warm, Norah thinks, looking at her husband. The last thing he needs is an attack of hypothermia.

The strong current beneath them is fighting their approach. For hours, they move down the Banka Strait. June falls asleep from exhaustion or trauma. Ena holds her close, her little head resting on her shoulder as they tread water. The sun is finally setting on this terrible day and visibility on the water ebbs away. Closer now, they watch the fires burning on the shore they are struggling to reach.

None of them sees the raft until it has passed by. Several swim after it, grabbing hold and then dragging it back for others to cling on to. With exhaustion threatening to overwhelm everyone, Norah and Ena help each other onto the raft. As complete darkness engulfs them, they huddle together. Most of those on the raft fall into a deep sleep.

'*Waltzing Matilda, waltzing Matilda*
  You'll come a-waltzing Matilda with me
  And he sang as he stowed that jumbuck in his tucker bag
  '*You'll come a-waltzing Matilda with me . . .*'

As night settles, Nesta finds herself alone, but realises that singing is of some comfort. The plank she grabbed hold of several hours earlier has become her home. With no strength left to paddle, she makes the decision to climb on and let the current take her.

Lying on her back, she looks at the stars above, the same stars her family and friends back, in Australia might also be gazing up at. She thinks of the vast skies of her hometown in rural Victoria, which she has marvelled at for most of her life, and imagines her mother and father are looking up too. She sends them a message.

I will survive and be with you as soon as I can. I know you never wanted me to go to war. I haven't made your life easy, for that I am sorry. I promise when I get home, I will not leave you again.

She thinks also of Dr Rick, who she met when they were stationed together in Malaya, there to tend to the Allied soldiers positioned, they believed, to see off the invading Japanese Army. She remembers the first time Rick spoke to her, the last time he spoke to her, and wonders whether he made it out of Malaya safely, and where he might be now . . .

She had agreed to cover Betty's night shift so she could accept a dinner date. As midnight draws closer, Nesta moves through the ward, ensuring the men are all sleeping, all comfortable. When she returns to her desk to record her notes, the night-duty doctor joins her.

'Everything all right, Sister James?' he asks.

'Sleeping like babies. I think all the men here can be discharged tomorrow,' Nesta replies, in hushed tones. It wouldn't do to wake sleeping soldiers.

'Do you now? Wanting my job are you, Sister?'

Nesta realises what she has just said. Mortified, she stands, her four foot, ten inches dwarfed by the much taller doctor.

'I am so sorry, that was inappropriate. I'll make my notes in each file for the morning shift to read,' she stammers.

'It's OK, I'm sure you're right. Especially with that amount of snoring going on. My money is on Dr Raymond agreeing with you. Take a seat, no need to stand to attention.'

'Thank you, Dr Bayley,' Nesta mutters as she sits down.

'I'm Richard, but my friends call me Rick. I have never heard of anyone called Nesta, can I ask where you got your name?'

Nesta laughs. 'It's Welsh. I was born in Wales and my parents moved to Australia when I was a child.'

'Ah, that explains it, some very different names come from Wales, am I right?'

'Yes, they do like to be different. No one from Wales wants to be thought of as English.'

Rick sits on the edge of the desk, moving files away, scanning the ward, before turning back to her.

'Would it be rude of me to ask what you were doing before enlisting and now sitting here with me tonight?'

'Well, briefly, I came to Australia from Wales when I was eight, lived in Shepparton.'

'That's in northern Victoria, isn't it?'

'Yes, farming country, mostly orchards.'

'Go on.'

'Always knew I wanted to be a nurse and trained at the Royal Melbourne.'

'Is that where you were before you came here?'

Nesta laughs again. 'No, far from it – I was in South Africa.'

'Wait, where? This I want to hear. Hang on a minute while I grab another chair. By the way, you have a lovely laugh, I've been hearing it for weeks now. I think you laugh more than anyone I've ever known.'

With a chair placed in front of the desk, Rick leans forwards, all ears.

'Like I said, I was in South Africa.'

'Why?'

'Are you going to let me tell the story?' Nesta says with a cheeky smile.

'Sorry, sorry. Do go on.'

'Don't get me wrong, I loved working at the Royal Melbourne, but I wanted to do more, use my skills for healing and not just caring for patients.'

'Ah, so you wanted to be a doctor.'

'Are you going to let me finish?'

'Sorry.'

'I saw a small advertisement in the paper for nurses to work in the gold and diamond mines in South Africa. I had no idea what was involved, but at the time, I was looking to do more, have something of an adventure. I applied, got accepted and went. I worked in a mine in the Johannesburg region.'

'Bad?'

'Some days really bad. Wounds from accidents, landslides, mine collapses, beatings. I certainly dealt with injuries I had not previously seen, and there wasn't always a doctor on the site.'

'So, you did what you had to do, made your own decisions regarding, shall we say, discharges.'

Nesta laughs again. 'Something like that. Yes. Anyway, I was there for two years, then, one day, it was a Sunday, we—'

'Who were the others?'

'Oh, there were nurses from England and Scotland and some local ones, not as well trained as we were. Anyway, we were sitting around the break room having lunch when one of the English girls picked up the paper that had been lying around and told us that both England and Australia were at war. You have to understand, we got very little news from the outside world, most of us didn't really want it, we just wanted to do our job, make a difference where we could. I knew immediately I had to go home, that my role was now helping my own people. It took quite a few months, but eventually I got back to Sydney and enlisted. And here I am. Here we are.'

29

'You are quite the adventurer, Sister Nesta James.'

'Thank you for asking and listening, I've not told my story to anyone other than Matron.'

'You should, I'm sure your colleagues would be fascinated to hear of your exploits. I'll leave you to your rounds, come find me if you need me.'

'Good night, Doctor.'

'Rick, my friends call me Rick . . .'

Dozing, Nesta doesn't see the beach until her raft runs ashore. She has no idea how long she has been in the water, but it must be the middle of the night; only the stars provide light on this moonless evening. She has a powerful thirst. Scrambling to sit up, she looks beyond the small beach into the black of the jungle. Rolling off the raft, she crawls ashore, collapsing onto the sand. A light catches her eye and, turning, she sees a lighthouse, a beam of light spinning and shining far out to sea.

Nesta shakily gets to her feet, all four foot, ten inches of her, and she strides towards the building. She finds the door and knocks.

Slowly, it creaks open and two local Malayan men peer at her.

'Please, can I come in?' she asks.

Their perplexed looks tell her they have not understood her. She pushes gently on the door, and they step aside. Nesta scans the small room. There is a bed, table and two chairs, and a bench laden with rudimentary kitchen equipment.

'English?' she says.

'A little,' one of the men responds.

'You live here?'

The men exchange glances and words in Malay.

'Dutch man lived here, he's gone.'

'Water? Can I have some water, please?'

Before they can respond, the door bursts open and two Japanese soldiers storm inside. The Malayan men flinch. Surprised to see Nesta, the soldiers raise their rifles, bayonets drawn, inches from her stomach. She doesn't flinch.

One of the soldiers lowers his rifle and walks around Nesta slowly, looking her up and down. Nesta puts her right hand into her uniform pocket and feels the money, the one hundred pounds, still in place, wet but intact. The soldier notices this movement and jerks her hand free. Turning her around to face the wall, they stand back, chattering and jeering. Nesta doesn't see them leave, but one of the Malays turns her around.

'Gone. You go too,' he says.

'Water, please.'

'You go, go now.'

The men give her some water, which she gulps down before she is ushered out of the door.

Nesta leaves the lighthouse, walking slowly away. She heads to where beach meets jungle and drops down by a large tree. Hidden here, in the dark, she waits for the sun to rise and give her a new day.

'This oil just won't wash off,' Norah complains, rubbing at her skin.

As the sun comes up, Norah, Ena, John and June struggle, with the others on their raft, for a comfortable position. The chill morning air is soon warmed by a searing sun. Too soon, they are burning up. They take turns to lower themselves into the cool water, all the while clinging on to the raft. They are desperately thirsty.

'Maybe there's a hot shower or a bath waiting for us, with good soap and thick towels when we find land.' Ena manages a joke, but no one is smiling.

'How are your hands?' John asks them.

The sisters hold out their torn and weeping hands for inspection.

'Oh, my goodness, I had no idea you were injured,' one of the women says. 'You should have said something.'

'We'll be fine once we can get ashore and hopefully find some of the nurses who were on board with us,' Ena replies.

They watch the sun pass the midpoint in the sky.

'We have been in the water for over twenty-four hours,' a man says. 'And not a drop to drink.'

A silence falls over the group.

They hear the engine before they see the launch heading towards them. Not knowing who is on board, several of the men and women slide off the raft into the water.

Cutting its engines, the launch pulls alongside the bobbing raft. Two airmen are on board; one so young he still looks like a child, the other John's age.

'Hello! Hello! It's great to find you. We're RAF. How about we get you aboard?'

Several of the women begin to cry; the men extend their hands to shake those of their rescuers.

'What ship are you from?'

'The *Vyner Brooke*.'

'Ah, sorry to hear that. Pass the little one over first,' the older airman says, pointing to June, who is still clinging on to Ena.

Ena attempts to untangle June's arms from around her neck, but the little girl holds on tighter and buries her face in Ena's neck.

'It's all right, June. I'm just passing you to the kind officer. I'll follow, don't worry.'

'Can we hurry this up?' one of the women says, as she attempts to clamber on board the launch.

'Stay on the raft, madam, we're taking the child first,' the airman tells her.

June allows herself to be lifted and placed into the launch and the others quickly follow. With a gentle push away from the raft, the launch fires up and heads towards land. Norah watches their plank of wood disappear. It has saved them from the sea; its job is done.

'Water?' John croaks.

'I'm so sorry,' says the airman, handing him a canteen. 'Do pass it round.'

John takes a gulp, and the canteen is hastily passed around the group, barely quenching their thirst.

'Have you found any other survivors?' John asks.

'Not from the *Vyner Brooke*.'

'Where are you taking us?'

'We don't have much of a choice, I'm afraid. Muntok is not far away, and we will take you to the pier. I'm sorry to say this, but we'll be delivering you to the Japanese.'

There are cries of fear and anger amongst the group. How can these men be delivering them into the hands of the enemy, the very army which destroyed their ship and machine-gunned civilians from the air?

'Can't we come with you? You can't just abandon us to the Japanese,' Norah says, aghast.

'We're surrounded. If you're caught with us, then you'll really be in trouble. This is all we can do, I'm sorry, I . . .'

The airman doesn't need to finish his sentence. The group falls silent. At least there is some relief in finally escaping the water.

'There's the pier ahead. We're going in hard and fast, please disembark as quickly as you can so we can get away.'

The launch slows down as they approach a bend in the Strait. Peering around, they see a long pier reaching into the sea from the land.

'Go, go, go!' the older airman tells his young colleague who is steering the launch.

The survivors are thrown back into their seats as the boat lurches forwards at top speed. They hit the pier with a thump, just beside the wooden ladder for disembarkation.

'Quick, quick.' The airman points to a young man. 'Up you go, I'm sending June after you; that's your name isn't it, sweetheart?'

The little girl nods.

'Help her and then the others as I send them up. We must move very fast now.'

The man clambers up the ladder, and June makes her own way up with shaking legs but a courage and determination beyond her years. Ena follows, stumbling on the steps, her legs also like jelly after hours in the water. Her lacerated hands are agonisingly painful as she grips each rung. As the last survivors struggle up the ladder to the pier, they hear shouting and feet pounding towards them.

'Go, go, go!' the airman yells, pushing the remaining survivors onto the ladder.

As the last one places his hands on the bottom rung, the airman guns the engines. A hail of bullets chases them away. When they are on the pier, Ena, Norah and John stare at the Japanese soldiers, still running towards them, rifles firing at the departed RAF men. Beyond the soldiers, they see that the pier is littered with other survivors, sitting on their suitcases, on boxes, watching in horror, terrified the newcomers are about to be shot. The launch disappears around the bend. The Japanese soldiers turn and walk back the way they came, leaving the survivors from the *Vyner Brooke* to wonder what happens next.

'I suppose we just sit here and wait like everyone else,' John says.

CHAPTER 3

Muntok, Indonesia
February 1942

'Is anyone there?'

As the sun cleared the horizon, Nesta slunk further into the jungle, moving slowly, quietly, her senses on high alert, flinching at every sound. The jungle, however, was alive with noise, the rustle of birds in the branches, the whistle of the wind in the trees, the ever-present rasping of insects. But now she hears a human voice, and then gagging, choking, again and again.

'Is there someone there?'

Nesta drops to the ground. It's coming from the beach. Crawling on all fours through the thick vegetation, she is once again at the edge of the jungle. Her heart racing, her head ringing, it takes her a moment to register what she is looking at.

There is someone on the beach, spluttering and choking, struggling to stand. They have clearly just come out of the water. A young woman, who, failing to make it to her feet, topples over.

Nesta watches and waits. The woman gives up and lies still. Nesta's nursing instincts kick in, instincts which are far more powerful than her fear. More powerful than her terrible thirst and mind-numbing exhaustion. She runs across the sand towards the survivor. The woman is lying on her side, her clothes sodden and coated in thick black oil, which also coats her face, hair and body. When Nesta gently turns the woman onto her back, a pair of bright dark eyes peer up at her, and a tiny smile says, thank you.

'We need to get off this beach,' Nesta tells her, matching her smile for an instant. 'We're too exposed.'

Much taller than the diminutive nurse, the woman allows Nesta to pull her to her feet, and together they hobble back to the safety of the jungle.

'Are you hurt?' Nesta asks.

'No, but I think I've swallowed a lot of seawater.'

'Lie down. You'll be fine in a moment.'

The woman seems only too happy to be off her feet again.

'Are you a nurse?' she asks. 'You look like one of the nurses that was on the boat.'

'Yes, I'm Nesta. Nesta James.'

'Phyllis Turnbridge. Australian?'

'Yes. English?'

Phyllis nods. 'Have you found anyone else? Any more survivors?'

'No, but I'm sure there will be others, probably washed up somewhere further up or down the beach.'

'What should we do?'

'Rest here a bit, there's a lighthouse not far away. I've been there already, didn't get a warm welcome though.'

'Japanese soldiers?'

'Two local men seem to be living there, though I did meet two soldiers.'

'Really? And they let you go?'

'Didn't seem that interested in me. The locals told me to leave, so I came here to watch and wait.'

'Should we go back? I badly need some water.'

'You up to walking?'

To answer, Phyllis stands on wobbly legs, stretches, shrugs her shoulders. 'Let's go.'

Slowly, they head for the lighthouse, remaining just inside the jungle, and peering around them all the while.

'What were you doing in Singapore?' Nesta asks.

'I work for British Intelligence,' Phyllis replies.

'You're a spy?'

'Hardly, administration.'

Nesta is intrigued but decides not to probe.

The local men are still in the lighthouse and the women gesture imploringly at their mouths. It is understood they are hungry and thirsty and, reluctantly, they are given a small quantity of rice each and some water.

'Can't stay, you must go,' one of the men insists.

'Where? Where do you suggest we go?' an emboldened Phyllis asks.

'Muntok. Go to Muntok.'

The two men herd the women out of the lighthouse and onto a path that leads into the jungle. 'Muntok.'

'I guess we're going to Muntok,' Phyllis says matter-of-factly.

'I don't have any other ideas and I'm not going back into the sea,' Nesta replies.

Not far along the path, Nesta and Phyllis come across a small group of *Vyner Brooke* survivors, dazed, disoriented, arguing about which direction to follow. Before Nesta can say a word, one of the women lets out a high-pitched scream. The group startles and begins to wildly scan the jungle for the threat. They see it. Japanese soldiers are walking towards them, bayonets held aloft. They move fast to form a circle around the survivors, letting them know, with a nudge of their rifles, which way to go. There's nothing they can do and so they begin to walk, and not long after, they enter the village of Muntok.

They are marched through the village, which is nothing more than a small collection of huts, with street vendors selling fruit and vegetables from mats on the ground. There are mothers with children, faces peering from windows, men spitting at the survivors in a show of support to the Japanese. At the far end of the village, a pier stretches out into the ocean and there Nesta spies hundreds of men, women and children sitting in the blazing sun. There are more soldiers here, standing watch over the displaced survivors. She looks desperately into the masses for a familiar face, a familiar uniform, but there are too many people. Nesta, Phyllis and the rest of their small group are led into a nearby building. One of the survivors translates the sign above the door: it is the Customs House.

'Can we sit, please, darling? Can we all just sit down?' John says and Norah can see that he is about to faint.

Norah, Ena, John and June are standing in the baking sun, trying to take in their surroundings. Norah is watching the soldiers close by, desperate for a sign of what fate has in store for them.

Taking his hand, Norah guides him down onto the wooden planks of the pier. June snuggles up to John; thankfully, it seems as though she feels secure with any of her three rescuers. They sit close together, trying to shield John and June from the sun.

'You look terrible,' Norah tells Ena, trying to distract them from what lies ahead.

'Thanks, Norah. You should see yourself – pot, kettle and all that,' Ena responds, and the sisters share a forced smile despite the pain in their hands and their overwhelming thirst. 'How can we get this oil off?' Ena asks.

'Let's try to help each other. My hands don't work, but my feet do. John, can we please have your singlet? You can keep your shirt,' Norah says with a cheeky grin.

John begins unbuttoning his shirt, but his hands are shaking and, watching him struggle, June pushes his fingers aside and pulls off his shirt, before helping remove his singlet. Handing the vest to Norah, she helps John put his shirt back on.

'Let's see, how can we do this?' Norah ponders, examining Ena, nudging the strip of cloth towards her feet.

Grasping the garment between her toes, Norah tries to wipe the oil from Ena's arms. The sisters twist and contort as they successfully remove some of the tarry steaks from the arms and legs of the other. Their laughter reaches others up the pier, who watch in amusement. When Norah attempts to wipe Ena's face they both nearly roll off the pier. As they regain their composure, June takes the now very dirty black vest from Ena and gently wipes both sisters' faces. She is rewarded by hugs from both women.

Others around them share in this funny moment, laughing and pointing at the sisters' comic attempts at bathing.

'Your hands need attention,' John tells them, having joined in the laughter.

Norah is delighted that John seems buoyed by this ludicrous scene. He must feel better if he can take a moment to appreciate the absurdity of their actions in this idyllic setting of lush jungle and brilliant tropical flowers, set against serene blue waters and the white sandy beach. She feels like they're in a painting.

'Be my life short or long, I'll remember this moment forever. How, in the worst possible circumstances, two women, whom I love more than life itself, found a way to laugh and make me laugh. Thank you, my darlings.'

Ena and Norah pause in their efforts to give him a kiss on each cheek.

Once the singlet is too thick with oil to be of any more use, Norah and Ena sit with John and June, looking at the human mass on the pier.

'I don't recognise anyone here. But they have their luggage and clean clothes. I'm guessing they're from another ship,' Norah says.

'How about I go and talk to some of them?' Ena suggests.

'Girls, please don't do anything dangerous,' John pleads.

'Of course we won't,' Ena says. 'There're no soldiers near us – and the ones over there aren't paying anyone much attention. I'll be quick.'

A new group of soldiers arrives and Ena hurries over to the nearest group of prisoners. Norah watches her speak to them briefly, before she returns with the news that their ship, *Mata Hari*, had been attacked, her passengers loaded into the ship's launches and brought here. Men, women and children sit, lie down, stand to stretch their legs, surrounded by their belongings.

'Do any of them know what's going to happen to us?' Norah asks.

'They don't know any more than we do, which is nothing. Wait and see, I guess.'

'John needs medication, I'm so worried about him,' Norah says, looking at her now-sleeping husband. His head is in her lap and she strokes his hair tenderly. 'He's burning up and being under this sun is making everything worse.'

'Do you want me to ask one of the soldiers if we can get a hat or something?'

Before Norah can reply, June, who is also fast asleep, grabs their attention.

'Mummy! Mummy!' she cries.

Ena takes her in her arms, whispering soothing words, rocking her, holding her tightly as the little girl awakes, disoriented. Soon, her screams become sobs and then she falls asleep again.

'What should we do with her?' Ena asks, stroking the girl's arm.

'Care for her, love her and hopefully we'll find her mother shortly.'

John stirs at June's distress, but not for long.

'I don't know if he is sleeping or unconscious,' Norah says quietly.

Ena looks at him; his breathing is ragged but regular. 'He's sleeping, don't worry,' she tells her.

The sisters fall silent; the sun is relentless in its attempts to burn them alive. They can see that others on the pier have hats and spare clothing to cover and protect their skin and faces. The unspoken looks the sisters exchange confirm they feel the same despair.

Norah reaches out and takes Ena's hand and lies back to doze. But within minutes, there is a commotion, and they start awake; both instinctively checking on June and John, who are still asleep. Japanese soldiers are pacing down the pier, yelling, and stabbing at the survivors with their bayonets. The message is clear: stand up, it's time to move on. Being at the very end of the pier, Norah and Ena have time to gently nudge John and June to their feet. While others struggle with their possessions, they walk unencumbered.

'Where are they taking us?' Nesta wonders aloud.

Nesta and Phyllis are escorted from the Customs House to join the hundreds of men, women and children exiting the pier.

'Looks like a cinema,' says Phyllis. It is a cinema, a single storey made of timber and iron. Inside, there is just one large room and a small projection pod.

'Stay close,' Nesta says, taking Phyllis's hand as the survivors vie for space. 'Hey!' she calls. Across the room, she has spied several of her colleagues. They rush into each other's arms and begin to share stories of their survival.

'Water!' Phyllis cries as the soldiers move amongst the survivors handing out banana-leaf pouches filled with rice and cups of water.

They are heartened that, throughout the rest of that day and into the night, more survivors are pushed through the doors. Friends and families separated when the *Vyner Brooke* sank reconnect in emotional scenes that affect all around them.

Norah, Ena, John and June have claimed some wall space. There is no room to lie down, but at least they are out of the punishing sun.

As night falls and the room grows dark, Norah can no longer make out the other figures in the room, but she can still hear the babies and small children crying with hunger. It feels like a long time since they were given a handful of rice. Norah can't get comfortable, can't shut out the noise and constant motion all around. When sleep comes, it is brief and full of dreams of Sally.

As daylight finally breaks, Norah looks into the faces of the survivors and knows they feel just like her: lucky and grateful to still be alive. As she and John and Ena and June struggle to their feet, stretching limbs and muscles assaulted by days of punishment, the doors are flung open.

'Thank God,' she says. 'We can finally get out of here.'

'Out! Out!' a Japanese soldier yells.

Several soldiers enter the room, pushing and shoving anyone in their way with their rifles and their fists. Norah and everyone else scramble and stumble from the building. Once outside, she turns around to see the last survivor exiting the building; there is blood streaming down his face from a blow to the head, and his distraught elderly wife is holding him up. As they are all marched through the village, Norah wonders what their unknown future holds in store.

CHAPTER 4

'Ena, what are we going to do? We can't lose John. He won't survive without us,' Norah whispers.

In full sunshine, the prisoners, after walking or stumbling with their children, reach a barracks-like compound. They are ordered through the gates, where the men are immediately separated from the women.

'Maybe it's just for sleeping. Please, Norah, just stay calm until we find out what's happening.' Ena wisely tries to placate her sister, but she is just as anxious.

They guess that the barracks were built to house local workers for the now-disbanded tin mine close by. Sleeping huts surround an open central area with one well the only source of water. A long concrete trough nearby, they are told, is where they will wash. Several women are already scooping water over their heads to cool down. In the land behind the huts are the toilets – long pits dug out of the earth.

The women and children, who outnumber the men, are ordered into huts on the left of the barracks. John is pulled away from Norah and pushed into a hut on the opposite side. Norah nudges Ena and, with June, they head for a hut almost opposite John.

'But where do we sleep?' a woman's voice calls out.

Attached to the walls are shelf-like sloping concrete slabs.

'On these, I suppose,' another voice calls.

Choosing a spot for themselves and June, the women begin to exchange names. There are several mothers with children. June finds a little girl her age and, with encouragement, joins her in play.

An older woman amongst them introduces herself as Margaret Dryburgh, sharing her background as a missionary teacher with nursing training.

'I also have a passion for music,' she tells the women who gather around.

'My sister, Norah, trained at the Royal Academy of Music in London,' Ena pipes up.

Margaret approaches the sisters. 'It's a pleasure to meet you. You never know, maybe one day we will sit around and sing about this experience.'

'Sounds interesting, but I don't think any expertise I might have in music will be needed here,' Norah says, peering into the dark corners of their hut.

'You never know. But I'd love to hear about your training one day.' Margaret turns to the wider group. 'I can see many of you don't have any possessions with you,' she says, observing the oily rags some are wearing, and the smart dresses of others. 'You have only the clothes you stand in?'

'And our lives,' Ena quips.

'And your lives, you're quite right, I'm sorry if I sound insensitive. Ladies, I am sure we can find some clothing and other necessities to share with those in need. What do you say?'

45

As the women with suitcases begin to rummage through their belongings, they hold up skirts, blouses, dresses.

'You're sisters?' Margaret asks.

'Yes. I'm Norah and this is my sister, Ena.'

'Your hands! What on earth happened to your hands?'

'When we had to abandon ship, we made the mistake of holding onto the rope as we slid into the sea. I don't know why, but it didn't occur to me that I would be shredding my skin. Then Norah did the same thing,' Ena tells her.

'May I have a look?'

The sisters hold out their hands for examination. Margaret turns them over to see if any damage or infection has spread to the back of each hand.

'How long were you in the water?'

'I don't know for sure; it was after lunch . . .'

'Which we didn't have,' Ena adds.

'Which we didn't have, and I guess it was later the next morning, or around lunchtime again, that we were picked up by a launch and dropped at the pier,' Norah concludes.

'I'm starving,' Ena says.

'I'm sure we will be given something to eat shortly. But you should know that the salt water was good for your hands. They don't look infected but I'm sorry to say, ladies, the rope burns are going to take some time to heal and I wouldn't recommend you use your hands at all until they do.'

'How long?' Ena asks.

'Under normal conditions, with medical assistance, it would take weeks. The skin is still shedding. All of that has to fall off before the skin below can heal. There'll be scars, I'm afraid, but, given where we are, I think that is the least of our problems.' Margaret pauses, looks around the room. 'I'd like to find something I can use for bandages, and they'll need to be changed every day. In this climate, you need to keep your wounds clean and dry. Since they'll be bandaged, I suppose that will remind you not to use them. There's enough of us to look after you and your daughter—'

'Oh, she's not our daughter. Just a little girl we found in the sea. She became separated from her mother, so we've been looking after her,' Ena tells Margaret.

'Oh, but she just looks so attached to you; I thought one of you must be her mother.'

Ena glances at Norah, who has turned away. She gives her a hug. 'Sally will be fine, Norah.'

'I'm sorry, have I said something?' Margaret asks.

'Norah has a little girl – Sally, she's eight. Just a few days before we sailed, she left on another ship with our other sister and her family,' Ena tells Margaret.

Norah finds herself remembering their agonising decision to send Sally away from Malaya ahead of them when they fled for Singapore. She and John had been reunited in Singapore, only to send her away from them a second time, in those desperate days as the island they'd thought was a safe haven fell so quickly to the Japanese.

Kuala Terengganu, Malaya – December 1941

Norah is packing clothes, books and dolls into their suitcases. She turns to look at John, who is by the window, his gaze intent on whatever is happening in their backyard. As she snaps the cases closed, she joins him, placing a comforting arm around his waist, and together they watch Sally, who is filling shallow bowls with water. Their garden borders the jungle and all its dangers.

47

'We need to bring her inside soon; the tiger cubs will be here and Mumma tiger won't be far away,' Norah says softly.

But they remain still, their eyes on their daughter as she goes about her task.

'I wish we didn't have to leave,' Norah begins.

'I know,' says John, not taking his eyes off Sally. 'I know.'

'It's so soon.' Norah's eyes fill with tears. 'I'm not ready,' she whispers.

John turns towards her now, takes her in his arms.

'We'll never be ready, my darling. But we can't stay here. The Japanese are close now. We'll put her on the bus tomorrow, trek overland ourselves, and be reunited with her in Kuala Lumpur. Then we'll all get to Singapore and safety together. It will be fine, I promise you.'

They remain like this, hugging, giving each other the courage to keep moving.

Finally, John pulls away and turns back to the window, which he slides open.

'Sally! Sally, it's time to come inside, my honey. The sun's nearly gone. You can watch the baby tigers drink from the window with us.'

Sally places the last bowl on the ground, peering into the thick foliage of jungle, on the alert for movement, any movement. Seeing none, she looks up at her parents. 'Coming.'

Nestled in her father's arms, Sally watches as five small tiger cubs run from the safety of the jungle onto the lawn. They play, fight, find the bowls of water and drink greedily.

Norah notices that John can't tear his eyes away from the mother tiger who is watching her babies from amidst the dense grasses. She doesn't take her eyes off the cubs and John doesn't take his eyes off her.

Norah knows what he's thinking: that a parent should never be parted from her children, that they must keep Sally safe at all costs.

'Play something,' he whispers to her.

Norah doesn't need to ask him what or why. She picks up her violin, never far from her hands. She can't stop the tears that come as the beautiful notes of Brahms' 'Lullaby' soothe a sleepy Sally, who leans back against her father's shoulder.

'I'm sure she is fine. Now come on, let's see what I can find that can be made into these bandages.' Margaret instinctively knows that a bit of bustle is the way to snap Norah out of her misery.

The mood lightens as Margaret lifts petticoats and bloomers from her suitcase, along with starched blouses and skirts. Clasping a cotton slip between her hands and teeth, she tears off strips of fabric.

Nesta and the nurses are allocated a hut to themselves. For the first time, they are alone, unsure of where they are or who is missing. Nesta quickly counts heads.

'Thirty of us. Sixty-five boarded the *Vyner Brooke*. We have to hope and pray others will join us when they're found. Come on, girls, let's work together to make the most of our new home.'

'Should we explore outside? We need to find a bathroom and some water,' someone asks.

'It's not like any of us have anything to unpack,' another adds. 'What I'd give for a new uniform, even one without a petticoat.'

The nurses from Nesta's division burst out laughing, the others look puzzled.

'What's up?' one asks.

'You tell them, Jean. You can tell it best,' Nesta says.

49

'Well, it was like this. When we first got to Malaya, we had our heavy, hot uniforms from home. They just weren't appropriate for us in the tropics. Matron got permission for a local tailor to make us more suitable, you know, lightweight uniforms. Made from cotton, with short sleeves.'

'And?'

'Oh, they were lovely, we really liked them until . . .'

The nurses burst out laughing again.

'Until what?'

'It happened a week or two after we'd been wearing them. We'd noticed that on night shift the soldiers we were looking after kept asking us to come to their bedside and when we got there, they didn't really need anything. We thought they just wanted company and didn't think anything of it. Anyway, I was working one night when Matron stopped by. She immediately ordered me out of the ward and told me that the night lighting in the soldiers' room made our uniforms see-through; they could see right through to our underwear.'

'Guess who was always offering to cover night shift?' another nurse calls out.

'You? Was it you, Nesta? Oh, my goodness, how did you feel when you found out?'

'Oh, once you get to know our Sister James, you will learn that she just laughs everything off. No one laughs as much as she does,' comes the reply.

When the nurses return from surveying the camp, several share the news of a dormitory that might possibly be used as a hospital. Three doctors are already installed, and the women asked if they could work with them. Those back in the hut, on hearing the news, hurry to the vacant hut, introduce themselves to the doctors, and, with an energy that none of them really possesses, set about making it ready.

'I'll speak to the Japanese soldiers and see if we can get some beds and blankets, and of course equipment and medication,' one of the doctors says.

'Do you think they will give you anything?' a nurse asks.

'Don't know until we ask. It will tell us just how they expect us to take care of our most basic needs, medically speaking.'

As they are relaying this information to the nurses back in their hut, an older woman enters the room.

'Hello, all. I'm Margaret Dryburgh and I'm in the hut two down from you.'

Nesta steps forwards, her hand outstretched.

'Nice to meet you, Margaret, my name is Nesta, we are—'

'Australian nurses, yes, I know. The word has spread. It's lovely to meet you.'

'I wish I could offer you something, but, as you can see, we're a little low on supplies.'

Margaret smiles wryly.

'Thank you, I do believe we have the same accommodation. But maybe there is something we can give to you.'

The nurses exchange glances amongst themselves.

'Let me explain. I know you have only the clothes you stand in. I was on the *Mata Hari* and lucky enough not to be shipwrecked. We were allowed to take a few meagre possessions. Others here have whole wardrobes of clothing, shoes and toiletries. Looking at you, I can confidently say there is nothing I have which would fit or suit any of you. But many of the other women have extras and we would like to offer you all a change of clothes. Some of the servicemen across the barracks have spare shorts and shirts. They won't resemble uniforms, but they're clean and fresh and haven't endured a sea soaking.'

'On behalf of us all, thank you. If there is anything we can do for you, you only have to ask,' Nesta tells her, too moved to say more.

'Something tells me you'll be our lifesavers. Already, there are women and children here who need some help. Now, come with me and choose some clothes.'

They follow Margaret to her hut, where the residents stand in the dirt aisle running up the centre of the room, the concrete 'sleeping' slabs either side displaying an assortment of clothing.

'This is better than Grace Brothers' women's department,' one of the younger nurses exclaims.

'What's that?' Margaret says.

More laughter. 'It's a clothing store in Melbourne,' Nesta tells her.

'Well, ladies, happy shopping – except, there is no cashier here to take your money.'

Slowly, the nurses walk down the aisle looking at the garments laid out before them. They don't move to pick up a single item.

'Oh really, come on, let's see how this looks on you,' one of the women announces, grabbing a dress and holding it up against a young nurse. Other women do the same and soon the hut resembles a house party.

One of the English women announces she has been given a sewing kit by a woman from a hut along the way, home to the Dutch internees. Alterations can be made if necessary.

'Is that who we saw when we arrived here?' one of the nurses asks.

'Yes, I've learned there were many Dutch families living here. I don't know what happened to the men, but the women and children were moved here from their homes,' Margaret says.

52

'They live here? Permanently?' Nesta asks.

'Their husbands probably ran the mines, so yes, they were here before the Japanese arrived and, well, they're now like us – prisoners of war.'

Margaret watches the fun. She sees that Nesta has decided on a sarong and pair of white Navy shorts.

'Excuse me, Nesta – can I call you by your name or should we be calling you "Sister"?'

'It's Sister James, but Nesta is fine.'

'Thank you. You might hear me being called Miss Dryburgh: there are some women here who know me from my previous life and won't hear of using my first name.'

'Can I ask what you were doing in Singapore?'

'I was a missionary and a teacher. I've been away from England for many years: first in China, then in Singapore. But enough about me, there are two women here I would like your opinion on. They have terrible rope burns from when they abandoned ship.'

'Were they on the *Vyner Brooke*?'

'Yes, and, like you, only have the clothes they were wearing.'

'Will you take me to them?'

The sisters are holding up dresses, inspecting them to see whether they might fit.

'Norah, Ena, this is Sister James . . .'

'Nesta, please.'

'You're one of the Australian nurses, you helped us on the wharf with my husband and we saw you on board. You sang that lovely song as we left Singapore,' Norah says.

'Of course, I remember you.' Nesta pauses, looking around.

'John, my husband, he's here in a hut opposite,' Norah says.

'I'm very happy to hear that. Is he all right, and can I ask what is wrong with him?'

'It's typhus. He was bitten by a rat in the jungle when we were escaping overland to Kuala Lumpur so we could get to Singapore. The bite got infected, and he got ill.'

'We have some doctors here and we're setting up a small hospital. Bring him over when you can.'

'Thank you!' Norah exclaims gratefully. 'Oh, and thank you for the singing. It was the strangest thing, watching Singapore burn to the sound of your lovely voices.'

'Is "Waltzing Matilda" your national anthem?' Ena asks.

'A lot of people would like it to be, but no, it's not. Our anthem is the same as yours. Can I have a look at your hands?'

Margaret gently unwraps the bandages from Norah's hands. 'I trained as a nurse, but it's been a long time since I've worked in a clinic or hospital,' she tells Nesta.

Nesta looks closely at the raw, seeping wounds on Norah's hands. She turns to Ena. 'Are yours the same?'

'They are.'

'Then don't unwrap them. Given we have no medication or sterilised bandages, I'm afraid all we can do is keep them wrapped up and change them as often as you can until they begin to heal. Then we'll let the fresh air take over. Margaret, this hut doesn't need us nurses; they're very lucky to have you.'

'I wanted a second opinion,' Margaret says.

'My opinion is that you both should be sent immediately for medical treatment at the nearest hospital, but that isn't going to happen. I'm sure Margaret will take great care of you, and if there is anything I can ever do for either one of you, please come and find me. But, right now, we just don't know whether we'll be given access to medicine or bandages.'

* * *

'I want to go and see John, will you come with me?' Norah asks her sister. After Nesta has left, there is only one thing on her mind.

'I'm not sure if we are allowed in the men's hut.'

'I'm going to try. I need to see him.'

'If you're going, I'm coming with you,' Ena reassures her sister. 'June will be fine here for a few minutes playing with the other children.'

As they leave their hut, they pause to see who is around, who is watching. A few men and women walk up and down the path dividing the men's and women's huts; there are no soldiers to be seen.

'I think we should just walk boldly across the barracks as if we have every right to be there,' Ena suggests.

Heads up, shoulders back, the two women cross the path and enter the hut they had seen John hustled into earlier. It takes them a moment or two for their eyes to adjust to the dark. All eyes in the room turn towards them before a serviceman steps forwards.

'Can I help you, ladies?'

'We're looking for my husband, John. We saw him come into this hut,' Norah tells him.

'Ah, John, yes. Come with me. I think he's sleeping. We gave him a change of clothes and tried to make him comfortable, he's clearly unwell.'

At the end of the hut, Norah and Ena kneel beside a sleeping John, curled up on the cold, damp concrete. Norah lays her arm across his forehead, and he stirs at her touch.

'Hello, my darling. How are you feeling?' Norah asks.

John struggles to sit up, so the women help as best they can, before settling down either side of him.

'I was asleep,' he says.

'You needed it. You have to get better, and sleep is the best way,' Ena tells him.

55

'It looks like you've enlisted,' Norah says.

John looks at his shirt and shorts. 'Yes, the British Navy, by the looks of it. Well, given the amount of time I've spent both on and in the water lately, I do believe I'm qualified.'

'It's great to see you've still got your sense of humour,' Ena says, grinning widely. 'Why don't I give you a few minutes alone.'

As Ena walks away, Norah guesses she is thinking of her own wonderful husband, Ken, and her heart aches for her sister.

'What's the matter, darling?' John asks.

'It must be hard on her seeing the two of us together. She hated leaving Ken.'

'Well, she has you.'

'That's not enough, John. Ken isn't here and she doesn't know where he is.'

'I'm sure he's with your parents, taking care of them like he promised.'

'But for how long? And Sally?'

John finds the strength to place his arm around Norah. She rests her head on his shoulder.

As the sun sets on their first day in the barracks, Japanese guards arrive carrying a few large cauldrons of rice and a small quantity of tin mugs.

'This is not enough food!' is repeated over and over as the women take a mug containing a single ladleful of rice. When one woman complains directly to a guard, she is slapped in the face and knocked to the ground.

Margaret Dryburgh walks along the line of women and children. 'Just take what they give you and say nothing,' she repeats.

'Is this all we are expected to live on?' one of the women fires back at her.

'We don't know yet. This is just our first day – we're going to have to be patient and see what tomorrow brings.'

A couple of days later, the nurses cheer when Sisters Betty Jeffrey and Blanche Hempsted, who had been with them on the *Vyner Brooke*, enter the camp. Betty has terrible rope burns on her hands, and both women are badly bruised.

'Come with me,' Nesta tells them both. 'We have a small hospital set up. I want one of the doctors to take a look at you.'

'A hospital?' Blanche asks.

'Well, I'm using the term very loosely. There's a hut we intend to turn into a hospital when we can get beds and supplies. In the meantime, we're calling it the hospital; in reality, it's where the three doctors are camped and where we go to help.'

'What supplies do we have?'

'Nothing. We boil what water we can get hold of, which isn't much, and have torn up spare clothing, mostly petticoats. No one here needs a petticoat, and they make good bandages.'

With Betty's hands bandaged and their other wounds treated, they return to the nurses' hut, where everyone gathers around to hear their story of survival.

'We got on a raft which was terribly overcrowded,' Betty begins. 'Several of us took shifts in the water clinging on, but our progress was so slow. The two of us and Matron Paschke took turns rowing all night. When Blanche and I weren't rowing, we got in the water.'

Pausing, Betty reaches out to Blanche with a bandaged hand. 'I'll never forget how you looked after everyone. She was just wonderful,' Betty tells the nurses. 'Whenever she wasn't rowing, she was in the water, checking on those clinging to the raft, swapping them out with those on board to rest. If she couldn't fit them

57

on the raft, she was keeping their spirits up, showing them how to paddle to conserve energy, and insisting that it wouldn't be long before we were rescued.'

Blanche wraps her arms around Betty, wiping away the tears that flow unashamedly down her face. The nurses wipe away their own tears.

'We saw fires burning on the beaches,' Betty continues. 'And smoke from what I presume were other ships, but none of them came near us. I told myself that surely the British Navy was looking for us, that they'd find us soon. One even got close enough for us to shout at, but they didn't see us. Each time we got near to the beach and I thought this time, this time we'll land, the current got hold of us and pushed us back out to sea.'

'Did you see anyone else in the water?' Nesta asks.

'A ship's officer floated past us on a piece of wreckage and told us where we should head to make land. He wished us luck as he was dragged away by the current,' Blanche says.

'We finally saw the lighthouse and tried desperately to paddle towards it,' Betty continues, 'but the current was just too strong. Next thing we know, we're surrounded by several large motor-boats with Japanese soldiers. They circled us, one came up really close, then they all turned and left us there. We saw and heard guns firing and watched as we floated past Muntok. We realised we were getting nowhere but tried to keep the conversations lively. We were both in the water clinging to the raft when a huge wave hit us and snatched the raft away. I can still hear Matron calling us as their raft sailed away, and . . . and they're not here.'

Blanche takes over.

'We had trouble staying together in the water. We kept waving at each other, to stay in each other's sight-line. The current finally pushed me into a mangrove swamp. I clung to a fallen tree and eventually Betty saw me and made her way over. We were both exhausted. We wrapped our arms around that dead tree and fell asleep. When we woke up, we joked about how we're now qualified for the Aussie swimming team.'

'Endurance swimming, not racing,' Betty adds.

'Yes, long distance for sure. We paddled and swam through the mangroves for hours, which is how we got so badly cut up. When the tide went out, we clung to whatever we could, waiting for it to return so we could swim again. We saw a few crocodiles, which was terrifying, but we eventually found a river and swam up it until we found some land. We made a bed out of palm leaves and tried to sleep through the night.'

Now Betty picks up the story.

'The next day we found a village; they gave us water and food. A Chinese man who spoke good English offered to take us with him to Java. It meant getting back on a barge, and we weren't having any of that. He then told us he had heard there were quite a few white people in Muntok who had been taken prisoner by the Japanese. Then a truck arrived and the next thing we knew, we were surrounded by Japanese soldiers. We had to get in the truck with them and here we are.'

A silence falls across the room. No one knows what to say. Eventually, Nesta breaks the spell.

'I think you both need to rest.'

'Does anyone know what happened to the others, to the matrons?' Betty asks.

'No. But you made it and you're safe. Let's hope they all turn up soon,' Nesta tells them firmly.

Later, while eating their afternoon allocation of rice, Nesta takes the opportunity to talk to the nurses about bathing.

59

'From now on, we don't go alone, no matter how badly you want to have a wash. I don't want the prying eyes of the soldiers on any of you.'

'I was going to change the dressing on my hands later and thought I'd do that while having a wash,' Betty says.

'Then I'm coming with you,' Nesta tells her.

'Why don't you go now while everyone is eating,' Blanche suggests. 'I'll come too. Hopefully, all the soldiers are busy still handing out rice.'

Finding only one other woman at the trough, Betty strips off, while Nesta carefully unwraps her bandages. Betty bites her lip against the pain of skin tearing from her hands.

'Looking good, Betty,' Nesta tells her. 'No sign of infection, but I don't want you getting any of this water on them. Who knows what bugs are in here.'

Stepping into the trough, Betty clumsily picks up a ladle. She scoops dirty water and pours it over her shoulders, down her back.

Behind them, they hear a twig crunching underfoot. They turn to see two Japanese guards only a few feet away watching Betty bathe.

'Get out of here! Get the hell out, you perverted bastards!' Nesta screams, running at the men.

The guards, surprised at the anger of the tiny woman, begin to go for their rifles. But Nesta is in their faces now, and, they are forced to back up. She advances as they retreat and, eventually, they turn and run.

Betty dresses quickly and the women celebrate this tiny victory with a hug.

'How are you so brave, Nesta?' Betty asks her, aghast at her friend's courage.

'I didn't feel brave, let me tell you,' Nesta says, sombrely. 'And you'd have done exactly the same thing and you know it. Up close, so many of those soldiers are just frightened little boys.'

'Bully's here! Bully's here!' the cry goes up.

Nesta's nap is disturbed by squeals of delight. They've been here two weeks and she was beginning to lose hope she would ever see another nurse from the *Vyner Brooke*.

Pandemonium erupts as the nurses gather round to hug Sister Vivian Bullwinkel, urging her to tell her story. Where has she been? Is she well? they ask.

With bare feet, her uniform grubby with dirt and oil from the *Vyner Brooke*, Vivian staggers, and Nesta catches her.

'Vivian, sit down. Girls, don't crowd her. Oh, you can't imagine how wonderful it is to see you.' Nesta kneels on the ground by her chair, squeezing her hand. 'Tell us everything, won't you?' But then Nesta catches a glimpse of Vivian's feet. 'Oh, my God, what happened to your feet?'

'I don't know, Nesta. My goodness, I didn't think I would see any of you ever again. Who else is here?' Vivian stammers.

A chorus of 'me, me, me' brings a smile to her face as she nods to each of the nurses.

'Matron Paschke? Is she here?' Vivian asks.

The hut falls silent.

'No, not yet,' Nesta says. 'Or Matron Drummond.'

'That makes you the senior, then, Sister James,' Vivian tells her.

'I guess, but we're not really operating on a hierarchy at the moment.'

Nesta registers Vivian has not let go of her water canteen. Its strap around her neck, she holds it tightly to her side.

61

'Are you alone, are there any of the others with you?' Nesta probes.

Vivian can't speak. No one speaks. Everyone is holding their breath in hope.

'They're all dead,' Vivian whispers.

'What do you mean? How can they all be dead?' one of the nurses asks.

'I have something I need to tell you and I don't know how,' Vivian says, looking at each nurse, seeing the fear seeping into their eyes.

'Let's sit down at the back there, where prying ears won't hear you.' Nesta takes her arm and leads her to the far end of the hut and onto a concrete slab, where the nurses gather in a tight circle around Vivian.

All eyes are on Bully. The only sound in the room is quiet sobbing for their dead friends. Nurses huddle together to comfort one another as Vivian begins to talk.

'We were still on the ship when I heard Matron Paschke tell us it was time to go. I took off my shoes and remembered Matron telling us to hold our life jacket firmly under our chins when we jumped. When I surfaced, the hull of the ship was so close I could have touched it. Someone shouted at me to get away from it, so I doggy-paddled as fast as I could. I found an upturned lifeboat and hung on to the rope it was attached to. Before long, others joined me, clinging to every part of the lifeboat. Rosetta and Clarice had joined me, and before we knew it, it was dark.' Vivian falls silent, wiping away a tear.

The nurses look at each other. They know Rosetta and Clarice aren't here.

Vivian presses on. She finds herself drifting away and reliving the story.

Vivian's story
Radji Beach
February 1942

'*I think I see a light. There on the beach. It's a fire! Someone's lit a fire.*'

'*Where, Bully? I can't see it.*'

'*It's behind you, Rosetta, just turn around. Come on, everyone. Paddle. Let's go.*'

'*Are you sure? I still can't see it.*'

Vivian pivots Rosetta around.

'*There. D'you see it now?*'

'*I see it,*' *says Rosetta, suddenly excited.* '*Come on, Clarice.*'

With a new-found energy, the group begin to swim hard for the beach. The light from the fire is beckoning them ever closer.

'*Bully! I think I touched the bottom; I can feel sand under my feet. Come on, everyone. We can walk from here.*'

Vivian takes Rosetta's arm to help her onto the beach, but then notices the wounds to her back and shoulder. Her uniform is torn open and, by the light of the stars, she sees the shredded flesh beneath.

'*Rosetta, you're injured! Let me take a look.*'

'*I'm OK. I'm OK. I think I was hit with shrapnel; I can't really move my right arm at all.*'

'*Hang on a minute. Clarice! Clarice, where are you?*'

'*I'm over here, Bully. Over here.*' *But it's so dark, she is just a voice.*

'*We can't see the fire, but keep talking and we'll follow your voice.*'

Rosetta and Vivian stumble towards Clarice, who has begun to sing in a loud, clear voice, without pause.

'*There you are!*' *cries Vivian.* '*Rosetta is injured. Are you OK?*'

Clarice has stopped singing. She briefly touches her chest. '*A bit of pain here and I think I've got a head wound. What about you?*'

'Wobbly legs, but no injuries,' says Vivian.

'Rosetta?' asks Clarice, noting that her friend is struggling to stay on her feet.

'Ladies, are you all right?' a voice calls in the dark.

'Who's that?' says Vivian.

'It's Miller. I've checked on the others – some minor injuries, all exhausted. We've missed the fire we saw, but not by much.'

'Jimmy! We're OK.'

'Is that you, Sister Bullwinkel?'

'Given our situation, I think you can me Vivian, Jimmy. What do we need to do?'

'Find the fire! I was thinking a couple of us could go and look for whoever lit it.'

'You go, Bully, I'll wait with Rosetta,' insists Clarice.

'Are you sure?'

'Go, we'll be fine.'

Jimmy and Vivian set off along the beach. Thankfully, the skies are clear and the starlight is bright enough for them not to wander back into the sea.

'I'm hoping they're just around the bend ahead,' pants Jimmy. It's hard going on the sand and they are already exhausted.

'Look!' exclaims Vivian. 'You're right. There it is – a bonfire, a beacon. Hey, over here, over here!'

A voice peals out into the dark. 'Sister Bullwinkel, is that you?'

'Matron Drummond! Yes, yes. Oh my goodness, we found you.'

'It's Bully, everyone. Bully's here.'

'Matron, this is Jimmy – Mr Miller – he's an officer on the ship.'

'Was an officer,' grins Jimmy. 'Hello, Matron, it's damn good to see you.'

'And you, Mr Miller. Are there no others with you?'

'Yes, they're not far away, just around the bend in the beach.'

'Clarice and Rosetta are with me, but they're injured.'

'Well, it's a good thing we have a doctor or two with us. Come on, let's find them and get our girls.'

'There are several others as well. I haven't been able to assess them, it's just too dark.'

'Then we will bring them to the light.' Matron Drummond turns to a middle-aged man huddled close to the bonfire. 'Doctor, we need you to accompany us on a short walk to where some injured survivors have landed.'

'I will not be going anywhere,' the doctor says bluntly. 'If you have injured survivors, then bring them to me.'

'But, Doctor,' pleads Vivian, 'they need help now, and I'm not sure if they can all walk. Please, it's not far.'

But the doctor is insistent and rude. 'Matron, tell your subordinate I do not take instructions from a nurse. If you have injured, bring them here. I will not leave the main group.'

Matron pulls herself up to her full height. 'And you call yourself a doctor? I'm going to get my girls.'

Vivian, Matron and Jimmy turn away and head down the beach. They walk in silence, each of them appalled by the belligerent medic.

'That's them,' says Vivian finally, as their small group comes into view. 'We're coming,' she calls.

'Matron, is that you, Matron?'

'Yes, Sister Halligan. Come on, let's get you to the fire so we can see what's what.'

Slowly, the new group of survivors heads back to the bonfire. Rosetta is limping badly, but Clarice and Vivian support her until they find a space for her near the warmth.

'Are you OK, Sisters?'

'Yes, thanks, Jimmy,' says Clarice.

Altogether, around eighty survivors are gathered on the beach: men, women, children and nurses.

Matron points out a large group of British servicemen. 'I think they're plotting what to do when the sun comes up.'

One by one, people begin to doze off. They have survived a shipwreck and the treacherous current. For the moment, they have found safety and it isn't long before the beach is filled with the sound of gentle snoring.

'Wake up! Wake up, everyone. We need to talk.'

Matron is the first on her feet. The sun is rising over the sea. It will be another day of pounding heat; it's the only thing she can be certain of.

'And who are you?' she asks.

'Good morning, Matron. I'm Bill Sedgeman. I was the first officer on the Vyner Brooke,' he replies and then turns to the wider group. 'Can I have everyone's attention please? It's obvious the Japanese are on this island, but our priority is to look for food and fresh water. I'm calling for volunteers, just a small party to venture inland and see what we find.'

'I'll go,' calls a voice, and then another, 'And me.'

'Count me in.'

'Let's get going.'

'That's five, that will be enough,' the first officer says. 'The rest of you try to find some shade and we'll be back as quickly as we can.'

'All right, Sisters, let's help move anyone who can't move themselves.'

The daylight has brought with it intense heat, and for the next hour, the nurses help those who are too weak or injured into the *shade of the giant cool foliage. There is nothing more to do now but wait.*

'Matron, they're back, the men are coming back.' Vivian races out of the jungle and onto the beach, desperate for news. 'Oh, no!' she calls to the group. 'There are Japanese soldiers with them. Mr Sedgeman is talking to them.'

'These are the people I told you about,' the first officer is explaining. 'We surrender and want to be prisoners of war.'

'What did he say?' A murmur of confusion passes through the group.

The soldiers come face to face with the group of exhausted survivors and raise their bayonets. Everyone gets slowly to their feet. They are ordered out of the jungle.

'What do you think you're doing?' The first officer is indignant. 'I've just told you we're surrendering. You don't need the guns.'

The soldiers ignore him and begin to pull the men away from the women.

'Matron, why are they doing that?'

'Everyone, please stay calm,' says Matron, although her own voice is cracking.

'They're taking them away!' cries Vivian as the group of men is marched away. 'Jimmy!'

'It's OK, Vivian,' calls Jimmy. 'Please look after yourself, it was a pleasure getting to know you.'

Jimmy, the soldiers and all the other men disappear around the bend of the beach. What follows are sounds that Vivian will never forget.

'NO! NO! OH, MY GOD, NO!'

'Quickly,' shouts Matron. 'Sisters, block the children's ears, they shouldn't be hearing this.'

67

The sound of the gentle lapping of the waves on the shore, the calls of birds and insects from dense forest, all is made mute by the ferocious staccato of gunshots erupting into the air.

'Matron! They're killing them, they're killing the men!' Vivian weeps.

'Everyone, stay close together now,' Matron orders. 'We must do exactly as they say.'

A nurse pipes up from the stunned crowd. 'Why don't we make a run for it? Those of us who are strong swimmers can head into the water, the others into the jungle. That way, at least some of us might escape.'

'No, Sister, we're not going anywhere. Can't you see there are people here who need us? Yes, they have probably killed the men, but all our training and everything we stand for means we do not abandon those who need our help. I want you all to remember that where there is life, there is hope.'

'I'm sorry, Matron,' sobs the nurse. 'I'm sorry.'

'We're all scared, Sister, but we're all scared together.'

The soldiers have reappeared and are making their way steadily towards the group. Some are using bloody cloths to clean their bayonets. They indicate for everyone to head down to the sea, pointing first at the people and then at the water.

'OK, Vivian, you and Sister Kerr help Sisters Halligan and Wight to their feet. Let's just do as we're told,' says Matron. 'All together, girls, hold hands.'

One by one, the women step into the sea. They are all so hot that the cool water is a momentary relief.

'Such a beautiful day, such a beautiful place. How could anything so terrible happen here?' Vivian is struggling to resolve the reality *of the ravishing landscape with the brutal attack on the men. She imagines them now, fatally wounded, just a few feet away.*

A feeling of terrible dread settles over the women. The nightmare is not yet over.

'Oh, Mother,' whispers Vivian. 'I am so sorry you will never know what happened to me. I love you, and I guess it will be great to see Dad again.'

'GIRLS!' yells Matron Irene Drummond. 'I WILL CARRY YOU ALL IN MY HEART. YOU HAVE NO IDEA HOW PROUD I AM OF EACH AND EVERY ONE OF YOU.'

Before Vivian turns away from the beach and focuses all her attention on the horizon, she has noticed the machine gun being set up at the water's edge. She turns around; she doesn't need to see this. For the second time that morning, gunfire pierces the tranquil skies.

Vivian comes to slowly. First, she opens her eyes to see the startling blue above her, and a bright white sun. She blinks, dazzled by its brilliance. Am I alive? *she asks herself, incredulous. She is on her back in the shallows.*

She doesn't move, terrified the soldiers are still close by. She shuts her eyes and tries to steady her breathing. She's in pain, knows she's been hit, but right now, she can't locate the source. Play dead, *she tells herself.*

When she opens her eyes again – did she fall asleep? – the sun is lower in the sky. She can't hear anyone else and risks raising her head to look at the beach. It's empty.

It's then the pain strikes in earnest. She has been hit in her side and back. She carefully runs her hands over her body. No major organs, thank God, *she reassures herself. It is when she raises her head once more to peer into the waters around her that she sees* the bodies of her friends floating there. It is a terrible moment and she wonders if she'll ever gather enough strength to leave this burial ground and find safety.

Slowly, inch by inch, she raises herself into a sitting position. She has to find somewhere to hide. Away from the beach.

The jungle!

Vivian crawls out of the sea, along the sand and into the shade of the forest. Her thirst is terrible; she can think of little else now, other than cool water sliding down her throat.

From the shelter of the trees, she flinches when she hears Japanese voices, but then they're gone. She'll wait, rest, and then go back to the sea to check for survivors.

Vivian listens hard and that's when she hears it, the gurgling of a stream. Her injuries forgotten, she's on her feet and stumbling towards fresh water. And when she reaches it, she buries her entire face in the lapping brook.

'Where have you been?' A voice snaps her out of her reverie.

Vivian turns around to see a young man, obviously British Army, lying wounded at the edge of the jungle, half his body on the sand.

'Who are you?' she asks, aghast.

'Kingsley, Private Kingsley.'

'You're injured.'

'Isn't it obvious, nurse? When they didn't finish me off by shooting at us, one of the soldiers ran his bayonet through me. Twice. I managed to crawl up here after they left.'

Thirst quenched, Vivian stands and approaches the young soldier.

'Can I take a look at you?' she asks gently.

'I'd be grateful. But aren't you injured too?'

Vivian manages a smile. Her wounds are painful, but right now, she has a patient.

'I am. But let's see what's going on with you first.'

'What's your name?' asks the private as Vivian kneels beside him.

'Vivian, Vivian Bullwinkel. I'm a sister in the Australian Army.'

Vivian peels away the private's bloody jacket and shirt. She sighs.

'These bayonet wounds; I'm afraid they're already starting to look infected. You really need a doctor.'

'Well, you're all I've got right now.' Private Kingsley attempts a laugh, which turns into a fit of coughing. Vivian lays a hand over his.

'I'll need to dress these wounds, but, as you can see, I don't have anything we can use for bandages. I'll go back to the beach and see what I can find.'

'The beach?' he exclaims. 'I don't think you should go back there.'

'Well, we can't stay here; I'll be right back. I promise.'

'The jungle is still crawling with Japanese. Can't we just wait?'

But Vivian is already on her feet and moving towards the sea. The pain in her side is throbbing, but at least blood is no longer flowing from the wound. If she doesn't think about it, then she can just keep going, keep placing one foot in front of the other, keep taking care of those who need her. She knows how to do this, if nothing else.

There are no soldiers on the beach, no one at all in fact. Vivian doesn't dare look out to sea; the bodies of her friends floating in the water might just undo her.

Where beach meets jungle, she finds two life jackets and a canteen for water. She goes a little way into the foliage and begins to tear off some fibre from the coconut trees. This should do, she tells herself and heads back to her patient.

Private Kingsley is asleep when she returns, and he doesn't stir as she binds his wounds using the only materials she can find. And then, when she is satisfied with her work, she lies down beside the solider and falls asleep herself.

Vivian wakes with a start, disorientated, in pain. But her first thoughts are for the private. He is awake, watching her.

'How long have I been asleep?' She sits up slowly, stiffly.

'Not long enough, but you clearly needed the rest.'

'What we need is food, Kingsley. I'm going to go and see if I can find something. Maybe there's a village close by.'

'What if the villagers turn you in?'

'I'm prepared to take that risk,' Vivian says firmly. She reasons that if she doesn't, they'll just starve to death in this jungle.

She heads off once more, weak, but determined to bring something back. It's early, so the sun hasn't yet begun its relentless pounding. Vivian reasons that the village First Officer Sedgeman found can't be too far away. Probably no more than half a mile. She hasn't walked five hundred yards before the smell of cooking renews her resolve to keep going.

Vivian feels tears prick her eyes when she spies the outskirts of the village. She is surprised that no one is paying this wounded, bedraggled, half-starved woman much heed as she enters. But she has to get their attention! Using a combination of the few words of Malay she knows and gesturing repeatedly to her mouth and stomach, she hopes she has made herself understood. And just in case she hasn't, she says, 'Food! Food! Hungry!' over and over again.

She can't understand what they're saying, but the elder men of the village are angry, indicating she retrace her steps and leave the village. In the end, a couple of women chase after her with parcels of food as she makes her way back to the jungle, saving the day.

* * *

'Kingsley! Wake up. I have some food.' The soldier has fallen asleep again. Vivian is worried his wounds are infected. But what can she do?

He slowly opens his eyes and focuses on Vivian's face. He struggles to sit up.

Vivian unwraps two banana leaves containing some cooked rice and pineapple slices. She figures they can make this meagre food stretch to at least a couple of days.

'Are you all right?' Kingsley asks.

Vivian wipes away her tears before they fall into her food. She shakes her head.

'I'm not all right, Kingsley. Look at us. Look at you.' She lays down her banana leaf and gestures towards the beach. 'My matron and my friends were gunned down right next to me. I watch it happen again and again and again. We all knew we were going to die, and what did we do? We didn't cry out, we didn't run away – it would have been a futile attempt in any case – we just looked at one another. I knew that if we had to die, at least we were all dying together. And then ...' Vivian swallows a sob. 'The guns ...' She raises her eyes to the young private, tears falling freely down her cheeks. 'Why am I alive, Kingsley? Why was I spared?'

'I don't know, Sister,' he says softly.

'I'm really worried about you. I don't think we can stay here any longer.'

'What are you saying?'

'We need to surrender. We need to find the Japanese and put our lives in their hands.'

'You can't be serious!'

Vivian knows that if she's haunted by the slaughter of her friends, then so is he.

'There are only two of us, Kingsley. We have to hope they'll just take us prisoner. We can't tell them we survived the slaughter on the beaches, or they'll probably just finish us off; if we say we were shipwrecked, we might have a chance. But one thing I do know is that if we stay here, we'll definitely die.'

'I can barely walk.'

'I'll make a crutch for your good side and support you on the other.'

It is decided.

'We'll fill up our canteen of water and leave first thing in the morning,' says Vivian.

When Vivian finishes speaking, the sound of women weeping fills the hut. The nurses are huddled together for comfort, supporting each other in their grief. But Nesta is worried that Vivian will exhaust her final reserves of strength before telling them what happened when she went in search of help. They need to hear the rest of her story.

Vivian is holding a water bottle tight against her tummy.

'The Japanese came after we surrendered in the village. They searched us for weapons but found nothing, of course. We were interrogated for hours and then a car arrived and brought me here.'

'Vivian,' Nesta begins, taking her hand. 'I can't imagine how you're feeling . . . everything you've been through. It's too awful. And your injuries, we need to take a look at them.' Nesta gazes around the room, meeting the eyes of the other nurses. 'But first, you, me, all of us, need to make a vow. What Vivian has just told us can never be repeated to anyone. Ever.' Nesta pauses to confirm that her words are striking home. 'Vivian is a witness to a brutal crime and if any Japanese soldiers know she survived, they'll kill her too. And if they think we know, we can expect the same fate. Agreed?'

Heads nod vigorously as the reality of Nesta's words sinks in.

'Come on then, Sister Bullwinkel,' Nesta says, with a little more cheer in her voice. 'You need to lie down so we can examine those wounds.' She extends a hand to Vivian, who gets shakily to her feet, still holding the water bottle to her tummy.

'Shouldn't we take her to the hospital and have one of the doctors examine her?' Jean asks.

'We can't risk it,' says Nesta. 'No one must know what happened and that includes the doctors. We take care of our own. Right, Bully?'

'Thank you, Sister James, I couldn't be in better hands than with all of you.'

Nesta gently takes the water bottle from her.

'It's OK, Bully, it's done its job, you can have it back when we've finished.'

Vivian reluctantly releases the bottle, and they get their first look at the exit wound on her stomach.

The nurses form a circle around her.

With bandages crafted from a torn Navy shirt, Nesta pronounces the wound free from infection and healing nicely. She apologises she has no food to give her; some will arrive in a few hours, hopefully.

'It's OK, they gave Kingsley and me a drink and something to eat at the village while they were interrogating us. If it's all the same with you, I'd like to sleep even if it is on concrete. I'm finally with friends and I feel safe for the first time in a long time.'

'All right, girls, let's get out of here so Bully can get some rest,' Nesta orders.

Before they leave, each woman gives Vivian a hug, a kiss, a few words of support.

Nesta hovers outside the hut, deep in thought.

'What are you thinking, Nesta?' Jean too is lingering, equally dazed by Vivian's story.

'I'm thinking we do have to tell someone else what happened, in case . . .'

'. . . In case we don't survive? Is that what you're thinking?'

'I am. Vivian witnessed the mass slaughter of unarmed people. These are serious, brutal crimes. When the time comes, those accountable should answer for their actions, and if her story can't be told, then they won't.'

'Who do you suggest we talk to?'

'I don't know yet, but I'll find the right people.'

That night, one of the nurses gently shakes Vivian awake. 'Come with me, there's someone who wants to see you in the hospital hut.'

Bully is met at the entrance by a British nurse.

'Thank you for coming, Sister Bullwinkel, there's someone here asking for you. He's fading fast, I'm afraid,' the nurse tells her.

Halfway down the hut, Vivian pauses by the bedside of a patient she immediately recognises as Kingsley. She sits down beside him and takes his hand.

'I'm here, Kingsley, I'm here. It's Vivian.'

Kingsley stirs, and slowly opens his eyes.

'Sister?'

'Yes, Kingsley, Sister Vivian.'

'Thank you . . . for everything . . . thank you,' he stammers.

'Is it time, Kingsley?' Vivian asks softly. Without a real hospital, the young private is never going to make it, she knows that much.

'It is,' he sighs.

'Then thank you, Kingsley. I'll never forget you.'

'You . . . should . . . go now,' says the young soldier, closing his eyes. Vivian feels the slightest pressure as he squeezes her hand.

She doesn't move until sometime later, when the nurse returns and lightly feels for a pulse.

'He's gone,' she says.

'I know,' sighs Vivian. 'He died about twenty minutes ago. Is it OK if I sit with him for a little longer?'

'Of course. But not too long, you need your sleep.'

'Leave him alone!' Norah shouts. 'Can't you see he's sick? We need to stay together.'

The next morning, when the men, women and children are informed they are to move camp, they are taken to the pier and, once again, the Japanese soldiers begin to separate the men from the women. Norah can't help but lash out when they approach John.

Ena grabs Norah's arm, pulling her away as the soldier raises his hand to strike her. Released from her grip, John is yanked towards the men's group.

'Ena! Do something! We have to stop them,' Norah cries.

'Norah, please. Don't make it any worse or they'll take it out on him.'

'John!' Norah calls.

Her husband turns around. Slowly, he raises his arm in a wave. 'Look after yourself, my darling. Look after yourself, I'll be fine.'

And he and the other men are gone.

Norah drops to the ground, sobbing. Women and children walk around her, no one says anything or does anything to help her. They are all feeling the same pain.

Ena helps Norah to her feet; Norah knows they must keep moving, and they join the throng of women and children walking onto the pier. She no longer knows who the tears she sheds are intended for: her sister, herself, her husband or her beloved daughter.

CHAPTER 5

Camp II, Irenelaan, Palembang, Southern Sumatra
March 1942–October 1943

'How long do we have to stay here?' Jean wails.
'Jean, please think about something else, won't you?'
Nesta pleads.

Nesta can feel the hours passing on this pier, can feel the sun pounding them all into hopeless submission. There's nothing she can do for anyone.

They're all still here the next morning. Nesta watches a beautiful rainbow in the sky overhead as dawn breaks. Two aged, dilapidated freighters approach the dock and drop anchor a little way off. As several small launches make their way towards the pier, the Japanese soldiers become agitated, pushing through the crowd, roughly pulling anyone still sitting onto their feet.

'Well, at least we'll be out of the sun.' Nesta tries to reassure the nurses, but everyone looks too exhausted to respond.

As each launch pulls up to the pier, the prisoners are shoved forwards, loaded onto the boats and taken to the freighters. This carries on until the pier is empty and the ships begin to heave their way through the Moesi River, slowly navigating through the jungle. As they move through the oil-slicked water, Nesta can't take her eyes off the hulls of partially submerged ships, wondering what stories they could tell.

Late in the afternoon, they arrive at another set of docks: Palembang, Sumatra. The sick and sorry human cargo shamble off the freighters and are led to a clearing at the end of the pier.

Once again, hours pass, but Nesta and her nurses sit quietly, knowing that a quick slap or a prod with a bayonet will be freely given should they raise their heads above the parapet. Just when everyone thinks they're about to pass out, a convoy of trucks rattles up and loads the women and children on board. They pass through villages, down dusty roads lined by locals cheering, waving small flags adorned with a red disc emanating rays of sunshine – the flag of the Rising Sun.

'Boo, boo!' one of the nurses calls out.

'Boo, boo,' echoes a chorus of brave voices.

The locals stop jeering, stunned at this challenge. Several of the nurses stick their tongues out, making gestures they would deem vulgar at any other time. Japanese soldiers run up to each truck driver, shouting at the women and ordering the drivers to speed up.

It is dark when the trucks stop outside what is obviously a school. For the first time in nearly two days, they are given something to eat and drink before finding a classroom to bed down in for the night. But sleep doesn't come easily; the guards insist that all lights must remain on, and the mosquitoes are relentless.

Later that evening, a serviceman appears at the entrance of the hut. One of the nurses points him out to Nesta, who hurries over.

'Hello, I'm Sister James.'

'Nice to meet you, Sister. I hear you need to speak to the commodore.'

'I do. Can you arrange it?'

'I already have. I spoke to him a short while ago and he's agreed to meet you tomorrow. Apparently, there's something he wants to talk to you about too.'

The next morning, the nurses are asked to assemble at the far end of the school. They don't have to wait long before an imposing-looking British officer approaches.

'I'm Commodore Modin, Charles Modin.'

Nesta steps forwards. 'Sir, I'm Sister Nesta James of the Australian Army Nursing Service.'

'I'm sorry we are meeting under these circumstances, Sister James.'

'I am too, sir.'

'I was told of your arrival last night. I immediately spoke to the senior Japanese officer here and requested that the nurses were to be treated as military personnel, not citizens. It makes a difference to be called a prisoner of war instead of an internee and you should be entitled to certain protections, as well as access to the Red Cross.'

'Thank you, sir, we—'

'Sister James, I'm sorry to say that they refused. I did and said all I could to persuade them, but they wouldn't budge.'

Everyone is instantly deflated. The brief smiles they shared fade and, once again, despair ignites amongst the women.

'Could we talk to them?' Nesta asks.

'They won't speak to you, Sister. Unfortunately, the Japanese opinion of women ... well, let's just say it isn't the same as mine, ours.'

Nesta looks at her nurses. She can feel the words on the tips of their tongues; only their disciplined training is keeping them silent.

'Again, I'm sorry. All I can do is wish you luck.'

'I'm not sure how much luck is going to be on our side, but we do appreciate that you tried. Before you go, Commodore, may I remind you that I asked you for a meeting?'

'Ah, yes,' the commodore says, and Nesta instructs all but Vivian and Jean to return to their classroom.

'Sir, may I introduce Sister Jean Ashton and Sister Vivian Bullwinkel? Vivian has something to tell you.'

'I'm not sure what I can do to help, but do please go ahead, Sister Bullwinkel.'

'We don't want you to do anything: we simply want you to listen.'

Vivian begins to tell the story of the massacre on the beach and as she does, the colour drains from the commodore's face. His staunch military bearing sags, but he remains respectfully silent until Vivian stops talking.

'We don't know what will become of us, but it's crucial someone else knows what happened on Radji Beach,' says Nesta grimly.

'Thank you, Sister Bullwinkel. What happened to you, to your colleagues and the others on that beach constitutes a crime. To gun down unarmed prisoners of war is against the rules of this confounded conflict. I cannot tell you how sorry I am to hear what happened to you. There are no words. But you have been very brave and the army is grateful to you for helping Private Kingsley.' The commodore's eyes are shining. He lays a hand on Vivian's shoulder. 'I can't even ask you to give me a list of all the people who were murdered; if it was found, none of us would make it out of here alive.'

Nesta watches Vivian while the commodore is speaking. She is visibly shaking; telling her story once more has taken its toll. She places a comforting arm around her distressed friend, holding her steady.

Commodore Modin steps in front of Vivian and straightens up to his full height before saluting her. He takes her hand.

'I served in the Great War and I've been fighting in this one for two years. I thought I had seen and heard the worst of humanity. But today, just now, you have shown me that human brutality knows no bounds. What happened on that beach will not be forgotten. I'll find a way to make it known and all I ask of you is that you say nothing to another living soul until you are safely back at home.'

Vivian can't speak, but she nods, and the commodore turns and leaves.

'Well done, Bully,' Nesta whispers. 'That can't have been easy, but we're all so proud of you.'

'Come on, Norah, you have to get up,' Ena pleads. Ena and her sister are in one of the small classrooms, along with many other women and children.

'What's the point?' Norah mumbles. She is lying flat on her back, gazing up at the ceiling. 'Sally's gone, John's gone. My family . . .'

'The point is that you need to get them back and you can only do that by getting up and carrying on.'

June lies down beside Norah, snuggling up to her. 'Please get up,' says the little girl. 'I'm so hungry and we have to go outside to eat.'

'June's right, Norah, they've set up the food outside. You know as well as the rest of us that we have to eat when we can.'

Norah slowly sits up, reaching for Ena's extended hand. Ena pulls her to her feet and hugs her tightly. June wraps her arms around their waists.

'I'm sorry, Ena,' Norah sighs. 'Especially because I know how worried you are about Ken. I'm being selfish.'

'My darling sister, you don't ever need to apologise to me. I'll always be here, whenever you need me.'

'Me too,' pipes up June and the two women stroke the girl's hair.

'You sweet girl, thank you,' says Norah.

While the women and the little girl share this precious moment of warmth, Margaret Dryburgh appears.

'Ladies, I've put aside some rice for you. Are you coming?' Margaret waits by the entrance and takes Norah's hand. 'I can't imagine how you're feeling right now, but I want you to know I'm here to help you.'

'Thank you,' says Norah, and adds, 'Is there any news?'

'There is. Apparently, we're moving on shortly. This is just a temporary stop.'

'Where to?' Ena asks.

'They didn't tell us anything other than that we're leaving. I wish at least one of them had a few words of English, but that's all I could make out.'

The next morning, the women and children are lined up and marched off the school grounds. Curious eyes follow them through the town as they walk towards the countryside. Eventually, they are led into a small village where two rows of houses face each other across a central street. The soldiers begin to divide the prisoners into groups.

'They're giving us actual houses?' exclaims Nesta. A soldier has approached the nurses, roughly counting them before aiming his rifle at the women and gesturing for them to split into two groups.

'Looks like it,' Jean says, 'but it's a shame we can't all be together.'

One group, led by Nesta, enters a house with the number 24 on the front door and Jean leads the second group into a house two doors down. Dutch settlers must have occupied these houses before they arrived and it's clear they had been moved on in a hurry. Their possessions are everywhere. In the kitchens, the nurses find a couple of tins of European food; the bedrooms have children's clothing hanging in the wardrobes. There are squeals of delight heard between the houses when soap and toothbrushes are found in the bathrooms, and even more delight when they turn on the lights to find there is electricity. Food being the most pressing of their needs, Jean instructs her nurses to build a firepit in front of the house where they can cook.

Nesta leaves her house and joins Jean and together they watch the firepit take shape. They hope they will be given something more than the few tins of food they found in the kitchen to prepare.

'Can we all get together when they're finished? I'd like to talk about how we should use our skills for however long we're here,' she tells Jean.

'Excellent idea, I'll gather my lot up shortly and join you.'

When Nesta returns to her house, she finds the girls gathered, waiting for her.

'What's wrong?' Nesta asks, unable to make out the silly grins on their faces.

'We have something for you,' Betty chortles.

'What?'

'It's in one of the bedrooms. It's a real bed and we all want you to have it.'

'Ha! That's lovely, but I'm more than happy with the floor. One of you can take it.'

'No, we can't. This is for you, just come and look at it.'

Playing along, Nesta follows them into the bedroom. The girls have formed a wall in front of the 'bed' and, with a flourish, they stand aside to reveal a baby's cot.

'You're the only one of us who can fit in it,' Betty says as all the girls burst out laughing.

Nesta examines the cot, pushing down on the firm little mattress. 'How do I get in? I'm not climbing over the top.'

'We can fix that,' one of the nurses says as she and two others set about removing one side of the cot.

Nesta sizes up the petite bed, before swinging up her legs and lying down. 'Perfect,' she says. 'I'll take it.'

The nurses of number 26 congregate in number 24. Nesta calls them to order and they gather around.

'Jean and I have been talking about how we can make ourselves useful. We'll find out what the hospital facilities are, offer our help, but we're thinking more along the lines of district nursing. You all know what this means. We'll visit the other houses and identify any small concerns the women have before they become big problems.'

There is a loud knock at the door and all heads turn. Jean opens up and four women enter, each carrying a large basket of food.

'Welcome,' says one in a strong Dutch accent. 'We are in number 25, the house in between yours. We hope this small contribution will help you settle in.'

The nurses all stand aside as the women take the baskets into the kitchen. 'There is some soap and basic toiletries in here also,' one of them calls.

'How long have you been here?' Nesta asks.

'We live here, well, in Palembang. Our husbands ran the mines, but when the Japanese invaded, they took them away. They took all the men away. Now it is just us and the group of nuns from the local mission.'

'Did they let you bring your possessions with you?'

'Some – clothes, pots, pans, plates, things like that. We're quite well set up, considering.'

'Were there people living in this house before we came?'

The two women glance at each other; Nesta finds it difficult to read their expressions.

'Yes, there were. Our friends. We don't know why they were taken away and not us.'

That night, the nurses eat together, reluctant to be apart. It is only the lure of a little space to lie down that finally sends some of them back to their own house.

When Nesta finally crawls into her cot, she announces her guilt at having a soft mattress while her friends are curled up on the floor beside her.

'Don't feel bad; none of us is interested in trying to wrap our bodies around that tiny space. It's all yours!'

Once the nurses have been housed, everyone else is shoved into homes with no thought to nationality or family. Norah finds herself in a hut full of strangers, but now, with the soldiers gone, she and everyone else set about finding their loved ones, rearranging themselves to be with their friends.

Finally, reunited with her sister and the little girl they rescued, they sit curled up in a corner of the bare but somehow stuffy room.

'How long are we going to stay here?' June whispers, cuddling up to Ena.

'I don't know, my sweetheart. Hopefully not too long and we can all go home.'

'Do you know where my daddy is?'

'I don't. Hopefully, he's still in Singapore waiting for his little girl.'

'I hope so, too.'

'Get some sleep, June, we'll explore in the morning, find some of the children you've been playing with.'

Norah listens to this exchange, her heart breaking, and she thinks of Sally; where is she, and more importantly, is she safe?

CHAPTER 6

Camp II, Irenelaan, Palembang
April 1942–October 1943

'We have something for you.' One of the Dutch nuns, Sister Catherina, has stopped Nesta in the street on her way to make her rounds of the camp. Earlier that day, she organised the nurses into pairs to work a roster visiting their neighbours, when they have been instructed to make friends as well as to tend to minor ailments. Somehow, she knows that community spirit is going to be essential if they are to survive their incarceration.

Sister Catherina is from the Charitas order who run the local hospital in Palembang: their leader is Mother Laurentia, she tells Nesta.

The nun reaches deep into the pockets of her habit and takes out three packs of bandages and some painkillers. Nesta is overjoyed. This is better than bananas; now, she has a few tools of her trade to help those in need.

'We have to be careful, and it's not much,' the nun tells her. 'But we will bring what we can.'

* * *

'Good morning. I am Ah Fat, translator for Captain Miachi, your camp commandant.' Ah Fat is a short, bespectacled man in civilian clothing, who has the habit of pushing his glasses up his nose as he speaks.

Two weeks have passed since their arrival and the women had been settling into the routine business of survival, until one morning when word began to spread that they were all to assemble the next day at noon. No further information was revealed, although rumours abound. Might they be about to be released? Or moved again? But, alas, not.

'Dr McDowell is your internee commandant,' Ah Fat continues, indicating a woman standing nearby. 'If any of you have problems, you will go to her, and she will speak to me and I will tell the captain. Understand?'

The captain's uniform displays colourful insignias. Short in stature, his hair parted immaculately, his swagger confident, he smiles at the women.

The women remain silent, and Ah Fat nods at the captain to continue.

'There will be some changes,' Ah Fat translates for the women. 'When you hear the word *tenko*, you will come outside. One of you will count everyone else in your house and this number will be reported to us. Understand?'

No one speaks. The captain briskly walks away as another soldier steps forwards.

'*Tenko!*' he screams.

For a moment, the women glance at one another, unsure what to do.

'*Tenko!*' he screams again.

Dr McDowell steps forwards. 'Ladies, I'm Dr McDowell,' she says in a soft Scottish accent. 'Those of you who have had the misfortune of needing medical treatment will have already met me. I'll get to know the rest of you, I'm sure. But, right now, you've all heard the command, so I suggest, before there's any trouble, you return to your houses and get counting.'

At the word 'trouble', the order finally hits home. Chaos erupts as the women scramble to get back to their houses.

Norah finds Ena and June and they quickly return home and wait outside for the others to arrive. Margaret is back last, strolling, not in any hurry to jump at the orders of the Japanese. 'Now, who wants to do this dreadful count?' she asks.

No one speaks, until Norah finally steps forwards. 'I will.'

A knock on the door of number 24 wakes the inhabitants. It is early – still dark. Nesta extricates herself from her cot and, with everyone else by her side, goes to check. It is their Dutch neighbours, the three women who brought them food on their first day.

'We've come to say goodbye,' one says.

'Where are you going?' Nesta asks.

'We don't know. As usual, we've been told to take only what we can carry and be ready to leave at breakfast.'

'I'm so sorry. We'll never forget your kindness. We couldn't have asked for better neighbours.'

'We have left some clothes and other things that might come in useful in the house. Please help yourselves before the soldiers throw everything out.'

The nurses hug the women and, tearfully, the Dutch turn to leave.

As the nurses in number 24 prepare breakfast, their discussion turns to who their new neighbours might be and whether, morally, it is

OK to ransack the house before they arrive. Nesta tells them she will talk with Jean and come up with a plan for what's OK to take.

Before the nurses can get on with their day, a Japanese officer strides through Nesta's front door. He is accompanied by Ah Fat, Captain Miachi's interpreter. Behind him are the nurses from number 26.

'We were told to come here, no explanation,' Jean whispers to Nesta.

Ah Fat begins to translate for the officer.

'You must move. Captain Miachi has two new houses for you. Just few doors down. Get ready. Quick, quick.'

Nesta sees several of her nurses opening their mouths to object, but she gives her head a sharp shake and they close them again. They can take their possessions, but the houses must be left clean and tidy.

The vacated houses will be an officers' club, Ah Fat continues to interpret for the officer. Once the club has been established, the nurses will become . . . hostesses.

No one speaks as the officer and interpreter leave.

But once they've gone, the room erupts into angry chatter. Defiance thrums through the group.

'I'm not doing it!'

'No way!'

'I'd rather die!'

Nesta and Jean watch their nurses vent their anger.

'Girls – please, girls. Let's just all calm down,' Nesta says.

'Nesta, I don't care what you say, I'm not letting one of those bastards put his hands on me,' one yells.

'Nobody is putting a hand on any of us. It will be over my dead body before I let them near us. However, we have more immediate things to worry about. Moving.'

'What are we taking?' a nurse calls out.

'Everything,' Nesta replies angrily. 'Absolutely bloody everything.'

'Does that include the stove?' Betty asks in jest.

'That includes the stove. And, of course, my bed.'

As the women are packing what they can, disconnecting the stove, moving Nesta's cot ready for the transfer, Margaret appears with Norah and Ena.

'Word's got round, so we've come to help,' Norah informs the nurses.

'Thank you! Three extra pairs of hands are just what we need,' says Nesta.

Margaret pushes the door wide open. 'There's more than three of us!'

Dozens of women are gathered outside the nurses' houses, ready to help.

'I have a plan,' Margaret announces.

'We're all ears,' grins Nesta.

'We form a human chain from number 26 to this house, then another from here to your new places. It will save a hell of a lot of walking backwards and forwards.'

'Great idea,' Betty says, the mood amongst the nurses beginning to shift as they acknowledge the kindness and effort of the volunteers.

Nesta turns back to her girls. 'When I said everything, ladies, I meant *everything*. If it isn't part of the structure, take it.'

'I'm not sure I can pass the stove or the cot along,' Betty says, smiling broadly.

'Not to worry. We can leave them 'til last and carry them together.'

It isn't long before the first pot is handed out and the procession begins.

A crack of lightning, a boom of thunder and the skies open to dump a tropical downpour on the women. But not a single person leaves the human chain. As they pass the home of the Dutch nuns, Sister Catherina hurries outside to ask what is going on. Within minutes, she has assembled twenty-five nuns, including their Mother Superior, to help with the move. They shuffle into line, seemingly oblivious of the fact their heavy habits are soaking up the rain.

Sister Catherina has become a fast favourite with both the women and children. She is in her early twenties, and her energy and curiosity are dedicated to helping others. She does not limit herself to one position in the line but hurries up and down, lending a hand with heavier objects. Children run around the line, chasing each other in and out of the volunteers. Little hands reach up to pass things along. Singing breaks out sporadically, jokes about joining construction sites when they return home, helping to make the work go quickly, and all too soon, the new houses hold everything the nurses will need. Wishing them luck, the women and nuns wander back to their own accommodation, wringing out sodden clothes.

Over the next few days, the nurses walk past their old homes to report back the activities of local labourers. Beds, settees and even a piano are moved into the 'officers' club'.

While the work is still going on, Nesta receives a visit from two Englishmen, Mr Tunn and Mr Stephenson. They are also internees, being held in the town prison, along with several other Englishmen who lived and worked here before the invasion. They have been asked to speak to the nurses.

'Fetch Jean, and everyone else,' Nesta instructs Vivian. 'We all need to hear this.'

When they are all gathered, Mr Tunn begins.

'I'm sorry, ladies, but we're here to deliver orders from our captors.' He pauses for a response; none is forthcoming. He continues, 'They are demanding that five of you attend their club. Tonight.' He pauses. Again, nothing. 'I am so sorry; they are threatening dire consequences if you don't obey. If it helps, Mr Stephenson and I are to act as barmen in each house and we will be able to keep an eye on you.'

'It doesn't help,' a voice fires out from within the ranks of nurses.

'Sisters, if you don't come this evening, they are threatening to start executing internees.' Mr Tunn removes a scrap of paper from his trouser pocket. 'Here are the names of those they've selected.' He reads out five names, including Nesta's.

Mr Stephenson hasn't raised his eyes from the ground the entire visit. Nesta sees his fists clenching as he struggles to contain his anger.

'Thank you, gentlemen. We know the way,' Nesta tells them.

As the two men beat a hasty retreat, Jean suggests they go out into the backyard of the hut to discuss next steps.

'Can I start by stating what I see as the common denominator amongst those they've chosen?' Jean remarks.

All eyes turn to the five nurses whose names are on the list.

'That we're the prettiest?' one says, not even trying to suppress a smile.

'Well, there's that, but I was thinking more of your size and the colour of your hair. There isn't one of you over five feet and you all have dark hair.'

'Hey, I'm five feet, two inches – four if you can find me a decent pair of heels,' another announces.

'I see what you're saying. We're too *petite* to physically intimidate them. And I guess they don't like blondes,' Nesta quips.

'You could be quintuplets,' Vivian says.

Everyone manages a small laugh. The tension is easing, but the problem still stands.

'They only asked for five,' another nurse pipes up. 'But what if all of us went – you know, strength in numbers and all that. See what they do.'

For several moments, no one speaks, but then they begin to mutter amongst themselves. They will all go, smile and be pleasant, stick like glue to each other and put the onus on the Japanese to send them away.

'Or,' adds the nurse, picking up a handful of dirt and rubbing it on her face, down her neck, 'we make ourselves as dirty and as unattractive as possible.'

'And have muddy bare feet with torn clothes,' Betty contributes.

'Let's do it. Everyone, look your worst and we'll gather back here at sunset. Let's show these men who they're dealing with,' Jean orders.

As the sun begins to set, the nurses gather and get to work ripping up their dresses and smearing even more dirt across any bare patches of flesh.

'Er, we have a problem. Will you step forwards, Pat?' says Jean.

Everyone looks around for the nurse named Pat.

'What did I do?'

'You have the misfortune of looking too bloody beautiful no matter how hard you try not to be,' Jean tells her.

'I do not. I'm just as ugly as the rest of you.'

'Nah, you're not,' Nesta says.

'Well, give me a minute.'

Pat grabs a handful of dirt and smears it into her shoulder-length hair. 'There.'

'Nope – if anything, that's made you look even more gorgeous,' Vivian says.

'Sorry, Pat,' Nesta laughs. 'It looks like there's nothing you can do to hide your beauty. I want you to stay behind.'

'And miss out on all the fun?' Pat complains.

'We'll tell you about it, don't worry. And I'll leave a few others behind to keep you company. Right, who hasn't managed to look revolting enough?'

Several others reluctantly agree to stay behind with Pat. And, once more, the nurses begin to scrutinise their friends, adding an extra dab of mud here, some twigs in the hair there. When they're all satisfied with their appearance, they march proudly down the street; several women, including Norah, Ena and Margaret, come out from their houses to cheer them on. Curious eyes peer from windows; word has spread.

Standing outside their former home, now an officers' club, the nurses exchange glances.

'Ready?' Nesta asks.

'Ready, ready, ready!' they shout.

The Japanese officer who opens the door of the club looks stunned at the sight of the grinning, grubby nurses. Before he can respond, Nesta pushes past him into the house, the other nurses on her heels. Inside, they stand in a tight group. The officers present watch them, open-mouthed. Finally, in broken English, a Japanese officer stutters, 'W-Would you like something to drink?'

'No, thank you,' reply the nurses, as one.

'What do Australian women like to drink on a Saturday night?' he presses.

'Milk,' Jean responds.

He translates this remark to his fellow officers.

Before anything more can be said, Mr Stephenson appears holding a tray with glasses of soft drinks. He hands them around. 'Keep it up, girls. You look disgusting.'

After a period of chatter amongst the Japanese, the English-speaking officer speaks up again. 'Why are you so dirty? You must wear powder on your faces, lipstick on your lips. If you don't have any, we will take you into Palembang to buy some.'

'No, thank you,' Nesta tells him with a smile. 'Nurses don't need to wear makeup.'

A long silence follows. Mr Stephenson returns with a tray of biscuits and peanuts. The nurses' resistance folds as they grab the food and stuff it into their mouths. The Japanese men continue to ogle them in silence.

The food relaxes the women and they talk amongst themselves, openly ignoring their hosts. After a while, the men too begin to talk amongst themselves.

It is not long before both the nurses and the Japanese soldiers are exhausted.

The English-speaking officer turns to the women.

'All of you will go now. Only five of you are to stay.'

'We all go, or we all stay,' Nesta says firmly.

The officer raises his voice, no longer bothering to hide his displeasure, and repeats his statement.

The nurses huddle in a tight circle; their fear can no longer be disguised.

'Hurry up!' an officer shouts.

Fives nurses break free of the huddle and step forwards.

Nesta ushers the remaining nurses from the room. The last to leave, she turns back to the five volunteers, who give her reassuring smiles. Mr Stephenson approaches Nesta. 'I'll keep an eye on them.'

When Nesta joins the women outside, Betty is furious. 'What are we going to do? We can't just leave them there.'

'We're not going to,' says Nesta firmly. 'Come on. Let's stand on the other side of the road – we hear anything we don't like, we go in. Agreed?'

The nurses position themselves behind the shrubs and bushes lining the street. Silently, they stare fixedly at the door. It is not long before it opens, and five Japanese officers emerge, each of them holding the arm of one of the nurses.

'They're taking them back to their huts,' Jean whispers.

Before Nesta can respond, one of the nurses breaks into a raucous cough, doubling over, as if she's about to be sick. The others follow her lead, coughing, choking and gurgling in the faces of their captors. Instantly, the Japanese officers push the girls away, grabbing for their handkerchiefs and pressing them over their mouths and noses. The coughing intensifies and soon all five officers have turned and fled.

The women hiding in the bushes emerge and run to their friends, unable to contain their laughter. They mimic their actions and soon everyone is spluttering and gagging.

'Let's go home,' Jean says, finally.

The next morning, none of the nurses wants to go on her rounds; they are terrified there will be repercussions for their behaviour, but it isn't until that afternoon that the English-speaking Japanese officer walks into Nesta's house. She rises to her feet and approaches him.

'You will send four girls tonight to the club. They will be clean and tidy. Eight o'clock.'

He doesn't wait for an answer but leaves as quickly as he arrived.

'Go next door and get the others,' Nesta tells Betty.

Once again, the nurses are in the backyard, talking quietly amongst themselves.

'Girls.' Jean calls them to attention. 'We need to discuss this as a group.'

'What's there to talk about? We're not going. Right?' one says.

'And we're all agreed?' Nesta asks.

Everyone is agreed.

'What do you suggest we do?' Jean turns to Nesta. 'Tell them we're not coming, or simply not turn up?'

'I think we should get a message to them. I'll talk to Dr McDowell and ask her to do it.'

Sleep is hard to come by that night. The doctor was firmly on her side when Nesta explained their decision, only too keen to pass on her message. Nobody came banging on their door tonight, which Nesta takes as a good sign. But the next day, when they receive no food, it is clear the repercussions have begun.

'No food for you. You know what you must do,' a soldier stops to shout at them before delivering food to the other houses.

Their neighbours have come outside to gather their own supplies.

'Anyone who gives them food will be punished. No food for the nurses!'

Late that afternoon, Dr McDowell knocks on Nesta's door.

'Hello, Doctor. We've been waiting to hear from you.' Nesta invites her inside.

'Oh, Sister, I don't know what to say.'

'Just tell us what happened.'

'I'm so sorry, so sorry, but my demands and threats fell on deaf ears.' Dr McDowell looks genuinely upset. 'I was ordered out of Miachi's office with the threat that he would close the hospital if I didn't leave immediately.'

'What are you saying?'

'I don't know what to suggest, I don't know how to help you. But please understand that I am not telling you to go to them. You mustn't. Stay away and continue to call their bluff.'

'It's OK, Doctor.' Nesta lays a hand on her arm. 'Thank you for trying.'

'Please don't thank me, I couldn't help you. I feel so useless, and so angry, and I don't know what to do with that anger.'

'Be a good time for a stiff drink, if only we had some,' Betty says. 'But I can't even offer you rubbing alcohol.'

The doctor smiles sadly, her curly hair limp in the heat. 'You are all very brave,' she whispers, then leaves.

The nurses look around at each other, determined yet fearful of what tomorrow might bring.

When the food cart approaches the next morning, the officer repeats his orders. 'No food for nurses.' He then points to Nesta. 'You come.'

As Nesta makes to follow him, Jean grabs her arm.

'What are you doing? You can't go with him!'

'I must. Don't we want to know what they have to say?' As she walks away, she turns back with a big smile. 'If I don't come back, don't fight over my cot.'

'That's not funny,' Jean yells back.

Now she stands before Captain Miachi and Ah Fat. The captain walks around his desk to confront Nesta face to face, even though she's several inches shorter than the man. He says a few words, which Ah Fat hastens to translate.

'You have been ordered to provide girls for our officers' club and yet they do not come.'

Nesta says nothing.

100

'It is your duty to do as you are told,' Ah Fat tells her. 'You are to service our gracious officers.'

'Service your officers?' Nesta can barely contain her disgust. 'With respect, that is not going to happen. We are nurses!' The captain may be standing over her, but she will not meet his eyes.

'You insult our emperor and the Japanese Army. This will not be tolerated!' Ah Fat translates.

'I wish to contact the Red Cross,' Nesta says, gathering her courage.

But Ah Fat doesn't need to translate these words, the captain knows all too well about the Red Cross. He barks out a few more words.

'Your Red Cross is far away from here. They have no power anyway and you will obey Captain's orders,' Ah Fat insists.

'No, sir, we will not.'

'Then you will die. Are you prepared to die, Sister?'

'Yes, I'd prefer that.'

With her head still bowed, Nesta doesn't see the captain raise his hand. The slap sends her reeling across the room.

'It's fine. It's just a slap.'

All the nurses from both houses have been awaiting Nesta's return. Nesta is shaking but feels strangely calm as she comes through the front door.

'But your face,' Jean says. 'He hit you.'

Nesta has no desire to linger on the violence and moves on.

'They are insisting four of us go to their club tonight.'

'What did you say?' Betty asks.

'Over my dead body.'

'You didn't,' Vivian says.

'I did, and I meant it. I was very clear with him; I am prepared to die rather than submit.'

The next day, none of the nurses bothers to come outside when the food cart is due. Consequently, they are not aware the cart doesn't come at all.

That afternoon, Norah and Margaret knock on their door. Margaret immediately registers Nesta's red and swollen face, the imprint of a hand still visible. 'Oh dear! Are you all right?'

'I am,' says Nesta. 'For now.'

'I can't believe what they're asking of you. It's not right. What can we do?' Norah asks her.

'Nothing. There's nothing anyone can do. They will try to starve us out, then, well, as I told Miachi, I will die before we submit to them.'

Nesta catches the anxious look Norah and Margaret briefly exchange.

'What is it?'

'I can't say,' Norah replies, biting her lip.

'Just tell me, Norah,' Nesta insists.

'It's not just you they're starving, I'm afraid,' Margaret says.

'Meaning?'

'They've stopped all food coming into the camp. It seems we are all to be starved, until—'

'Until we give in and give them what they want,' Betty interjects.

'I'm afraid so, and we're here to tell you that if that's the way it has to be, then so be it. We can only hope they don't deny the children – surely, they couldn't be that inhuman,' says Margaret.

'We don't know what to say.' Nesta is visibly moved. 'It never occurred to me they'd punish the rest of you.' She turns to her nurses. 'I think we need to talk.'

'No!' Norah insists. 'You don't. There is right and there is wrong, and, in these circumstances, there is no ambiguity. And I've spoken to the Mother Superior, and I'm to pass on the message that she and her nuns also stand with you.'

'Her exact words were, "united we will stand, divided we fall; we will fall together, united",' Margaret says.

Several of the nurses begin to sniff. Norah hugs Nesta tightly.

'Thank you. Please thank everyone,' Nesta tells them, before escorting her friends to the door.

After Nesta and Norah have left, Vivian speaks up. 'Everyone. Outside.'

This time, they sit in a tight circle in the yard outside the house, holding hands.

'Suggestions?' Nesta asks.

'We can't let the children be punished.' The first opinion is offered and cheered. 'Heaven knows they get little enough food as it is.'

'I can't believe they're doing this. It is one thing to punish us, but how could they? How dare they?' Betty rages. 'There must be something we can do.'

Nesta and Jean allow all the nurses to voice their thoughts. They rant and rage, many weep, but one statement continues to resonate: 'I would rather die.'

'Is that an option?' Jean asks and everyone falls silent.

'Is what an option?' Vivian asks.

'Well, if we're not here, then they can't punish the others,' Nesta says.

'You mean if we're all dead?'

Still, no one speaks. Nesta looks around the circle, taking in the mood of the women. She feels it too, feels the precipice upon which they stand. But would they really die for this cause?

'I'm in,' Betty says, finally.

'Now wait . . .' Nesta begins.

'Me too.'

'Me too.'

'Lead on.'

The nurses volunteer in a chorus of agreement.

As they all agree to lay down their lives, Nesta has never felt prouder. She has not shed a tear since the *Vyner Brooke* was bombed, but now, now she's crying.

And then all heads turn as a single nurse stands up and announces, 'You don't need to die. I'll do it.'

There is a moment of silence and then Vivian says, very quietly, 'Do what?'

'Go to their club. Submit. Whatever it is they want.'

'No! You won't, you can't,' Betty says, also jumping up.

Another nurse is on her feet. 'I'll go with you.'

All eyes swivel to the new volunteer.

'I'll go too. And do sit down, Betty,' says a third.

'Make me number four.' Another nurse rises, her hands reaching for the other volunteers.

Everyone is on their feet by now, loudly challenging the women who would sacrifice themselves for the camp. Nesta and Jean allow them to go on for a few moments longer before calling everyone to order.

'Do you understand what it is you're volunteering for?' Jean asks.

The four women look at each other. 'We know,' one says.

'Then why?'

'I look at all of you; you're so young, you will leave this place, fall in love, get married, have babies. That's not something I ever considered for myself.'

'You're only three years older than me,' Vivian says.

The nurse laughs. 'Only three years, huh? Vivian, please let me do this, not just for you lot, but for the other women and children. I'm fine with my decision.'

For hours, the four nurses defend their intentions to the rest of the group and finally, with heavy hearts, their great sacrifice is accepted.

'Betty, will you do something please?' Nesta asks.

'Anything.'

'Please will you run to Margaret's and ask her for a Bible?'

'Why?' Jean asks, perplexed.

'I want each and every one of us to swear that what has been agreed today will never be revealed to another living soul. The names of' – Nesta's voice breaks as she recites the names of the four women – 'shall remain with us until our dying day.'

Betty runs out of the house to fetch the Bible, almost colliding with Sister Catherina, who is about to knock on their door.

'I'm sorry, I'm sorry,' Betty gasps.

'Sister Betty, I was on my way to see you. We need to talk about what is being asked of you by the Japanese.'

'OK, but not now, Sister, I'm in a hurry.'

'Where are you going?'

'I need a Bible; I'm going to borrow Miss Dryburgh's.'

'Come with me, then,' says the nun, taking her arm. 'If there is one thing we have plenty of, it's Bibles.'

They run to Sister Catherina's house. There is a pile of Bibles on the kitchen table. The nun picks one up and hands it to Betty. 'You can keep it.'

Betty returns to find all the nurses have come inside. All the doors and windows are shut.

Jean takes the Bible from Betty and, holding it up, she begins.

'I swear that the decisions made today, the sacrifice made by the four volunteers, will never be spoken about to another living soul. The names of the four will be carried to our graves. I swear.'

Betty moves around the room, presenting the Bible to each nurse in turn, who places her right hand on the holy book and repeats, 'I swear.'

After Nesta has sworn, she takes the Bible from Jean and flicks through a few pages.

'Betty, where did you get this Bible?'

'Oh, I ran into Sister Catherina; she offered it to me.'

'Did you know it was in Dutch?' Nesta says.

The sombre mood in the room lifts a little, and finally someone asks the question they are all thinking. 'Does it still count if you've sworn on words you can't read?'

'It's a Bible,' Betty proclaims. 'It's a bloody Bible! What difference does the language it's written in make?'

'No difference at all, Betty,' Nesta tells her with a hug.

The next morning, Nesta reports back from her visit with Dr McDowell.

'Well, she's promised to get a message to the senior doctor in the nearby men's camp and the hope is that he'll be able to tell someone higher up the chain exactly what's going on here.'

Every night, and with a heavy heart, Nesta watches the four volunteers leave for the officers' club. But even their safe return brings her little relief.

How much can they endure?

CHAPTER 7

Camp II, Irenelaan, Palembang
April 1942–October 1943

'We're using the garage of number 9, which we've renamed The Shed, to hold church services every Sunday,' Margaret Dryburgh tells the nurses as she makes her way around the camp letting everyone know that spiritual comfort is available should they want it.

'Thank you, Margaret,' Nesta says. 'Lord knows we need a blessing.'

The following Sunday, the nurses attend a service. It is the first time Nesta hears the beautiful singing voices of Margaret, Norah and Ena's small choir. She sees, also for the first time, the musical brilliance that must be kept secret. Surely, they would be punished for doing something which gives them so much pleasure. For a few moments, Nesta forgets where she is, what her nurses have sacrificed and loses herself in the music.

'As camp commandant, it's time we appointed a deputy,' Dr McDowell announces to the women gathered in the camp's central clearing. 'I'm too busy with the hospital to do it all alone, I need help.'

'Mrs Hinch!' a voice calls from the crowd.

'Yes, Mrs Hinch,' cries another, and then another, and soon all the women are chanting Mrs Hinch's name.

'I think you've chosen well,' Dr McDowell says. 'She's the very picture of diplomacy, and charming to boot.'

A laugh ripples through the crowd.

'I'd be honoured to accept,' says Mrs Hinch graciously.

'What is it about her that's so different to the other English ladies?' Nesta wonders aloud to Jean on their way back to their hut. 'She's very funny, and . . .' Nesta drifts off, admiring the woman's confidence, her dignity in the face of their squalor.

'Well, she's not English for one thing,' Jean laughs.

'What do you mean? She's not an Ozzie!'

'She's American, Nesta. She's married to an Englishman and has spent many years in Singapore surrounded by the English. She's actually got an OBE, believe it or not, for her YWCA work. She may have adopted a little of the English accent but not the stiffness of the people.'

'How do you know this?'

'I've had tea with her a few times when I've been treating one of the ladies in her house.'

Nesta shakes her head and smiles. 'She's definitely not someone I'd like to reckon with! It's good to know she's on our side. I wonder what her first name is?'

Jean laughs again. 'Even if I did know it, I'd never have the courage to use it unless she gave me permission – can you imagine?'

Nesta laughs too, and the two women feel buoyed, just for a moment, by the presence of two forthright and capable people for camp commandant and deputy.

'I must say,' Norah says to Ena one afternoon, on their way, with little June, to Mrs Hinch's house for a committee meeting, 'she's a real powerhouse, isn't she?'

'I'll say.'

As soon as Mrs Hinch was appointed, she began organising committees and assigning captains at every house in order to address the everyday running of the camp. There was comfort in being busy, of staking out a little bit of order in an environment that was otherwise out of one's control.

'She's got us all on work rotas and now the nuns will run classes for the children. I don't know where she gets her energy.'

When they reach the house, they find it full of chatter and high spirits.

'Her energy is infectious, isn't it?' says Ena.

'It's already rubbing off on me,' remarks Norah, giving Ena a pinch. 'You too, dear sister, I can see it in your face.'

'I need a volunteer for the entertainment committee,' Mrs Hinch says, calling the meeting to order.

'I'll do it,' Margaret offers.

'I think you should be chief organiser,' says Norah and everyone agrees.

Many of the women in the camp who don't visit Margaret's church service share her passion for singing. Norah and Ena have been regular churchgoers and have two of the finest singing voices of all the internees. And what none of the women counted on was the day-to-day boredom that accompanies the drudgery in the camp. What better than to use their talents? So Mrs Hinch, in her typically straightforward way, has decided an entertainment committee should be organised.

'Well, what would we all like to do?' Margaret asks the women. Suggestions come thick and fast, from choirs to concerts.

'I love all your ideas and, depending on how long we are here, we should be able to satisfy everyone. However, can I suggest we start with something completely different, something that won't require rehearsal time but some participation from you all nonetheless?'

'What do you suggest?' Norah asks.

'I think we should start a newspaper,' Margaret announces. 'Something we can put together and distribute to everyone. One of the houses has a typewriter and some paper. As well as sharing news, we can highlight birthdays.'

'There's enough of us, can't we do the newspaper and a concert?' Norah suggests.

'We can,' Margaret says. 'And Norah and Ena, you must be on the music committee. Your knowledge and your lovely voices have to be heard.'

'What about me, can I sing too?' June asks, glancing between Ena and Margaret.

'Of course you can, little one; we will find a special role just for you,' Margaret tells her.

On their way home, June runs ahead to play with her friends.

'I'm worried about June,' Ena says.

'Really? She seems fine to me.' Norah is watching June with her friends as they play tag.

'She hasn't mentioned her mother for several weeks,' Ena continues. 'She used to ask me about ten times a day if I thought her mother would come soon, but earlier today she called me *mummy*.'

'What did you do?'

'Nothing.' Ena looks stricken. 'I didn't know what to say. I just gave her a hug.'

Norah's heart goes out to both Ena and to little June. Their bond has become so strong, but her mother could be out there somewhere, missing her daughter and desperate to know what has become of her. A picture of Sally leaps into Norah's mind, and a lump forms in her throat. But she pushes it down – her sister needs her advice. 'Do you want me to say something to her?'

'Like what?'

'Oh, I don't know, perhaps something like, Aunty Ena and I are so happy you are going to be part of the concert. If you tell us a favourite song of your mummy and daddy's, we could all sing it for them.'

Ena nods her head. 'So, you think if you mention me as aunty and her parents in the same sentence, she will get the message?'

'Can't hurt, and every chance I get, I'll refer to you as Aunty Ena.' Norah squeezes Ena's arm.

Ena wraps her arms around her sister. 'I knew you'd have an answer.'

A week later, the first edition of the *Camp Chronicle* is released. It is agreed only two copies will be produced; there is not enough paper for more, especially if they want to carry on. The paper will be passed from house to house, with a request for content and ideas placed on the first of the eighteen pages. One of the women has put her drawing skills to use and produced a masthead. Barbed wire circles the name of the paper.

In their house, Margaret holds up one of the two inaugural copies, flicking through the pages. She reads aloud several of the headlines.

'*Making Soup out of Fish Heads – A Recipe*. Mmm, sounds yummy. All we need are fish heads. The Dutch System of Childcare. Oh, I see this is part one of a three-part series. Now, who came up with the idea of a gossip column, I wonder?'

Margaret looks at the women on the newspaper committee. They are smiling and slowly turning to look at Betty.

'I might have known,' Margaret says. 'The title has given you away, *Miss Know-All's Diary*. I can see this column only getting longer.'

'You haven't mentioned the headline on the front page,' Norah says.

Margaret reads aloud.

'"At the Sunday Service the Choir Will Be Performing a Special Hymn".' Margaret beams at the women. 'Thank you for the mention. It will be a momentous day when we sing the hymn for the first time.'

'It was a privilege to write not only the music, but also the words – words that will rise to the heavens on Sunday, words that will give us all strength and hope. And I know what we should call it.' Margaret is grinning broadly. '"The Captives' Hymn"!'

And, as one, the women chant, '"The Captives' Hymn"!'

'Have you seen how many people are here?' a nervous Norah asks the choir as she watches the women and children making their way to The Shed long before the service is due to start. Very soon, the small space is filled, and people spill out across the modest front lawn onto the street.

'I have. I had to push my way past everyone to get inside,' Betty says.

'It's going to be like singing at St Paul's,' another quips, reducing all of them to howls of laughter.

112

'This place couldn't be more removed from St Paul's if it tried. Where are our stained-glass windows?' Norah jokes.

'You don't need thousand-year-old bricks and beautiful stained glass to be one with the Lord,' Margaret says.

'If I had the choice of singing at St Paul's or here with all of you, this is where I would want to be,' Betty says.

'Come on, ladies, it's time,' Margaret tells them. 'I'll make my opening sermon short; after all, the mob out there haven't come to hear me drone on, they've come for you. Thank you for the gift you are about to give me and everyone else here.'

The crowd parts as the choir heads to the small vacant space at the rear of the garage, where packing crates have been upended to form an unsteady stage for the women to balance upon. Earlier, Norah and Mrs Hinch gathered chairs from every home to form three rows of seating. Mother Superior and Sister Catherina, along with the nuns, fill the front row, apart from the centre seat. Mrs Hinch is also the usher, sitting the children on the floor, insisting they stop pushing and shoving. No one questions her authority.

As Mrs Hinch makes her way towards Margaret and the choir, the talking stops, and the children outside cease their running around. Norah, Ena and the other choir members form a semi-circle behind Margaret. They are holding hands. No one sees June sneak up onto the stage behind Norah and Ena, wriggling her way between them. The sisters smile at each other as June avoids eye contact with her aunties; she doesn't want to be sent away.

Mrs Hinch takes her seat in the front row, her work for the moment done.

'I am not so silly as to believe that you have come to hear me preach the ways of the Lord,' Margaret begins, with a big smile.

113

'Thank you so much, each and every one of you, for being here today to hear these amazing choristers sing my humble words and music. We present to you "The Captives' Hymn".'

Turning back to the choir, Margaret raises her right hand. As she gently lowers it, the full choir collectively take a deep breath and sing.

'*Father in captivity*
We would lift our prayer to Thee,
Keep us ever in Thy Love.
Grant that daily we may prove
Those who place their trust in Thee,
More than conquerors may be.'

The intensity and strength of their voices rises as they sing the remaining four verses. Quiet sobbing travels beyond The Shed, onto the lawn and into the street beyond.

As the final notes ring out, Margaret drops her conducting hand and lowers her head. When she finally looks up at her choir, tears unashamedly roll down her face. The choir tighten their circle around her as they all weep; the significance of the words, of the music they have just made, has deeply moved each of them. Margaret touches each one softly on the cheek. Finally, she turns back to the congregation.

'On behalf of all of us, thank you, thank you from the bottom of our hearts. I don't think there is anything more I need to say today. Thank you.'

The choir's exit from The Shed goes on for over an hour as women embrace the singers, seek comfort from them, try to find words to express what being here today has meant to them. Margaret laughs off remarks such as, 'I don't believe in God, but today you have given me hope, a faith in myself and all of us here.' Words such as these are repeated over and over.

114

Accepting the hugs and words from the last of the congregation, Margaret spies three Japanese soldiers standing on the opposite side of the street. She stares at them, daring them to make a move. Norah and Ena, with June still squashed between them, surround Margaret. One of the soldiers nods towards the women, before all three scurry away.

'Have they been there throughout?' Margaret asks.

'Yes,' says a woman next to her. 'I even saw one wipe away a tear.'

Wiping away her own tears, Nesta looks at the nurses standing nearby, all openly weeping. Jean catches her eye, her head nodding towards the four nurses who have sacrificed themselves as 'hostesses' to save the others. Nesta observes them embracing, quietly sobbing and comforting one another.

Jean pushes her way through the crowd to Nesta.

'I don't know how much longer I can bear it,' she whispers.

CHAPTER 8

Camp II, Irenelaan, Palembang
April 1942–October 1943

'Oh, my God – how are we supposed to choose what to put in the paper?'

Submissions have been pouring in since the *Camp Chronicle* was announced, and the women have assembled in one of the houses, to sort through the offerings.

'I mean, look at this stuff.' A volunteer holds up dozens of scraps of paper covered with hastily scrawled articles, book reviews, puzzles, stories for children and recipes.

Another volunteer is reading, '"One Hundred Ways to Cook Rice". It says one hundred ways, but she's only written three!'

The article sparks a conversation about food and the editors revive happy memories of mealtimes, of Christmas dinners and Sunday lunches. And, in a strange way, once they start talking about food, they can't seem to stop, despite the ever-present gnawing hunger in their stomachs.

But it is Betty, the editor compiling *Miss Know-All's Diary*, who receives the most submissions.

'Well, the Japanese aren't going to let us put this in the paper.' Betty is reading an account of one survivor's journey to the camp. 'We're going to have to get creative.' She has a little twinkle in her eye. 'We're going to have to *help* the reader to read between the lines,' she says. 'I never thought I'd want to run a newspaper, but this is really fun.'

'It's weird to say it,' chimes in Jean, 'but over the last few weeks, things have really changed around here.'

'I feel it too,' agrees Betty. 'I mean, our only problem is going to be finding paper.'

'Oh, we've found loads of scraps in the rubbish thrown out at the back of the admin building,' Jean tells her.

'So we've got a paper and a theatre company and a choir now,' Betty says. 'I mean, can you believe we've had to move The Shed to our house because it's not big enough for the audience?'

Jean points to the piano in the corner of their living area. 'And there's that too.'

The nurses are excited, busily preparing for their performances. What had started off as just one concert has increased to more, as both performers and audience find so much to enjoy in the musical shows. Nesta watches their growing enthusiasm for the concerts and a shadow crosses her face.

'Girls, can you all give me a minute?'

All eyes turn to her.

'What Margaret, Norah, Ena and others have given us is, without question, a great gift. We've been able to forget where we are and really enjoy ourselves, but I'm worried we're getting carried away. We mustn't ever forget we are here at the mercy of the Japanese, who have shown us, time and time again, they

117

control every aspect of our lives. So far, they've let the concerts go on, but you have to remember that all this can change in an instant.'

'What Nesta is saying, and I agree with her entirely, is be wary of our captors, let's not give them any reason to shut us down,' Jean adds.

'I don't want to be a party-pooper, I just want you to be safe. Now, go and enjoy yourselves,' Nesta says with a big smile.

'Have you seen how many are out there?' Norah is breathless. 'It's our biggest crowd yet, so we are all going to have to sing really loud to be heard outside.'

'Well, that's what we're good at,' Ena tells her with a wink.

The Saturday night concert is a great success and their largest yet, featuring the choir, a glee club, dancers, comedy turns and recitals. The house is buzzing inside and out, and those unlucky enough not to have found space inside join in the singing from the street.

'What an evening!' Margaret announces when it's over. 'I haven't laughed this much in such a long time, and I know you all feel the same way. I want to thank these wonderful performers who have entertained us tonight, and I want to thank you for coming and being part of this special evening. We will all remember it for as long as we live. I think it is fitting we end the evening singing "God Save the King", "Land of Hope and Glory" and the national anthem of Holland.'

The applause is long and heartfelt as each of the anthems is bellowed into the balmy night air.

When all the last notes have faded, a silence lingers in the crowd. And then the women stomp their feet, clap their hands, and turn to embrace the woman next to them. They will remember this night forever.

'Be my life short or long,' Nesta whispers to herself. 'Just please don't let it be short.'

CHAPTER 9

Camp II, Irenelaan, Palembang
April 1942–October 1943

'You have made such a difference in the camp; you know that, don't you?' Nesta tells Norah.

'I hope so,' Norah agrees. 'I've been eavesdropping on the camp as they practise "The Captives' Hymn"; it's wonderful.'

Norah has spent the past week hunting down scrap paper to produce copies of both the musical score and lyrics, which she has happily distributed to the women.

'Norah, I spoke to the nurses a couple of days ago about the concerts.'

'And?'

'I just reminded them how quickly the Japanese can turn; and that we mustn't take their approval for granted. I'm concerned someone will say – or sing – something that offends them.'

'Mmm, I think you're right. I must admit I've become complacent about seeing the soldiers in the audience, and yes, I'm a little surprised they've let us continue. I think I should speak to everyone too and remind them to be careful.'

Norah waves goodbye to Nesta; she will talk to the others, but right now, she has something else on her mind, something so momentous that she can no longer bear to hold it in.

'What is it Norah, are you all right?' Margaret is just leaving the house as Norah arrives.

'Is Ena inside?' she asks.

'Yes. Do you need her?'

'I need both of you.'

Margaret goes back inside the house and reappears a moment later with Ena by her side.

'What's going on?' Ena asks, laying a concerned hand on her sister's shoulder.

'I've got an idea and I have to say it out loud. I want to know if you think it's crazy,' Norah says, the words tumbling out of her mouth.

'You are never crazy, dear sister. Just say it,' Ena urges.

'There's something missing from our concerts.'

'What?' ask Ena and Margaret together.

'An orchestra; we don't have an orchestra.'

There is a moment of stunned silence from Ena and Margaret.

'Are you suggesting we ask our captors to provide us with instruments?' Margaret says eventually. 'You should know that I don't think they will.' She laughs. The idea is preposterous.

'It would be nice, but no, I can't see them doing that either. So, I've come up with the next best thing.'

'Well, tell us, then,' says Ena. She's wondering whether, after all, her sister is a little crazy.

'I want to form an orchestra. An orchestra of voices. Voices I can turn into instruments.'

Margaret and Ena once again fall silent, exchanging glances of utter bewilderment.

'Well, what do you think?' Norah asks, a little impatiently.

'My dear, I have never met a more brilliant, capable musician than you. I don't know how you'll do it, I confess, but if it's something you want to try, you have my complete support,' Margaret says.

'She won't just try, Margaret, she'll do it. There is nothing my brilliant sister can't do. If she says she's going to create an orchestra of voices, then, by God, she will.'

'You don't think I'm being stupid?' Norah asks anxiously.

'Maybe a little crazy,' grins Ena. 'But I can't wait to hear *your orchestra* – how amazing does that sound?'

At that moment, June comes running out of the house.

'Aunty Ena, are you crying? Are you all right?'

Ena kneels to wrap the little girl in a hug.

'A little tear of joy, June. The best kind.'

'Nesta, what's wrong? Has something happened?' Margaret asks the nurse as they linger in the street, the latest performance due to start very soon.

The sun has set and the few camp street lights begin to glow. An air of excitement is building around the 'concert hall'. The performers have gathered outside the house, chatting nervously about their impending acts. For several, it is the first time they're singing, dancing or acting in front of an audience.

'Haven't you seen?' Nesta says, her eyes wide. 'We have visitors.'

'Visitors? Good visitors or bad ones?' Margaret asks.

'Bad, I think.'

'You'd better tell me what's going on.'

'A few minutes ago, six soldiers, including Miachi and Ah Fat, walked into the house and made the women in the front row leave their seats so they could sit down.'

The other women have gathered around, listening intently.

'They want to be entertained too, I'm guessing,' says Margaret, eventually. 'And if that's what they want, then let's do it.' But she doesn't sound confident.

The room is silent when the performers enter. The presence of the Japanese has hit the audience hard. They have no idea whether the night will end in celebration or a beating.

Margaret steps onto the makeshift stage and bows to the gathered soldiers in the front row.

'We have some guests tonight; welcome,' she says. 'Let's begin the evening with the first song on your programme.'

The performers start to sing 'The Captives' Hymn', and, hesitantly at first, the audience joins in. As the last words are sung, everyone applauds and the Japanese officers politely join in.

And so the evening continues. Those listening forget their captors just a few seats away, and laugh, sing, clap the beautiful dancing and poetry. Every act is applauded by the officers; they even laugh when the women laugh. It is clear they are enjoying themselves.

When it's over and the applause has died down, Margaret steps forwards once more.

'Thank you, everyone, and a special thank you to our guests,' Margaret says, with a low bow. 'And now we will end as we usually do with our national anthems.'

'God Save the King' receives a gusty rendition and then the Dutch national anthem, 'Wilhelmus', follows with the same boisterous energy. The level of passion rises as everyone sings 'Land of Hope and Glory'. When the singing has finally ended, the Japanese officers stand and applaud enthusiastically.

'Again, again,' Miachi says.

'I'm sorry?' Margaret says, approaching the captain.

'Sing. Please sing again,' he asks.

'Which song?'

Miachi mumbles a few words to Ah Fat.

'The captain likes last the song. So beautiful. Please sing it again.'

The room falls silent; all eyes are on Margaret.

'Ladies, Captain Miachi has asked we sing our last song once again. He says it is beautiful. Are we ready?'

The Japanese officers stay standing as the women proudly sing what they are now calling 'the camp anthem', and they once again join voices in 'Land of Hope and Glory'. The officers are applauding even before they finish.

Miachi approaches Margaret. 'Thank you,' Ah Fat translates. 'Most entertaining, we will be back next Saturday night.'

The women move aside for the departing soldiers, bowing as they move through the crowd. The officers, to their astonishment, are smiling.

'Well, that was unexpected,' Norah announces.

Margaret and Norah have remained behind in Nesta's house after everyone else has left.

'Unexpected, certainly, but good too. It means we can carry on; they clearly enjoyed it. I didn't know what to do with my face when Miachi asked for an encore,' Margaret says.

'I could have a problem,' Betty admits, looking sheepish.

'A problem?' Nesta asks.

'Well, it's like this, I've been working with some of the girls.' She looks around the room at the others involved, all of whom are trying to suppress their laughter. 'I – I mean we – have written and rehearsed a new version of a well-known song. They may not like some of the lyrics.'

'I think they will definitely not like some of the lyrics,' one of the nurses adds. 'I'm sure that Ah Fat will translate everything we say.'

'Do I want to know what they are?' Nesta asks.

'No, no. I think under the circumstances we might have to make some alterations,' Betty says.

'Well, I know the song you have submitted for the programme, I will trust you not to do or say anything to upset the officers,' Margaret says.

'Can we see the lyrics in advance?' asks Norah. 'Maybe everyone who's performing at the next concert needs to run their acts past us.'

'Sadly, I agree with you. It goes against the grain, censorship, but we can't take any chances,' Margaret adds.

When the nurses are alone again, Nesta notices their four 'hostess' colleagues sitting apart from everyone else. It has been two weeks since they began their nightly visits to the officers' club.

'Oh no!' Nesta turns to Jean. 'How must they be feeling with their violators in their house? I need to do something. I have to talk to them.'

'Let's do it in the garden,' says Jean. 'I'll take them outside.'

The six women move to the rear of the garden. Nesta begins by apologising for not immediately realising how painful it must have been to find the Japanese soldiers at the concert.

'How were you to know they'd turn up?' one asks.

'We weren't, but it's a big problem and we have to fix it.'

'You could stay in our house next week, skip the whole thing,' Jean suggests.

'No way,' says another. 'Haven't they taken enough from us? It's our concert too. But I don't want to perform for them.'

That night, sleep doesn't come easily for Nesta. She continues to berate herself for the pain she has caused the four nurses who have made a sacrifice no woman should ever make. The self-doubt she has kept at bay over her ability to be a good leader to her colleagues, who have become her friends, and now her family, taunts her. Nothing in her training has prepared her for this role.

CHAPTER 10

Camp II, Irenelaan, Palembang
April 1942–October 1943

'How are the rehearsals for Saturday coming along?' Nesta asks Norah. They are walking through the camp, watching the children play.

'I've censored Betty's lyrics,' says Norah. 'But I think we'll be fine. Ena's been going over the other acts and, let's say, a few changes have been made.'

'Are you singing this Saturday, June?' Nesta asks.

'No, not this week. Oh, look, there's Bonnie!'

'Who's Bonnie?'

'She's a stray dog June and some other children have befriended,' Ena explains.

'Bonnie! Bonnie, here, girl,' June calls.

Dogs have found their way into the camp, and just like the women and children, they too are starving. Children befriend them by sharing their meagre rations. Mothers go without to give their children their share. Seeing the smiles on their sons' and daughters' faces outweighs the concern for any diseases the animals may bring. Young girls are seen singing to the dogs; boys do what boys do when they have a pet dog, throwing twigs and sticks for them to fetch. For the most part, the Japanese soldiers ignore them, and the children quickly learn which soldiers to avoid, coaxing the dogs away from the threat of a bayonet.

June and two of her friends have a special stray they look out for, sneak food to and cuddle.

Today, out walking with Norah and Ena, she has been on the alert for her friend, Bonnie.

The dog reacts to her name and turns towards them but is then startled by the sight of a soldier bounding towards her, rifle drawn, screaming. Behind the dog is another soldier, frozen in place.

'Nooooo!' yells Ena, throwing herself onto June, and they hit the ground as a shot rings out.

Nesta and Norah turn to see the dog bolt away but the soldier behind falls down, grasping at his chest. June screams while Ena holds her close. Nesta runs to the fallen guard.

'Take her back to the house,' Norah tells Ena, and to June she says, 'Bonnie's fine. She ran away.'

Ena pulls June to her feet and, wrapping her arms around her, she hurries away.

Norah looks at the solider who fired the shot; now it's he who stands frozen. Norah runs over to Nesta and the injured man, while other soldiers stream onto the street, some heading for the wounded soldier, others towards the man who is still trying to comprehend what he has done.

'How is he?' Norah asks, kneeling beside Nesta.

'He's dead.'

Soldiers grab Nesta and pull her away. But Norah takes her arm, and the two women quickly leave, warning those who have come out of their houses at the sound of a gun firing to go back inside. This is a reminder, thinks Norah, more alert than ever to the danger they're in. A reminder and a lesson: any one of their lives could be snuffed out by a poorly aimed bullet, with few, if any, repercussions.

Nesta is pleased the concert the following Saturday is a success. She despised Miachi and his soldiers in the front row, loudly applauding every performance, and felt her heart contract.

Her four volunteer nurses stood apart from the crowd, in the doorway to the kitchen, where they could enjoy the evening without being spied by their rapists. It was with a grateful tear she watched them sing an encore of 'Land of Hope and Glory' at the tops of their lungs.

CHAPTER 11

Camp II, Irenelaan, Palembang
April 1942–October 1943

'I wish they would hurry up; the suspense is killing me,' Betty whispers to the other nurses.

'Shush, Betty, I don't want you getting into trouble for talking,' Nesta tells her.

'Everyone else is talking,' Vivian counters.

'Talk quietly, then. I'm just on edge. I have no idea what's coming.'

'Those aren't soldiers outside the admin block, are they?' Jean asks.

'They look more like locals. And they don't have rifles, just revolvers,' Betty says.

The buzz of the previous evening still lingered amongst the women the next day, until Mrs Hinch announced the women were to assemble for an announcement at noon. Rumours run rife in the crowd. It's hard not to hope for freedom.

Well before the appointed hour, the women line up in rows outside the administration block at the end of the street.

A hush falls over the camp as the door to the administration building opens. Miachi strides out, with Ah Fat, surrounded by young men in simple, unadorned uniforms. He comes to a stop in front of the women. A crate is placed before him, and he steps up and begins to talk. Ah Fat yells over Miachi's statement. The women in the front rows grasp enough to send the translation down the lines.

'The honourable, brave Japanese soldiers have gone to fight, and we are now being guarded by local police. We are to treat them as if they are Japanese. Do not be in any doubt that they will punish bad behaviour.'

All the nurses gather in Nesta's living room and quieten down as she and Jean call them to order.

'Well, wasn't that the best news we've had for a while?' announces Nesta.

A chorus of 'Oh yes!' and 'Best ever' is echoed back.

'There are four of us here for whom it means so much more.'

Four nurses look at one another, wiping away their tears, as their colleagues move in to hug them and offer words of comfort.

'We – and I don't mean just those of us here, but every woman and child in this camp – owe you a debt we can never repay. Whatever any of us can do for you, you just have to ask,' Jean says.

'Thank you. We don't know how we're going to feel in the weeks and months ahead, but to know that we can talk to any of you, should we feel the need, is the best thing you can offer us.'

'And take our names to the grave,' another of the four adds.

Each of the nurses calls out, 'To the grave.'

They are interrupted by a knock on the door. Mrs Hinch steps into the room.

'Well, wasn't that the best news?' she beams.

'The very best,' Nesta agrees.

'I've come for you, Nesta. Dr McDowell and I met with the captain and she has some news for you.'

'Thank you, Mrs Hinch. I'll go right away.'

'I'm sorry it's taken so long for your nurses to be freed, Nesta,' Dr McDowell says as soon as Nesta enters her small windowless 'office' in the makeshift hospital. 'I should have spoken to you sooner, but I wanted you to know that yesterday I heard back from the doctor at the men's camp. He spoke to a Commodore Modin, who was absolutely furious at what has been asked of your nurses. The commodore apparently stormed off to see the Japanese general and remonstrate with him. Apparently, he told the general, *It's just not cricket*. Can you imagine him saying that? I'm not sure the Japanese general knew what he was referring to, and now it doesn't matter since they've gone, but your nurses are safe. Even if they come back.'

'You can't begin to imagine how relieved we all are,' says Nesta.

'I'm so sorry it happened, and that it took so long to be resolved. You all have my greatest admiration.'

Nesta runs back to report the conversation. No one can suppress a laugh at the commodore's, *It's just not cricket.*

'I'd have used different words if it was me,' Betty says.

'And what would you have said?' Vivian asks.

'I'd have threatened to do them some grievous bodily harm and spelt out exactly where that harm would be inflicted.'

Walking home one evening from rehearsal, Norah loops her arm in Ena's.

'What's going on?' Ena asks her.

'I just want to feel close to you.'

'OK, but something's on your mind.'

'You know me so well. I'm sure what I'm thinking about is also what you're thinking about.'

'Ken and John?'

'Yes. Do you think John's OK? I think I would feel it if he wasn't. At least, I want to think I would.'

'You would. Just like I'd know if anything happened to Ken.'

'But he was so sick when we left him. So ill he needed a hospital.'

'You know how strong John is and he has everything to live for, you and . . .'

'Sally. I'm convinced she's safe with Barbara. But I miss her so much. It should be Sally who's here with us, not June.'

Ena stops walking and turns to Norah.

'Oh, I'm sorry, Ena. I didn't mean it like that, I didn't mean we shouldn't be looking after June; heaven knows she gives us someone to love and care for.'

'I know what you meant, it just hit me how hard it must be for you seeing her with me all the time. But, Norah, I'm glad Sally's not here with us, we don't want her living like this. God knows we don't want June living like this. None of us should be here.'

'June definitely shouldn't be here, you're right. And it's up to us to care for her until she can get back to her father – if not her mother.' They both know it's unlikely June's mother survived the sinking of the *Vyner Brooke*. Norah pauses, her eyes drawn to the opposite side of the street. 'Hello, Nesta,' she calls. 'Out for a walk?'

'Oh, yes! I needed some time to myself. You two look very serious, though, everything OK?'

'Yes, we're fine, just talking about the men in our lives and how much we miss them,' Norah says.

'John and Ken, is that right?'

Ena nods. 'And you? Is there a special man in your life?'

Nesta smiles. 'No, not really.'

'Aha, that smile tells me there is someone. Care to tell us?' Norah says, smiling warmly.

'He's not someone special; our relationship never really got off the ground. But he's someone I enjoyed being with and, well, who knows, if things were different, if we hadn't had to flee Malaya, then maybe ...' Nesta drifts off. What's the point in maybes out here?

'Do you want to tell us his name? Just saying it might give you something to hold on to.'

'Dr ... Er, Rick, his name is Richard, but everyone calls him Rick.'

'And he's a doctor?'

'He is. We often found ourselves sharing night shifts and, well, you know, we had all those hours with nothing to do but sit and talk.'

'Look up at the stars, Nesta,' Ena says.

All three women look skyward.

'We are all under the same sky, and who knows? Maybe somewhere John is looking up and thinking of Norah, Rick is somewhere thinking of you and Ken is somewhere thinking of me,' Ena muses.

For several minutes, the three women gaze at the brilliant overhead display of southern stars.

'You know what?' says Ena.

'Tell us,' Norah says.

'I'm going to sit in the garden and by the light of the full moon I'm going to write to Ken. It's our anniversary, you know.'

'Oh, my darling sister,' Norah says with feeling. 'I'm so sorry I didn't remember.'

'Don't worry, it's fine. Will you keep an eye on June?'

'Of course – take all the time you need.'

The next morning, Norah finds a scrap of paper beside Ena's sleeping mat. She reads the first line before folding it up and tucking it under her sister's pillow.

My darling Ken, she has written. *Eight years ago today we were married . . .*

'Look what I've got,' Betty whispers to a few of the nurses as they sit outside.

'It's a piece of wood,' Vivian says, bemused.

'Well, I wondered whether we might work together to make a gift for Nesta.'

'You want to give our senior nurse a piece of wood?'

'No, I want to take this piece of wood and make it into something.'

'Like what?' Jean asks.

Norah watches the nurses, smiling at their love for their leader. As their first Christmas approaches – plans for a concert are already afoot – it is agreed by all that every woman and child should receive a small present. Those who arrived with suitcases of useless possessions such as formal ball gowns hand them over to make dresses. Silk handkerchiefs are destined to become treasured gifts. Norah and Ena have a special plan for June.

'When we were living in Malaya,' Betty continues, 'while most of us went to the beach on our days off, Nesta spent her time with some of the patients and doctors, playing mahjong. What if we make her a set of mahjong tiles?'

'I like the idea of it, but how can we do that – we don't have anything to cut it with,' Vivian observes.

'We have kitchen knives, don't we. And this wood is quite soft; it was one of the rafters which must have fallen off a roof. A while ago, I found two old metal files. We can use them to smooth the tiles and I'm sure the Dutch nuns would lend us some paints from the schoolroom to paint the characters.'

'Do you know what the characters look like?'

'Of course I do. What d'you say?'

'I say, let's do it,' Vivian replies enthusiastically and to Betty's relief. 'We'll set up a roster for the work, but we must keep it a secret. I think we should surprise her.'

Rehearsals for the Christmas concert take place every day, but one morning, a session is interrupted when several of the Dutch women internees burst through the door.

'English men . . . English men at the back of our house,' one of the women announces.

'What are you talking about?' Norah asks as the singers gather around.

'They were speaking English! We saw them walking through the trees behind our house.'

'Please take us there now,' Norah says, as they all move towards the door, and together they head towards the houses where the Dutch women are living and into the first one. Through the front door, living room, kitchen and out into the backyard they stream.

'We're here! We're here and we're English! Is there anyone there?' Norah shouts.

They peer through the dense jungle that buffets the back gardens. They can't see a soul.

Suddenly, a loud cockney voice.

'Same time tomorrow, lassies.'

Urgent, angry Japanese voices follow, and the women hurry back inside.

Word of the encounter spreads quickly and everyone descends on the Dutch house. The women are abuzz with speculation, until Mrs Hinch, in her quiet but firm manner, moves to the front of the crowd and holds up her hands.

'Ladies, ladies, please. We can't all talk at once. Why don't we let those who were there tell us what happened?'

The first Dutch woman, not used to being the centre of attention, uncomfortable with her command of English, steps up to the front.

'I was outside and heard something in the trees. I thought it might be an animal and was about to run inside when I heard a voice, a man speaking in English, and then another man said something back to him. I got closer and through the trees I saw lots of men with shovels. Japanese men yelling at them. They walked right behind our house, then back into the jungle. That's when I ran and told Norah.'

'What happened next?' Mrs Hinch asks.

'I can answer that,' Margaret says, stepping forwards. 'I wasn't the first one there; I'm sure you can all appreciate I can't run as fast as the young ones. I didn't see anyone, but we called out to them and one of them called back.'

'What did he say?' yells a voice.

'He said, *Same time tomorrow, lassies*,' Norah relays. 'We should come back tomorrow, see if we can talk to them.'

'Well,' begins Margaret, a note of caution in her voice, 'I know you will all want to be here, but I must warn you, these men are guarded by Japanese soldiers, and we don't want to put their lives at risk.'

'Well, maybe no more than five or six women? I hope we'll be able to share a few quiet words with the men as they pass,' Mrs Hinch suggests.

'And who is going to decide who they should be?' another voice calls out.

'I will,' Mrs Hinch says with an authority the others know not to challenge. 'I promise if we are able to make contact with them you will all know immediately. You're welcome to come back and wait out front.'

Squashed in the crowd of women, Norah clings to Ena. 'Do you think John is with them? Oh, my God, Ena, could he be here, on the other side of the fence?'

'I don't know, we can only hope he is, and soon we'll find out.'

The next day, the women gather. Mrs Hinch has chosen a handful of women, including Norah, to approach the prisoners, with Margaret leading the way. The rest of the camp waits outside the house for the women to return.

Norah is glad that the men are in the cooling shade of the trees, given the blistering weather.

Within half an hour, they are back inside. Margaret steps forwards to announce their news.

'We saw them!' she begins. 'There were dozens of them marching through the trees. A Japanese soldier was out in front, so we waited a bit before calling out. It was an Englishman who told us there are Dutch amongst their group.'

'They're being held in a prison and every day they're taken to work on a camp a few miles away that they'll soon move into,' Norah adds. All these expectant faces beam up at her as if she is delivering their freedom. 'They've been at it for some time and the camp is nearly ready,' she continues. 'They didn't give us any names – it was too risky for us to talk too long, anyway. But I don't see why we can't go back every day.'

'Thank you, Norah,' says Mrs Hinch. 'We haven't worked out what time they return in the afternoon and some of us could take turns in the backyard to wait and watch,' she suggests.

The following morning, Norah and the women gather again in front of the Dutch house. In an orderly manner, they file inside and out into the backyard and wait in silence. The nurses remain at the back of the crowd: there won't be anyone they know amongst the male prisoners, but today they want to be part of this. They give thanks that their fathers, brothers and boyfriends are safe back at home in Australia. Once again, Nesta thinks about Rick, wondering what it would be like to suddenly be so close to seeing him again.

The silence is finally broken by the sound of footsteps crunching through the forest. As the Japanese soldier in charge of the men appears, Margaret holds up her arm before slowly letting it drop. She is leading the women in song.

Beyond the wire, the men hear sweet voices raised to the heavens; just for *them*.

'*Oh come, all ye faithful*
Joyful and triumphant . . .'

Norah's heart fills as she sings a Christmas carol for their fellow prisoners, communicating in the only way they are able.

The men in front pause for a moment before they are shoved on their way. She can see them peering between the trees, hoping to catch a glimpse of the women who are serenading them. Other Japanese guards stop and turn towards the singing. Through the leaves and branches, the women watch the men remove their hats and shirts to wave at them.

'Thank you,' they hear the men calling out, both in Dutch and English, before being moved along.

'I didn't see John,' a distraught Norah tells Ena afterwards.

'I couldn't make out anyone; it's impossible to know,' Ena soothes. Norah knows that Ena harboured her own wild hope of seeing Ken.

The next day at the same hour, the women gather once more, silently waiting for the moment when they will hear the crunch of footsteps approaching and their voices will send the message of hope to the unknown men.

As they strain to make out any noise from the jungle, the men's voices filter through the trees. Hearts full of hope and fear, they begin singing.

'Oh come ye
Oh come ye
To Bethlehem . . .'

Once again, the men pause, but they are silhouettes in the dappled light of the jungle. Norah can't make out a single face, but she sings with all her heart. When the final notes ring out, the song is sung again, this time in Dutch.

The women weep, clinging to each other, desperate to call out, but heeding Mrs Hinch's words:

'You must do nothing that might put the men in danger.'

Already, Christmas 1942 is like none Norah has ever known; it has been a wonderful moment, powerful and uplifting, but when it is over, she and everyone else is once more mired in the stark reality of their circumstances.

As the men pass by the following day, they call out their goodbyes: this is the last time they will walk the path from their prison to their new jungle camp. This time, the women don't hold back, calling out their own goodbyes.

'John!' Norah screams desperately. 'John, it's me, Norah. Are you there? Please be there!'

Caught up in the emotion, Ena also calls out, 'Ken, my darling Ken! It's Ena, I'm here, I'm here.'

But no one calls back to them.

CHAPTER 12

Camp II, Irenelaan, Palembang
April 1942–October 1943

'It's Christmas! It's Christmas!' June squeals, waking not only Ena and Norah but all the women in their house.

'Yes, it is, dear girl,' Ena says, giving her a big hug, 'and look what we've got for you.'

Ena and Norah hand her a small gift. June is delighted with the doll Norah fashioned from a rice sack, with a big lipstick smile painted on its face. It is wearing the pretty lace dress she painstakingly stitched together. Christmas is all about the gifts for a five-year-old.

Ena watches Norah wipe away a tear and quietly whispers, 'My darling sister, Sally is safe. She is waiting for you, and John. I know it.'

Norah turns away, sniffing, remembering.

'Mummy, Daddy, he's been, Santa's been, look what he left me,' Sally calls out to Norah and John who are making their way down the stairs on Christmas morning.

'Merry Christmas, Sally. What have you got there?' Norah asks, gathering her daughter in her arms as John folds them into a hug.

'It's a doll and a doll's house and a pram for her. It's so beautiful.'

'Not half as beautiful as you are, my darling. Merry Christmas,' John says.

Turning back to Ena, Norah buries herself in her sister's arms.

'Merry Christmas, Ena,' she whispers. 'I am so blessed to have you here with me, even though I wish you weren't, that you were right now with Ken, that we were all together.'

'We will be, hopefully this time next year.'

Several of the others approach June, bearing small gifts. As they are being handed over, Margaret intervenes.

'Plenty of time for that later, June. Right now, it is time we all get ready and head over to morning service. Come on now.'

As the women turn away, duly chastened, Margaret approaches June.

'Merry Christmas, sweet girl, you bring so much joy to our lives, thank you,' she says, handing her a beautifully made lace handkerchief.

June wraps her arms around her. 'Thank you, Aunty Margaret. Merry Christmas!'

Nesta and her nurses have skipped the morning Christmas service to begin cooking, working creatively with the extra rations the local guards have supplied. But preparations are paused when they are called into the street by the guards.

'Come outside. Please, ladies, come outside.'

The nurses join the other women cautiously exiting their homes. About a dozen guards stand in the middle of the street holding large baskets full of food. They note that a couple of them contain plucked chickens and slabs of beef.

One of the guards attempts an explanation.

'This from the English men.'

'What do you mean, English men?' Norah calls.

'English men in the other camp sent to you. They asked their guards to send food to the women nearby.'

With that, all the guards place the baskets on the ground and step back.

The women slowly approach the offering.

'Look how much is here.'

'How did they do this? Aren't they starving like us?'

'It must come from the men we sang to; they must be nearby.'

'Oh, my goodness, this is the best Christmas present I have ever received.'

'They buy from local traders,' offers a guard.

As the rest of the women and children leave the church service, they are stunned to see the overflowing baskets of food.

Mrs Hinch is keen that everyone acknowledges the unfathomable generosity of the men. 'Ladies, we have been blessed with a wonderful gift. While we were singing and giving thanks to God, we were graced with this bounty.'

Margaret joins Mrs Hinch. 'Ladies, would you bow your heads and pray for the men who have made this selfless act in sharing their food on this day of giving and receiving.'

'Welcome to our home,' announces Nesta. 'We hope you all enjoyed the services; we enjoyed preparing this spectacular feast for you, made possible by the gift of the food.'

The nurses have invited occupants of several other houses to share their rations and join them in what they had only recently assumed would be a humble meal. Tables have been carried through to the spacious backyard and the guests take their seats, filled with anticipation at the forthcoming meal.

Nesta holds open the back door and the three nurses who helped her cook march outside, carrying heaving and steaming pots, bowls and plates. Laying them on the table, they return to the kitchen to fetch even more.

'I don't believe this; I'm eating potatoes *and* beef,' Betty cries.

'I have an onion with mine, can you believe it? Steak and onion; this is the best Christmas dinner I've ever had,' Vivian cries.

Jean calls for attention. 'Before we begin eating in earnest, can we please thank Nesta and the others who have slaved away for hours preparing what Nesta correctly called a feast. Thank you all so much, this is wonderful.'

And everyone toasts the cooks with glasses of tepid water.

When they have eaten, they clear everything away and gather to sing a few Christmas carols. Soon, the women grow weary and everyone returns to their own homes. The nurses retreat to their bedrooms, a quiet corner of the living room, the backyard, now wet and muddy from a brief tropical downpour. It is time for the women to be alone, to think of family, friends and loved ones, at home, or in other camps just like theirs.

Before they retire to bed, Christmas presents are finally exchanged. Nesta's mahjong gets a loud cheer. She turns the hand-carved, hand-painted tiles over and over in her hands, unable to say a single 'thank you' because she's crying so hard.

'This is not how any of us thought we would see in 1943. I wish I could tell you this year will be better than the last. Whatever happens, we must not give up hope that this war will end, and we'll be at home with our families this time next year. I want you to know how incredibly proud Jean and I are of you all. It has been truly humbling for me to watch you go about making this place a home, being part of the camp, working in the hospital, and all of it without complaining,' Nesta tells her nurses.

'I've heard Betty complaining many times,' Vivian pipes up.

New Year's Eve is not celebrated. The women have endured the worst year of their lives, and any hopes for 1943 are voiced quietly amongst small groups, in the houses they have attempted to make into homes. The younger nurses accept an invitation to a party in The Shed, the original concert room. Spontaneous plays are improvised, songs are sung and an award given to the woman who can make the best animal noise. Their evening is cut a little shorter than they would have liked when a passing guard tells them to go to bed.

Nesta shuts the door when the last of her nurses is back. Everyone is still up.

'Yes, well, we have all complained from time to time, thank you, Vivian. Including me. But that hasn't stopped any of us from doing our duty, caring for ourselves and others.'

'You're so busy caring about all of us, I'm wondering how you're doing, Sister James,' Vivian says.

'Well, Bully, about the same as the rest of you. I'm tired, hungry – more hungry than tired to be honest, despite our Christmas Day feasting.'

'You don't show it,' Betty says.

'Doesn't mean I don't feel it. But, most of all, I'm bloody angry. Angry that this war began in the first place, angry that we got chased out of Malaya, angry at losing so many of our men in Singapore. Furious about what happened when we tried to leave.

But this doesn't even begin to describe how I feel about those friends we fled Singapore with who are not here with us now.'

'Oh, Nesta! Nesta, I'm so sorry. Every single one of us shares our anger and frustration with you all the time, you are so strong for us, and we've never asked you how you feel, I'm sorry,' Betty says, hugging her senior, her colleague, her friend.

Everyone in the room gathers around Nesta, wiping away their own tears, wiping away Nesta's, vowing to take care of her just as she takes care of them.

Nesta tries to apologise for being so unprofessional but is shouted down and reminded that she is just as human as the rest of them.

'It was lovely hearing "Auld Lang Syne",' Ena whispers to Norah as they settle down to sleep.

As the doors to The Shed closed behind them after the concert, the women sang 'Auld Lang Syne' as they walked home. Soon, they heard the same song being sung inside each house, behind closed doors.

'I would have loved to join in but didn't want to wake June,' says Norah.

'We'll sing it again and again.'

'Do you remember the New Year's Eve party in Singapore the first year after John and I married?'

'How could I forget? The friends, the food, the champagne; it was a spectacular night. We were all so happy, weren't we? And Father kept making Mother dance with him even when he was worn out.'

'That's because Mother loved to dance.'

'Ken and I were still getting to know each other. He proposed just a few weeks later.'

'What I do remember is that you never let him go all night.'

'And I remember you panicking when midnight struck, and John had gone to get a drink or something, and you were so worried he wouldn't get back in time to kiss you as the clock struck midnight.'

'I know. All I could see were Ken's arms around you, Father's around Mother, and when the clock chimed twelve, I was standing on my own.'

'Not for long, you weren't. After Ken kissed me, I turned around and the two of you were in each other's arms.'

'It was a wonderful night.'

'And we'll have more of them, just not this year. It seems silly to say Happy New Year given our circumstances, but Happy New Year, my darling sister.'

'Happy New Year, Ena,' says Norah. But her warm memories fade with sleep and her dreams are filled with soldiers wielding bayonets running after her.

CHAPTER 13

Camp II, Irenelaan, Palembang
April 1942–October 1943

'What now?' Nesta is indignant that Miachi has once again commanded an audience for an announcement.

'Maybe he's leaving and wants to say goodbye,' Vivian says hopefully, as she and the other nurses make their way onto the street.

'Don't wish away Miachi, girls – better the devil you know and all that,' Nesta tells them.

The street is filling up as women stand in small groups in front of their homes. Nesta sees Norah and Ena and wanders over.

'Any idea what today's announcement is about?' Nesta asks them.

'Nope. Rumours are Miachi is unhappy with the sloppy attitude of the local guards, something about them spending too much time staring at the younger women in skimpy clothes,' Ena says.

'Well, if so, then that applies to me. We've got no clothes other than the ones we make, and it's so hot anyway.'

'I think it's those wearing bra tops and short shorts he's referring to,' Norah adds.

Margaret approaches the women. 'Everyone is genuinely scared the Japanese soldiers will be back. I didn't know what to tell them,' she says.

'That's an awful idea. All that fear and intimidation, the guns being pointed at us for no reason.'

'Oh, here he comes,' Nesta says, spying Miachi with Ah Fat in tow, exiting the administration block. She hurries across the street to join the other nurses.

The women hear Miachi ranting before they see him. He walks down the street, barking orders, Ah Fat running along beside him.

Miachi's instructions are translated and repeated by Ah Fat as the two men pass along the street.

'You will clean camp. You will cut the grass, pick up rubbish, toys. There must be nothing left outside. No one will get any food until whole camp is clean. Captain Miachi will inspect tomorrow morning. There is a special visitor coming tomorrow afternoon, all women will be nicely dressed, no skin,' Ah Fat insists.

Having walked to the end of the street, Miachi turns around and walks back repeating his orders. The children laugh at the diminutive translator stumbling up the road. His message is now reduced to: 'Cut grass. No skin. Clean drain. No skin.' Mothers hold their hands over the mouths of their giggling children, only letting them go when Miachi has passed by.

Norah looks at a group of guards, nudging Ena, who snorts out a laugh; the Javanese guards hold their stomachs as they openly laugh out loud at the spectacle they too have witnessed.

Mrs Hinch calls out to Nesta to join her and Margaret.

'I think we'd better have a meeting and set up work details. He was serious about wanting the camp spick and span.'

149

'That was one of the funniest performances I think we've seen,' Margaret says. 'I was worried for the children who couldn't control themselves.'

'I think we should be very grateful the soldiers have gone; they may not have been as tolerant as the guards,' Mrs Hinch says.

'I'm not sure how we are to cut the grass, we don't have any mowers,' Nesta points out.

'Inchi, Inchi, where are you?' Ah Fat calls out, running towards them.

'Oh, he's back,' Mrs Hinch sighs.

'Inchi! Inchi!'

Turning to the exhausted Ah Fat, who stumbles towards them, she says, 'What do you want now? We got the message.'

'Inchi, please have women clean properly. Captain Miachi will be very angry if you don't.'

'We will try, but we don't have any tools. How are we to cut the grass?'

Reaching into his pocket, he opens his palm. 'Here, you have these.'

'Scissors? You're giving me two pairs of scissors to cut everyone's grass?'

'You share, you cut all the grass out front.'

'Oh, so we don't have to cut the grass at the back of our houses?'

'Just out front, and clean drains. Nothing is to be seen in the street, OK?'

'Run along, Ah Fat.'

'Thank you, Inchi.'

'Well, who wants to cut their lawn first?' Mrs Hinch says, brandishing the scissors.

Nesta takes a pair. 'He's kidding, isn't he?'

'I don't think so. Come on, let's come up with a plan.'

'Right then,' Norah tells the groups assigned to clean the common areas. 'Let's get started.'

Norah and the volunteers clean the drains and street outside their house, offering to continue down the camp and help their neighbours. Others in the groups are given knives and sent outside to cut the grass on their hands and knees.

'I see you have actual scissors,' Norah calls over to Betty, who is hard at work snipping the grass in front of their house.

Nesta joins Norah who is dragging rubbish from the drains in which there is free-flowing sewage.

'Nice job,' Nesta says.

'Hmm.' Norah is using banana leaves to carry the grunge to the end of the camp to dump.

The sun beats down and the workers begin to struggle.

Nesta hands out precious water for the women to share, while the guards walk up and down the street pointing at mounds of rubbish and uneven grass cutting. Nesta watches them hovering outside her house. She follows their gaze. A young nurse, Wilma, is the object of their attention. Nesta sees suddenly that Wilma has taken her top off and is working in her bra.

'Wilma! Wilma, can I see you for a minute?' Nesta calls out to her.

'Coming. I'm sorry if we're going slow, but it's impossible to cut grass with a knife, it's hopeless.'

'You're doing good work, don't worry, but you have to put your top on.'

'Why? It's so hot, and I'm not the only one wearing just a bra.'

'Mrs Hinch and the other house captains will talk to them. I know we've got away with wearing little clothing – heaven knows we've hardly got anything – but for today and tomorrow, can I ask that you cover up?'

'I'm sorry, I didn't mean to upset anyone.'

'That's it, you're not upsetting anyone, quite the opposite.' Nesta nods towards the guards who are still watching Wilma.

That evening, a representative from each house meets at Nesta's house. Those who came into the camp with suitcases of clothes bring a variety of dresses, skirts and blouses with them.

'Check everyone's clothing first thing in the morning, anybody you think isn't appropriately dressed send over here. We'll kit them out with something more modest.' Mrs Hinch gives a small wink.

'*Tenko!*' the guards cry the following morning.

Within minutes, Miachi, with Ah Fat running to keep up with him, is pacing the street, stopping at each house to inspect the women and children. Every woman he deems inappropriately attired is slapped in the face.

The women who need to change hurry to the nurses' house to select more modest dresses.

'I'm here for my fitting,' one says on entering the house.

'Over here, madam. We have a fine selection for you to choose from, do tell us the occasion you are dressing for,' Nesta quips.

'Well, I have a little thing this afternoon. I'm not quite sure what it is, but I want to look fabulous. You never know who you're going to meet at these events.'

'Bully, would you help Madam find the perfect ensemble?'

'Come this way, miss,' says Vivian with a small bow. 'I'm thinking Paris chic with just a touch of conservative London.'

'Oh, you know me so well.'

The atmosphere in the house is one of triumph as the nurses overdress the women who have suffered Miachi's wrath. One is wearing layers of white with a lace petticoat fixed to her hair.

'I don't think they're taking this seriously,' Jean says to Nesta. 'She looks like she's about to get married.'

'Clearly. But who cares as long as they walk out of here all covered up?'

Lunchtime comes, and no food appears. A short time later, '*Tenko! Tenko!*' is bellowed up and down the street.

The women and children stand to attention.

Miachi leaves the administration block with several highly decorated Japanese officers. An escort of snappy, well-dressed soldiers with rifles held high accompanies Miachi and the officers as they slowly walk up and down the camp. No one speaks, no orders are given. When the party finally makes their way to the administrative building, the women continue to stand quietly, not knowing what to do, until Mrs Hinch steps out from her line.

'Go back to your homes, ladies, business as usual.'

'I don't think I can stand any more of this rain!' Jean announces, looking out of the window at the latest monsoon shower.

'I know,' sighs Nesta. 'It was good for a bit, being able to take a warm shower, but it's not fun anymore.'

'Everyone's feeling it,' Jean says, also sighing. 'We're all bored of it. What's the point of cleaning when the floors are just going to get muddy again?'

As January turns to February, a contingent of Japanese soldiers returns. Miachi calls one of his meetings to address the women.

153

This time, they crowd together in front of the administration building, their feet squelching the wet dirt. Miachi appears with Ah Fat. Behind them stands a line of unfamiliar soldiers. Standing on his crate, Miachi barks out his message. The look of exasperation and fatigue on Ah Fat's face, as he tries to outshout the captain, makes it difficult for the women in the front rows, the only ones who can see him, to keep a straight face.

'These soldiers will train the locals who have let you get away with being lazy, untidy and not dressing properly. *Tenko* will be called every day and anyone who is late to line up will be punished. The orders of the Japanese High Command will be obeyed. Go back to your houses. *Tenko! Tenko!*'

The women all race back to their homes and line up. The new Japanese soldiers begin their inspection from the top of the camp. Betty quickly counts the nurses in their house. Across the street, Nesta watches Margaret counting the women in her house.

Slowly, the soldiers make their way towards them. Opposite her, she sees a soldier, about her height, but as wide as a barrel. He is yelling at the women in Japanese, pushing and shoving them as he attempts to do his own count.

'That one we'll call Grumpy,' Betty whispers to her.

Nesta suppresses a grin as she watches the soldier at the house next door. She is startled when he raises his hand and slaps one of the women across the face, screaming in broken English, 'No lipstick! No lipstick!'

She tries to look at her nurses, some of whom appear to be wearing pale lipstick. And then he is standing in front of her.

'How many?' he yells.

'Sixteen!' yells Nesta.

The soldier wanders over to Jean's house, coming to a stop in front of one of the youngest nurses. Nesta glances at her, sees she is not wearing lipstick, and breathes a sigh of relief. She doesn't see his hand come up and slap the nurse across the face. 'More clothes, more clothes,' he spits.

Nesta moves out of line as the soldier strides off. She rubs the woman's back, comforting her in the only way she can right now. And then she heads off after the abusive soldier. One of the local guards steps in front of her in an attempt to stop her. She brushes him aside and gets up behind the soldier. He is looking intently at another woman now, she sees his hand come up and nimbly steps in front of him, taking the full force of the slap. Nesta goes down, but quickly gets up and meets the soldier's eyes. He moves off, ignoring her entirely.

'Nesta, what are you doing?' Jean calls to her.

'We're going to have to watch this one,' is all she says.

They watch him castigate another woman for wearing lipstick. Everyone holds their breath. 'No lipstick!' he yells in her face. But there is no slap this time and he walks on.

With *Tenko* over, the women go back indoors. The nurses gather around Nesta and the other nurse who was assaulted. Wet cloths are produced and held on red, swollen cheeks.

'I think we are returning to the good old days of abuse and punishment,' Vivian says.

'Bloody Lipstick Larry!' Betty exclaims to snorts of laughter from the nurses, but they all agree a code name is a good idea for when he's out and about. 'What else do you think they will do?'

Smiles fade from their faces as all heads turn to the four nurses who have already sacrificed so much.

'No! That will not happen again!' Nesta vehemently insists.

'She's right. We won't let it. Dr McDowell will intervene in any case,' Jean says. 'We stay strong together on this, right, girls?'

Vivian opens her mouth and begins to sing 'Waltzing Matilda' and in no time the house is buzzing with their voices.

The women outside hear the glorious singing. Standing on their front lawn, Margaret, Norah, Ena, Sister Catherina and dozens more quickly gather, and soon this vocal tribute to unity and solidarity fills the street.

'I have some news,' Nesta announces as she walks into the house. She has just been called to Miachi's office while the nurses awaited her return. 'Does anyone know the Japanese word for nurse?' Nesta asks them with a big grin.

A chorus of *no*.

'Well, the soldier kept calling us *kangofu*; I wasn't sure if that meant nurse or he was referring to us as kangaroos,' Nesta says. 'He wants a full list of our names to send home, can you believe it? Our families haven't heard from us for a year, and he is offering to get them a message. Of course, I gave him what he needed, including the names of those no longer with us. Bully, I didn't tell him how I knew some of them were dead, so no worry on that score. Thankfully, he didn't ask. The others we can only hope have been rescued or captured and are somewhere safe. He also said we can write a letter home and he will give us some pens and paper soon.'

'Did you believe him?' Jean asks.

'He was pleasant enough, but I don't know. I can only tell you what he said. I guess we'll just have to wait to see if the pens and paper turn up.'

'Even if it does, how do we know the letters will be sent home?' a nurse asks.

'We don't,' comes Nesta's retort.

She knows it's a generous offer, but she has no idea whether the Australian authorities will ever be told of their existence.

* * *

For the women with children, especially those with boys, there is no such generosity of spirit, she notes drily, when, the next morning, during *Tenko*, all the boys are ordered to line up in front of the other occupants of their house. Everyone watches in horror as each boy is told to drop their pants and their genitals are examined. Regardless of age or height, any boy showing signs of pubic hair is immediately yanked away from his mother.

'Too old! Must go to men's camp,' a Japanese guard says as the boys are marched away. When their mothers chase after them, they are knocked to the ground. Everyone witnesses the barbarity of young children being wrenched away from their mothers, but no one looks away.

June buries her head in Ena's skirt. The little girl is safe, for now, because of her gender, but she is not saved from bearing the pain of her friends and neighbours.

CHAPTER 14

Camp II, Irenelaan, Palembang
April 1942–October 1943

'Any idea what's going on?' Nesta asks Margaret and Mrs Hinch.

The sound of trucks pulling into the camp has brought many of the women out onto the street.

'None. But I think we're about to find out. My goodness, how many trucks are there?' Mrs Hinch wonders.

'I can count seven, but there might be more on the other side of the gate,' says Margaret.

The trucks are parked, and now soldiers and guards begin to scream orders as women and children are forced out of the back of the vans. Very soon, hundreds of frightened new arrivals stand clutching the hand of a child, or a bag of possessions, or to steady an older internee. Without any explanation, the soldiers and guards march the newcomers down the street, pushing a few of them at a time towards each house they pass.

'What's happening?' Jean wonders.

'I wish I knew, but it looks like we've got company.'

'We have to do something.'

'Agreed. Before anyone gets too comfortable, go and tell your nurses to pack up everything they have and bring themselves over to our house. Let's put our new residents next door. If they're anything like us, I think they'd be happier if they weren't split up the minute they arrive.'

Norah has become fast friends with Audrey Owen, a New Zealander she shares her house with. On cloudless nights, the women sit outside, and Audrey talks to her about the constellations, providing brief moments of respite where the women forget where they are and live amongst the stars.

Tonight, Norah and Audrey wander outside to get a feel for how many internees are being disgorged into their camp and what their nationalities might be. They watch as soldiers hold out their hands to help the women now stepping down from the back of the last truck. 'That's strange,' Audrey observes. 'I wonder who they are?'

'They're smartly dressed, aren't they?' Norah notes.

'And they're wearing makeup. I mean, look at them, they're really pretty.'

'I wonder . . .' Norah begins but doesn't finish.

'What?'

'D'you think they're here to . . . well . . . "entertain" the officers?'

'Really? Look, they're taking them away. Let's follow.'

'But let's keep our distance, we don't want to be mistaken for one of them if that's what they're here for.'

'Norah!'

Casually, Norah and Audrey stroll along, keeping well back as the women are escorted out of the camp and down a gently sloping bank. They lose sight of them for a moment before seeing them cross a narrow stream and begin to climb the hill on the other side. At the top of the hill are several small huts. One by one, the women enter and the guards follow them with their bags.

'I'm thinking a new officers' club,' Audrey says.

'A club on the hill. Well, that's certainly going to be a relief to the nurses. Nesta was saying they are all terrified Miachi will come back for them.'

Shortly after, Norah and Audrey visit Nesta's house and are surprised to find the sisters from next door have moved in. They are busy sorting out sleeping arrangements.

'Can we tell you something?' Norah asks Nesta.

'Just me or all of us?' Nesta says.

'I think all of you should hear what we have to say.'

The nurses stop what they're doing. A feeling of dread permeates the room. What now?

'Well,' begins Norah. 'We were curious about the new arrivals and took a walk to see who was being dropped off. And then a truck arrived – the last one, I'm guessing – and there were these women being helped down.'

'You mean, dragged off, surely?' Betty interrupts.

'No. That's the thing. Like I said, they were *helping* them. And carrying their bags. The women were from Singapore, I'm guessing. They were smartly dressed and made up,' Norah continues.

'Naturally,' Audrey adds, 'we were curious, so we followed them. They were taken to the huts across the stream, which I suppose is where they'll live.'

'Who are they?' Vivian asks.

'We think they may be here to *entertain* the officers,' Norah says, trying to gauge the nurses' reactions.

160

'Really?' Nesta says.

'Obviously we don't know for certain, but I think so. Why else would the Japanese be carrying their bags?' Norah says.

'And they were all young and very beautiful women, I think Singaporean Chinese. I don't want to second-guess their previous occupation, but we saw plenty of ladies in Singapore who acted as escorts for the visiting colonials,' Audrey asserts.

'Why don't we go and talk to Mrs Hinch? Let's see if she can find out what's going on,' Norah suggests.

'Ladies, thank you. This could be good news for us,' Nesta tells them.

'But maybe not so great for those women,' Vivian adds, glancing at the four volunteers. They must know better than anyone what lies in store for these women, and, willing or not, it is anything but good news for them.

'Inchi! Inchi!' shouts Ah Fat, poking his head into Mrs Hinch's house.

'What do you want, Ah Fat?' Mrs Hinch is in no mood for one of Miachi's rants. She has just had to move house and there's not nearly enough room for everyone to sleep.

The new arrivals have added to the stress of camp life. The houses are overcrowded, and language is a problem. The new-comers are mostly Chinese women from Singapore with limited English. Over the past few days, the internees sorted themselves out so they were more or less living with those speaking their own language. Food, always an issue, has become contentious, with fights breaking out over distribution. Lipstick Larry and Grumpy don't have to look very far for reasons to berate and beat squabbling women.

'The captain wants to see you.'

161

'Why?'

'Come now; the captain will tell you.'

'I'll be there shortly. Now run along.'

'Inchi, come now.'

'Shortly, I said,' Mrs Hinch snaps. She doesn't want him to think she's at his beck and call, so sometimes being stubborn has its uses.

Crestfallen, Ah Fat trudges out of the house.

Mrs Hinch's visit to Miachi brings both good and bad news. News spreads that a local trader is to be granted permission to come into the camp two days a week selling food, toiletries and various other small items that might come in useful. He is prepared to trade for anything of value. Naturally, this sends a shiver of excitement through the camp. The chance to buy food feels like a dream.

The following afternoon, Gho Leng enters the camp with his bullock-drawn cart. The women flock around as he displays bananas, mangoes, limes, peas and beans. There is tea, butter, flour and rice that comes with free protein-packed weevils. The women who were lucky enough to bring their luggage have money or jewellery to trade for goods. Everyone else looks longingly at the overflowing cart. Nesta can almost taste the mangoes, her mouth waters, but, somehow, she just can't look away.

'Well,' she says, her eyes fixed on the ripe orange fruit, 'if we don't have any money, we'll just have to earn it.'

Norah finds June curled up on her bed indoors instead of playing outside with her friends.

'What's wrong, my sweetheart? Are you feeling OK?' Norah lays a hand on the little girl's forehead. But she doesn't have a temperature.

'I'm OK.'

'Are you sure? You don't look OK.'

'It's just, well, Charlie wouldn't let me have a bit of his banana. It looked so good and I thought he was my friend and that he'd give me a bite.'

Norah wraps June in her arms. 'Darling girl, I'm so sorry. Do some of your friends have special food?'

'Yes! Today Charlie had a banana, and yesterday Susan had a mango. They said their mummies told them they weren't to share.'

Ena comes into the room and sees the concern on Norah's face. 'Everything all right?'

'Charlie had a banana and wouldn't let June have a bite,' Norah tells her.

'Can you get me a banana, Aunties? I'd share mine.'

'I know you would, dear girl. Why don't you go outside and play, and Aunty Ena and I will try to work out a way to get you a banana?'

Reassured that soon she may have her own banana, June is happy to go outside again.

'I don't believe this!' Norah laments. 'We can't get our little girl something as simple as a banana. Just think of the thousands we saw rotting on the ground before we came here and now I'd give anything to be able to get hold of just one, even a rotten one.'

'We'll work it out, Norah,' Ena reassures her sister. 'June will have her banana. But this is getting ridiculous; we've become a camp of haves and have-nots.'

Ena is right, there is inequality within the camp and she wants something done about it. The camp committee is called to an urgent meeting and Margaret and Nesta head over to Dr McDowell's house, joined by other house captains along the way.

163

'We have to do something to control the mood in the camp. It wasn't long ago we supported and cared for one another and now everyone is tense and upset,' Dr McDowell says.

'It's because of Gho Leng,' a house captain remarks.

'It's because a few of us can actually buy stuff and the rest can't,' Margaret adds.

'It's not our fault that some of us have our valuables; would you rather we gave them to the Japanese?' another points out.

'No, of course not. But it would be nice if you shared your bounty with those who have nothing. That's all I'm saying.' Margaret may speak softly, but there is never any doubt when she's cross.

'You're sticking up for the nurses, that's what you're doing,' Margaret is told. 'But isn't it also true that the nurses arrived with barely a stitch of clothing?'

'We're quite capable of sticking up for ourselves,' snaps Nesta. 'But we're not the only ones who came here with nothing. What little we have has been made possible by the generosity of others.'

'How many of you have had one of the nurses visit your house, tend to you or your family?' Margaret asks.

No one responds.

'And how would you feel if they now want to charge you for taking care of you or your children?'

'They wouldn't! That's not what nurses do,' a woman blusters.

'Exactly. So, we expect them to give, for you to receive, to *take*, and that's fair? Is that what some of you are thinking?'

'If I may, I have a suggestion,' Mrs Hinch says. She doesn't want this meeting to turn into a row. 'Why don't we form a shop committee? I think we need to agree right now, before things get any worse, that whenever Gho Leng comes into the camp, everything we buy is evenly distributed.'

164

The women, some begrudgingly, agree and the meeting ends. A shop committee of six members is appointed.

Gho Leng's visits to the camp become regular and word spreads to nearby villages that the internees have 'money' to spend. Soon, other local traders approach Captain Miachi; they too want a piece of this pie.

Miachi finally agrees to allow a second local trader to visit the camp twice a week, as long as the women continue to share the purchases, he confirms.

When it's time to trade, the six designated shoppers are enthusiastically assisted by the women, who gather to view the goods on offer.

'Oh, my goodness, Betty! Look at this, he has lipstick. Can you imagine if we all put some on, even the children? What would Lipstick Larry do then?' Vivian says.

'He would have a heart attack,' Nesta laughs. 'He wouldn't know who to wallop first.'

'I think we stick to buying food,' a woman interjects wryly.

Norah appears at Betty's side. 'Are there any bananas?'

'Yes, and we're taking all he's got.'

'If I could just have one, for June. We don't need anything else. Just one banana.'

Betty plucks a single banana from a bunch and hands it to Norah.

'How good a cook are you?' Betty asks.

'Very good actually. I did all the cooking for our dinner parties. Why d'you ask?'

'We're having a cookery class tonight in our house for some of the ladies from Singapore; they want to learn how to cook English style. They're paying too. Would you like to be one of our chefs? We'll split the money with you.'

Norah hugs Betty, careful not to squash her precious fruit.

'What time?' she asks with a wink.

'I know there's been a lot of talk about us having a ceremony to acknowledge the anniversary of our leaving Singapore. But for Vivian, it's all about surviving what happened on Radji Beach. We should talk to her,' Nesta says to Jean.

Nesta has noticed that Vivian is not socialising or joining in their card games. She has always been the first to volunteer for the dirtiest of jobs or to attend a sick child in the middle of the night. Now, she spends most of each day sitting quietly on her own.

They find Vivian sitting under a tree at the back of the garden; she seems oblivious to the downpour that has soaked right through her thin dress to her skin.

'Can we join you?' Nesta asks.

'If you want to. You do know it's raining, don't you?' Vivian says.

'Well, I'm glad that *you* know it's raining; I wasn't sure when we came outside. You seem so far away these days,' Jean says.

'Where I come from, we can go months without seeing the rain, so I don't mind it.'

'We've been talking,' Nesta says. 'We don't think we should do anything big to mark the year since we left Singapore, but what if we share stories of those who are no longer with us, but especially the ones who were with you on the beach?'

Jean picks up on Nesta's thread. 'We would like you to lead a service. That's if you feel up to it.'

Vivian looks at both women, sniffing as she wipes away a tear.

'I can't believe it's been a year; I can still see their faces. We walked into the water, and we looked at each other and I remember we were all smiling. We knew what was going to happen, that this was the end, but it didn't matter, we were together.'

'This is exactly what I mean,' Nesta says gently. 'We want you to share their stories, hear Matron Drummond's last words again.'

'I'm sure the girls would love to share their stories about the women too. There are so many funny, lovely memories we have talked about since we left home. What do you say?' Jean asks.

'I say, thank you, I'd like that,' Vivian replies with a small smile.

Now on her feet, Vivian holds out her hands to help Nesta and Jean up.

'Let's get out of this rain,' she says.

Word of the nurses' planned remembrance day spreads through the camp. Nesta and Jean are approached by many wanting to join them, particularly Norah, Ena and other survivors from the *Vyner Brooke*.

The night before the event, Nesta and Jean call all the nurses together.

'We have a dilemma; I know you have all heard that many of the women, and the English women in particular, want to come to our remembrance tomorrow,' Nesta begins. 'I know this is something we planned on doing privately, but Jean and I have been talking and we think it would be unfair to not include the women and children who were with us on the *Vyner Brooke*. What do you all think?'

'I say that's a good idea,' says Vivian.

'We'll allow in anyone who wants to attend. And after everyone's gone, we'll have our own very private remembrance. Agreed?'

Without exception, all the nurses agree it is the best, the safest, way to remember.

On the day itself, the nurses' house is full. The windows are thrown open as many more women stand outside. Several of the Dutch nuns have brought with them the candles last seen on Christmas

Day. Margaret and Mother Laurentia lead everyone in prayer before inviting anyone who wants to speak. Ena talks briefly on behalf of herself, Norah, John and little June. Others from the *Vyner Brooke* remember family and friends who are no longer with them. As the evening wears on, Margaret speaks on behalf of all the women and children who, while not on board the *Vyner Brooke* on that fateful day, made their way to the camp by boat and overland. No matter how they arrived, what matters is that they are all here now, together.

Finally, when everyone has said what they wanted to say, the event draws to a close. Goodbyes and hugs are exchanged.

'Well done, girls, I'm so proud of you,' Nesta says to the nurses. She notices how tired they look, but there is still plenty they need to express.

With the windows now securely shut, they sit in a circle, each one holding hands with those either side.

'Bully, thank you for your courage in talking to us now,' Nesta adds warmly.

As Vivian recalls her time in the water, of scrambling onto the beach and reuniting with friends and colleagues, every nurse is crying softly. When she repeats the words of Matron Drummond as they walked into the surf, louder sobbing breaks out, but Vivian doesn't falter.

'I came ashore when it got dark and now I'm here with you.' It's no surprise that there's a tremble in Vivian's voice. Nesta is amazed she has got through the whole terrible episode in one go.

She scrambles over to Vivian and hugs her tightly, giving her the permission to join the rest of them in letting her tears flow.

Nesta waits until the nurses are cried out, before asking if anyone would like to share a story of one no longer with them.

It is late when the last story is told. The tears now come from laughter at the antics of their fallen friends' adventures in Malaya and Singapore.

The women finally drag themselves away to their makeshift beds, exhausted, but each one hugging Vivian before they settle down.

'I'm hungry, Aunty Norah, can you get me another banana?' June pleads.

'I know, my darling; I promise we'll try to get you some more food this evening. You should sleep now.'

'She should be playing outside but she's too weak,' Ena says, the concern in her voice evident as she gently strokes June's hair.

'She doesn't understand how only a few weeks ago we had plenty, well, just enough, and now we don't.'

'She can have my ration tonight; I don't need it,' Ena says.

'How about we each give her half our ration; we need a little something if we're to keep going, for her sake.'

Across the street, Nesta is discussing the same issue with Jean.

'I can't believe we're back to where we started in the first camp; there's just not enough food to get by.'

'I know what you mean, I thought Gho Leng would go on forever, but he's gone.'

'We should have known he can only get hold of seasonal food. We'll just have to wait until the fruit ripens. In the meantime, I'm getting worried about some of the young nurses. Look at them, they're wasting away and they're in the prime of their lives.'

'Vivian told me she caught a couple of them taking their rations to the hospital to give to the patients.'

'That doesn't surprise me. I'm humbled by them every day, dragging themselves on home visits and to the hospital, but I don't know how we can help them, when everyone's in the same boat,' Nesta says.

At that moment, the front door swings open, and a young nurse enters.

'Nesta, can I talk to you a moment?'

'Of course, do you want to sit down?'

'No, I think if I sat down, I wouldn't get up again.'

Nesta eases herself up. 'Come on, let's go outside.'

Shutting the door behind them, Nesta asks, 'So, how are you doing?'

'As well as anyone here, but I'm worried.'

'About?'

'I've just been with one of the Chinese families, one of the mothers waved me down on my rounds and asked me to come and see her children.'

'Are they ill?'

'I'd like you to take a look, but I think they might have typhus.'

Nesta gulps. This is the last thing their depleted bodies need.

'OK, this is serious. Take me to the house, and then go and fetch Dr McDowell. But be discreet, we don't want to frighten anyone.'

A short while later, Dr McDowell appears at the home of the Chinese family, the young nurse in tow. Nesta has cleared the room, except for the mother of the two children who lie on the floor, sweating, shivering and groaning with delirium.

'How long have they been like this?' Dr McDowell asks, kneeling quickly to examine the children.

Nesta has to force the mother to focus on the doctor's questions.

'Two or three days,' she says.

Dr McDowell stands up and turns to the young nurse. 'What's your name?'

'Eileen, Doctor.'

'And you told Nesta you think these children might have typhus.'

'Yes. I'm sorry, did I get it wrong?'

'No, you got it very right. I want to thank you for reacting so quickly.' The doctor turns to Nesta. 'We need to move these children to the hospital straightaway, but we also need to alert Miachi. I'm going to go and arrange for some help. Will you go and tell Mrs Hinch that she needs to find her favourite friend, Ah Fat, and let him know the gravity of this situation so he can pass it up the line. I'll try to quarantine the children, along with their mother, as best I can. Eileen, do you mind staying here until I return?'

'No, Doctor.'

'Let's go, Nesta.'

Before she leaves, Nesta turns to the young nurse. 'Good job, Eileen, a *very* good job – you may have saved these children's lives.'

Within days, more internees from the same house are diagnosed with typhus. To protect the rest of the camp, they quarantine the house, with the nurses providing round-the-clock care. Dr McDowell visits several times a day.

But there is panic amongst the Japanese guards, who fear disease as much as they fear their human enemy. Miachi asks to see Mrs Hinch and Nesta in his office.

'Captain Miachi wants to know how bad is the sickness?' Ah Fat asks the women.

'We have it contained in the one house, but there are fourteen patients inside confirmed with typhus,' Nesta tells him.

'Captain wants to know what can we do to stop it.'

'We need clean water, not the contaminated water dragged from the well. We need more firewood to boil the water, and to clean surfaces.'

Miachi takes his time to respond.

'And we need it now,' Mrs Hinch chimes in.

Miachi talks rapidly to Ah Fat, who translates.

'Captain will allow women to leave camp and get water from the stream. They can also get wood from the jungle for fires.'

Being allowed out of the camp to fetch water and firewood lifts the spirits of the women. They use the situation to their advantage and allocate bathing areas downstream. Fires burn all day, boiling the water they drink and use to rinse the food. The outbreak of typhus remains restricted to the one house, and all but an elderly grandmother survive.

Miachi and his officers have been keeping their distance in the camp, and for a glorious, but all too short, period there is no *tenko*, no abuse, and Lipstick Larry stays away.

'I want to be in Sister Catherina's class for all my lessons,' June announces to Ena and Norah one morning.

'Darling, she's the art teacher,' Ena tells her.

'She's my favourite.'

'She's everyone's favourite, including the adults. I think I might take her art class too, what do you think?' Norah says.

'Oh, Aunty Norah, you're too old to go to school.'

'You're right. Now let's get you to your class and you never know, you might have an art lesson later today, or tomorrow.'

Vivian and Betty are also leaving their house as Norah steps outside with June.

'Hello, Sister Betty and Sister Vivian, I'm off to school, but I don't have Sister Catherina as my teacher except for art,' June calls to them.

'Hello, June, Norah, you have a wonderful day,' Betty calls back.

'Are you teaching us today too?' June asks, as they all make their way up the street towards the Dutch houses where the classes are being held.

'Well, we've decided there are a lot of very clever people here already, so we're going to be the fun teachers and play with the children,' Vivian says.

'Really? Can we play instead of going to class?'

'After class. But there are a few boys who don't want to go to school right now, so we're going to play with them.'

'A game?' asks June, peering up at Vivian.

'We're going to draw some lines on the ground and play a game called hopscotch, and then we'll have a go at tag.'

'I know those games!'

Norah pauses a moment to watch Vivian's exchange with the reluctant boys.

'Hey – we're over here!' Vivian calls to a group of pre-teenage boys loitering at the back of the camp, kicking at the dirt, their hands stuffed in pockets; none of them makes eye contact with Betty and Vivian.

'So, have any of you made a slingshot?' Betty asks.

'What's a slingshot?' one asks.

'It's a bit like a bow and arrow, but a stone instead of an arrow and a sling instead of a bow.' Betty realises she's not doing a very good job of describing the toy. 'Let's all find some Y-shaped branches and we'll take it from there.'

'We're going to scavenge for the materials we'll need and then Betty and I will help you make them. What do you say?' Vivian adds.

The boys shrug.

'It's a weapon, you know,' Vivian adds, with a grin.

Now she has their attention. They look at her intently.

'You're going to love it. Now, into two teams and we'll start foraging for the bits and pieces. First one to make a weapon is the winner.'

'Can I make a slingshot, too, Aunty Norah?' June asks as they set off once more.

'Maybe,' says Norah. 'When you're older.' A lump forms in her throat. She doesn't want the little girl to grow older in this camp.

'Come on, June. It's time to get up. You have your favourite lesson this morning – art with Sister Catherina,' Ena pleads with her young charge.

As the weeks roll by, class attendance falls, mostly due to the fact the children have little strength to make it out of the house. Those who do manage to get to school struggle to retain their lessons, so focused are they on their rumbling stomachs. By June of 1943, the scarcity of food, plus the lack of firewood to boil contaminated water, has begun to take its toll on everyone in the camp.

'I'm too tired and my tummy hurts.'

'I'm sorry, my love. I'll go and see if Aunty Norah has found any rice.'

Norah is outside, clearing the drains that run past their house, with Audrey. Ena watches, her heart breaking to see her sister on her hands and knees scraping mud and sewage onto the street, knowing full well that when the rain comes, the same chore will have to be repeated.

'Hi,' she says, a false cheeriness in her voice.

'Hello, Ena, we're just finishing here,' Audrey replies.

'I'll go and get a bucket of water to wash your hands,' Ena says, heading off to the well.

'Something's bothering her,' Audrey remarks.

'I agree, but she'll tell me when she gets back.'

'Why don't I take over here and you go and talk to her?'

Norah finds Ena on her way back with a small bucket of water. They walk to the edge of the street where the drain is flowing freely. Ena tips the water over Norah's hands, while her sister scrubs them clean.

Shaking out her dripping fingers, Norah says, 'You're worried about June, aren't you?'

'You know me so well. She won't get up, she's so weak. I don't know what to do, I can barely look at her. What kind of carer am I if I can't even feed her the bare minimum she needs to survive?'

'Ena, you have been the best thing in her life since we all went overboard. It's not your fault there's no food, but we do need to find something for her. I'll go and see if Nesta has any ideas.'

The sisters hug.

'Oh, one more thing,' says Norah, before they part. 'Audrey heard a rumour that Miachi is leaving.'

'Really? Did she hear when?'

'No, and like I said, it's just a rumour.'

Betty answers the door to Norah.

'Hi, Betty,' she says and then looks beyond her into the living room. The nurses look a little bit sheepish. 'Is Nesta around? I wanted to have a word.'

'Er, no, not right now, but she should be back soon.'

'I'll come back later then. Can you tell her I stopped by?'

'Sure, unless one of us can help?'

'No thanks, I'll talk to Nesta.'

As Norah turns to leave, Nesta bursts into the living room from the back door.

'Vivian was right,' she exclaims to the roomful of nurses. 'There's a burial happening right now!' And then she sees Norah at the front door. 'Oh, Norah, hello. I didn't realise you were here.'

'That's OK, I was just leaving. I'll catch you later?'

'No, wait, wait. What do you say, girls?' Nesta asks the expectant faces.

'OK, let's tell her what we've found. We don't know if it is going to be doable yet, so why not?' Jean says.

'What's going on?' Norah steps back into the house and closes the door behind her.

'A few weeks ago, Vivian was scavenging behind the hospital . . .'

'I didn't know you could go behind the hospital, I thought the fence line was right up to it,' Norah says.

'It is, but I'm so skinny now, I managed to get right round the back. I wanted to see what I could reach through the fence, and I saw something,' Vivian says.

'She could just make out some people walking through the trees,' Nesta adds. 'Then they stopped for a while, and when they moved away, she could see it was a cemetery. They had just buried someone.'

'So?'

'I saw that they'd left some food and fruit on a grave,' Vivian adds.

'We think it was an offering to the dead,' Nesta says, 'and it just rots away, or animals get at it. So, each day at the same time, one of us sneaks behind the hospital and waits to see if there is another burial. It was my turn today and there's a burial happening right now.'

'What are you going to do?' Norah asks.

'We've made a small gap in the fence and I think I can fit through; we're going to wait for an hour or so for them all to leave and then I'm going after that food,' Nesta says triumphantly.

'Nesta, the reason I came here was to ask if you have anything to spare for June. She's just fading away.'

'Then why don't you come with me? I don't know how much there's going to be, but I'm taking it all.'

'You're not worried about disrespecting the dead?'

'No, I'm worried about the children in this camp and what we can do to help them carry on living,' Nesta says.

'Then yes, I'd love to come with you.'

'Afterwards, we'll distribute anything we can get hold of to those with children. Come on, let's go and see. It's not too bad, the waiting, as it's so shady back there.'

Nesta and Norah casually walk down the middle of the street towards the hospital, swinging a water bucket each. Approaching the door, they check to see if anyone is close by. There isn't and so they nip along the side of the hospital towards the back of the building. Nesta stops at a small opening, and the women crouch.

'They're leaving,' Nesta whispers.

Norah peers through the thick undergrowth and makes out some movement a short distance away. They watch for a while, trying to catch a glimpse of the grave.

'I can see a mound of something. I don't know if it's food or flowers,' Norah whispers.

'I'll go and take a look, stay here.'

Norah watches as Nesta squeezes through the hole in the fence before crawling through the undergrowth towards the cemetery. She disappears for a few minutes before Norah spots her again. Nesta is walking towards her, her arms full of . . . something.

'Here, Norah. Take this quickly, I'm going back for more.'

Nesta passes mangoes, potatoes and onions to Norah before scurrying away. She returns a few minutes later with two bananas, a woven basket of cooked rice and two unrecognisable, but reassuringly large, fruits. Norah takes the food, piling it into their water buckets.

Back at the house, Norah and Nesta are greeted as returning heroes. Norah takes one of the bananas, leaving the nurses to distribute the rest of the food amongst the families with children.

'June, wake up, honey, Aunty Norah has something for you.'

'I don't want anything.'

'Even a banana?' Norah teases, revealing it from behind her back.

June's eyes light up with pleasure. It is a small moment of respite, but deeply savoured all the same.

'This is Sergeant Major Kato, your new commandant. Please be good and nothing will happen to you,' Ah Fat tells the assembled women.

The rumour about Miachi is proved to be true when the women are called to *Tenko*.

When the announcement is over, Kato and Ah Fat quickly stride back to the administrative block. The women wander back to their houses or to the well, hoping there will be some water to collect.

'Well, I wonder what this one's going to be like,' Mrs Hinch says to Norah.

'He could give us more food, but I bet nothing will change.'

'I'll arrange to talk to him and stress we either need more food from them, or he needs to find us some local traders to come back,' Mrs Hinch decides.

'Well, good luck,' says Norah, with little hope that something will come of it.

'If somebody had told me two years ago that I would be sifting through garbage, looking for any grubs that can be eaten, I wouldn't have believed them. But you know something, I quite like it.' Mrs Hinch grins widely.

'Dr McDowell, do you have a moment?' Nesta asks the frantic doctor, who is running between rooms to tend to her feverish patients.

Conditions have worsened in the camp, with outbreaks of both typhus and dengue fever. Very soon, the hospital is full of the seriously ill. The nurses rotate between house visits and working in the under-resourced, poorly sanitised hospital. Nesta's shifts, however, are all at the hospital.

'How can I help you, Sister?'

'There's a patient who came in with some of the others, but I can't tell whether she has typhus or dengue fever.'

'Tell me her symptoms,' the doctor replies wearily.

'Her headache is severe; she doesn't have a bad rash but keeps complaining her stomach hurts.'

'Could her stomach pain be because of hunger?'

'We're all starving and no one else is complaining specifically of stomach pain like she is.'

'Mmm, I wish I could say conclusively that it was dengue; it sounds serious enough, though. Just keep her comfortable for now and I'll alert everyone to be on the lookout for tummy pain. It could be the distinguishing symptom.'

Morale in the camp reaches an all-time low. Many women can be seen walking up and down the street in a daze, making little effort to avoid the torrential rains that arrive every afternoon. The drains clog with mud, overflowing sewage and camp rubbish. Without being asked, Norah and Audrey take it upon themselves to clean out the drains on their side of their street. Two of the nuns do the same on the other side. They are often the only women doing so.

Margaret walks the camp during the downpours, talking to the many women whose stupefied appearance is as much a concern as any physical illness. One day, she and Norah approach a young woman who is staggering along the street. Norah notices she is not looking straight ahead as many others do, but down at the muddy cesspools she is trudging through. Margaret takes the woman's arm.

'Tell me your name, my dear,' Margaret says.

The woman with the dead eyes turns to Margaret, a puzzled look on her face as she tries to make sense of what she is hearing.

'I'm Sonia.'

'I have an idea for you, Sonia. Look up,' she says softly. 'Look up, my dear.'

Sonia slowly raises her head, as the rain soaks her face, shaking her out of her stupor.

'What are you saying? What do you want from me?'

'Just to raise your eyes.'

The woman turns on Margaret, grabs her by the shoulders and starts to shake her. Norah attempts to pull her away.

'Norah, please, leave her alone,' Margaret says, stumbling, her own hands coming up to take hold of Sonia's arms.

'I don't need your preaching!' Sonia screams at Margaret. 'Where is your God? He's not here, that's for sure. Why don't you go and save someone who wants to be saved.' She lets go of Margaret, and once again, her eyes fall to the mud around her sodden feet.

'I'm sorry, my dear. That's not what I'm trying to do, I don't want you looking up to find some higher power, some God. I want you just to see the sky, the tops of the trees, the birds. Soon, the clouds will be gone, and the sun will come out. There is more than the mud and squalor beneath your feet.'

The woman looks up as the rain peters out. At that moment, the clouds part and the sun streams down. From the nearby trees, a flock of birds launch themselves over the camp, whooping loudly. Sonia smiles, then her tears begin to fall. Margaret carefully takes the women into her arms.

'It is beautiful,' she sobs. 'I've always loved being outside. The jungle around our home in Malacca was magnificent. My husband . . . my husband . . . we . . .'

'I know . . . I know, but this beauty is still all around us, we just have to look up.'

Sonia spies Sister Catherina in the street and extricates herself from Margaret's arms and rushes over to the nun.

'Sister! Sister, look up, look up at the sky. Isn't it beautiful?'

Margaret watches as Sister Catherina raises her eyes, sees the smile come to her lips, and the two women embrace.

Norah takes Margaret's arm and they continue along the road.

'Can I borrow that?' Norah asks.

'Borrow what?'

'Your "look up". I think those two little words might just be what makes a difference around here. Thank you.'

'Why are you thanking me?'

'For showing us another way to live, to endure, to get through these blasted days. You have given so much to all of us, and you keep on giving; how do we ever repay you?'

'Dear Norah, nobody here owes me anything. You and your sister, along with so many others, bring music and, for a while anyway, we can escape this camp. That's just as valuable as any spiritual message I might bring.'

Norah nods. She knows Margaret is sincere but wonders if music and spiritual nourishment will be enough.

PART 2

Deep in the Jungle

CHAPTER 15

Camp III
October 1943–October 1944

Mrs Hinch walks slowly out of Sergeant Kato's office. Her shoulders droop as she heads back to her house. Norah watches her come inside.

'Mrs Hinch, what is it? Has something happened?'

'I've just had a meeting with Kato; he's told me to get the women ready. We're moving camp.'

'Oh no! Not again. Do you know when?'

'He wants the nurses and the first three houses on both sides of the street to get ready to in a hour today. The rest of us are leaving tomorrow morning. I know we're all tired and hungry, but we need to start gathering our things. Norah, can you tell Nesta? I'll go and tell the other houses and then everyone else.'

'I need to find Ena and June too, and tell the nurses,' says Norah. 'Oh God, not this again!'

'Don't forget to pack.'

'Pack what? We only have the clothes on our backs.'

* * *

Jean answers Norah's knock at the door and ushers her in.

'Where is everybody?' Norah asks.

'Either at the hospital or on home visits. What's going on?'

'You're moving, I'm afraid. Well, we all are, but Mrs Hinch has been told to tell you and a few of the houses that you're leaving in one hour and to hurry and pack your things.'

Jean blanches. 'Are you joking?'

'I wish I was. Do you need some help to pack? We're not leaving until the morning.'

'I need to find the others and get them back here.' Jean shakes her head, visibly upset. 'I don't believe this.'

'Where's Nesta?'

'At the hospital, where she is every day and most nights. I've come back for a rest.' Jean sighs. Norah can't help but notice how exhausted her friend looks. 'Will you let her know while I find the others?'

'Of course.'

The two women nod at each other in grim solidarity before heading off to their respective tasks. There is nothing else that they can do.

Norah enters the hospital and comes to an abrupt stop. All around her are sick patients. Slouching off chairs, lying on the floor. Nurses move amongst them, soothing foreheads, offering water. Dr McDowell and Nesta are talking at the far end of the room. They turn as she approaches.

'Norah, are you ill? You look so pale.'

'I'm fine, I just have some bad news.' She sighs as she takes in Dr McDowell's and Nesta's questioning expressions. 'It's . . . well, Mrs Hinch was summoned to Kato's office a short while ago and told we are moving camp.'

186

'When?' Nesta asks.

'You and some other houses are to leave in an hour, the rest of us tomorrow morning.'

'Impossible!' the doctor exclaims. 'This is ridiculous. We can't just up and move. I need to speak to Kato.'

'I don't think he's going to change his mind; I'll speak to Mother Laurentia to get you some help for the next twenty-four hours. I can only presume he wants the nurses moved today so they can prepare the hospital at the new camp for your arrival.'

'Thank you, Norah. Nesta, take your nurses and go. I'll see you tomorrow.'

Nesta quietly asks each of the nurses on duty to come with her, and with Norah, they head back to the nurses' house.

They arrive in time to join the others packing up their kitchen, along with the few clothes they share. Their uniforms are lovingly folded and tied together in a blanket.

'How can we help?' Audrey calls as she pushes through the front door.

'You could start in the kitchen. Only problem is we've no boxes or bags to put things in.'

'Let's just bundle them into sheets like a swag,' Betty says.

'A swag?' Norah queries.

'Ah, I know the answer to that,' Audrey says with a proud grin. 'It's a bundle of your possessions that you carry on your back.'

'Do you have them in New Zealand too?' Vivian asks.

'No, but I know you Aussies do. Come on, let's make up some swags.'

The sound of a truck horn brings the nurses into the street, along with their pots and pans, cutlery accumulated along the way, and a few books borrowed and not returned. At the head of the

187

camp, women and children are being loaded into two trucks. Everyone else comes out of their homes to wave them off.

'We'll see you tomorrow,' Norah yells, as the trucks begin to pull away.

Ten minutes later, the women arrive in their new camp in the jungle. They stumble down from the truck and take in their surroundings. They are only about a mile away from Irenelaan, and the camp – more prison-like than the houses they have been living in – is a collection of barracks, hemmed in by barbed wire, with four sentry boxes, one at each corner, and a guardhouse next to a gate, through which the women are led.

'Where the hell have they brought us?' Betty asks.

'It looks like a rubbish dump. And, oh my God, what's that smell?' Jean gasps.

The walkways between the barracks are strewn with broken furniture, with litter and rotting mounds of food waste. There are rats everywhere.

The soldiers approach, jabbing the women with their bayonets, indicating for them to move on, into one of the many huts that line both sides of the small street.

'Who on earth lived here?' Jean asks to no one in particular.

One of the Japanese soldiers nearby starts giggling and they realise he has understood what Jean said.

'Do you speak English?' Nesta asks him.

'Little, some.'

'Why are you laughing?'

'Who live here before? It was Englishmen, Dutchmen, other white men. They made mess when they left.'

'I don't believe it. Look at the place,' Betty says.

'Surely, they didn't live like this,' Jean replies.

'I, for one, don't believe they did. They wouldn't have laid waste to everything if they knew there was any chance we would be brought here,' Nesta says. 'Come on, let's make the most of it, see what we've got to work with.'

'Let's choose a hut and explore,' Jean agrees.

'There seems to be a bigger building down the back, maybe we can turn that into the hospital, so let's get a hut close by,' Nesta suggests.

As they walk towards the back of the camp, the same soldier follows them, pointing to two open-fronted buildings. 'You will wash here.'

The nurses peer into the huts. Each has one long concrete trough for washing and a row of holes dug into the earth along the back wall for their toilet. Nearby, there are three wells. Looking inside, they find they are full of rubbish, and the small amount of water at the bottom smells rank. Dumping their bundles into the hut Nesta has chosen for the nurses, they check out the larger building nearby. It is one long room containing a few broken beds. Slashed mattresses lie scattered on the floor.

'We've got our work cut out for us before the others get here,' Nesta says.

The next day, the rest of the camp arrives. Norah, Ena and June find themselves crammed into a hut with sixty other women and children. There is barely enough room to lie down.

'We'll be like sardines,' says June, not letting go of Ena's hand for a second.

'But we'll be sardines together,' Ena reassures her.

'The rain is coming through the roof, Aunty Ena.' Norah and Ena look up to the thatched ceiling to see drops of rain pouring through in a steady stream.

'We'll find a few palm leaves,' Norah tells her, trying to stay upbeat, but failing. 'That should keep the worst of it off.'

'I don't think I'm going to like it here,' says June. 'It feels like a prison.'

She's right, thinks Norah, watching a line of tiny ants climbing the wall. In a few days, everyone will be watching out for these biting insects, whose attacks are so painful their victims can only claw wildly at the hot stings. Within days, infections abound.

When she realises this is their home for now and she needs to do whatever she can to make life easier, Norah speaks to Audrey.

'We have to do something to improve the sanitation here; will you help me?'

'Do you have any ideas?'

'We need to get rid of effluence in the drains each day, otherwise we will all get sick. Let's look around and see what we can find to help us. You with me?'

'Of course. Let's go.'

Norah and Audrey scavenge the entire length of the camp and beyond. They discover several badly dented cans that once held kerosene. Putting them aside, they break up branches, measuring them across the length of their shoulders. From nearby palm trees, they tug away large strips from the fronds to make ropes. Sitting under a tree, resting from the exhaustion of their efforts in the tropical heat, they admire their results.

'So, the plan is to fill the kerosene tins with the sludge and then tie them onto each end of the branch so we can carry them away on our shoulders?' Audrey says.

'I think that should work, shouldn't it?'

'Well, it should. Only one problem – how do we fill the tins?'

'Mmm, we can't use the pots we have, they're needed to cook and carry water. We'll have to come up with something else.'

They sit for a little while, thinking, enjoying the respite from the heat and the work.

'I know, what are we sitting beneath?' Audrey says, breaking into a huge grin.

Norah looks up at the coconuts hanging above their heads. 'You're brilliant. Of course. Now all we need to do is get them off the tree, cut them in half and we're set.'

'Can we sit for just a little longer? I'm wilting from the heat.'

'I have an idea. You stay here, I'll be right back.'

It isn't long before Norah returns with Jack, a young boy teetering at the edge of adolescence. He is excited and runs beside her.

'Hello, Jack, what's she roped you into?' says Audrey.

'It's all right, she asked me mum and she said I could help,' Jack explains.

'I take it she's sending you up the tree to get us some coconuts.'

'Yeah, that's what she said. That's right, isn't it?' He turns to Norah.

'It is. Come on, I'll give you a leg-up.'

'I'll help,' Audrey says, cupping her hands together for Jack to step into them.

Jack looks at Audrey before turning back to Norah. 'I'm bigger than she is.'

Norah laughs. 'Yes, yes you are. Sorry, Aud, it's not your fault you never had a growth spurt. I'll do this.'

'Hey, my parents were on the small size; what chance did I have?'

Norah and Jack step up to the tree. 'For once, my height is going to be a good thing,' she says, bending her knees, cupping her hands for Jack.

With one hand on her shoulder, Jack bounces, steps into Norah's hands and hoists himself up, scrambling to grab hold of the lowest branch. Wriggling away, he beams down at the women. 'I'm OK.'

'Now, don't do anything silly, young Jack. Hold on tight and try to get to the nearest coconut,' Audrey instructs.

But Jack doesn't need to be told twice. He shimmies along the branch, reaching up to a coconut above him. It takes some effort to dislodge, but finally it drops to the ground.

'How many do you want?' he calls out.

'As many as you can reach, please. It will save you from having to do this again,' Norah calls.

Before long, a pile of coconuts lies on the ground. Jack ignores Norah's offer of help and leaps down.

'That was fantastic, I loved being up there, you can see for miles.'

Norah and Audrey give him a hug. 'Will you help us carry them back to our hut?' Audrey asks.

'I can even get some friends to help you break them open if you like,' he says.

While Jack and his friends smash the coconuts apart, Norah and Audrey plait palm strands into rope. When they have enough, they tie the kerosene tins on each end of the branch. Ena has rounded up a group of women who sit scraping the raw coconut from the shells. Some of the precious milk is saved, most of it goes to waste as the overexcited boys are too keen to split the hard nuts in two.

'Why are you doing this?' a woman asks Norah and Audrey.

'Somebody has to do it – why shouldn't it be us?' Norah tells her.

'Need a hand?'

Norah and Audrey look up from their work to see Nesta, Betty, Vivian and several other nurses grinning down at them.

'Not fair that you have all the fun,' Betty says.

'Find yourselves a sharp twig and start scraping out the pulp,' Norah tells them.

The next morning, women stagger out of the huts and watch as Norah and Audrey place their yoked tins on the ground and, with half a coconut shell, scoop the vile contents of the drains into them. When they think they have all they can carry, they hoist the branch onto their shoulders and carry the stench away to an area at the back of the camp where the contents will run downhill.

With this shining example set by Norah and Audrey, it dawns on the women that if they are to survive and make the camp habitable, they must join this effort.

'Outside, please, everyone,' Norah calls up and down the camp. Once everyone is present, she makes her announcement. 'It's time we sorted out who's doing what.'

'Right-oh!' says Mrs Hinch. 'Tell us what needs doing.'

'There's firewood to chop, the wells to clean out so we can have fresh water. And if anyone fancies it, they can help us clean out this drain.'

Only a few raise their hands for drain duty.

'It's great we're cleaning the camp,' Nesta tells Jean one morning as they make their way up the street. 'But it's too late for some.'

'It's those bloody ants,' says Jean. 'And the food. It's rotten.'

'I'm more worried about infection than diarrhoea,' Nesta says, watching a woman scratching hard at her legs as she pauses in her chores. 'Dr McDowell's had no luck getting any medicine from the Japanese. And these bloody mosquitoes!' she squeals, swiping at the air.

'I'm off to the hospital,' Jean says. 'I'll see you there later.'

Nesta is about to enter the huts of the Dutch women when Norah intercepts her.

'Nesta, oh, please! You have to help her!' she cries.

'Who? Quickly, tell me what's wrong.'

'It's Margaret, she's sick. One of the women in her hut came and told me she can't rouse her; she's burning up.'

'Let's go,' Nesta says, leading the way as they run towards their friend.

Inside, several women are standing around Margaret's groaning body. One, Marilyn, is pressing a wet cloth to her forehead. They step back when they see Nesta.

With no equipment, no supplies, only the skills she learned back in Melbourne, enhanced in a mine in South Africa, perfected on the battlefields of Malaya and Singapore, Nesta gently examines Margaret. Undoing her clothes to expose her burning torso, turning her gently to see the rash that covers her back.

'How long has she been like this?'

'For the past two or three days, she's been a little more subdued and slower than usual,' Marilyn explains.

'I asked her yesterday if she was OK and she said it was nothing, just a little headache. She seemed to be rubbing her eyes as if that was where the pain was,' a housemate offers.

'Can you please get me some rags and as much water as you can spare? We need to try to cool her down and get some fluid into her.'

Nesta lifts Margaret's skirt to confirm the rash on her front and back has spread down her legs. When a bucket with precious

194

water and some torn-up garments are brought, Nesta first dips one end of fabric into the bucket, then gently forces Margaret's mouth open. Placing the tip of the rag into her mouth, she squeezes and slowly drips the water into her friend's mouth.

'This is the best way to hydrate her without wasting any,' she explains.

When she is satisfied Margaret has swallowed some water, she drops the rags into the bucket. Squeezing them out, she lays them over Margaret's near-naked body.

'The quicker we can lower her temperature, the better. You must cover her all over with these rags, not just her forehead.'

'What's wrong with her?' asks Marilyn.

'It might be malaria, but I think it most likely is dengue fever. I saw cases of it in Malaya.'

'Is it contagious?' another woman asks, backing away.

'No, you won't catch it, not from Margaret anyway. She's been bitten by a mosquito that was infected.'

Without warning, Margaret begins to shake and shiver.

'Help me get these rags off her and find me whatever you can to wrap her up. Blankets, coats, anything.'

One of the women produces a heavy fur coat 'Have this. I haven't had the need to wear it recently, may as well put it to good use,' she says, raising a couple of laughs.

Nesta takes the coat and wraps it around Margaret. And then, to everyone's surprise, she snuggles up to Margaret, folding her arms around the delirious woman's violently shaking body. She stays with her until the seizure subsides.

Margaret finally falls into a deep sleep and Nesta stands, stretching her limbs.

'She will be like this for several days, I'm afraid. Are you able to take care of her or do you want help to move her to our hut?'

There is a chorus of 'we'll take care of her' and 'she'll be OK with us now we know what to do.'

'Just remember, if she's burning up, use the wet rags. It would be better if we could use cold water, but this is where we are. Get some fluids into her as frequently as possible and then wrap her up when she starts to shiver. Somebody should sit with her all the time.'

'We'll take turns,' Marilyn tells her. 'Don't worry.'

'I'll come back later today and check on her,' Nesta says.

'I'm so worried about her,' Norah says as she and Nesta walk away.

Nesta smiles. 'She's got a rough few days ahead of her, but I have never known anyone as strong as Margaret Dryburgh.'

'I'll look after her,' Norah tells her. 'I won't leave her alone.'

Two days later, Ena and Audrey enter Margaret's hut to find Norah dozing and starting awake on the floor beside the sick woman.

'Norah,' says Ena, laying a hand on her sister's arm and pulling her to her feet. 'You need to go and get some rest, some proper rest.'

'I . . . I can't . . . I need—'

'You don't need to do anything. You've done so much already,' Audrey insists. 'You've barely been home; you're here all the time.'

'And how do you think Margaret will feel when she wakes up to find you're sick because you haven't been looking after yourself?' Ena adds. 'June needs you at home, with me.'

'But I have to help her,' Norah wails.

'What can you do that the others can't?' Audrey asks her.

'I don't know, but there must be something.'

'Time – she needs time,' Ena tells her.

Norah is quiet for a moment and then her eyes light up. 'I've got it. Music! We'll get through to her with music.'

'You want us to get the choir to sing to her?' Ena asks, equally enthusiastic.

'No, it needs to be something different, something special. You two, you're a start. I have an idea and I just need two others. They're in one of the Dutch huts. Come on, why are you just sitting there? Let's go.'

'It's getting late, Norah; can't this wait until tomorrow?' Audrey says.

'No, it can't.'

Ena has known all her life not to argue with her sister; Audrey too has learned that Norah is an unstoppable force, and they follow across the road to a hut, home to some of the Dutch women.

Thankfully, two of the women in the hut were part of the original choir, Margarethe and Rita. They look on in amusement as Norah explains her idea.

'I'm going to sing Tchaikovsky's "Andante Cantabile for Strings",' Norah says.

'What do you mean, you are going to *sing* it? It's written for violins and a cello. We don't have any instruments,' Rita says.

'I know. You are all going to be my instruments. Just listen.'

Sweetly, gently, Norah oohs and aahs the simple melody. The other women in the hut crowd around. Opening her eyes, Norah looks at her chosen choristers.

'What do you think?'

'Well, you sound amazing, but we can't do that.' Margarethe is bemused.

'If I can do it, so can you. All of you have much better voices than me. Please, will you at least try?'

'Is this what you want us to sing to Margaret?' Audrey asks.

'Yes, we need to give her something special, something unique. I believe if she hears you singing this piece, she'll wake up.'

'Well, I'm up for it. What do you say?' Audrey turns to her three choir mates.

'How long have we got to learn it?' Rita asks.

'Tonight, and tomorrow. But the next day I want us to visit Margaret.'

'Let's do it!' Ena says.

'I think we should start humming just the first line; I want to hear the shades and rhythms in your voices.'

The second line is sung, then the third, and so on until the four women have created a sound unlike anything their audience has ever heard.

'Now let's string them together,' Norah says, raising her arm.

The next day when Norah, Ena and Audrey arrive at the Dutch hut, the women are waiting for them. Over the next few hours, they perfect their parts in readiness for their performance of Tchaikovsky.

Saying farewell to Margarethe and Rita, Norah sends Ena and Audrey home. She is going to stop off and visit Margaret, even though it is late, but she needs to see her.

Knocking gently on the door, she is let inside and she tiptoes with Marilyn to Margaret's bedside.

'No change,' Marilyn says.

'Not getting any worse though?'

'Not that Nesta has seen. If anything, she is resting for longer periods between the shivers and seizures.'

'Is it OK if I come back tomorrow morning with four others? We would like to sing to her.'

'Of course, it certainly can't hurt.'

* * *

The next morning, Norah, Ena, Audrey, Rita and Margarethe wait outside Margaret's hut for Nesta to update them on Margaret's condition. They pace and worry, scuffing at the dirt beneath their bare feet. Finally, Nesta appears. She isn't smiling, but she isn't frowning either, which Norah takes as a good sign.

'She's no worse, not as many fevers overnight, but that is what I would have expected. This fever has a long recovery. Go on, go inside and see her. Do you mind if I come and listen?'

Norah loops her arm through Nesta's, and the six women enter the hut. There are so many women inside; word has spread that Norah and the others are going to sing to Margaret and everyone wants to be there, to witness a hoped-for, prayed-for miracle.

Gathered around her mattress, Norah positions her choir. Nesta sits beside Margaret holding a damp cloth to her forehead, wiping sweaty hair from her face. Raising then slowly lowering her hand, the first notes slide from Margarethe's lips, as the others join in. Softly, sweetly, the golden sounds of the women's voices reach out to grab at the souls of all the women present. Nesta involuntarily squeezes Margaret's hand. The notes ebb and flow and soar and fall. The air vibrates with their voices and when the short piece is complete, each of the five women bends down and kisses Margaret on the cheek. Nesta walks out with them. She hasn't said a word inside the dark, rat-infested hut, but outside in the brilliant morning sun, she turns to the women.

'There can be no medicine, no tonic, to compare with what I just heard. Thank you, I shall never forget it.'

As she walks away, the five link arms and head back to their chores. 'There's some cesspools to be cleaned,' Audrey tells Norah.

* * *

That evening, an excited Audrey bursts into Norah's hut.

'You have to come quickly. She's waking up. You did it! Oh, my God, you beautiful women, you did it, you've given us back our leader.'

'Get Nesta,' Norah tells her as she and the others race to Margaret's hut.

The door is open; chatter and excitement bombard them as they enter. The women part, allowing the five singers through, reaching out to pat their shoulders and give their arms a rub as they pass.

Margaret lies still, her eyes fluttering. Norah kneels beside her. She is vaguely aware that Nesta has entered the hut, but for now is focused on the older woman.

'Hello, it's good to see you, my friend. How're you doing?' Margaret says.

'I'm so happy you're awake! Tell us how you're feeling, won't you?' Norah asks.

'Oh, a bit tired. Think I may have caught something, but I'll be all right.'

'You will,' Nesta says. She reaches a hand to Margaret's forehead. 'Temperature seems normal. Welcome back, Margaret.'

'Where have I been?' a perplexed Margaret asks.

'You've been very unwell, but you're on the mend. You'll need to take it easy for quite a while, but you will be fine. Someone fetch me a cup of water please.'

Gently lifting Margaret's head, Nesta helps her drink.

'What was it?' Margaret asks.

'Dengue fever, I think. I can't know for sure, but that's my best guess.'

'I would take your worst guess any day. Thank you for taking care of me.'

'Oh, don't thank me, it's the others in the hut who have looked after you and got you through this, I just checked in on you every so often.'

'More like ten times a day,' Marilyn calls out.

Margaret looks around, a worried expression on her face. 'Music, did somebody find a record player? I have this vague memory of such beautiful voices.'

'You heard—' one of the women starts to say.

'Let's talk about that when you are stronger,' Norah says quickly.

'I know what you did, Marilyn told me. Tchaikovsky, was it?' Margaret says, giving Norah's arm a squeeze.

Margaret has continued to improve. She is helped outside each morning to sit under the shade of a coconut tree. Norah visits her every day. Sometimes they talk, other times they sit in peaceful, companionable silence. Today, they talk.

Norah laughs. 'I figured someone would, sooner or later. Yes, it was his "Andante Cantabile for Strings". Do you approve?'

'Oh, my dear, how can I ever thank you? It is quite simply the most precious gift I have ever been given, and to think you and the others did that for me.' Margaret reaches over and squeezes Norah's hand. 'So, what are you going to do with this ... this *voice orchestra* you have created?'

'Ah, glad you asked. I was thinking maybe I – I mean, we – could expand, have a go at something a little more challenging. What do you think?' Norah looks nervously over at her friend.

Margaret smiles. 'I think if anyone on God's green earth could do it, it's you.'

'I'll get started while I wait for you to recover.'

'No need to wait for me,' Margaret says. 'Take that training you received at the Royal Academy of Music, add it to your God-given gift and I can't wait to hear the results.'

Norah finds Ena and Audrey sorting through their evening meal of rice. The dirt and weevils are plucked out and discarded.

'I need recruits,' Norah says.

'*I* need recruits,' Ena fires back. 'You can help with the rice.'

'Forget about the rice, Ena. I need recruits for the voice orchestra.'

Ena looks up, puzzled. 'Voice orchestra?'

'Yes, that's what I'm calling it. Margaret agrees we should expand. What do you say?'

'I say, that is a wonderful idea. When do we start?' Audrey replies.

That evening, Ena asks one of their housemates to mind June while she, Norah and Audrey go out for a couple of hours. They are warmly greeted as they arrive at the Dutch hut. It is not long before the small hut is overflowing with volunteers.

'Thank you all so much for being here,' begins Norah. 'I am truly overwhelmed. If I could, I would take all of you and form a symphony orchestra. I'm afraid all I can possibly manage is a chamber choir at the moment, I do hope you understand.'

The next hour is spent auditioning the women. Norah wants no more than thirty members. When someone suggests they should ask the women from the English women's huts and the nurses if they want to be part of the group, Norah assures them that once they are established, they will look for others, maybe another ten or so.

When she has her number, she shoos the others from the kitchen. They can listen from next door.

'Now, I need to sort us into sections. I'm thinking three sets of six women, maybe more in the strings.'

'Have you thought about what we're going to perform?' Rita asks.

'Has she thought about it? What do you think?' Ena jokes.

When the laughter dies down, Norah shyly tells them. 'Margaret and I have been working on that very question and we want to start with something from Dvořák's *New World Symphony*.'

'Which piece?' Rita asks.

Norah pulls something from her pocket. It is just a scrap of paper torn from an old notebook, but it is covered with bars, chords and the brace. 'Largo, anyone? Shall we start with the largo?'

Norah hums the melody, and the women's eyes begin to shine.

'Do you really think we can do this? I mean, where do we start?' Margarethe asks.

'We start by trusting Norah to teach us, to train our voices to bring out their best harmonies,' Ena assures them.

'We need a place to rehearse,' Rita says.

Someone shouts from the living room, 'Here, you can rehearse here!'

'Thank you. Let's turn this kitchen into the rehearsal room for the inaugural voice orchestra,' Norah says.

Everyone bursts out laughing, and the audience whoop with delight, as they are getting front-row seats to the creation of a unique performance.

'We start tomorrow night,' Norah says and the whooping breaks out once more.

CHAPTER 16

Camp III
October 1943–October 1944

'We'll meet twice a week to rehearse,' Norah explains to her voice orchestra. 'I'm going to divide you into three sections, based on the pitch and quality of your individual voices.'

'Can you explain?' asks Margarethe.

'Of course. I'm sorry, I forget not everyone is familiar with musical terms. Those of you with soprano and alto voices will be the string instruments, the voices a bit lower will be woodwind and those of you with the deepest voices will be the brass section. All clear?'

The women nod and the rehearsals begin.

It is a couple of weeks later when Norah is conducting the melodic voices that she waves a hand to stop the rehearsal.

'Audrey, what's wrong?'

'Nothing, nothing at all.'

'You're crying?'

'No, she's not upset, dear sister,' Ena says. 'She's moved. And we all feel the same. I can't believe we are producing such beautiful sounds.'

Norah looks at the sniffling Audrey. 'Is that it?'

'Yes! Oh, my God, you all sound so wonderful, so powerful. I know I'm singing with you, but you're taking me to another place.'

Norah looks at her orchestra, all nodding, all sniffing. 'Do you want to take a break?'

They shake their heads.

'Oh, my God,' Ena exclaims, pointing to the window. It is not just the women present who openly weep at this moving interpretation of Dvořák's symphony, but anyone who is passing by the hut, pausing to listen, feels their eyes welling with tears.

'Shall we start again, then? From the beginning?' Norah is smiling, proud that the orchestra is already doing its job of entertaining the internees.

The brass section begins with deep humming, the woodwinds wait for their cue and imperceptibly thread their voices into the music. Norah signals for the strings to merge and the entire orchestra now vibrates. The lump in Norah's throat expands until she too is crying.

'Norah? Norah, are you all right?' Ena says, pulling her sister towards her for a hug.

'I heard what you heard,' she mumbles into Ena's shoulder.

For a moment, the women cry freely, turning to one another for comfort.

'Do we need to start from the beginning again?' Audrey says, finally.

'I need to compose myself before I can conduct the rest of you,' Norah replies with a grin.

When she calls 'time' on the rehearsal, she asks the women if they would be prepared to learn another piece.

'Wouldn't it be nice to perform an actual concert, not just one piece?'

With trepidation, they all agree.

The next day, Norah visits Margaret, who is recovering well.

'I need more advice,' she says, perching at the corner of Margaret's sleeping mat. 'We've decided to expand our repertoire. I was thinking of Mendelssohn's Songs Without Words, one of Brahms's waltzes and the "Londonderry Air".'

'Perfect,' exclaims Margaret. 'Absolutely perfect.'

'I'll need to adapt them for the female voice, though.'

'Well, if anyone can do it, my dear, it's you.'

Norah painstakingly copies out the scores on scavenged scraps of paper. She asks Ena if she will sing the final song with the backing of the orchestra. Her beautiful soprano voice will complement the orchestra's performance of the 'Faery Song', from *The Immortal Hour*. Humbly, Ena agrees.

That piece, too, is written up and copied by hand, over and over. With no access to the original sheet music, Norah's eidetic memory for musical scores astonishes everyone.

'None of us expected to be still here for a second Christmas, yet here we are,' Nesta announces to a roomful of nurses. 'We won't have a feast and none of us will get presents, but it's still Christmas and I think we should mark it.'

The girls exchange glances.

'What do you suggest?' Jean asks.

'Well, I'd like to just sit here together for a while,' Betty says.

'Maybe some of us would like to share what a typical Christmas Day was like back at home,' Vivian adds.

'That's a lovely idea, Vivian. Why don't you start?'

'Well, the first thing I remember about my childhood Christmases is that they were always bloody hot in Broken Hill.'

'Of course they were, Bully! Tell us how it was,' Betty calls out.

'You'll never believe it, but my mum still insisted on upholding the English tradition of serving a hot roast meal in the middle of the day, followed by an even hotter steamed pudding. There were just the four of us – Mum, Dad, my brother John and me. Dad was a real trooper and ate everything Mum put in front of him. John and I whinged about the heat and shoved the food around our plates. But we knew if we wanted to get our Christmas presents, we'd have to eat up. Which we did, with a little help from Joey, our dog, who hid under the table. Dad used to catch us, but he never said anything, just gave us a wink now and then. What I wouldn't give to be sitting around that table, no matter the temperature, no matter how hot and overcooked my mother's food was, and believe me, it was.'

The following day, the camp is filled with the sounds of children playing, sharing the simple games and toys lovingly made for them. Norah sits under a tree with Ena and Margaret watching June playing with the other children.

'Are you ready for tomorrow?' Margaret asks.

'It's time,' Norah says.

'Time for our voice orchestra to show you what we can do,' Ena quips.

'Tomorrow it is then,' Margaret says.

'We have something special for you tonight,' Margaret tells the assembled women, agog to hear this highly anticipated performance.

'After weeks of rehearsal, I want to introduce to you the one and only Norah Chambers. Norah felt there was something missing from our entertainment programme. With some amazingly talented women, she has created for you … a voice orchestra. Please welcome them for the first, but not the last, time.'

The performance is to be held in the camp's central clearing. The crowd parts as Norah's orchestra make their way through the eager women.

Norah organises her singers into a semicircle and the audience cheers and applauds with enthusiasm.

Her back to the audience, Norah mouths soothing words of encouragement to her singers, before slowly raising her right arm.

Norah Chambers, captive of the Japanese Army, barely surviving in the jungle of Sumatra, closes her eyes. Norah Chambers, conductor, opens them. Slowly, she lowers her arm and the clear, soulful opening notes of the largo from Dvořák's *New World Symphony* sweeps over the first rows of women, arriving in an explosion at the back. As the piece gathers momentum, rising and falling, up and down the scale, the audience gasps in disbelief. The singers, their eyes fixed on Norah, following her every gesture, do not falter. Held by the beauty and strength of this music, written in a time and place unimaginable to the audience … in this moment, they are free.

As she drops her arm, Norah's head bows, eyes close. The silence in the clearing seems to last an eternity. She turns to the sound of one person clapping and then, all at once, the women erupt into applause and cheers, wiping away the tears that began to fall from the very first note. Her orchestra is weeping too, hugging one another.

Margaret steps up to the front, biting back her own tears, but trembling with the emotion another musician feels when they have heard something extraordinary. She embraces Norah, who slumps in her arms, overcome with emotion. 'Thank you so much, dear Margaret. Without your beautiful transcription work, this orchestra would never have been possible.'

'Encore, encore.'

The calls for more do not end. Norah looks at her orchestra, her eyes questioning. The women all nod, 'yes!'

'Chopin?' she asks.

Again, the women nod.

Margaret once again holds up her hands. That is all that is needed to silence the audience.

'I believe it is going to be Chopin?' she says, looking at Norah, who smiles.

'Ladies, I give you the "Raindrop" prelude by Chopin,' Margaret announces, stepping away.

As the final notes hang in air, still washing over the women, Norah whispers, *'Mendelssohn.'*

Floating, falling, the delicate introduction to Songs Without Words transports the women above the filth and squalor of their camp. Now they are dressed in the finest of gowns, sitting in the most famous opera houses of Italy, Paris, London. To the heavens above, the women's hearts soar, washing away their pain. How can simple notes of music be so sad, so beautiful, uplifting and transformative, Norah wonders to herself.

The last note is so quiet, so delicate, that it is heard by only those lucky enough to be in the front rows. Norah drops her head. Exhausted, overcome with emotion, she and her orchestra experience their own escape from this place and time. Slowly, they come back, and the noise is thunderous, the sobbing louder than the clapping and cheering. Whether their lives will be long or short, every woman present will remember the night the angels came to this desolate place, to give them hope, and beauty beyond words.

'Ladies,' Margaret addresses the audience, 'what we have experienced here tonight is quite simply the most beautiful, extraordinary music I have ever heard, or will ever hear again.'

She turns around to smile broadly at the orchestra.

Norah whispers something to Margaret.

'Ladies, we have not heard the last from our remarkable women. Before we sing our national anthems, they have one more performance for you.'

The cheering erupts again.

Ena steps out of the line and she and Norah exchange a smile. Norah nods 'ready?' to her sister. Ena's eyes answer, 'yes!'

Representing the wonderous tones of the harp, Betty launches the music, the other voices join hers and then Ena's glorious soprano voice rings out the opening words to 'Faery Song' from *The Immortal Hour.*

'*How beautiful they are,*
the lordly ones . . .'

The women in the audience who were standing collectively drop to their knees, their eyes reaching for the stars, and the sobbing stops abruptly; they need to hear these words, the majesty, the gift Ena is giving them.

'*In the hollow hills . . .*'

Ena holds the final note long after the other voices have stilled, long after Norah drops her hand.

The voice orchestra stare into the jubilant faces of the women in the audience. They have seen for themselves the effects they have had on all present. They gave it their all, and now they allow the applause, the grateful sobbing, to envelop them and provide sanctuary for a few brief moments.

June pushes her way between Norah and Ena. 'Why are you crying, Aunties?'

She breaks the spell, and the women now laugh and hug her.

With no sign of the applause ceasing, Margaret once again holds up her hand and silence falls.

'In four days, it will be 1944; I hope it will be a better year for all of us. I have no words, just as you have no words, to thank the women behind me for what they have given us tonight. Perhaps we can all try by singing for them our national anthems. *God save our gracious king . . .*' Her powerful voice rings out.

The audience all stand and join in.

'. . . *Long live our noble king.*'

Before the women return to their huts, they circle the orchestra, hugging, finding tears they thought had all been cried out, to give their personal thanks. Finally, with June skipping along behind them, Norah and Ena walk Margaret to her hut.

'Can I ask what you're working on next?' Margaret asks.

'It's a difficult piece, but so many of the Dutch ladies have been coming to our rehearsals that I've been trying "Bolero" with them,' Norah says.

'Oh, my dear, I can't imagine Ravel ever considered his piece being performed by voice alone. But if anyone can do it, it is you, and I can't wait to hear it.'

'I'm going to the well – anyone want to join me?' Nesta asks one morning.

It is the new year and the mood amongst the campmates is altogether different to how they felt when they arrived three months earlier. Efforts are redoubled to clean out the wells; the rainy season is back, and the wells are trapping precious water.

'I'll come with you. Wait a minute while I grab a pot,' Vivian says.

Nesta and Vivian join the queue of women waiting to collect water. Nesta ties the rope to her bucket and slowly lowers it into the well. Leaning over to see how much further she has to go before she hits water, all it takes is a gentle clattering of the bucket against the well wall for the rope to give. The bucket crashes into the water below, clanging against all the other pots consigned to its depths.

'Oh, no! I don't believe it! Another one,' Nesta says, hauling up the empty rope.

'Do you think I can reach it?' Vivian asks.

'No, it's way too deep.'

'Sister James, there's only one thing you can do.' Sister Catherina, also waiting in line to collect water, speaks up.

'Really, and what's that?' Nesta asks.

'You're quite small, aren't you?' asks the nun, sizing up Nesta's tiny frame.

'You've only just realised that?' Vivian exclaims.

'No, but it's the first time I've thought it might be very useful.'

'Useful for what?' Nesta says with apprehension.

'I would be very happy to help Sister Bullwinkel lower you into the well; what do you say, Sister?'

'Oh, yes, count me in, there's nothing I'd like to do more than lower my senior head first into a well,' Vivian says, grinning.

'You're both joking, aren't you?' Nesta is aghast.

'Not at all. Oh, and while you're down there, can you chuck up some of the other buckets and pots? Everyone would be most grateful.'

While Vivian is tying a frayed rope around Nesta's waist, several other women arrive and get caught up in the adventure, offering suggestions and words of encouragement.

As Nesta climbs over the wall of the well, she says anxiously, 'Please hold tight! Do you need extra hands, Bully?'

'I can help,' pipes up Margaret, who has just arrived. 'Word has already spread around camp that Sister James is going into the well. I thought I needed to see this for myself. We've got you, Nesta!'

'Come on then,' says Vivian. 'Grab onto the end of the rope with me.'

'Slowly, take it slowly,' Nesta calls out as Vivian, Sister Catherina and Margaret lower the tiny nurse into the dark well. Nesta looks up to see dozens of faces peering down at her. 'I can't see. You're blocking out the light. You all need to move away,' Nesta shouts.

There is a shuffling as everybody takes a step back.

'I'm here. I'm nearly at the water,' she calls.

'Grab as many buckets as you can, and we'll pull you up.'

'OK, give me a minute.'

'Shout when you're ready, all right?'

'Slowly! Slow down, aahh, I've tipped over. I'm upside down,' Nesta cries.

'We've got you, just hang on.'

'Hurry up.'

'Have you got the buckets?' Sister Catherina calls to her.

'Yes, my arms are full. That's what tipped me over.'

'I can see her legs. Oh, my God, she looks like a baby being born feet first,' a cheeky commentator observes.

The women gathered around roar with laughter as Nesta is yanked out of the well, her dress over her face. Buckets hang from both arms and hands. Two of the women grab her around the waist and drag her away, dropping her unceremoniously on the ground.

Vivian pushes her way through the women and helps free Nesta from the rope, restoring her dignity.

'The others back at the house are going to kick themselves for missing this,' Vivian says.

'Happy to have entertained,' Nesta replies, looking at the grinning women circling her.

Nesta and Vivian walk back to the house, Nesta now carrying a bucket full of water, Vivian the pot.

'I guess there's no way we can keep this little event a secret, just between you and me?' Nesta says hopefully.

'Not a chance, Sister James, not a chance.'

'They've said we can have a vegetable garden,' Nesta announces to her nurses. 'So let's join the effort and get on with it.'

'Thank God,' Jean says. 'We're practically starving.'

'Betty, Vivian, it's our turn to work the plot; we've got the morning shift. Jean, can you find two others not rostered on home visits to take over from us this afternoon please?'

'Of course, Nesta. I'll be free this afternoon and will join them.'

Arriving at the designated spot, they are each handed half a scooped-out coconut shell.

'Has someone got the tools?' Betty asks.

'If you mean the axe handle or the shovel blade, then yes. The rest of us get the coconuts,' Betty says.

'Hands and knees, girls,' Nesta instructs, kneeling in the dirt and beginning to loosen the soil with her shell. They have had to sacrifice a small portion of their rations to provide pips and seeds, which they will plant this afternoon.

'Do you really think they will let us eat what we grow?' Vivian asks.

'We can only hope,' sighs Betty. 'But we've put a lot of work into clearing this garden, surely we can eat the spoils of our efforts.'

214

'There's no telling really, all we can do is our best,' Nesta concludes. 'Having said that, I don't want anyone keeling over in this heat. If you need a break, just say so.'

'We'll stop when you stop,' Betty says, nudging her friend.

For once, the women see the benefits of living in the tropics; once planted, the food springs up and is shared amongst them. They also scavenge the immediate area, looking for other edible plants, bark from trees that could be boiled until soft to go with the spinach and beans that have sprouted up. As always, the first mouthfuls go to the children.

One day, as Norah is working outside, June runs up to her, clenching something in her fist.

'Look, Aunty Norah, look what I've got.'

She gently uncurls her hand, showing a few precious grains of cooked rice.

'Where did you get that?'

'I went with the boys and we found it under the hut.'

'What hut? And, come to that, what boys?'

'Just my friends. Normally only the boys go, but I told them I was going to scream if they didn't let me come too. We crawled under the guards' hut, there are little gaps in the floor and when the guards are eating, some of the rice falls on the floor and rolls through the gaps. We lie there with our hands open, and this is what I caught,' June says with the pride of a hunter returning to his cave.

Norah is lost for words. She looks around to see if anyone is listening to June talk of the risks she and the boys are taking. Wanting to tell her she can't do it again, it was wrong to be anywhere near the guards' huts, she looks into the smiling eyes of the little girl and sees once again the pride; her heart breaks. All she can do is hold her tightly and try to hide her pain, pain for not being able to feed and care for a child, not her own, but one she has willingly accepted responsibility for and who has won her love.

Pulling away from Norah, June excitedly says, 'I'm going to go and share it with Sammy, he wasn't there. OK?'

As June skips away, Norah collapses, with her face buried in her hands as she sobs quietly. Vivian is the first to find her.

'Norah, what's wrong?'

Norah looks into the caring eyes of a woman who, under normal circumstances, she would never have known, a woman from another country, a woman she now calls her friend. A friend who not only understands her pain but shares it.

'I'm not hurt, don't worry, I'm just . . .'

'Oh, Norah. Come on, let's go back to your hut, we can talk there.'

When Norah enters her house, with Vivian's supportive arm around her shoulders, Ena looks up from her sewing.

'What's going on? Has something happened?'

'She's OK,' Vivian says soothingly. 'She's not hurt.'

There are other women in the hut, who are all gazing up with concern, but Norah shakes her head.

'I'm fine, honestly. Just being silly,' she says with a watery smile.

'Let's go outside,' Ena suggests.

In the small yard, the women find some shade to sit down and Norah lays her head in Ena's lap.

'Do you know what happened?' Ena asks Vivian.

'Not really. I saw her talking to June, and when she ran off, Norah collapsed.'

'Is it June?' Ena asks anxiously. 'Is she OK?'

'She seemed OK. Like I said, she ran off.'

'Norah, please tell me what's happened,' Ena gently coaxes her sister.

'What's happened? Let me tell you. June and a group of boys hide under the guards' hut in the hope of catching the few rice grains that spill from their plates onto the floor and through the cracks. That's what's happened. We can't feed her, so she risks a beating, her life, for a handful of infested rice.'

'She told you this?' Ena probes.

'Told me and showed me the seven – yes, I counted them – seven grains of rice in her hand.'

'Oh, Norah, I don't know what to say,' Vivian says.

'What's more,' Norah continues, 'she wanted to actually *share* them with her friend. What is there to say, Vivian? We've failed this little girl.'

Norah puts her hand up to her face and weeps, her head still in her sister's lap. Ena and Vivian exchange a look; they are unused to seeing Norah break down like this.

'Please don't think that, Norah,' Ena says, stroking her sister's hair. 'Her mother is almost certainly dead and if it wasn't for us, who knows where she might be, if she even would have made it out of the sea. I hate seeing you like this. We're doing all we can. And don't think I don't know that you give her all your food some days.'

'As do you. Oh, Ena, you should have seen her face, she was happy, excited. It was like she'd gone hunting and returned with a moose. I'm just worried about her.'

The three women sit alone, each lost in their private thoughts. There is nothing they wouldn't do for June, and yet, in the face of such daily desperation, it all seems very little. Will they ever make it out of this camp?

'Ladies, I have something for you.' Ah Fat is with two guards at the gates. Weeks have passed since the women planted beans and spinach; it has all been eaten and the plot lies barren. They have been forbidden, at the whim of Kato, to resow their seeds.

Norah and Ena, who are taking a stroll in the late afternoon, stare at Ah Fat, too stunned to speak.

'Rice! Here is rice to share,' he beams.

The guards drop two small sacks on the ground and step back. The sisters hurry forwards and gather the meagre offerings.

'I have something else for you,' Ah Fat continues. He thrusts a kerosene tin at them. 'Oil,' he says. 'Oil for you.'

'Thank you,' Norah says finally, taking the tin. She looks at Ena and gives a sigh of relief. 'We need this,' she remarks. 'I'm sick of boiling banana skins to make soup.'

Norah tries to read the label on the tin. 'Do any of you know what this is?' she asks the others when she returns to her hut.

The women all look at the label but shake their heads, *no*.

'I'll take it to Mother Laurentia, I think it's in Dutch. We really should know whether it's edible or should be put in a truck.'

Norah hurries across to the nuns' hut.

'Yes!' Mother Laurentia exclaims. 'It is Dutch, and it says, "Red Palm Oil". Perfect for cooking – if only we had something to cook.'

'We also got some rice,' Norah tells her. 'I daresay we could make fried rice.'

'Yes, and we could also add some roots or any greenery you can find, but . . .' The nun sighs.

'But what?'

'You might want to think about saving some of the oil for the hospital. The locals in Malaya used to apply it to infected cuts and injuries. It has proven medicinal qualities.'

'Like honey.'

The nun smiles. 'Yes, like honey.'

'Thank you, Mother Laurentia, I'll let the others know, as I'm sure they will want to share it with the hospital. We'll get some of the rice and oil to you as soon as we have portioned it out.'

Inspired by the oil, the women begin to cook very basic meals with the rice, all the while describing what they would do with it 'back home'.

'You know what, Norah?' Ena is reading an old issue of the *Camp Chronicle*.

'No, I can't begin to imagine,' her sister replies.

'I think we should relaunch the recipe sessions from the *Chronicle*, where women jot down their favourite memories of preparing meals.'

'Won't that just make us hungrier?' Norah is staring into the empty pot on the stove, their rice rations consumed for the day.

'Maybe, but it was so good too. Ham and eggs, dinners out in posh restaurants, *pudding*. It will take our minds off having nothing, don't you think?'

'Well, it would certainly take our minds off the camp,' Norah quips.

'My only problem is we have nothing to write these recipes on so we can share them,' Ena laments.

'Mmm, here's a thought. I was visiting Margaret last week and one of the women in her hut waved around a chequebook she found in her suitcase, joking she could write cheques to buy us all food. She even laughed about how she and her husband had enough money in their bank in Singapore to buy the camp and wondered what the sergeant would take for it.'

'I would have loved to have heard that conversation. But what does that have to do with recording recipes?'

'I think we all agreed the cheques were useless, but the backs of them are blank; they might be just the right size to write down a recipe. What do you think?'

'I love it, it sounds perfect!'

With the chequebook graciously donated in exchange for providing the first recipe, Ena, Audrey and Norah decide a cookbook would be the best way to share the delicious food memories. They speak to everyone in the camp, asking for inspirational national dishes.

The nurses' hut is the last on their list, and one evening, the three women knock at the door. Jean lets them in and those nurses not in the hospital or visiting a sick patient at home listen intently.

'So, you want us to come up with one recipe that represents us? A unique Australian dish?' Betty says.

'Yes, anything you like,' Ena replies.

'Well, there's only one dish, isn't there, ladies? As Australian as we all are,' Vivian says.

'Don't you dare say pavlova,' Audrey protests, catching the eye of as many of the nurses as she can.

'Of course, it's pavlova! We invented it,' Betty says.

'No, you didn't. It's a New Zealand dish; everyone knows it was invented there. It was created for the Russian ballet dancer who was touring at the time, Anna Pavlova,' Audrey counters, standing firm.

'You lot might have named it, but it was invented in Melbourne. Isn't that right, Bully?' Betty says, equally belligerent.

'I don't know about Melbourne, but everyone knows it's Australian,' Vivian states.

'Invented in New Zealand, named in New Zealand, it is a Kiwi dish.'

Norah and Ena watch the argument play out, back and forth like a tennis match.

'What do you think, Norah? It's a New Zealand dish, isn't it?' Audrey says.

'No idea,' she replies. 'Can't you say it's from both countries, or just choose another dish that you don't have to fight over?'

'One day the argument will be settled,' Audrey says, one final parting shot as they leave.

Many of the Englishwomen are unable to provide the recipes for their favourite dishes. After all, they were prepared by their cooks. For Norah, reading the recipes isn't enough. And one day, she goes to the guards' hut. She doesn't crawl underneath, but instead heads for the back of the building where the Japanese throw out their rubbish and it is here she finds scraps of paper. She smooths out the scrunched pieces and creates a notebook, held together with a piece of wire she punctures through the sheets.

Sitting quietly in a corner of the hut if it is raining, or outside, leaning against the back fence, if it is not, she tries to imagine her life back in Malaya with John and draws up a budget, with no idea of the value of anything. She allocates her husband a sum of money to buy season tickets to the theatre, or a sporting club he might like to attend. She dreams up the cost of newspapers, how much to spend at the butcher, the baker, train tickets, meals eaten out. She designs her perfect home, puts a price on furniture and furnishings, nominating the colours she wants for curtains, for carpeting. She allocates a monthly allowance to buy a growing June new shoes, dresses and, of course, school fees at the best school. Norah puts together a weekly menu, describing in detail the ingredients needed to make roast duck and apple stuffing; *pâté de foie gras*; roast potatoes; coffee and chocolate. She escapes

221

from her prison into an unknown world, one which comes easily when she closes her eyes, picturing every detail of every room, every dish on the table at mealtimes. In the distance, she can almost hear June practising at the piano in the drawing room.

With her passion for things domestic, Norah asks if she can be put in charge of the cooking. A shortage of fuel for the open fires has resulted in communal cooking shared between several huts. With the combined cooking comes the need for combined meal preparation. Squads form for the rice sorters to hand over the weevil-plucked rice to the washers. Vegetable choppers hand over to vegetable cooks. Others carry water and collect firewood; some serve, some wash up. Even with so little to prepare and cook, the women still turn up for their allocated chores.

'Can you pass me the meat, please?' Norah says to Betty, who is busy sorting the rice from the insects. 'It's time to add it to the vegetables and sauce.'

'Of course, Chef. Prime rib of beef coming up,' Betty says, handing her a small quantity of rice in a banana leaf.

'Excellent. If you would now lay the table? Use the silver cutlery, won't you? It goes so well with my fine china. I'll serve up.'

'Yes, Chef. June, can you please run and tell the others dinner is being served,' Betty says.

June giggles and skips away, returning with a line of women and children each carrying their own small bowl or banana leaf. From Norah, they accept their scoop of rice before sitting down together and eating with their fingers.

'Inchi, Inchi? Where are you, Inchi?' Ah Fat calls, running into Mrs Hinch's hut.

One of the women, prone on the floor and suffering from the heat, casually points to the backyard before rolling over and closing her eyes.

'Inchi, I need you,' Ah Fat says, spying Mrs Hinch sitting under a tree at the far end of the yard.

'Really? What now?'

'You come with me; we have to talk to the nurses.'

'What about?'

'Come with me. I will tell them.'

Putting her hand out for Ah Fat to help her up, Mrs Hinch leads him to the nurses' hut. Finding Nesta at home, she tells her Ah Fat has something to share.

'So, go on, man. Say what you want to say,' Mrs Hinch instructs him.

'OK, Inchi. You have to make room for men. Captain says they are to stay with you.'

'What are you talking about?' says Nesta. 'What's he talking about, Mrs Hinch?'

'What *are* you talking about?' Mrs Hinch glares at Ah Fat.

'Local men coming here for us to train, and the captain says they have to live here with you.'

'Well, that's not going to happen,' Mrs Hinch says.

'Inchi, it is. The men must live here, with the nurses, while we train them.'

Mrs Hinch draws herself up straight. 'Train them for what?'

'To be guards, to guard prisoners like you.'

'And what if we don't let them in?' Nesta asks.

'Then you will be put outside. You share or live outside.' Ah Fat looks genuinely upset at the news he is imparting. He sighs. 'Sorry, I don't like them either.'

'What do you mean, you don't like them?' Mrs Hinch asks, aghast.

'Local men. I prefer you ladies.'

'But what if they attack us? What's to stop them if we're living in the same house?' Nesta objects.

'They won't, we will slap them.'

'How will you know?'

'We will slap them anyway; they won't hurt you.'

'I'm sorry, Nesta, what can we do to help? Do you want to spread around the other huts?' Mrs Hinch asks.

'We'll have a meeting, maybe there's a way we can share, give them room or something,' Nesta says, trying to come up with a solution for this problem. 'Do you know how many are coming?'

'Twenty-five men,' Ah Fat says, averting his eyes. He can no longer look at either Nesta or Mrs Hinch.

'I'm worried about the so-called training these men are getting,' Jean says to Nesta and several of the other nurses; they are sitting outside one evening trying to enjoy the gentle breeze, and a brief respite from their hot, sticky, overcrowded hut.

'Their training?' Nesta comments. 'What about the fact we have to live with them?' The local guards had been given timber, which they used to put up a wall dividing the small living space in the nurses' hut into two.

'I don't want to live with them either, Nesta. But I don't like the way the soldiers are treating them. Slapping them, poking them with their bayonets. It's not right.'

'I know what you mean – are they learning that this is the way to treat prisoners once they're in charge?' Nesta says.

'I guess we'll find out soon enough if they start hitting us,' Betty comments. 'Does anyone know how long they're staying with us?'

'Mrs Hinch spoke to the captain and was told three to four weeks,' says Nesta, shrugging.

The next morning, the sound of the soldiers yelling in the street startles everyone. The nurses run out of their hut to see several women and children being chased and hit by the Indonesian guards.

'Stop it! Stop it, you brute! Leave her alone!' Nesta screams at the guard kicking a woman on the ground. She hits him square in the back and sends him sprawling. Nesta helps the woman to her feet before placing herself in front of her. The guard takes a swing at Nesta, who ducks easily under his arm. There is chaos all around. Women and children cry out, the soldiers are laughing, the Indonesian men are yelling.

'Come on, ladies!' screams Vivian. 'There's way more of us, let's get them.'

As the man threatening Nesta turns around to see what's going on, Nesta raises both her arms, and, growling like a bear, she charges him. The guards are being herded together by hundreds of angry women. Deciding they need to break things up, the soldiers move in and shepherd the men away. They do not return to the camp.

Word of Mary Anderson's death spreads through the camp.

'She's the first of us to die,' Mrs Hinch tells Norah, as the women gather outside Mary's house in vigil. 'Poor thing never had a chance with all the infection, the hunger.'

'Well, we should bury her immediately. This heat . . .' Norah says.

'I'd like to see her first,' says Mrs Hinch. 'Then we can talk.'

Norah and Mrs Hinch enter Mary's house and head for the crowded room in which the residents sit around her body, covered with a tatty sheet. Kneeling, Mrs Hinch closes her eyes in prayer.

'I think we have to keep her in the house while our captors decide where and how to bury her,' Norah says, when they are outside once more.

'And how long will that take?'

'I don't know, but I doubt we'll have an answer today.'

'Will you let me know as soon as you hear something? The women here will look after her. Oh, look, here's Nesta.'

'Mrs Hinch, Norah, I'm so sorry,' says Nesta, sighing deeply. 'I just came to pay my respects and ask if there is anything I can do.'

'That's very kind, we'll look after Mary until the sergeant tells us what we can do to give her a decent burial.'

'I don't think you should keep her in the house. With this weather, it will very quickly become unpleasant for everyone,' Nesta says.

'You're quite right. How about we move her to the school building? That way, the air can circulate,' Mrs Hinch suggests.

'I worry about the rats, and those feral dogs that wander the camp at night,' Nesta says.

'We'll stake a lookout for all of that,' Norah says.

The school is closed, and Mary is moved to the open-fronted building. For the remainder of the day and overnight, friends take turns to chase away the rats and mice attracted by the smell. The next day, permission is granted for Mary to be moved outside the camp, just beyond the guardhouse. Ah Fat has instructed them to leave her there until he can have a coffin made.

'Well, that's not going to happen,' Margaret asserts. 'We'll move her, but she will not be alone, not for one minute, until she is buried underground.'

Moved outside the camp, volunteers once again take turns sitting with Mary. The day passes, another night comes and goes, and no coffin appears.

The next morning, Ah Fat finds Mrs Hinch talking to Norah and Audrey.

'Come with me, please,' he says to the group.

The three women follow him outside the camp, past Mary, and several hundred yards into the jungle to a small clearing.

'We will give you something to dig a hole, this is where we will bury people,' he tells them.

Returning to the camp to fetch more volunteers, they see a simple wooden coffin has been placed beside Mary. Everyone helps to move Mary's body into her final resting place.

'Well, she's protected now,' Mrs Hinch says. 'Ah Fat is getting us, hopefully, some shovels, so we can clear an area and dig a grave. Go and get something to eat and drink, and we'll let you know when we are having the burial,' Mrs Hinch tells the women.

A few hours later, the shallow grave dug, Margaret leads a long line of women to the coffin, where six of Mary's friends gently pick it up and carry it to the gravesite. Norah and Audrey move towards Nesta and Jean who are representing the nurses, watching as the coffin is placed in the ground.

'Where's Ena?' Nesta asks.

'She's stayed behind with June. As much as we tried to protect her and the other children, they know someone has died and we thought it was better Ena stay with her and try to explain what is happening,' Norah says.

Margaret reads from her Bible. Several of Mary's friends speak of their friendship, telling stories of the life they knew she had enjoyed *before*.

Margaret concludes the brief service. 'We thank you, Mary, for everything you were and all that you gave, and may you now and forever rest in peace with the certain knowledge that you were, are, and will always be dearly loved and terribly missed. Farewell.'

'Amen.'

Using their hands, the women take turns placing the soil back in the grave.

CHAPTER 17

Camp III
October 1943–October 1944

On April Fool's Day, Kato appears to have vanished and a new camp commandant arrives with pomp and ceremony. His name is Captain Seki. He demands that every woman and child is presented to him, to bow and pay homage. He is accompanied by Ah Fat.

Norah watches as he takes a seat behind a small table in the school shed and awaits her turn to be called.

'Norah Chambers,' Ah Fat calls finally.

Norah steps up to the table, bows and immediately wants to laugh. It's as if she's being presented to the King of England.

'Norah Cham . . . Chambers,' Seki says, nodding. She can hear her campmates laughing as he struggles to pronounce her name.

Afterwards, Seki stands and delivers a long-winded, rambling speech, which Ah Fat stutteringly translates.

'Oh, no,' Norah whispers to Ena. 'Not again.'

'Cutting our rations?' Ena exclaims while Ah Fat still rambles on. 'And we have to work for the little they're going to give us?'

'Well, at least they're giving us a bit of land back to grow some food,' Norah says.

'Will we grow bananas, Aunty Norah?' asks June, taking her hand.

'I'm afraid not, my sweetheart, but you do love spinach, don't you?'

'A bit,' says June.

Having threatened a cut in their food allocation, it becomes clear that Seki did not know how much food the women had been receiving up to that point. Or its quality. Immediately, the women notice that the rice features far fewer insects. They are now given sugar, salt, tea, curry powder and maize. Betty meets Norah at the distribution point.

'I can't believe they're giving us sugar!' Betty whispers.

'I know! And look at your rice,' Norah urges.

Betty peers into her banana leaf. 'It's not moving!'

'Well, that's going to put Margaret out of a job: no weevils to pick out. A real treat!'

'Another way of looking at it is that we've just lost our source of protein. But I'll live without it.'

'I think we have to tell everyone to keep quiet about the extra food. We don't want Seki to know he is giving us something we weren't getting before.'

But while there might be more rice and sugar, it is the drop in the vegetable rations that worries the nurses most. They are what is needed for growing bones.

Norah and Ena stand at the entrance to the camp to watch the trucks rumble through the gates.

'It's lovely to see friends reunited, isn't it?' Norah says. Women climb out of the vehicles, and stand dazed, looking around them.

Some of the camp inmates rush forwards, recognising survivors from the *Vyner Brooke*.

'Poor nurses,' says Ena, watching the sisters troop dejectedly back to their hut. 'They were hoping to see some friends.'

Norah stares after the nurses.

'There's no reunion for us either,' she says. 'The only person we know who might be possibly on the island is John, and he was so sick.'

'Oh, Norah, he's strong. I know he's here somewhere, just waiting, and so is Sally.'

'And we don't know where she is, or if they made it.'

'Of course they made it, Norah. Like we discussed, you'd know if something happened to either one of them. You'd know it here,' Ena says, tapping her own heart.

'What does your heart tell you about Ken?'

'That he's safe with our mother and father, waiting for our turn to be reunited, and in the meantime . . .'

'In the meantime, we keep doing what we're doing here: caring for June and staying alive.'

'And you're keeping alive the spirits of every woman and child in this camp. And it looks like you now have a whole new audience to entertain.'

'I couldn't do this without you.'

'That's what sisters are for. Aren't we lucky to be together?'

'Now,' Norah says, standing up. 'I have to go and rehearse – that's the other thing keeping us all going.'

Norah joins her orchestra at their twice-weekly rehearsal. The improvement in the camp food has given them back the energy needed to prepare for their next performance. It will include the difficult, what many considered impossible, to learn, 'Bolero'.

* * *

230

'Betty, have you got a minute?'

Betty is about to leave for the next practice when two other nurses approach her.

'I'm on my way to rehearsal, but sure, how can I help?' Betty asks Win and Iole.

'That's what we want to talk to you about. Could we come with you?'

'Can either of you read music?' Betty asks.

The two nurses exchange a look. 'No,' says Iole.

'Never mind, half the orchestra can't. Come on, I'm sure Norah will love to have you.'

As Betty predicted, Norah welcomes the women and is overjoyed to hear their beautiful voices; their enthusiasm is inspiring. The Dutch singers outnumber the others and their friends still turn out for every rehearsal. Norah and Margaret have added a Mozart sonata to their repertoire; Norah's brilliant understanding of the voices her singers produce has made her change the opening chord in the very simple Sonata in C into A flat major. The clear bell-like melody is now suited to a range for women's voices. At the next concert, they will begin with Mozart, giving the women the confidence they will need to tackle Ravel. But, first, Norah must make more copies of the 'Bolero' score, for those who can read music, while she conducts those that can't.

Norah asks Sister Catherina if she has any idea where she can get some paper and a pen. In one of the huts, a woman produces her husband's business letterhead from her possessions. She happily donates sheets of paper, along with several pens, to Norah.

Norah and her orchestra make their way through the audience for their special performance.

'God knows we need this,' Norah says to Ena from the front of the room. Ena is also watching the audience.

'Everyone looks so ill. So thin,' she whispers.

'That's why we need it. We have to believe there is still some beauty in this world.'

When the audience has settled, Ah Fat appears.

'Move, move, move away,' he says, pushing the women aside. He is followed by Seki and several other soldiers. 'Captain Seki would like to hear your concert,' Ah Fat tells Norah.

'Please tell him he is most welcome. Let me get the two of you some chairs,' Margaret offers, very deliberately indicating she will only ask a couple of women to give up their seats in the front row.

With the captain and Ah Fat seated, Seki says something to Ah Fat which is translated.

'Begin.'

Margaret bows.

'We welcome Captain Seki to this evening's concert.'

She bows again.

'Tonight, you will hear music from Mozart and Beethoven. And how can we have a concert without our beautiful largo – and remember the first time we heard it? None of us will ever forget that evening. These wonderful musicians behind me are going to give you another special performance tonight. When Norah started humming the song to me, that beautiful voice moved me beyond words. But it was difficult, and there were times when I didn't think we could do it.'

She laughs and continues. 'Everyone agreed. Do you think she listened? Of course not, there are no such words as "can't be done" in Norah Chambers' vocabulary. We all know how she is the first to volunteer for the dirtiest – can I say, shittiest – jobs.'

Margaret waits for the laughter to subside before continuing. Captain Seki frowns.

'Anyway, she didn't listen to me or any of the forty-four women you are about to hear from, because she knows there is no limit to what we can do when we put our minds to it. Inspired by her confidence, I'm so thrilled that I was able to get Dvorak's beautiful music down on paper for you all. The last piece tonight will be from the wonderful composer Ravel. His haunting, complex "Bolero".'

When Margaret takes her seat the applause becomes ecstatic. Norah lets it wash over her and her girls. She holds up her hands for quiet and mouths, 'Thank you, let's give the captain something to remember.'

Suppressed smiles from the audience disappear as Norah turns towards her orchestra and raises her right arm. With the flick of her hand, the jaunty notes escape and float over the audience, building and receding as the voices bring the music to life.

A standing ovation greets the final notes. Waiting for quiet, wanting everyone to hear every note sung, Norah leads the singers into one of Beethoven's minuets. She doesn't need to turn around to know the women are swaying. In their heads, they are on the dance floor, in full-length dresses, in the arms of their loved ones. Norah closes her eyes and lets herself drift back into John's arms, dancing on the lush green grass outside their home in Malaya. Surrounding her, the jungle, from which she hears a tiger calling its mate. She sees Sally looking down on them from her bedroom window when she should be asleep.

The music ends all too soon, the applause this time not instantaneous. Norah turns around and sees so many other women like her, their eyes closed, in another place and time. It is Seki who begins the applause and soon everyone has joined in.

Ena steps up to Norah. 'That was unbelievable, you should have seen them, they were swaying, moving – it was so beautiful.'

'I thought they would. It was a good choice. Remind me to thank Audrey for suggesting it. Now, let's give them the largo.'

The stirring opening notes send the women back to the first time they heard the orchestra. They are no less affected this time. For many, this music is better sung than played by instruments; they can hear the passion in the singers' voices, the vibrating energy of their emotions.

The applause when it concludes is strong but brief; the audience is keen to hear what's next.

On cue, Rita makes the quiet thrum of a drumbeat; gasps from the audience drown out the flutes, but not for long. This they want to hear. The clarinets follow, the harps, then the oboes. At the first step up in intensity, Norah clutches both hands to her chest; her girls don't need her to conduct them as their voices merge and meld together. Rising, rising, the tempo thuds inside Norah's chest, and all she can do is gaze in wonder at the women in front of her. She sees the joy the singing brings to each of them as she looks from face to face, each one smiling with their eyes a *thank you for making me do this*.

As the orchestra reach for the final pounding notes, Norah raises her arm again, and the music stops.

This is the first time the orchestra whoop, holler and stamp their feet, along with the audience.

Once again, they have heard something so magical, it takes their breath away.

When Norah turns around, she sees Captain Seki and Ah Fat are also on their feet, clapping loudly.

It seems to take forever before Margaret kicks off the national anthem, and while the women remain standing, Seki and Ah Fat sit.

234

When 'Land of Hope and Glory' has been sung, the women know to remain where they are until Seki has left. Finally, he stands and looks around, before saying something to Ah Fat, and nods to Margaret.

'Is that all?' Ah Fat asks.

'Yes, the concert is over, for tonight.'

Ah Fat has a further exchange with Seki.

'Captain Seki says he would like you to sing a Japanese song – any song, but it must be Japanese.'

Margaret beckons Norah over and tells her what has been requested. They exchange a few words before Margaret turns back to Seki. She says, smiling sweetly, that they do not know any Japanese music.

The message is conveyed to Seki, and a further conversation takes place between him and Ah Fat. Once again, Ah Fat translates.

'Captain Seki would like you to learn Japanese music and perform tomorrow night.'

'No!' gasps Norah. 'How?'

Hearing the vehemence in Norah's voice, Seki begins yelling. Ah Fat translates as he rants.

'You will learn Japanese song, or he will punish you,' he says, pointing at Norah.

'Please tell the captain that even if I did know any Japanese music, I will not have my orchestra or the choir perform it. On that I am clear.'

Ah Fat translates to Seki, who yells something further before turning and striding away. The Japanese soldiers quickly follow him.

'What did he say?' Margaret asks.

Pointing at Norah, Ah Fat says, 'She is to come back here tomorrow morning. Just her.'

As Ah Fat walks away, Norah is immediately surrounded by her girls. They offer to try to find some Japanese music.

'No. Thank you, but no, we will never perform for them. We can't stop them coming to our concerts, but we do not perform *for* them. Please support me in this.'

'But you will be punished, you don't know what they will do to you,' Margarethe says.

Ena puts her arms around her sister. 'I think Norah knows and it doesn't matter. We must respect her wishes.'

The next morning, Norah, with half the camp behind her, walks to the middle of the camp clearing where Seki and Ah Fat are waiting for her.

'Will you sing Japanese music?' Ah Fat asks.

'No.'

Seki thrusts his arms down to the ground. Norah doesn't need to be told what to do and stands tall, her hands by her side, her head straight ahead.

'You couldn't get her to change her mind?' Nesta asks Margaret. Both women have joined the crowd to support their friend.

'I didn't try.'

As Seki walks away, Ah Fat calls out to the women. 'You stay away, anyone who goes near will join her. Understand?'

Norah smiles, looking at the women around her. 'Go back to your huts and get out of the sun, I'll be fine.'

Slowly, most of the women walk away. Ena, Margaret and the entire orchestra of forty-four remain.

'I will have a nurse here throughout the day with instructions to help her if they feel they must,' Nesta whispers to Margaret.

The sun is merciless, as if its sole focus is to bring Norah to her knees. She sways, stumbles, but stays on her feet.

* * *

'No, Ena!' Nesta has arms around Ena's waist, stopping her from running to Norah.

The afternoon sun is relentless.

Ena goes limp. 'I know. I know,' she wails.

'We'll all get a beating if you go to her. Just think about that. One of you needs to be there for June at the end of this,' Nesta says, letting go of Ena. 'Where is she now?'

'She's with the Dutch women,' Ena says. 'I didn't want her to see Norah like this.'

'Or you,' adds Nesta, with a weak smile.

The soldiers rotate from their place in the shade. Two nurses at a time stand on duty, ready to react if they think Norah's condition has become life-threatening. When Norah doubles over, gasping, Ena finally approaches one of the soldiers.

'Let her go!' she pleads. 'I beg you, she's my sister and you're killing her.'

Ena receives a resounding slap across the face for her efforts, knocking her to the ground. Audrey is right beside her, helping her to her feet.

Norah lifts her head, and slowly, painfully straightens up, trying to smile with cracked, sunburnt lips. She mouths: 'I'm OK, I'm OK.'

As the sun slips over the hill, Ah Fat strides towards Norah.

'You can go now.'

He hasn't even turned away before Norah collapses. Nesta runs towards her, trailed by Ena and Audrey and nurses Betty and Jean.

'Leave her for the minute,' Nesta tells Ena, who is trying to pull Norah to her feet. 'We need to have a look at her and get some water down her throat.'

Audrey has a bucket of water, a small tin cup and a rag ready.

'Gently sit her up,' Nesta tells Ena.

237

Sitting behind her, Ena gently raises her sister into her arms, her body nestled into hers. Nesta takes the rag and pours a little water over it. As she places it on Norah's temples, Jean tilts her head and slowly dribbles water into her mouth. Norah attempts to gulp the water, but Jean pulls it away.

'Slowly, Norah, slowly. We've got you.'

Margaret appears and kneels beside Norah, gently taking her hand.

Norah gives her a small smile: 'I couldn't let them win.'

Margaret sobs. 'Oh, my dear girl, my dear, dear girl.'

'I woke up this morning, Margaret, I will go to sleep tonight, and I will wake up tomorrow,' Norah mumbles.

With her strength returning, she attempts to stand. Ena and Nesta wrap one of her arms around each of their necks and half walk, half carry her back to her hut. On entering, they are surrounded by every woman who lives there. They have all saved a portion of their evening meal for her. Nesta retrieves a small quantity of the precious red palm oil for the burns on Norah's face and issues clear instructions for her to rest all day tomorrow.

Seki never mentions the Japanese music again.

CHAPTER 18

Camp III
October 1943–October 1944

Norah, Ena, Audrey and a few others are finishing up clearing the patch of land just outside the camp, ready for planting. They have been allowed to start planting vegetables once more. The women are surprised when a young Japanese officer approaches them carrying a sack, which he empties onto the ground.

'These from Captain Seki for you to grow,' he says with a small smile.

None of the women attempts to examine what is being spread out on the ground. All except Audrey, who decides to take a closer look.

'Thank you,' she says with a small bow.

'These for you to grow, make food,' the officer says with pride.

Audrey picks up and inspects several of the seedlings.

The officer takes a few steps away, giving the other women the courage to approach.

'Beans,' says one. 'These will grow fast.'

'And sweet potatoes,' points out another. 'We need to get these in the ground quickly.'

Watching the women finally embrace his offering, the officer leaves.

'Well, we know what we're going to call him, don't we, ladies?' Audrey says.

'What?'

'Seedling!'

Working from five in the morning until six at night, seven days a week, the women have finally prepared the plot of fertile ground. They have fashioned rudimentary tools from branches. Working the sun-baked earth is back-breaking. The sweet potato, carrots and tapioca seeds will only flourish with daily watering, but the well feels like it's miles away and, still very weak, the women have to make multiple trips back and forth. From time to time, Seedling walks with them, offering quiet words of encouragement.

And then, without notice, storms hit the camp.

'It's not monsoon season, though, is it?' Norah asks Ena.

'No, way too early for that.'

The torrential rain and strong winds wash away many of the seedlings, but the immediate concern is the damage to the thatched roofs atop each hut. Sister Catherina becomes an expert roofer. Barefoot, with her habit hitched up around her thighs, her large veil sailing behind her, she is seen going from hut to hut patching up and tying down the huge gaps in the roofs with old rush matting. After rescuing the nurses from drowning in rainwater one night, she accepts their invitation to share the evening cup of tea, a concoction made from seeds, burnt rice and anything else the girls can get their hands on.

'How have you never fallen through a roof?' Blanche asks.

240

Sister Catherina laughs. 'I've come close, but I don't know, maybe someone' – she raises her eyes skyward – 'is looking out for me.'

'If I ever see a long arm stretching down from the heavens to catch you, then you can call me a believer,' Jean says.

'I don't ever see you gardening,' Betty remarks. 'Do you prefer men's work?'

'I only like to eat the rewards of gardening,' Sister Catherina replies. 'I much prefer to be useful elsewhere – fixing things, teaching the children. That is one thing about this camp. We all work to our strengths. I went into the convent when I was very young; I've spent the last few years in teaching with some wonderful colleagues and, of course, Mother Laurentia, but I have never seen a sisterhood quite like what we have here.'

'Oh, I don't know, we have our moments, don't we, ladies?' Betty says.

'Yes, but is there a person here who you would not help, defend, fight for?'

'You're probably right. You know, Sister, you should be a politician when we get out of here, you are so diplomatic,' Blanche says.

'Not likely. You know, I wanted to join the Navy? I couldn't see why, just because I was a girl, I couldn't be a sailor,' Sister Catherina remarks indignantly.

'Really, you wanted to be a sailor? I've never heard of women in the Navy, except as nurses of course,' Betty says.

'Well, I think one day it will happen, just probably not in my lifetime.'

After Sister Catherina leaves, the women sit around talking about the careers they would have liked to have had, had they not become nurses.

241

'I could fix any piece of farm machinery growing up; I could've been a mechanic,' Vivian says.

'Well, you kind of are, you put people back together again,' Betty says, with a laugh.

'Very funny – and what about you, did you always want to be a nurse?'

'No, not really. My father was an accountant. Other than sewing and being full of mischief, the main thing I got from my family was always to do my bit, help anyone and everyone. I didn't know what I was going to do with my life, which is why I was an old woman of twenty-nine before I started training.'

'And you're still an old woman,' Jean quips.

'Then what about you – nursing in your veins?'

'I think the bigger question is, did any of us dream of becoming a doctor?' Jean retorts.

The question has a sobering effect on the nurses. They shake their heads.

'Well, hopefully when we return home and tell the army what we've been doing, they will see that women are capable of being trained either as doctors, or as nurses who can treat – and not just care for – patients,' Vivian says firmly.

It is when the monsoon rains arrive that the crops begin to truly flourish and it is not long before carrots have pushed through the dirt, their lovely green tops waving to the women as they work. Peeking beneath the earth, the women spy the brilliant orange of a carrot ready to pluck. Calling Seedling over, they ask if they can start digging. Smiling, he enthusiastically tells them he will ask for permission and hurries away.

It is not long before he returns with Ah Fat in tow. The women understand his message all too clearly: none of the food they have planted and tended is for them – it is to feed the noble Japanese officers.

When the women of the camp hear this news, they gather in the central clearing. Mrs Hinch pushes her way through the crowd until she reaches the front. There is the small box that occasionally Seki perches on to deliver his missives.

'Give me a hand up, Norah,' she says.

With a hoist and grunt from Mrs Hinch, she gathers her pride and looks out over her audience.

'Quiet. Please,' she says in her calm, clear voice, and when Mrs Hinch speaks, others listen. 'So, you've all heard the news. Apparently, none of the vegetables you have gone to such lengths to cultivate are for us. If you will all just wait here, I think it is time I had a chat with our captain. Help me down, will you please, Norah?'

With a groan and grunt, Norah helps Mrs Hinch off the box.

'Come with me, Norah. Let's see what he has to say for himself.'

Mrs Hinch and Norah are met outside the captain's office by Ah Fat.

'Inchi, what are you doing here?'

'I demand to see Captain Seki.'

'No, no! You can't see the captain.'

'Oh, Ah Fat, step aside, I'm going to see the captain and you're not going to stop me.'

Ah Fat backs off, allowing the women to enter the office. Seki is sitting at his desk but jumps to his feet when he sees them advancing, Ah Fat reluctantly on their heels, knowing he will be required to translate.

'Captain Seki, I must protest. We have been told none of the vegetables the women have planted and grown under the most

243

horrendous of circumstances are for their use. If not for their use, why have they damn near killed themselves?'

Ah Fat struggles to translate, obviously trying to find the most diplomatic way of communicating their message. When Mrs Hinch thinks Ah Fat has finished speaking, she continues before Seki has a chance to respond.

'It is unforgivable to lead these women up the garden path so to speak, to let them believe their efforts would be rewarded with some decent food for once. We're starving. What have you got to say, man?'

Seki is initially stunned at being spoken to in such a manner by Mrs Hinch. Although he can't understand her, it is clear she is demanding something of him, and he is highly offended.

When Ah Fat has finished translating, it is time for Seki to speak.

'The captain wants to know where you are from?' Ah Fat asks Mrs Hinch.

'I am a proud citizen of the United States of America.'

It becomes clear Ah Fat has not appreciated Mrs Hinch is not English or Australian.

'American?' he whispers at the same time Seki roars, 'American!'

'Yes, American. What's wrong with you? Now, are you going to let the women eat the vegetables they have grown?'

'*No! No! No!*' is his response.

Ah Fat hurries the women from the room, as Seki continues to rant.

'Americans are very bad,' he tells Mrs Hinch. 'They are causing much damage to Japan.'

'Well, that's very good news!' she says. 'Maybe we'll finally get out of this blessed place.'

'Do not try to steal food, Inchi,' Ah Fat calls after them as the women are leaving the compound. 'There will be slaps if you do.'

As Norah and Mrs Hinch walk back to the clearing, Mrs Hinch loses some of her bluster.

'Oh, dear, while I'm glad to hear the US is winning this war for us, I'm worried the fact that I'm American has made the situation worse.'

'Maybe,' agrees Norah. 'But I don't think he was ever going to let us have the food.'

Not needing to be asked, Norah offers her hand to help Mrs Hinch back on the box.

'I am so sorry; I have failed in my attempt to get the captain to let us eat what you have grown. It seems it was never meant for us.'

The women react angrily, shouting about the unfairness. Mrs Hinch holds up her hand for quiet.

'Ladies, I'm afraid I also have a warning for you. Please do not attempt to take any of the vegetables; the captain has made it clear that anyone caught "stealing" their food will be severely punished. I have no doubt he will carry out that threat. I am so sorry.'

Norah's hand is already raised to help her off the box.

Norah has struggled to regain the energy she had prior to her punishment in the sun. Her orchestra had been the perfect tonic. It's been several weeks since their last concert, the one that went so terribly wrong for her. Ena and Audrey kidnap her one evening and take her back to the Dutch hut, where her singers await. After a rehearsal which is more fun than serious practice, Norah returns to her hut invigorated. Finding Margaret, she tells her it is time for another concert. She is surprised by Margaret's subdued reaction.

'What's wrong?'

'I'm sorry, my dear, Ah Fat has made it clear; from now on, concerts are to be approved by Captain Seki. I will ask Mrs Hinch to speak to him tomorrow, but I don't know what he will say.'

'That's not fair, all we're doing is singing, how can that hurt anyone? It's quite the opposite, in fact.'

'He didn't get what he wanted, and I think this is his way to punish us. But I will try to talk him round. Leave it with me.'

Two days later, Mrs Hinch is in her kitchen with Norah when she hears the familiar, and irritating, call of, 'Inchi, Inchi, where are you?' from Ah Fat.

'Oh, dear, what now?' Norah wonders aloud.

Mrs Hinch's only response is a loud sigh every other woman in the hut can hear.

'Inchi, Inchi,' he calls again from the living room.

'You'd better go,' Norah prompts her.

'I suppose I must.' Mrs Hinch takes several deep breaths before slowly walking into the room. 'What is so pressing, Ah Fat?'

'Inchi, I come to tell you captain say yes to concert, OK.'

'As he should.'

'But he is also very angry; he can't understand why you women want to sing when there is a war on, and you are starving, and you are sick.'

'That is precisely why we are singing. Please pass that on to the captain, will you?'

Downcast and brow-beaten, Ah Fat departs, dejected because he had clearly thought his good news would make him a hero in *Inchi*'s eyes.

'This is some good news, finally,' says Norah. 'A small victory, wouldn't you say, Mrs Hinch?'

'Looks like it.'

At the next concert, the women's applause as Norah and her orchestra walk to the front of the gathered crowd does not stop. They are on their feet, desperate to show Norah how much they love, appreciate and value her bravery in defying their captors.

Norah turns around to face the women, tears snaking down her cheeks. She is overwhelmed. Turning back to her orchestra, she fears they may not be able to perform, as they too are crying.

Margaret whispers to Norah, 'Why don't I start them off, then hand over to you?'

All Norah can do is nod and whisper back, 'Yes, please.'

'What are you starting with?'

'Beethoven.'

Margaret faces the orchestra, who catch on immediately.

'Beethoven,' she mouths.

Norah stands aside to let Margaret conduct, and for the first time she is an observer, watching her singers perform. From her position, she is also able to watch the audience. Their emotion has a powerful effect on her, and she struggles to catch her breath. As the minuet ends, Norah joins the audience applauding the orchestra.

Margaret takes a deep bow before holding her hand out to Norah to take over. As Norah steps in front of her girls the cheering is thunderous. Composed, Norah turns around, holding her finger to her lips.

As the concert resumes, Norah, her back to the audience, is oblivious to the soldiers circling the shed. The orchestra, the only ones aware of their presence, like true professionals, ignore them. A quick word amongst them when the concert ends confirms no one will mention their presence to Norah. She should be allowed to enjoy this evening sharing in the love and gratitude. When there are no repercussions from the captain in the days to come, Norah begins to relax.

However, everyone knows when the last concert is upon them. It hasn't been announced, but how can they possibly continue when they can barely stand after a day's chores? Both the choir and the orchestra struggle to rehearse. Norah knows that working long, hard days leaves them with little energy for singing, but she also knows how important their performances are to the women.

It is a different sort of evening for Norah. She sees that the women are trying to sing their hearts out, but nothing can hide the fact that they are exhausted and running out of hope.

CHAPTER 19

Camp III
October 1943–October 1944

'We have to speak to the captain about the violence,' Nesta tells Dr McDowell as she helps her staunch the flow of blood from yet another victim's wound.

The Japanese guards are showing less tolerance for the falling numbers at work each day. Any woman caught walking in the camp during the day, unless occupied with a chore, has her face slapped, the force sending her sprawling, and often in need of medical attention.

'We'll have to talk to Mrs Hinch.'

Both women stop what they're doing when they hear heavy boots approaching. Three soldiers have entered the hospital and have fanned out amongst the patients.

'What do you want? What are you doing here?' Dr McDowell says, marching towards them.

'Too many women in here, need to go to work,' a soldier yells at her.

'They're sick. How can they possibly work? Just look at them,' Nesta interjects.

He glances at a woman, who is struggling to sit up, alarmed by the sudden appearance of the soldiers.

'This one, she should work.'

Before Dr McDowell or Nesta can respond, the guard slaps the patient hard across the face. The other guards see this and immediately begin to attack the other patients.

'Stop it! Stop it at once!' Dr McDowell screams, advancing on the men. 'You do not come into this hospital and assault the patients – now get out!'

'Just go!' Nesta yells, shooing them back.

'We will go, but we will be back tomorrow for inspection. Women who should work will be punished by us,' he says, gesturing to his colleagues, before turning to leave.

'This has to stop,' says Nesta as she and Dr McDowell hurry to find Mrs Hinch.

Just outside the hospital, Nesta sees that Mrs Hinch is, in fact, rushing towards them.

'I heard! I was coming to see you – tell me what happened?' Mrs Hinch pants.

When Nesta has finished her report, Mrs Hinch turns on her heel.

'Leave it with me!' she says.

Returning a short time later, Mrs Hinch's customary indignance is wiped from her face.

'Believe it or not, the captain agreed the punishments, as he calls them, have gone too far. From now on, only women seen misbehaving will be disciplined. I argued no one is misbehaving, we're all just trying to survive. All we can do is hope he tells the guards to back off; if he doesn't, he can expect another visit from me. I'm sorry I couldn't do more.'

'Mrs Hinch, thank you. We all know how much you stand up for us and we appreciate it,' Dr McDowell says.

'I'll tell the nurses of your visit and warn them to be on their guard,' Nesta adds.

'Ladies.' Mrs Hinch addresses the women gathered in the camp clearing for her announcement. 'Given that the wells have dried up good and proper, we have permission to leave the camp and use the pump outside.'

'Thank God,' Norah says. 'I'll go right now, but I can only carry one bucket.'

'We'll go together,' Ena offers.

'No, Ena. You stay with June, she needs you. I'm so worried she's going to get sick; she can't go on like this without falling ill. Tell her a story, sing if you have the energy. She needs to know we're always here.'

'I'll come with you,' Audrey pipes up.

Walking to the well, they catch up with Betty and Vivian heading in the same direction. The women continue, stopping now and then to pull at shrubs and roots.

'Not much, is there,' Audrey observes.

'Well,' says Betty, 'we cooked the roots from this same vine a couple of days ago – didn't taste too bad and no repercussions, so we think it's safe.'

'Are there any more you can see? We're desperate to get something for June,' Norah says.

From the bucket she is carrying, Vivian pulls out several long, thick, dirty roots and hands them over. 'Take these and get them back to June. We'll find more, don't worry.'

Back at the hut with the water, Norah and Audrey twist and snap the roots into pieces, dropping them into boiling water together

251

with a few grains of salt. It takes a while, but eventually they boil down. Both women lift a teaspoon of the concoction to their lips and pronounce it 'not bad'.

Norah slowly feeds June the soup.

'This is the best roots soup I've ever tasted,' June says, licking her lips. 'Thank you, Aunty Norah and Aunty Audrey. I've saved a little for you.'

'We want you to eat it all, dear girl,' Audrey says.

'Oh, no, I couldn't. I'm full. Please,' she says, handing over her bowl.

'Inside! Inside!' yell the soldiers, streaming through the camp, hitting out at any woman or child in their path as they attempt to shepherd everyone towards shelter.

'Are they planes?' Norah screams, looking into the sky. 'Allied planes?'

'I scc them!' Ena shouts back. 'Look, above the trees.'

Norah picks out the outlines of planes above the towering jungle trees. But it's the explosion that follows that causes a panic in the camp.

'Where's June?' Norah yells. She and Ena had been inside when the skies began to rumble and they'd run out of the house to join everyone else.

'I don't know!' Ena says frantically. 'She went to play at one of the Dutch huts, but I don't know which one.'

Outside, the aircraft continue to thunder through the skies. It is a chaotic scene; the women are waving wildly, hooting and cheering to attract their attention, while their captors run in all directions, yelling to get inside.

Norah and Ena run towards the Dutch huts on the other side of the street.

As they exit the first hut, two soldiers run at them waving their rifles, ordering them back inside.

'We'll find her when this is over,' Norah shouts, dodging a bayonet.

It is then that the most unusual sound erupts into the camp. An air-raid siren.

The women and children wait indoors until the siren stops. Slowly, people begin to venture outside, looking for their missing children, their friends.

Norah and Ena find an excited June, who proudly tells them she saw the plane and describes over and over the sound of the explosion they all heard.

In their house, Margaret and Mrs Hinch make a headcount and are reminded that the three missing are in hospital.

When the siren stops, all the nurses run back to the hospital to check on their patients. They gather for a quick chat.

'Is this it? D'you think we're going to be rescued?' an excited Betty asks.

'I don't know what it means, we can only hope,' Nesta tells them.

'Maybe we should make a sign for the pilot?' Vivian suggests.

Dr McDowell interjects. 'I don't think that's a good idea, the tree canopy is too dense, and I can guarantee if a guard sees it, there'll be trouble.'

While they are talking, Mrs Hinch comes into the hospital.

'I've just spoken to the captain,' she tells them.

'And?' Nesta says.

'When the siren sounds, everyone is to enter the nearest hut and stay there. He plans on having every window boarded up immediately and anyone caught outside or seen at a window will be punished.'

'We'd better spread the word,' Dr McDowell says.

The next day, nurses Ray and Valerie make the mistake of opening their door to peek outside. Their timing couldn't have been worse. One of the soldiers sees them and bursts into the hut, where he is confronted by the entire household, all huddled together.

'Can I help you?' Nesta asks him.

'I saw two outside.' Beckoning with his hand, he says, 'You must come.'

The nurses don't move.

'I don't know what you are talking about, Officer. Can you identify who you think you saw?'

'I saw two – come or you all punished.'

The soldier puts his hand on his pistol, breathing heavily, a brutal look on his face.

The two nurses step forwards; Ray and Valerie will not let their friends be punished because of their mistake.

Nesta steps up beside them, bowing deeply.

'We are sorry for breaking the rules; wewill not do it again.'

Nesta does not see the hand slashing out at her until it connects with her face, sending her flying back into the arms of the nurses behind her.

Shoving the two culprits out of the door, the officer marches them away.

Several hours later, Ray and Valerie return to the hut.

'We got taken to Seki,' Ray says.

'Did he hurt you?' Nesta asks.

254

'Not yet, but tomorrow we have to stand in the sun. Like Norah. No hat,' Valerie tells them.

The next morning, the nurses give Ray and Valerie their rations of water, which they try to refuse.

'You need as much fluid as you can get down; you both know what dehydration does to a body,' Jean tells them.

'But we'll pee ourselves if we drink all this,' Ray says with a chuckle.

'I would rather you peed yourself than your kidneys failed,' Jean says.

The nurses all march to the centre space, where no shade touches the dry earth. Seki, accompanied by Ah Fat, strides out to the two nurses who stand with their heads bowed.

'I'm going to talk to him,' Jean whispers to Nesta.

'Do you think that's a good idea?'

'Ray has been with me since we first came to Malaya, and I know something about her that no one else does. She has a heart condition, we discovered it when she got malaria not long after we arrived.'

'OK, see what you can do but don't risk joining them. Ray wouldn't want that.'

Jean, head bowed, walks slowly towards Seki and Ah Fat. They watch her approach with curiosity.

'What you want?' Ah Fat asks.

'With deepest respect, can I please ask the captain to not punish Nurse Ray this way. She has a heart problem and standing in the heat would be very dangerous for her.'

Ah Fat translates; Seki's response, as usual, is long-winded and pompous. Ah Fat's translation is more succinct.

'No.'

Ray has heard this exchange and calls out, 'It's OK, Sister. I'll be OK.'

The nurses stand on duty in whatever shade they can find. Throughout the morning, Norah, Margaret and several other women bring them water when the soldiers' backs are turned. As the sun hits its zenith, it becomes clear Ray is in trouble.

Mrs Hinch and Dr McDowell plead with the guards to let her go. Their pleas are refused.

Watching as Ray stumbles, regaining her feet only to stagger again, has every woman crying out, 'Let her go.' It is not long before Ray collapses and it is clear she will not be getting up.

'Go and get her!' Mrs Hinch yells as she storms towards the unconscious nurse.

Every nurse is running now, along with Dr McDowell. The Japanese guards standing nearby, bayonets drawn and pointing at them, realise they are outnumbered and allow the women to push past them. Dr McDowell briefly examines Ray before telling the nurses to pick her up and take her back to their hut.

'I'll go with them,' Jean tells Nesta. 'You look after Val.'

Valerie stays standing, surrounded by her friends throughout the afternoon until the sun has set.

'Come on, enough, let's get her,' Nesta says, rushing to grab Val, who collapses in her arms.

By the time they get Val back inside the hut, she is unconscious. Nesta and Vivian tend to her. Jean has taken Ray to the hospital, as it's serious enough that she wants Dr McDowell to look after her.

Margaret knocks on the open door, peering inside. 'I know it is a stupid question, but is there anything I can do?'

Nesta stands and waves Margaret over to the comatose nurse, where wet cloths cover her entire body and head, only her face exposed.

'Thank you, Margaret. Other than arranging to get us all out of here,' she says sardonically, 'there's not really much to do. We will look after Val. Her pulse is coming back nice and steady, although, besides the sunburn, she will need a few days to recover from the heatstroke.'

Margaret's eyes fill with compassion. 'And what about Ray?'

'Jean has taken her to the hospital. She'll spend the night there.'

'Norah and her team are preparing the evening meal for you all, so you don't have to worry about lighting a fire and cooking. They'll be here shortly.'

'Oh, Margaret, I never even thought about food for the nurses.' Nesta's face twists in exhausted pain. 'What is wrong with me? I'm meant to be their leader.'

Margaret squeezes Nesta's arm. 'Sister James, you are a fine leader. I'm sure none of your friends have thought about themselves today either. Dinner will be here soon.'

'Well,' says Norah to Audrey, 'I think something has shifted.' The women are walking to the water pump a couple of weeks after the planes first appeared in the sky.

'I think so too,' Audrey says. 'The soldiers are spooked, which is good and bad.'

'Bad in that they're more likely to lash out at us.'

'And good,' Audrey adds, 'because we might be rescued soon.'

'At least the air raids are only happening at night now.' The women have reached the pump and Norah fills her bucket. 'Which means we're free to walk to the pump in daylight.'

* * *

Mrs Hinch is informed that there is mail for some of the women. Hearing the news, the nurses agree it will be very unlikely that there is anything from home for them. Instead of all of them lining up with everyone else to see if there is an envelope with their name on it, Nesta offers to go on their behalf.

The process of waiting for the soldiers to sift through the mail with Mrs Hinch's help takes a long time, or it just feels like a long time in the midday heat.

'I'm here to see if there is any mail for the nurses.' Finally, Nesta has made it to the front of the long queue.

Mrs Hinch smiles warmly. 'There's mail for Betty, Wilma and Jean. None for you, I'm afraid, my dear.'

'Thank you, I'll go and fetch them,' Nesta says, her eyes brimming. What she wouldn't give to hear from her mum right now.

Betty sobs when she reads her name on the battered envelope. It is her mother's handwriting, and the letter is two years old. Carrying it back to her hut, she holds the unopened message from home. Looking into the faces of her fellow nurses and friends, each of them desperate for news from their families, is too much for Betty to bear. She heads outside, to the furthest corner of the yard, and hides behind a tree to read the longed-for letter. It is dark before she returns inside. She tells everyone that she has no news of the war. Clearly her mother had been instructed as to what she could and couldn't write.

In Norah and Ena's hut, the sisters watch a few of their house-mates reading and rereading their letters from home.

'They look so happy, don't they?' Ena whispers to Norah.

'They do,' Norah agrees, trying to hide her own disappointment for her sister's sake.

'I wasn't expecting to hear from anyone. Ken and Mother and Father are probably imprisoned like us,' Ena says, unable to take her eyes off the women poring over their messages.

'True. But there's Barbara.' Norah's voice catches. She'd do anything to hear news of Sally. 'I wonder if she's tried to write to us.'

'Oh, Norah, Sally is safe with her, we just don't know where they are and we don't know what she's been told about our whereabouts.'

'You're right, of course. I don't mean to sound ungrateful, and I'm really happy news is getting through at all.'

The rations are late, and the women grow anxious, gathering in small groups by the fence. Several local traders have been allowed to visit the camp again, offering fresh food for anyone who can pay.

Norah wanders over to Betty, who is pacing nearby.

'Do you think it's coming?' she asks.

'Well, we haven't heard that it's not,' sighs Betty. 'But if you think about it, we had rations yesterday, but not the day before, so maybe they're only going to feed us every other day.'

'It's like they starve us to the point of death, then give us enough to get some of our strength back, then withhold it again. Do you think this could be part of some evil plan?'

'I don't want to think like that, but you could be right. How's June? Is she getting enough?'

'Define "enough",' says Norah, grimly. 'She's no worse off than any of the other children, better than most adults. Several of the Dutch mothers give her a bit of the food they buy from the locals.'

'Oh, to have money, or jewels, or anything at all to trade. We had to have the bad luck of ending up on a bombed ship.'

'We may have lost everything, but we hung on to our lives, though, didn't we? So many were lost.' Norah reflects for a moment on that terrible day and the horrors of floating around in the sea without any sense that help might come. 'I'm sorry, Betty,' she adds hastily. 'I didn't mean to sound insensitive, and I didn't mean to remind you of the lost nurses. I know there are so many who sailed with you and are not here today.'

'We think of them every day,' Betty says softly, her mind drifting to old friends who she may never see again.

'You never know,' Norah says, rubbing the young nurse's shoulder. 'They might have been found and imprisoned somewhere just like us.'

'I guess,' replies Betty, reluctantly.

As Betty wanders off dejectedly, Norah regrets the entire exchange. Their lives are hard enough in the day-to-day, without being reminded of who they have lost.

Jean and Vivian wander over to the far corner of the fence, where locals are trading with the prisoners. They have nothing to offer in exchange, but are riveted by the deals being made. They are rewarded for their proximity when a Dutch woman hands them two sweet potatoes.

'Mother Laurentia, you wanted to see me?' Nesta says, taking her hand. She has been asked to stop by the nuns' hut and now carefully takes in the Mother Superior's appearance for any signs of illness.

'I'm quite well, Sister James. You don't have to look at me like that,' the nun says with a smile before pulling out an envelope from an unseen pocket in her habit. 'I would like to give you this, for you and your nurses.'

Nesta looks at the proffered envelope. 'What is it?'

'Money, my dear. Why shouldn't you, who do so much for this desperate community, buy a little food now and then?'

'I can't take your money, Mother. Surely you need it?' Nesta counters, looking longingly at the envelope.

'It's not mine, if that makes it any easier to accept. Captain Seki gave it to me yesterday; it is from the Dutch Red Cross, and while, yes, it is meant for my fellow countrywomen, I do not see them going without like you women.'

Nesta is still reluctant to take the envelope. 'I really don't think my friends would be able to accept it, knowing it belongs to others in need. It was given to you by your government.'

'What can I say to persuade you?' The nun is still holding out the envelope, just as stubborn as Nesta.

Nesta thinks long and hard. She doesn't want to offend Mother Laurentia. She thinks of her friends, their hunger, their failing strength, their ever-waning hope of freedom. She has also seen the supplies being traded: eggs, fruit, dried fish, biscuits.

'Can I take it on one condition?' she says, finally.

'Anything.'

'We'll only agree if it's a loan, which we'll repay in full when we get out of this place.'

'Agreed.'

And Nesta gratefully pockets the envelope.

'Hello, ladies,' Nesta says cheerfully as she enters the hut.

'What are you looking so happy about?' Ena asks glumly. 'There are more weevils than rice in this batch.'

'I'm happy because I have something for you. Mother Laurentia loaned us some money she received from the Dutch Red Cross. We want to share our food with you and the others from the *Vyner Brooke* who arrived with nothing.'

'But it was given to you, for the nurses I presume,' Norah says, hurriedly getting to her feet. With food so close at hand, she doesn't know how long she'll be able to politely decline.

'You have nothing, Norah. Of course we're going to share what we have with you,' Jean insists.

Ena joins her sister on her feet. 'Thank you! I wish there was more I could say, but right now, I'm so worried about June, and the rest of us in the house, that any food at all will make a huge difference,' she says desperately.

Another batch of mail arrives at the camp, and Betty eagerly opens her second letter. Within seconds, she is crying, running from the hut into the garden. Nesta and Jean go after her.

'Betty, what's happened? Is it bad news?' Nesta asks.

Sobbing, Betty thrusts the letter at Nesta.

'Are you sure you want me to read it?'

Betty nods.

'Who's it from?' Jean asks Nesta as she begins to read.

'Oh, my God! It's from Phyllis.' Nesta's hands are shaking.

'Phyllis P?' Jean asks, trying to get a look at the letter.

'They made it! They got home,' Betty sobs.

Several of the nurses have come outside to check on their friend. Everyone knows that bad news is worse than no news.

'Girls! Betty's got a letter from Phyllis P. The others made it home, their ship got through,' Nesta tells them.

Within seconds, every nurse in the hut is in the garden, hugging and sobbing. The relief that their friends and colleagues who left Singapore the day before their ill-fated journey are safe at home surges through every woman.

'I'm going to the hospital to tell the others,' Nesta says, handing the letter back to Betty. 'Share the letter, it's exactly what we need.'

The letter is passed around the nurses eagerly, each of them desperate to read the words themselves to fully take in the news. Betty watches Blanche clutching the letter, sobbing quietly. She seeks out Nesta.

'I promised Blanche that if she didn't get any mail before I received another letter, I'd get her a cake. Is it wrong of me to ask for a little money to buy a moon cake for her?'

'A moon cake? Where are you going to get that?'

'One of the Dutch girls told me she only buys moon cakes from the traders. While everyone else gets vegetables or fruit or rice, she buys cakes.'

Nesta goes to the kitchen drawer where she keeps the money from Mother Laurentia. She hands Betty two notes.

'It's a day for celebrating – see what you can get.'

Betty returns and excitedly displays the results of her bartering: four small moon cakes, each the size of a golf ball, and two biscuits. She and Nesta take the sweets, along with a knife, and join the others outside.

It is just as the nurses are placing the last delicious crumbs into their mouths that Mrs Hinch appears in the garden.

'Oh, dear, I'm so sorry . . .' she begins.

'What's going on?' Nesta asks, swallowing her final morsel.

'Bad news, I'm afraid; the traders have been banned again.'

Nesta sighs inwardly.

'Well, ladies,' she says to her nurses, 'at least we got our moon cakes.'

'And they were weevil-free,' Jean adds.

CHAPTER 20

Camp III
October 1944

'Half of you will be leaving the camp tomorrow!' Ah Fat announces. Just minutes earlier, Seki had called a camp meeting. 'And, nurses, half of you will go tomorrow, be ready.'

Hearing the news, Nesta approaches Seki and Ah Fat as they turn to leave. Guards immediately brandish their rifles. Undaunted, Nesta walks up to the captain, glaring at him.

'We will not be split up,' she tells him. 'Either we all go, or we all stay.'

Seki walks away, but as Ah Fat attempts to follow him, Nesta takes his arm.

'Please, tell him not to separate us,' she pleads.

'Captain Seki has decided. Half of the nurses go tomorrow.' And then Ah Fat, bows his head. 'I'm sorry,' he says.

That night, the nurses talk until the small hours. They had felt close to rescue and now they worry they will never be found.

But they make a contingency plan should they be split up, deciding who should go in each group. It is obvious that Nesta and Jean will each take a group.

The following afternoon, sixty women, including half of the nurses, Norah, Ena, Audrey and June, are loaded onto a small truck and driven away, their meagre possessions clutched in their arms.

The sun has set when they arrive at the mouth of the river. They are ordered onto the waiting river boat. As they begin to settle down, the soldiers point out six women who are to disembark, Betty amongst them. Another larger truck has pulled up to the jetty and they are ordered to remove its cargo and take it back to the river boat. There are sacks of food, boxes of fine china, books, silverware, chairs; obviously the fine possessions of a wealthy homeowner. Amongst the wares are dozens of coffins.

'We have to find a way to help them,' Norah whispers to Audrey. 'It's not right that the six of them have to do all the work.'

'What do you suggest?'

'Here comes Betty with a box. I'm going to sidle up beside her and when she's about to load it on, I'll push her aside and take over.'

'But what if they see you?' Audrey says, unsure of this brilliant plan of Norah's.

'I have to try at least. If it works, you can do it for someone else. Not Sister Catherina obviously, but, surely, we all look the same to them, apart from her.'

Norah hurries over just as Betty is approaching the storage areas with a heavy box. As she bends to lower it, Norah catches her eye and signals her over. As Betty bends her knees to drop the box, Norah whispers, 'Stay down.'

When Norah rises and heads for the gangplank, she comes face to face with an apoplectic soldier, screaming at her to stay where she is. He turns to Betty, still crouched amongst the boxes and waves his rifle at her to get up and back to work. She ducks under the soldier's swinging rifle.

The commotion is heard on the pier and as the soldier turns away to tell the others what has just happened, Norah takes this moment of distraction to jump up and race back to the safety of the crowd of women on board, where she joins Ena and June.

'What was all that about?' Ena asks.

'Nothing. You know what they're like,' Norah murmurs.

The women and children spend the night anchored at the pier. When the sun is fully risen, the boat begins its slow journey down the river. The air is still, humid, energy-sapping. Hours pass before they leave the river mouth and enter the Banka Strait. The smell of salt water and a gentle breeze is a comfort to the exhausted women.

Peering over the side of the boat, Jean speaks quietly.

'This is where the *Vyner Brooke* sank,' she says, staring into the sea.

One by one, the nurses reach for the hands of their friends.

'And there's Banka Island,' says Jean.

'The massacre . . .' begins Betty, but the words get caught in her throat. It is enough to imagine; they don't need to talk about it.

The nurses huddle together, remembering their fallen friends. They can see the beaches of the island and wonder which inlet saw their friends murdered.

It is dark when the boat anchors off the Muntok pier. A foul-smelling junk boat pulls up alongside the river boat and the women are ordered to board. They are forced into the hold below, into two inches of kerosene. Their belongings are thrown down after them. As an air-raid siren sounds overhead, the hatch to the hold is slammed shut. In the dark, the fumes of kerosene overpowering, the women vomit and struggle for breath. They collapse into the pool of oily liquid.

'Everyone, please try to keep calm,' Jean calls out.

'We're suffocating,' a voice in the dark moans.

'We're going to die,' another calls.

'You have to stay calm. Try to slow your breathing down. It's the only way we can limit the amount of fumes we inhale. Please just have a go,' Jean urges.

'But the children . . .' a desperate voice pleads.

'Mothers, please help your children, get them to breathe with you. Slow, slow, slow.'

Soon, the crying stops.

'Are you all right, June? I can't see you,' Ena whispers.

Between gasps, June manages a few words. 'I'm fine, Aunty Ena, but I don't like the smell.'

'I know,' says Ena, finding the little girl's hand. 'Let's breathe together, shall we. Slowly now – one, two, three. It won't be too long now.'

'Can I suggest we don't talk?' Jean announces. 'Save your energy and shallow breathe through your nose.'

Hours later, the junk boat bumps up against the pier and the hatch is thrown open. Sick and almost too weak to place one foot in front of the other, the soldiers help the women out of the hold. Dumped on the pier like sacks of sand, the internees struggle to stand. They support one another on the long walk to the dock. For the first time since they were taken prisoner, they are grateful to see the waiting trucks.

Part 3
The Last Days of War

CHAPTER 21

Camp IV
November 1944–March 1945

'Nesta, Vivian, over here!'

Nesta and Vivian see Norah, Ena, Audrey and June running towards them.

'Finally, you're here,' Norah says, feeling something close to joy. The camp is about to be reunited.

'Do you know where Jean and the other nurses are?' Nesta asks.

'They're at the hospital waiting for you. Come on, we'll give you a hand. June, honey, run ahead to the hospital and tell them that Jean, Nesta and the others have arrived,' Ena says.

'On my way, Aunty Ena.' June runs ahead to deliver her important message.

'Finally!' Jean yells, sweeping Nesta into a hug. 'Wait till you see our huts!'

'Leaky roofs, no bedding, I can guess,' says Nesta, grinning.

'No! They're new buildings. Huge. They can sleep around one hundred people.'

'And the best thing,' says Betty, joining them and throwing an arm around Nesta's shoulder, 'there are grass mats on the ground with enough room around each to stretch out without hitting the person next to you. Can you believe it?'

Nesta is led to the centre of the camp where the large kitchen is pointed out, along with two further kitchens with small fireplaces for cooking. The huts that they are to sleep in are wooden, light and airy inside, a distinct change from their last camp.

'This is better,' Nesta says, finally relaxing. 'Toilets?'

'Bathrooms!' Betty says. 'Actual bathrooms. And . . . wait for it . . . nine concrete wells.'

'Clean water?' Nesta asks. 'This may very well save all our lives.'

A few days later, the number of internees swells when two hundred English women are marched into the camp. Amongst them are several Indo-Dutch young women dressed in beautiful clothes; they are led away by soldiers to several small huts on the hillside beyond the camp. It is obvious to all that they are the new 'entertainment' for the Japanese officers. Each day, the women observe the platters of meat, vegetables and rice delivered to their huts.

Within days, all nine wells are empty. Nesta complains to Mrs Hinch that the sick women will not get better if they are dehydrated on top of everything else. Mrs Hinch demands a meeting with Captain Seki, Ah Fat escorting her and Nesta into the commandant's new office.

Mrs Hinch enters the room already talking; they are beyond the niceties of polite introductions. 'The facilities are an improvement, and we're grateful. However, your wells are useless; there is not a drop of water left in any of them.'

'The women are ill and thirsty,' Nesta adds. 'We really need water.'

Seki listens to Ah Fat's translation. Following his long retort, Ah Fat bows to Seki before turning back to Mrs Hinch.

'Captain says more water will come when it rains.'

'W-When it . . . rains?' Nesta stammers.

'And when will that be? Do you have a reliable weather forecast for us?' Mrs Hinch says. 'This is preposterous.'

Ah Fat doesn't attempt to translate. Seki grins at Mrs Hinch and then at Nesta.

'What's he smiling about? This isn't funny, Ah Fat!'

Ah Fat doesn't attempt to hide his silly grin. 'Inchi, Inchi. I'm making joke. Captain Seki not a monster. He says you can get water from the stream nearby.'

Mrs Hinch is not amused. Neither is Nesta. Fighting to control her temper, she bites her bottom lip, nods to both men and storms out.

Norah and Nesta join a line of women carrying whatever they can find to fetch water, creating a path through a jungle ablaze with colour, the tropical vegetation bearing the lush reds, purples and orange hues characterising so much of this landscape. Equally luminous wildflowers carpet the ground upon which they walk.

'So much beauty,' Norah says to Nesta.

'And all we want is water,' Nesta responds. 'I'd trade all of these wildflowers for a tap.'

Down in a small gully, they find a babbling stream. Norah and Nesta exchange a glance and follow the other women, who are throwing off their clothes and plunging into the cool water. After they feel refreshed, they sit on nearby rocks, using the sand gathered from the streambed to wash their hair.

'It is so good to still be alive,' Nesta says.

'And not thirsty!'

On their way back to camp, clean, and bearing containers full of water, Nesta pauses to pick a bunch of the wildflowers.

'Ladies.' Mrs Hinch has called a camp meeting to relay Seki's latest edict. 'I've been told we need to form work details to carry out the jobs around the camp.'

'We have jobs!' exclaims a voice. 'Cleaning the toilets, the street, the huts.'

'Well, now we will have more jobs. They want us to build a barbed-wire fence around the hospital. There is also wood to be collected and stacked near the kitchens, and rice to be taken to the supply sheds. Do I have any volunteers?'

No one speaks, until, finally, Norah raises her hand.

'I'll help,' she says.

'Me too,' chime in Audrey and Ena at the same time.

Norah wonders at the wisdom of helping make the barbed-wire fence. With no gloves to protect their hands, the work is slow as they learn how to string the wire without slicing off their fingers.

'I guess there is an upside,' Ena says, sucking the blood from a cut on her finger. 'We're getting more rations.'

'True,' Audrey says. 'I heard shark was on the menu.'

'And Seki has even given us more oil,' Norah adds.

Deep-fried shark, mixed vegetables and rice washed down with copious cups of tea brings the women together. For the first time in her life, Nesta opens her mouth to lead the nurses in song. Within a few lines, every woman in the camp is singing 'Waltzing Matilda', as their voices carry up and down the street.

* * *

Nesta is working in the hospital when the front door bursts open. She looks up to see Vivian and Jean push inside, carrying a lifeless body.

'It's Betty! She's unconscious,' Vivian exclaims.

'Bring her over here,' Nesta says, pointing to a quiet corner of the room. 'Lie her on the floor and we'll get her onto a bed when we can.'

Dr McDowell joins the nurses to examine Betty. 'We need water and cloths: we have to cool her down quickly.'

Vivian and Jean run off to fetch what's needed while Nesta and Dr McDowell undress the poorly Betty.

'This bloody water is hot; she needs cold water,' Vivian groans when they return with water from the well.

'Yes, but we don't have any,' Dr McDowell says. 'This is what we have and we will make the most of it. Now, soak the rags and hand them to me.'

'Can you do it, Nesta?' Vivian says before turning to Jean. 'You grab a bucket and come with me.'

Before Nesta can object, Vivian has thrust a bucket into Jean's hands, grabbed one for herself and together they run from the room and head for the stream.

'Please tell Captain Seki that there is a fever raging through the camp. To get better, the women have to eat better. Why have you cut our rations again?' Mrs Hinch can barely get the words out. No sooner had the shark arrived than it disappeared, along with the vegetables. They are back to the weevil rice. Nesta has joined her for this audience with Captain Seki; standing by her side, she can no longer hold her tongue.

'We have to face facts,' she says. 'Women are about to start dying and we need to prepare. Just tell us how.'

'Everything you get is a gift from the Japanese. Be grateful for the food, Inchi,' Ah Fat says, before turning to Seki to deliver their messages.

After a terse response, Ah Fat clears his throat. 'Captain Seki is aware many women are very sick and will die. He said he wants you to bury them just outside the camp – there is a small place there, we have boxes to put them in, but you must do it.'

'Of course we must. Can we please have the tools to dig the graves and we will need timber to make crosses?' Mrs Hinch presses.

'Captain Seki will give you a machete to dig with and will find some wood for you to make crosses.'

'A machete? That's not much use. If we were clearing our way through the jungle it would come in handy, but how can we dig into the rock-hard soil with a large knife?'

'We will give you two machetes. That's all, now leave, Inchi.'

Without paying the captain the respect of a small bow, Mrs Hinch and Nesta hurry from Seki's office.

'Mrs Hinch, what's going on?' Audrey intercepts the two women on the street.

'We've just had the hardest conversation I've ever had with anyone. Poor Nesta had to say out loud that some of us are going to die, and die soon, and that we need to prepare.'

'That must have been awful,' Norah sympathises. 'But you're right. We've just been at the hospital and Jean told us there are several women there who they fear they can no longer save.'

'Inchi, Inchi, wait!' Ah Fat calls, hurrying towards them.

'Oh, no. I really do not need him right now,' Mrs Hinch says, before turning to Ah Fat and yelling, 'Unless you have good news for me, please go away.'

'Inchi, I have these for you,' he blurts, handing her two long machete-like knives.

Mrs Hinch snatches them from him, turning her back and walking away. Norah and Audrey hurry after her.

'I can't say what I am tempted to do with these two weapons in my hands, but I am thinking it,' Mrs Hinch says, a small smile crossing her face.

'We would do it for you, Mrs Hinch, you just have to say the word,' Audrey assures her.

'Well, thank you. However, we've been given them for another use.'

'What are they for?' Norah asks.

'These are what we have been given to dig graves,' Nesta replies. 'You don't have to say it, they are totally impractical, but they are all Seki will give us. We've also asked for some timber to make crosses.'

Audrey and Norah exchange a look.

'Why don't you give them to us and we'll look after the cemetery preparation. We will get others to help, but it will be our responsibility. Is that all right with you?' Norah says.

Mrs Hinch stops in her tracks, looking from one woman to the other. 'Are you sure? I don't know if this is a short- or long-term thing. It's a lot to offer and a lot for me to ask.'

'Let us make it one less thing for you to worry about,' Audrey says.

For a moment, Mrs Hinch's legendary demeanour falters, her voice quivering as she hands each of the women a machete. 'Thank you. You both have given so much to the women in this camp with your voices and now, now you are doing this.'

Within days, three women are dead and Audrey and Norah have dug shallow graves in an area just outside the camp where

277

wildflowers flourish. Seki has been true to his word and provided some wood for the women to carve small crosses.

Norah and Audrey are perched on small wooden stools in front of a raging firepit. They suffer the heat of the flames as they each hold a rusted screwdriver in the fire, before they burn the names of the dead women into the crosses. While time-consuming and exhausting, they nevertheless cherish this last act they can perform for the unfortunate women who have succumbed to disease. At the gravesite, Mother Laurentia and Sister Catherina conduct the services, and flowers are placed lovingly on the graves.

Mrs Hinch calls a meeting with Margaret, Mother Laurentia and Nesta.

'It is Christmas Day tomorrow; I have been told there will be some pork to go with our rice. By pork, I am to understand that two baby piglets will be given to us to prepare and cook.'

'Please . . . please don't tell me we have to k-kill them first?' Mother Laurentia stammers.

'I don't think so, but I can't be sure. However, if they come to us alive, I will have no problem dealing with them. Too many of us are too ill and too hungry to be squeamish right now. Am I right, Sister James?'

'You are, and I'll help you if needed,' Nesta answers.

'What we *need* is for the strongest amongst us to spend the morning getting the fires ready, plenty of firewood, as I expect it will take some time to roast a whole animal.'

Once all three kitchens have been stocked with firewood, the cooking pits are lit and soon are blazing. It is well into the morning before three soldiers arrive – two with the piglets (thankfully already dead) and the other a sack of rice. Placing the carcasses on the table, they draw their bayonets and remove the legs from the animals, before taking them away.

'Oh, well, we'll just have to make do with legless pigs,' Mrs Hinch says as she rolls her sleeves up to help prepare the meat for cooking.

The sun has set when the women and children leave their huts to eat. The mood is subdued, as yet more internees are dying, and Christmas isn't celebrated this year with handmade gifts. The women have brought their own chairs from the living blocks and now sit in the clearing in the middle of the camp, as they eagerly await the arrival of food. The smell of roast pork is the only topic of conversation.

Margaret calls on a few members of her original choir, who move with her to the centre of the gathering.

'I know we all think there is nothing to sing about, nothing joyous about this day for any of us. I am certainly not going to preach, the time for that has long past. However, if no one objects, might we sing a carol or two while we wait for our food?'

No one objects; in fact, small smiles appear around the table, but it's the children who look most excited.

'We'll start with "Silent Night",' Margaret tells the women of the choir.

The first notes spring forth as she slowly lowers her raised arm. One by one, the audience join the choir in a sweet rendition of the most beloved carol. The voices of the beaten, half-starved, sick and exhausted ring out through the camp: they are not yet broken.

As they move onto 'Oh Come, All Ye Faithful', patients from the hospital stagger towards them, supported by Nesta and her nurses. They add their weak and croaky voices to the music.

They sing a rousing chorus of 'Land of Hope and Glory' one more time as the food is finally served.

As they begin to sing, Captain Seki appears and stands just outside the gathering, a small gesture of respect for the song Captain Miachi had once requested as an encore.

Eating their Christmas dinner, Audrey watches Ena placing morsels of her food onto June's plate. Using wisdom and ingenuity beyond her years, June distracts Ena by pointing something or someone out, and sneaks the food back onto Ena's plate.

'What did you think of Seki turning up tonight?' Audrey asks Ena and Norah.

'I wasn't surprised,' Norah says. 'Just like Miachi, he seems to love that song, which is strange, to say the least.'

'I was talking to Mother Laurentia, and she asked me if the voice orchestra was ever going to perform again,' Ena replies.

'What did you say?' Norah asks.

'I didn't know what to say. I mumbled about how difficult it was to rehearse, how no one has the energy. I hope we can, but realistically I don't think so.'

'I would love us to re-form, but I think that time has come and gone. Still, let's not let that thought spoil tonight and how special this day has been,' Norah tells them both.

'I think we'll sing again one day; I have to believe we haven't heard the last of Ravel,' Audrey says, smiling at her two best friends.

The start of 1945 arrives without being marked, the women now burying many of their friends every day. Almost all of the nurses have malaria, now relying on the others to nurse them. Ena is stricken with Banka fever; Norah and Audrey carry her to the hospital, June hanging on tightly to her favourite aunt's hand.

'We'll look after her,' Nesta, thankfully free of malaria, assures them.

'What can we do?' Norah pleads. 'I'll do anything.'

'If you can bring us cool water from the stream, that will help lower her fever, and, of course, a three-course meal would go a long way to speeding up her recovery,' Nesta says, trying for a moment of humour.

'She can have my ration,' Audrey says.

'Mine too,' June pipes up.

'I know you want to give her your food, little one. But you're a growing girl and you need all the food we can get for you,' Norah says.

'I'm a big girl now, I'm eight.'

Norah looks away suddenly, choking back a sob.

'Yes, my darling girl, you are big now, but big girls also need to eat. OK?'

'June, what good will you be to Aunty Ena if she has to look after you when she's all better?' Nesta asks her. 'We'll get as much food into her as we can. You can stay and change her wet towels, that will be a great help.'

'I have somewhere to go, can you two look after her?' Norah asks Audrey and June.

'Where do you have to be that's more important than being here?' Audrey asks.

But Norah has already left, the door to the hospital swinging shut behind her.

Hurrying to the barbed-wire fence, she takes a quick look around and, seeing no soldiers nearby, she slips under the wire and runs in crouch towards the huts on the hill. Towards the homes of the women here to entertain the Japanese officers.

She knocks on the door of the first hut she comes to. When there is no answer, she nudges the door open.

'Hello, is there anybody here?' Norah calls.

As she steps inside, a woman appears from the kitchen.

'Can I help you?' she asks.

Norah begins to babble. 'It's my sister, she's so sick, you see. She needs food, and they don't give us enough, but I have to help her. She's my sister, the best sister you could hope for . . . and . . .' Norah drifts off when she sees the puzzled expression on the woman's face.

'Your sister is sick, I understand, but how can I help? I am not a doctor. I'm a—'

'No, no! I'm not asking you to see her.'

'Then what do you want from me?'

'Food. You all get extra food, so much of it. We've seen it being delivered. I want just a little. For my sister. I beg you.'

'What is your name? I am Tante Peuk.' Tante is smiling and Norah is immediately hopeful.

'I'm Norah, Norah Chambers, and my sister is Ena.'

'A pleasure to meet you, Norah.'

'I apologise again for my rudeness, but I'm desperate. If I could get some food for her, she might have a chance.'

'How long have you been a prisoner of the Japanese?'

'Since February 1942.'

'Oh. I'm so sorry, that's so long. Yes, I have extra food – have you got something to pay for it?'

'What? Pay? I . . . I don't have any money. I wouldn't be here if I had money. I have the clothes I'm standing in, that's all. Are you really not going to give me life-saving food for my sister because I can't pay you?'

Tante Peuk looks down at Norah's left hand. 'What about that?'

Norah raises her hand to catch sight of her wedding ring. She sighs; it's the only thing she has to remind her of John. It hangs halfway down her skinny finger, threatening to fall off.

'My wedding ring?'

'Do you want food for your sister or not?'

Norah plays with the ring before sliding it off. Kissing it, she hands it to Tante Peuk.

Over the next week, Norah feeds Ena with small quantities of vegetables and dried fish along with her rice ration. When her fever finally breaks, Ena's strength slowly returns. Audrey has asked repeatedly where she got the food from, but Norah can't bring herself to tell her she sold her wedding ring. Watching her sister improve, Norah has no regrets for having parted with it. She knows John will understand and applaud her for doing the right thing – the only thing. A ring can be replaced, a sister can't.

In the first month of 1945, seventy-seven women die. More foliage around the cemetery has to be cleared to make room for the growing number of coffins. A human chain of twenty of the strongest women ferry the dead from the camp to their graves.

'How long is this going to go on?' Norah says. She and Audrey are perched in front of the firepit most days, burning names and dates of death into small, misshapen crosses before forcing them into the hard earth.

'Please God, not much longer,' Audrey says. 'I know these crosses are to honour the dead, but it's a terribly sad and awful job.'

'The nurses have the worst job, though,' Norah observes. 'Those that aren't sick are taking care of everyone else.'

'And they've just lost Sister Ray. The first nurse to die.'

'It's horrible, isn't it? After standing in the sun that day; I'm sure that didn't help her fight off whatever she died of in the end.'

'Her uniform's ready.' Nesta had prepared Ray's outfit herself, giving it a good airing, dousing dirty smudges with a little water and scrubbing.

283

With no time to grieve, the nurses begin to dress Ray in her uniform.

'It's the first time we're wearing ours since we were captured,' says Betty. The uniform hangs off their emaciated frames. 'I'm just glad we've managed to hang on to them.'

'Ray will get the full honours,' Nesta says. 'The coffin's not up to much, but she has the respect of the Royal Australian Army.' Nesta's voice breaks as six nurses step forwards to carry Ray to her resting place in the cemetery. 'One last thing.' Nesta lays a small bunch of wildflowers on her chest.

The nurses line up behind the coffin-bearers and begin their slow march to the burial site.

'Look,' Vivian says, unable to hold back her tears. The street is lined with internees, standing as guards of honour as the procession heads towards the gates of the camp. Even the soldiers remove their caps as the women approach. Both Mother Laurentia and Margaret wait with Bibles in their hands. Dozens of women join them at the graveside.

A nurse steps forwards, a borrowed Bible in hand, and she begins to read.

'*They shall hunger no more, neither thirst anymore; neither shall the sun light on them, nor any heat.*'

The beautiful, brief service is over and Norah and Audrey begin to fill the grave with earth, before Nesta stops them.

'Thank you, but we'll do this – it's the last thing we can do for her.'

'Nesta, Nesta! I don't know if I can carry on,' Betty says, bursting out into the garden where her friend is taking a short break in the shade. Betty sinks to the floor, a sobbing mess.

'What's happened? Talk to me. Are you ill?'

'It's Blanche!' Betty explains through her tears. 'I can't stand not being able to help her. She practically saved me and so many others when we were stranded in the sea. It's not fair.'

Nesta gives her a quick hug and calls for one of the other girls to come and sit with her, before she hurries to Blanche's side. Kneeling beside the sick woman, Nesta gently takes her hand.

'I'm so sorry, so sorry,' Blanche whimpers. 'I should be up and helping.'

'It's OK, I'm here. I'm here.'

Blanche opens her eyes. 'Nesta, oh, Nesta. Will you tell the others I hate to be a burden?'

'Oh, darling Blanche, you are no bother. All you have to do is rest and get better.'

'I'm taking too long.'

'You'll get better when you're good and ready, and until then we'll take care of you.'

'I'm not going to get better, Nesta.'

Nesta gasps as she looks into the pale, watery eyes of her friend, whose trembling hand she is still holding. Now she understands why Betty is so upset. Lying down on the bed, Nesta wraps Blanche in her arms, Blanche's body convulsing as she fights the deep guttural sobs that wrack her emaciated frame.

'Sshh,' Nesta whispers. 'I'm right here and not going anywhere.'

It is dark when Betty gently shakes Nesta awake.

'Nesta, wake up. Blanche has gone.'

Blanche looks as though she's asleep, and more peaceful than she has ever looked in life, in this place.

'There's a coffin ready,' Betty tells Nesta. 'We'll bury her in the morning.'

'And flowers, she loves flowers.'

'We'll pick them fresh first thing.'

Nesta stretches her aching limbs. All the nurses are present, holding each other, softly crying. Another one of theirs has passed in this desolate camp, without ever knowing freedom.

Betty and Nesta march in front of the coffin, heads held high, as they make their way towards the cemetery. The weight of Blanche's last words are heavy on all their shoulders. The previous evening, the nurses had poured their hearts out, repeating those painful final words, Blanche's apology for taking too long to die, for not wanting to be a burden. Their anger towards their captors was vociferous, but eventually, exhausted and bereft, they fell asleep in one another's arms.

Ena, Norah and Audrey help the nurses cover Blanche's grave with jungle soil. Many have gone to gather wildflowers and soon the mound is covered with dazzling colour.

'You go home, I'm going down to the stream to get some fresh water. Audrey and I have a lot of crosses to make today,' Norah whispers to Ena as they head back to the camp.

'Do you want me to go?' Ena says. 'Unless you want the walk.'

'I could do with the walk before sitting in front of the fire all day. And anyway, you need to check on June; she was very quiet this morning, I'm worried she may have a temperature.'

Picking up a bucket, Norah heads down to the water. Several women are bathing downstream, others filling buckets, kerosene tins, whatever they have on hand to use as a vessel.

Stepping cautiously into the middle of the stream to fill her bucket, from the corner of her eye Norah spies movement on the hill beyond. A woman is staggering up the slope. She stumbles, hits the ground. Crawling towards her hut, she gets to her feet and pushes open the door, collapsing on the threshold. Norah recognises her as Tante Peuk, the woman she brought food for Ena from.

Norah crosses the stream and makes her way up the hill. Tante Peuk is lying in the doorway. Norah drops down beside her.

'Water, water,' Tante mumbles.

Norah remembers her bucketful of water and brings a palmful of the cool liquid to the girl's lips, before helping her to her bed.

Once Tante is settled, Norah checks that she has food: she has far more than Norah, June and Ena eat in a week. She pours the last of her water into a jug, which she places with a cup beside Tante's bed.

'I'll come back tomorrow to check on you,' Norah says before leaving. Tante looks like she's fallen asleep. 'And I'll bring more water.'

CHAPTER 22

Camp IV
April 1945

'We cannot, we will not, move again, do you hear me?' Mrs Hinch insists to Captain Seki. Norah insisted on accompanying her for moral support. Surely Mrs Hinch is tired of confronting the captain on her own.

'Captain says you will do as you are told,' Ah Fat tells her, bluntly, after a lengthy monologue from Seki.

'Let's start again, shall we?' Mrs Hinch will not leave before she says everything she wants to say. 'We have heard rumours from the soldiers that we are to move camp once more; please can you reassure me that this is not the case. The next time we leave this place is when the Allies storm in here to liberate us.'

Ah Fat looks at Mrs Hinch and then at Norah, who smiles at him. Seki grunts, prompting Ah Fat to say *something*, but even Mrs Hinch knows he won't tell the captain of her firm belief that the prisoners will be liberated.

'Captain says he is sorry, but you will be leaving camp in four days' time. You should tell the women to get ready.'

'Get ready? You can't be serious!' Norah explodes. 'What about the sick? The starving. We're *dying*. How do you expect us to move when so many can't even stand up? And where are we going?'

'Captain says you will carry the sick, but you are going. He cannot tell you where. That is all.'

Placing her hands on her hips, Mrs Hinch takes a step closer to Seki's desk, glaring down at him. Slowly, he rises to meet her glare. She turns and storms out of the office, Norah running to keep up with her.

Ah Fat catches the door before it slams behind them.

Norah takes some time out of the following few days to visit Tante Peuk, bringing her water, cutting up her fruit, pleased to see that she is improving. Norah has said nothing to the others of these visits; to do so would mean explaining how she knew her in the first place. She has no desire to confess to Ena she sold her wedding ring for food.

'This is the last time I can visit,' Norah tells the young woman. 'We're moving camp tomorrow.'

'I'm sorry to hear that. Where are you going?'

'We don't know. But I can't come again, too many of us are sick.'

'Come and sit beside me, Norah.' Tante Peuk pats her bed.

Norah takes Tante Peuk's hand. 'I'll never forget you. You saved my sister's life.'

'And you've saved mine. I think we're even. Please go and be with your family,' Tante says, hugging her friend.

'Nesta, can you come here a moment, please?' Sister Catherina calls.

The women were ready at 6 a.m. as ordered. They waited in the heat and intermittent rain for the trucks to arrive. Five hours later, they pulled into the camp. Once the stretchers had been loaded on board, the women climbed in. Once more, they sped towards Muntok pier, where this nightmare began. A small launch was moored there, ready to whisk them away to the awaiting ship.

And now, one boatload has left for the ship, while Nesta waits on the pier with the other nurses for it to return.

Sister Catherina is kneeling beside a stretcher patient.

'How can I help?'

'I think she's dead. Would you check?'

Nesta quickly examines the woman and sighs.

'You're right. I'm so sorry. Did you know her?'

'I did. I don't know what to do.' Sister Catherina is holding the dead woman's hand.

'When the launch gets back, we'll put her on board. I think the only thing we can do is bury her at sea from the ship.'

When the launch returns, Nesta and Sister Catherina place the body on board and Sister Catherina takes her place beside her.

As the deck of the ship fills up with stretcher patients, most of the women find themselves crowded together below deck, enduring the suffocating heat.

As the ship begins its journey, Nesta gathers the able nurses together on deck. 'I think the women up here need to rotate with those down below and give everyone a break in the fresh air.'

'Absolutely agree,' Jean replies. 'Only problem will be persuading those who have staked a claim up here to do the right thing.'

'I'm sure everyone will see it's the only thing – never mind the right thing – to do,' Nesta insists. 'First, we'll assess everyone above and below deck to see who needs the most urgent attention. Let's get as many children up here as we can.'

'Nesta?' Sister Catherina calls, approaching the nurses. 'I can see how space is a problem, so why don't we have the burial before we leave the Strait? It will help to make a little more room up here.'

Nesta feels her eyes well up. Looking at the young nun, she feels distraught that this kind and, yes, angelic girl should have to help lower a body over the side of a ship chugging through the ocean.

'Thank you, Sister. I think there are enough of us to manage the burial.'

The nurses split into two groups: one to assess women and children below deck and the other above. Nesta joins those heading into the bowels and is immediately joined by Norah and Audrey.

'What can we do to help?' Norah asks.

'Thanks, ladies. We want to get the children up here as quickly as possible and any women who are in real distress. My other nurses are persuading those on deck to take a shift below.'

By evening, the rotations are well underway. However, there are yet more deaths and more burials at sea. When the ship drops anchor at the mouth of the Moesi River, everyone is too sunburnt and suffering from heat exhaustion to feel relieved. They all know that while night-time will deliver a cooling breeze, it will be accompanied by platoons of mosquitoes.

'Looks like we're going back to Palembang,' Margaret says. Beside her, June is asleep in Ena's lap and Ena is gently stroking her forehead. Ena's feet and legs are swollen from beri-beri.

'Can I be honest with you, Margaret?' Ena says, with a grimace as she tries to find a comfortable position without disturbing June.

'Of course. But I think I can guess what you're about to say. It's what we're all thinking.'

'I'm losing hope.' Ena won't meet her friend's eyes, appalled to be saying these words out loud. 'Going back into the jungle again feels like it's the end for us. How will we ever be found?'

'I wish I could say something positive about this move, but I can't, I'm struggling myself,' Margaret says. 'All we can do is look after each other, take care of the children and—'

'Please don't say pray.'

'You're right, my dear. It's my default phrase. But I'm sure you won't mind if I pray for all of us.'

'I'm pra— I'm hoping you will,' Ena says and both women manage a smile.

As day breaks, the ship lumbers up the Moesi River, before dropping anchor off the Palembang wharf. Japanese soldiers await their arrival. When the women disembark, the soldiers stand to one side, offering no help at all. It is a depressing sight. Soon, the wharf is loaded with stretchers with the sick and dying, with dead bodies awaiting burial, and the exhausted, starving women. Finally, they are ushered over some railway tracks to a grassy area beyond, where they are given some water.

Several hours pass, during which the women doze and rouse, doze and rouse, until a train pulls into the station. The stretcher patients and the dead are placed in the cattle wagons; everyone else is ordered into the carriages. And there they remain overnight, shut in airless compartments, the windows securely closed.

'Finally,' yawns Nesta. The internees awake to the train's engine firing up. A long hiss of steam erupts and the train begins its journey.

Hours later, after rumbling through the countryside and past small communities, they eventually arrive at the village of Loebok Linggau.

Nesta stands along with everyone else and bangs on the door to be let out.

'You stay! You stay!' a soldier barks at her, waving his rifle at the window.

'For how long?' Nesta yells.

But the soldiers turn away from the women and leave them on the train to endure another sweltering night.

'Ladies.' Nesta calls over her nurses to let them know seven stretcher patients died in the night. 'Even more will die if they don't let us out soon.'

And then, just as the words leave Nesta's lips, the order comes. 'Out now! Out now!' and the prisoners disembark and are counted, over and again.

'Not the right number!' a soldier screams.

'That's because some of us died in the night,' Nesta tells him with as much venom in her voice as she can muster.

Finally, they are ordered to board the waiting trucks, and driven further into the jungle on roads barely wide enough for the vehicles to fit.

When they eventually come to a stop, Nesta is in the back of one truck helping to soothe the stretcher patients with nothing more than words. She feels a hand on her arm and turns to find Norah outside, her eyes alive with worry.

'Nesta, you have to come quickly. It's Margaret.'

Jean appears at Norah's side as if summoned by magic.

'I can handle this, Nesta. You go to Margaret,' Jean says, climbing in the back to take her place.

On the ground beside another truck, a large group of women have gathered around the frail figure of Margaret Dryburgh. They move apart for Norah and Nesta. Ena is on the ground cradling Margaret's head in her lap, while Audrey is gently ushering June away.

'How long has she been like this?' Nesta asks.

'She stopped talking the first night we were on the train,' Ena tells her. 'I said I wanted to get you or one of the nurses to look at her, but she said no, she was just tired and needed to rest. This morning when I woke, she could barely open her eyes.'

Nesta checks Margaret's pulse, takes her hand in hers. 'Margaret, it's Nesta. Can you open your eyes for me? Please? Just a little.'

Nesta feels a slight squeeze on her hand. Slowly, painfully, Margaret opens her eyes and looks at the women around her, and a small, radiant smile fills her face before she closes her eyes for the last time.

Howls of 'No!' travel down the tracks.

Mrs Hinch stumbles from her truck and runs towards Margaret, pushing her way through the mourners to kneel beside her beloved friend. She looks at Nesta, who shakes her head. For the first time since being captured Mrs Hinch allows herself to cry.

The new camp, Belalau, is a disused rubber plantation. The huts are dilapidated and dank, yet some are relieved to see the camp is bisected by a running stream. The weakest amongst them take the first huts available. Everyone else, including those on stretchers, must negotiate a small hill down into a gully and over a narrow wooden bridge to the remaining huts. The nurses stay on the hill side of the stream, and it is here they carry Margaret's body, placing it respectfully inside one of the huts.

While Norah and Audrey occupy themselves carving the names and dates of death into eleven wooden crosses to honour the women who have died since leaving the ship, the twelfth cross sits on the ground, daring them to start carving Margaret's name.

They watch as a steady stream of women visit Margaret's body. A queue forms outside the hut as they wait their turn to say a final thank you and goodbye to the woman who brought so much joy and light into their lives in the jungle.

'I can't do it!' Norah weeps, thrusting the twelfth cross at Audrey.

'I think we both should do it,' Audrey says softly. 'You should at least write her name, you were her dearest friend, and I'll do the rest,' she offers, handing the cross back.

Norah gives a small nod of agreement. She holds her screwdriver over the naked flame, not backing away from the intense heat, hoping that physical pain will take away some of the ache she feels acutely in her chest.

Audrey pulls Norah's hand away from the fire, as the screwdriver is glowing red. Norah snaps from her trance, looks at the cross in one hand and the screwdriver in the other.

Gently, she places the cross on her lap and slowly starts to burn in the letters: M . . . a . . . r . . . g . . . Her tears fall on the seared initials and hiss.

Audrey places her arm around Norah's shoulders, hugging her tight, both giving and receiving support for the duty they are undertaking.

Nesta steps out of her hut and watches the two women. Her hands are shaking, the rage inside her threatening to explode.

'Sister James! Sister James, can I have a word.' Mrs Hinch's voice splinters the roaring noise in Nesta's head.

'What is it?' Nesta snaps, turning her head. 'Oh, Mrs Hinch, I'm so sorry. I don't know what's wrong with me, I . . .' Her eyes return to Norah, still carving Margaret's cross.

'Are you all right?' Mrs Hinch probes.

'Not really, but that's not important right now. Did you need something?'

'I never thought I'd be doing this again, but I've been to see the captain about where we can put a cemetery. They showed me a small clearing just outside the fence and will leave us a few tools. But what I came here to say is, would you help me select the perfect place for . . . for . . .'

Nesta understands. 'Of course I will. Let's go now, shall we?'

Nesta and Mrs Hinch survey the clearing. Nearby, banana trees throw a cool shade across the middle of the patch of dry ground.

'How about there? In the shade of the trees,' Nesta suggests.

'It's perfect, and she'll be surrounded by those who love her.'

'I'll arrange to have the graves dug and . . .' Nesta pauses to look at Mrs Hinch. 'Do we bury them at the same time? I don't know if we should have a separate service for . . . for . . . I mean, so many of us will want to be here, and they may not have the strength to wait while we bury everyone. What do you think?'

'I think we bury her first.'

'You can't say her name either, can you?' Nesta sighs.

'Not yet,' her friend admits. 'It's still too raw.'

CHAPTER 23

Camp V, Belalau
April 1945–September 1945

'Inchi, Inchi!' calls Ah Fat. Nesta slows her pace, but Mrs Hinch doesn't. 'Inchi, Inchi!'

Grasping Nesta's hand, Mrs Hinch hisses, 'Nesta, I swear I'll . . . Not today. Just not today.'

But Ah Fat is now running along beside the two women and, eventually, Mrs Hinch stops walking, and takes several deep breaths before turning to the interpreter.

'Go away. Now,' she says forcefully.

'Inchi, oh, Inchi, very sorry. I heard about Miss Margaret, s-so sorry,' Ah Fat stammers. He wipes away tears with the back of his hand.

Mrs Hinch stares at him, not trusting herself to speak. Finally, she gives him the smallest of nods, the barest of smiles. Turning away, she walks off as Nesta hurries after her.

'You know my Christian name,' Nesta says to her, to break the silence that has fallen over them as much as anything.

'Of course I do.'

'But I don't know yours.'

Mrs Hinch manages a warmer smile this time, before leaving Nesta and heading off towards Mother Laurentia's hut.

Norah and Audrey lead the coffin-bearers as they follow Mother Laurentia from the camp. Ena, whose legs are still swollen from the beri-beri, is assisted by Dr McDowell and Sister Catherina. As the procession moves towards the cemetery, every woman and child in the camp still capable of walking either lines the way or follows behind. The guards stand respectfully aside, their caps removed. Ah Fat is openly sobbing.

Lowering the coffin into the shallow grave is difficult, cumbersome and uses the last of the women's depleted strength. But once it's in the ground, Mother Laurentia begins the service by reading a poem written by Margaret Dryburgh: 'The Burial Ground'.

And then Nesta gives the eulogy.

'How can we even begin to show our gratitude to this woman who gave us purpose and a reason to live, if only to hear her incredible music each Saturday night? She gave us back our voices to sing, with passion and pride, our national anthems. Margaret wrote plays, poems and songs, and never wavered in her belief that we could all survive, even while others around us perished. She created beauty where only sickness and death prevailed, and whether the duration of our lives is long or short, we will never forget her . . .' Nesta clears her throat, but finds she is unable to continue.

Norah steps forwards and takes Nesta's hand. 'We will carry on looking up even when all around us is squalor and sickness. That is her greatest gift to us all,' she says, her eyes shining.

'I would like to bring this service to a close,' Mother Laurentia tells the crowds of mourners. 'Margaret so loved to sing "Land of Hope and Glory" and there isn't a better song to bring us all together right now and to remember her.'

Birds soar into the skies from the giant trees, circling overhead as the women's voices ring out. They are not the most powerful voices, and certainly nowhere near as robust as they were a year ago, but the women sing with passion nonetheless; today their hearts are full of love, and that is enough.

Every woman wants to take a turn dropping a little of the soil into the grave. When Margaret is finally buried, banana leaves are laid over the entire mound. As everyone steps back, Norah and Audrey together push the little cross into the soil.

Margaret Dryburgh
21ˢᵗ April, 1945

Norah, exhausted, joins her sister, who is sitting on the ground just outside the cemetery clearing. June squeezes between them.

Reaching into her pocket for a handkerchief which is not there, Norah's fingers close around a small metal object. She pulls it out and stares disbelievingly at the gold ring in the palm of her hand. Her wedding ring. She thinks back to the moment she sat on Tante's bed, when she hugged her goodbye.

Norah sways suddenly, on the verge of fainting, before she feels Ena's steadying arm around her shoulders. Wrapped in her sister's embrace, Norah slips the ring back on her finger.

'Inchi, Inchi!' Mrs Hinch is chased down by Ah Fat as she and Norah return from the stream with buckets half full of water; neither of them has the strength to carry a full one. It's been weeks since they arrived at the camp, and along with the disease that is running rampant among the inhabitants, there have been torrential monsoons, and it is difficult for them to think of a time when they might be dry again.

'Hmm?' she grunts.

'Captain Seki wants to see you.'

'We will drop this water off then come to the office.'

'No, you come now. Leave water. Captain wants to see you now.'

'We will meet you there after we have dropped off this water, Ah Fat,' says Mrs Hinch, heading belligerently away. 'We've got little enough power as it is,' she explains to Norah. 'We have to take our small victories where we can.'

The women arrive at the hut deemed the captain's office to find Ah Fat waiting for them. Captain Seki stands from behind his desk when they enter and he speaks to Ah Fat.

'Captain says he is sorry to hear Miss Margaret died. He liked her, he liked her music.'

'Thank the captain for his words, I will pass them on to the women.'

Ah Fat translates. Seki nods and sits down.

'Is that it?' Mrs Hinch asks.

'Yes, you can go now.'

'But I have to talk to the captain about what's going on here.'

'Inchi, I said—'

'No!' Norah steps forwards. 'We need to tell the captain that we're in serious trouble.' Her grief and growing weakness are momentarily forgotten as she gets into her stride. 'The monsoon rains have flooded the camp. The stream has swallowed up the bridge so we can't get to the huts on the other side.' She takes a deep breath, preparing herself to say more, but Mrs Hinch is already speaking.

'We're ill and so weak we can't fight off any infection. Do you know that mice feed on our toes while we sleep? The winds have whipped off the roofs and rain pours into the huts ... and ... and ...'

'And the soldiers are doing their business upstream and it's pouring into the camp when the banks overflow,' Norah finishes for her.

Both women stand panting before Ah Fat and Captain Seki. Ah Fat makes no attempt to translate.

'Go now!' is all he says.

'Concert! Concert! Outside now!' the guards bellow, storming up and down the camp.

'What's going on?' Norah catches Ah Fat's arm as he joins the guards' cries.

'Captain Seki invites you to a concert!' he says. 'Just like Miss Margaret did for you, we will do for you. Outside now.'

The guards are now ordering everyone up the hill. Swinging long sticks, they corral the women, forcing them to walk faster. '*Hurry, hurry*,' they berate them.

Those living at the head of the camp scamper down the gully, and drag themselves up the hill, helping each other as they go. The sick are allowed to remain behind.

The large rubber trees provide shade, and the women look around to find themselves sitting in an idyllic setting overlooking the lush abundance of the jungle and the stream below, melodically tinkling over pebbles. They don't have to wait too long before Captain Seki leads a group of thirty musicians onto the hillside.

For the next two hours, they entertain the women with music consisting of German waltzes and marching songs. They are also treated to the beautiful male voice of what the women feel certain

301

is a Western-trained performer. For a brief time, the women lose themselves in the rhythms, the setting and the comfort of their friends around them.

'I wonder what Margaret would have made of all this,' Ena ponders.

'She would have appreciated the talent, certainly,' Norah says instantly. 'Some of them are excellent musicians.'

'And they have real instruments. How long has it been since we heard instruments?' Audrey adds.

'Oh, I don't know, what Norah did with her voice orchestra was pretty great,' Ena says, with a grin.

'It was better than great. I would listen to you again over the real thing any day,' Audrey tells them.

'We weren't bad, were we?' Norah agrees.

June and July of 1945 come and go before Mrs Hinch is summoned to the captain's office once more.

'I wonder if something's up?' Mrs Hinch wonders aloud, as she heads to his office with Nesta in tow.

'Like what?' Nesta asks.

'The soldiers, they're different. Haven't you seen them clustered together in groups around the camp, arguing?'

Nesta considers for a moment. 'I guess so, but, honestly, we're kept pretty busy just looking after everyone.'

'Captain Seki, how can I help?' Mrs Hinch asks the captain as Ah Fat leads the women into the office.

'Captain wants all women, including sick ones, to come to the hill now. Please go and get the women.'

Mrs Hinch opens her mouth to object but closes it again.

'There's definitely something going on,' Nesta concludes as they leave the office.

'He wouldn't look me in the eye; did you notice?' Mrs Hinch says.

'I'm more worried about how we're going to gather all of the women,' Nesta says with a sigh. 'I mean, so many are too ill or weak to leave their huts.'

'I'll help where I can, Nesta,' offers Mrs Hinch. And then, 'You're worried about Norah, aren't you?'

'I am. Her leg is badly infected after she was bitten by the ants.'

'It's not just the sick we're going to have to help. Everyone else is heartily bored of Seki's ranting and railing.'

'Well, we'll just have to do our best, won't we?' Mrs Hinch decides.

In the end, Nesta has to enlist the help of Dr McDowell, Ena, Audrey and all of the nurses to help her persuade the women to assemble.

Nesta helps Norah up the hill as she can no longer walk on her own.

As the women gather, Captain Seki, Ah Fat and several soldiers arrive. The captain puffs out his chest before launching into what the women believe is just another pointless speech, all the while praying they don't have to leave this place again. When he has said enough, he nods to Ah Fat.

'Captain Seki says the war is over, English and Americans will be here soon. We are now friends.'

If Seki is expecting the women to burst into whoops of joy, he is mistaken. The women don't move and stare uncomprehendingly at one another. Seki doesn't get his moment. He storms off the hill, the soldiers and Ah Fat scurrying after him.

Slowly, the women pull themselves to their feet and return to their huts. Their mood is sombre. How many times can they be tested like this? If the war is over, where are their rescuers?

Where is their sanctuary? No one amongst them can imagine leaving this place.

'Is it really happening?' Jean asks Nesta when they return to their huts. With no tangible evidence that anything has changed, she knows as well as every other nurse that they must carry on with their duties. Before Nesta can reply, the door of their hut bursts open.

'Come quick!' urges Mrs Hinch. 'To the gates. Come now.'

Nesta and Jean follow Mrs Hinch to the camp entrance, where a couple of trucks have pulled up and where soldiers are unloading large Red Cross parcels.

Nesta is handed a box, which she tears open.

'I don't believe it!' she exclaims. 'Medicine. Bandages.'

Jean digs further and pulls out a small parcel which unfolds into a mosquito net. Tears spring to her eyes as she rubs the simple fabric between her fingers.

'How many lives could this scrap of material have saved, Nesta?' she says.

'And to think they had it all along,' Nesta says with a sigh.

In the following days, there are more deliveries of the Red Cross parcels, more medicines arrive, and the women are allowed to eat as much of the fruit from the trees as they like. Allied planes are seen regularly flying overhead, circling ever lower to acknowledge the women waving at them from the jungle.

Slowly, in small groups of twos and threes, Nesta, the nurses and the women who are strong enough to walk test their freedom by leaving the camp, escaping beyond the wire fencing, before turning around and coming back. They have nowhere else to go.

* * *

'Do you believe it, Nesta? Do you believe the war is really over?' Norah stammers, too weak to sound enthusiastic. They are seated in the makeshift hospital, and Nesta is delicately unwrapping the bandage around Norah's leg. Stained yellow, the final layer is stuck fast to Norah's skin.

'Well, if it's true, I just don't know how they're going to get us out; there's barely a road and none of us can walk any distance.'

'I will crawl out of here if I have to. I must find John and Sally.'

'I'll crawl with you if I have to.'

'How is it looking?' Norah asks, as Nesta struggles to peel away her bandage.

'It's no worse, maybe marginally better. Let's hope the Red Cross medicines start working soon.'

'Are you telling me what you think I want to hear?'

'No, Norah, I wouldn't do that to you. The infection doesn't seem to have spread since yesterday. That's a good thing.'

'Thank you, I didn't think you would.'

Sunlight bursts through the door as Betty enters. She stands in the doorway, a silhouette in the dark hut.

'Men!' she gasps. 'Men are coming. Norah, they're British.'

Nesta jumps to her feet. 'The army, you mean? To get us out of here?'

'No, no. They're prisoners, like us. They've been released from their camp nearby, and apparently, they're on their way here. Now! Can you believe it? Men, our men!'

The news finally sinks in.

'John!' exclaims Norah. 'Oh, my God! Could John be one of them?'

'I don't know! I hope so, Norah. I really do,' Betty says.

'Wrap my leg, Nesta, hurry and help me get out of here. He's coming, John is coming. I just know it.'

305

'Lie still, I'll be quick, then I'll help you outside.'

With care, Nesta applies red palm oil sparingly onto the infected area of Norah's leg. Gently bending her knee, placing her foot on the ground, she wraps the clean bandage around the leg, tucking in the end to keep it in place. As soon as Nesta has finished, she helps Norah to her feet, supporting her around the waist as they limp outside. Norah gasps with the effort, Nesta being so much shorter than her.

'Oh, Norah,' says Nesta. 'You're so weak. Please hold on tight to me and we'll find somewhere to sit.'

Clinging to the tiny nurse, Norah makes her way into the sun. Nesta lowers her against the wall and then sits beside her.

'I'll wait with you if that's OK,' she says and Norah takes her hand.

'I'll need you, my friend. One way or another,' Norah says. If John is here, she will celebrate with Nesta, but if he isn't, she will need her comfort and consolation. 'He's coming, I just know he is,' Norah repeats over and over, as she reaches out to grasp Nesta's hand. 'But what if he doesn't come? I mean, he was so ill, and it's been three and a half years . . . and . . .'

'Norah, listen.' Nesta squeezes her hand and both women turn their heads towards the gates of the camp. A very unfamiliar sound has rendered them silent.

'They're speaking English.' They can hear the rumble of male voices snaking towards them. 'They're here,' whispers Norah, and then, louder, 'John! John!'

Nesta and Norah watch bedraggled and emaciated men stumble into the camp to be surrounded by the surviving English women, the nuns and everyone else looking on from a distance. There are cries of relief and exhaustion as husbands and wives are reunited. Howls of despair as man after man is told his wife and, in many instances, children have not survived. Frightened children hide behind their mothers, wary of the unkempt men claiming to be their fathers.

Ena runs towards the hut to find Norah sitting outside with Nesta. The sisters wait in silence, hands tightly clasped.

The flow of men into the camp thins out. Nesta pulls Norah close. Ena is fighting back her tears. She's not ready for this, not ready to find words of comfort should they be informed that John has died. Nesta closes her eyes, overcome, willing the tears that threaten to stay away. She feels, more than hears, Norah whisper.

'It's John . . .'

Nesta opens her eyes and looks at the stranger stumbling towards them.

'Ae you sure?' Ena says. He is so thin and looks so much older than John.

Norah holds out her arms as she struggles to find her voice.

'John, John,' she mouths.

In that moment, in that place and time, their squalor seems to fall away. The jungle heat, buzzing mosquitoes, emaciation and disease, all of it, just for an instant, is absent, as one woman watches the man she loves lock eyes with her. The lopsided smile she fell in love with so many years ago slowly spreads across his face as his hands reach out to her.

'Oh, my God, it's him, it *is* John,' Ena whispers.

Nesta stands and takes a few steps away. This is a family reunion, but not her family. She watches as John's eyes light up on seeing Norah. He comes to his full height, and the fatigue that has etched so many lines in his face recedes.

John tries to run, but his body, just like Norah's, can't sustain his joy. He stumbles, trips and falls a few feet from the sisters.

And then he's struggling to his feet, summoning all the strength he can muster, to place one foot in front of the other.

'Oh, my God, John,' Norah weeps. 'What have they done to you?'

Nesta doesn't bother telling her he looks just like his emaciated wife.

'Don't hurry, my darling,' she whispers. 'I'm not going anywhere.'

With one final lurch, John collapses on the ground in front of Norah. They embrace and hold on, never wanting to let go. Apart, they were broken, incomplete, but together they are whole again, or nearly: there is still one person missing from their family.

John sees Ena sitting beside his wife and now he hugs her too. They are all sobbing.

Squeezing between the two women, John wraps his arms around his wife and his sister-in-law, each of whom rests a tear-stained face on his shoulder. Nesta is weeping too, and while John has no idea who she is, he has a feeling she is a friend to the two women.

'Aunty Ena! Aunty Ena!' June calls out.

Shock hits John like a thunderbolt. 'Sally! Is it Sally?' he cries.

'Oh no, no, my darling. This is June,' Norah says.

'But where is Sally?' John is looking all around, trying to see through and past the crowds of men and women embracing, consoling each other.

Norah gently turns his head to look at her. 'It's not Sally, she's with Barbara and the boys, remember?' she whispers. 'June is a little girl who, well, I suppose adopted Ena. Do you remember when we were together at Muntok, John, before they took you away? There was a little girl clinging to Ena's skirts. It was June. We believe her mother died after the ship was attacked and Ena and I have become her aunties.'

June drops into Ena's lap, looking at the strange man sitting between her aunties. John struggles to control his breathing as he looks at the little girl. She's about the size of his daughter when he last saw her. She smiles at him and his heart melts. Cautiously, he reaches out and touches her hair.

'Hello, June, do you remember me?'

'No.'

'This is John, he's Aunty Norah's husband,' Ena tells her.

'Why did he call me Sally?'

'Aunty Norah and Uncle John have a little girl named Sally; he thought you might be her.'

'Uh-huh, I'm not, sorry. But you'll find her, don't worry. Just like I'll find my daddy.'

'Yes, you will, my darling,' Ena whispers, hugging her tightly.

Nesta is transfixed by the sight of this family coming together again. She is unable to move away, unable to speak, as so much pain, so much joy, is played out in front of her eyes. She suddenly feels very dizzy and slides down the wall.

A hand reaches out to her.

'Nesta? Are you OK?'

Vivian towers over her, her own eyes moist.

'Why don't we go and get some tea? We've even got the real stuff now.'

Nesta takes her hand and comes to her feet.

'It's time for you to have a break, Sister James, you've done your duty; your shift is over.'

Allowing Vivian to lead her away, Nesta looks up at her colleague, her friend, the one amongst them all who has witnessed, experienced and suffered so much more than anyone here.

'It's been a bloody long shift, Bully, a bloody long one.'

'Three years, seven months, but who's counting,' Vivian says, laughing.

The following week, excitement in the camp ramps up when two young Dutch soldiers and a Chinese military official literally drop in, by parachute.

Mrs Hinch, Dr McDowell and Nesta sit down with the visitors.

'We're an advance party,' the Chinese officer tells them. 'The Allies will be here soon. Just a little more patience and we'll get you back home.'

'How soon will that be?' Nesta asks.

'Well, we'd love to stay here and hear your stories, but the best way we can help you is to return to our base and let headquarters know we've found you.'

'I wholeheartedly agree,' says Mrs Hinch. 'How far away is your base?'

'We're at Loebok Linggau.'

'Oh, I know that place! That's where the train stopped before we were brought up here.'

'Yes, the train line ends there, but we can't move you until we work out how to get you all off the island. I'm sorry, but it might take a few days. But now we know where you are, you'll be getting airdrops of supplies.'

'Can I please ask you to do something for us?' Nesta asks.

'Of course, anything, if we can.'

'Can you get word to the Australian Army that you have located their nurses?'

The official looks long and hard at Nesta. 'You're a nurse?'

'With the Australian Army.'

'We will contact them immediately.'

* * *

310

Two days later, three men in military uniform walk into the camp. They are tall, fit, young, and two of them are wearing berets bearing the Australian military badge.

Vivian bursts into the nurses' hut.

'The Aussies are here! Oh, my God, the Aussies are here!'

Before anyone can react, two young paratroopers come through the door. Time stands still as the men take in the gaunt, broken bodies of the women.

'Are you the nurses?' one asks, unable to keep the shock from his voice.

Nesta steps forwards. 'Yes, sir. We are nurses of the Australian Army. I'm Sister James.'

'Sisters. I'm Bates and this is Gillam. Are you ... are you all right?'

'We are now that you're here. Are you really Aussies?'

'We are and our priority is to get you out of here. There are a lot of people back home wanting to know if you're still alive.'

'We are, but barely,' Jean tells them, 'and we have lost many. Are there just the two of you?'

'Three of us actually; we're here with Major Jacobs from the South African paratroopers – he's gone to find the Japanese administration office.'

All eyes have been on the officer who is speaking, Bates, and no one notices, at first, that Gillam is breathing heavily, clenching his fists, his right hand resting on the revolver at his hip.

'Sarge! Look at these women!' he suddenly explodes.

'It's OK, Gillam. We're here now, we've got them.'

Before anyone can respond, Gillam runs from the hut. 'I'm going to kill them!' he yells.

The nurses, led by Bates, follow him outside. Gillam has his revolver drawn and is running towards a Japanese soldier. Gillam pounces on him, knocking him to the ground, before yanking him to his feet and marching him towards two other soldiers he has spied.

Bates asks Nesta where the Japanese administration office is, and then bolts from the hut. He bursts in on Captain Seki, who, with Ah Fat's help, is talking with Major Jacobs.

'Sir, the Australian nurses,' Bates announces. 'We've found them, but they're a bloody mess. And Gillam has lost it, sir. He's threatening to shoot every soldier. You'd better come quick; he'll bloody well do it.'

Jacobs runs from the hut with Bates. They head towards a large crowd that is silently watching Gillam marching up and down a line of Japanese soldiers he has just rounded up. They stand with their backs against the barbed-wire fence while Gillam shouts and swears in their petrified faces. He is still waving his revolver. Major Jacobs slowly approaches.

'Gillam, Gillam, listen to me, son,' he says quietly. 'Don't do this. Now is not the time. They will be punished, but not by you. Put your gun away, there's a good chap.'

Gillam looks at his senior office, and back at the guards.

'Sergeant, I'm telling you to lower your weapon.'

Slowly, Gillam holsters his gun.

'I just hate their guts,' he tells the soldiers.

Bates turns to Nesta.

'I'll bring him back to your hut; can your nurses look after him? I need to speak to the major a minute.'

'Of course.'

'Tell me, Sister, how many of you are there – I mean, here, right now?'

'Twenty-four.'

'But you were a party of sixty-five. Am I right?'

'Not any longer.'

There is a long silence.

'Thank you, Sister.'

The crowd disperses as Gillam and the nurses head back to their hut. Bates returns to the admin office with Nesta.

'Major, I'd like you to send an emergency request to the Australian Army headquarters.'

'Certainly, Bates. Write your message down and I'll have it sent from their ops room.'

'Do you know how many women are in the camp?' Bates asks.

'There's around two hundred and fifty of us,' says Nesta. 'It used to be more . . .'

Bates nods to her and takes the notepad and pencil offered to him by Ah Fat.

He writes:

HAVE ENCOUNTERED AMONG 250 REPEAT 250 BRITISH FEMALE INTERNEES IN LOEBUKLINGGAU CAMP STOP SISTER NESTA JAMES AND 23 OTHER SURVIVING MEMBERS OF AUSTRALIAN ARMY NURSING SERVICES REMNANTS OF CONTINGENT A.A.N.S EVACUATED FROM MALAYA IN VYNER BROOKE STOP IN VIEW OF THEIR PRECARIOUS HEALTH SUGGEST YOU ENDEAVOUR TO ARRANGE AIR TRANSPORT DIRECT TO AUSTRALIA FROM HERE SOONEST STOP AM COLLECTING PARTICULARS MASSACRE OF A.A.N.S. AT BANGKA ISLAND FOR LATER TRANSMISSION

Reading the cable, Major Jacobs shakes his head in angry astonishment.

'It's beyond belief,' he says.

'And yet it happened,' Nesta says.

'Thank you, sir, Sister. We're going back to the nurses' hut, where Sister James' nurses are looking after Gillam. And we thought we were coming here to look after them.' Bates manages a small, tight smile.

'The irony is not lost on me, Sergeant,' says the major. 'I'll come and find you when it's time to leave, as we have a lot to plan.'

'Sister James,' begins Bates as they head back to the hut. 'Quite a lot has happened while you've been incarcerated in the jungle.'

'I can imagine,' Nesta says. 'But we won, and that's the main thing, right?'

'Yes. But the cost to all was too high.' Bates takes a breath. 'Two atomic bombs were dropped on the Japanese by the Americans, effectively ending the war.'

'Atomic bombs?' Nesta says hesitantly. 'But they're . . . they're . . .'

'Catastrophic for those unlucky enough to live in Hiroshima and Nagasaki.'

Nesta feels a chill run up her spine.

Bates lays a hand on her shoulder.

'Nasty business war, Sister James.'

But Nesta can only nod.

The day after Gillam, Bates and Major Jacobs leave, a low-flying plane appears above the trees, to parachute crates of supplies into the camp.

'This one's medicine! Get it to the hospital quickly,' someone shouts.

'And there's so much food. A banquet!' another announces.

'This one has a message on it.'

314

A large crate, reinforced with extra slats of timber, sits adrift of the rest.

Betty rushes to the box and begins to read.

'"Baked with love this morning from the cooks of the Royal Aus—"' Betty drops to her knees hugging the crate, sobbing. Another nurse takes over.

'"Baked with love this morning from the cooks of the Royal Australian Navy".'

The crate is prised apart.

'There's another message inside. Let me read it to you,' Jean says. As her eyes sweep over the words, she bites her lip. This will be tough. '"This morning, the cooks on HMAS *Warrego* and HMAS *Manoora* fought off their entire crews who attempted to enter the mess and take part in the cooking of this small token of our gratitude, respect and love for the brave women and children who have survived in the jungles of Sumatra. Please accept and enjoy scones with strawberry jam and cream. We'll get you home, ladies, each and every one of you. Lieutenant Commander Leslie Brooks".'

The food – fruit, vegetables, meat, eggs – is pored over, handled and passed around the women. Here is everything they need to nourish themselves and begin healing.

With military precision, tables are set up in the camp; the scones, jam and cream distributed between the internees. The men and women fall silent as they enjoy this bounty. The scones are declared the best they have ever tasted.

'What is this? Vege . . . Vegemite?' one of the English women calls out, holding up a small jar of thick dark brown syrup.

The nurses squeal and rush to inspect the jar.

'That smells terrible,' the English woman confirms, having managed to unscrew the lid and hold it to her nose.

Fingers are dipped into the jar and popped into mouths, to the pleasurable groans of the nurses.

'Is that how you eat it?'

Between moans, one of the nurses says, 'Yes! I mean, no – usually you spread it on toast or just plain bread.'

'There's bread here!' someone shouts. 'Let's all try it.'

Norah finds Nesta and the other nurses hard at work in their hut fixing up their uniforms in readiness for departure.

'You will all look so smart,' Norah tells them.

'Well, we've washed them and mended holes where we can,' Nesta says. 'But they don't fit right.'

'That's because we've all lost so much weight,' Jean says.

'I'm not mending the bullet hole in mine,' Vivian tells them. 'I never want to forget what happened.'

The room falls silent for a moment until Nesta gets up to hug her friend, and one by one the nurses offer Vivian a smile, a soothing pat on the arm and a few words of comfort.

'Want me to look at your leg?'

'Please,' says Norah. 'I think it's on the mend, but it's still so hard to move around.'

'Let's go into the garden,' suggests Nesta.

She helps Norah to shuffle the few steps to the back door. She pulls up a chair and Norah collapses into it.

'I want to put on a new dressing.' Nesta pulls a pack of bright white bandages from her pocket and gently hoists Norah's foot onto her lap. Norah winces in pain.

'How's John doing?' Nesta asks, unwinding the wrapping from Norah's leg. The infection is healing and she sighs with relief.

'He's so much better. Just longing to get home to our girl.'

'I'm happy for you, but I will miss you and Ena and June.'

316

'Oh, Nesta, you have no idea how much we'll think of you all. Of everything you've done for the women,' Norah says.

'I wish we didn't have to say goodbye,' Nesta says, fixing the new bandage in place. She gives Norah's leg a soft tap. 'You're done.'

Norah takes her hand. 'I mean it, Nesta. You have made this place just about bearable. And Margaret . . .'

The women fall silent, remembering their beloved companion.

'We'll carry her in her hearts. Always,' Nesta says, helping Norah to her feet. The women embrace for a long time and then Nesta helps her back to her hut.

Ena and John sit Norah down beside the mound bearing Margaret's wooden cross, her name so lovingly inscribed by Norah and Audrey.

'She wouldn't want us to weep for her,' Ena says.

'I don't care what she would want, how can I say goodbye to the finest woman I have ever known and not weep for her passing,' says Norah, barely able to control her tears.

Ena is crying too. Neither woman attempts to wipe away her tears, letting them fall onto the earth, onto Margaret. John is upset to see the women so sad. He doesn't belong here, and yet here he is. If he is to get to know Margaret, in even a small way, then he needs to understand the women's depth of feeling for her.

'Nesta is here,' John whispers.

Norah and Ena look up to see Nesta standing a few feet away, not wanting to disturb their grief. Norah holds out her hand and Nesta joins them. The three women embrace.

After a long time, Norah turns to Nesta. 'Will you say goodbye to . . . to your dead for me, I can't walk to their burial site, I'm so sorry.'

317

'Of course. And of course they'll understand. We are having a small service at sundown for them, here. We don't know when we're leaving, but it could be soon, and we need to say goodbye while we can.'

'Can I join you?' Ena asks.

'We'd like that. Thank you, Ena.'

As the sun sets, the surviving nurses, Ena, Mrs Hinch, Dr McDowell, Mother Laurentia and Sister Catherina gather at the cemetery, each clutching a small bunch of flowers. Walking slowly from grave to grave as Nesta says each name, Mother Laurentia gives blessings for the lives lived and taken too soon.

That night as the nurses lie down, waiting for sleep to take them away, they hear a gentle knock on their door.

'Sister James, can I see you for a moment?'

Nesta opens the door to Mrs Hinch. As she steps outside, Mrs Hinch takes her arm to lead her away.

'Hurry now. There's a telephone call for you in the administration hut.'

'One sec,' says Nesta, popping her head back into the hut. 'I'll be back in a minute. I have a telephone call!' She shuts the door, but not before she hears squeals of delight and anticipation.

Mrs Hinch accompanies Nesta to the office and stands beside her as she picks up the receiver.

'Hello, this is Sister James.'

'Hello, Sister James! It is wonderful to hear your voice. I am Flying Officer Ken Brown, Australian Air Force. I am going to meet you tomorrow at Lahat and fly you to Singapore. I've been told to ask you to have the nurses ready at 4 a.m. Major Jacobs will be there with a truck to bring you to Loebok Linggau, put you on a train and bring you to the airstrip. Sister James, are you there, did you hear me?'

'Yes! Oh, yes! Thank you, thank you so much! We'll be ready.'

'Sister James, you don't get to thank me, I thank you.' The officer's voice is thick with suppressed tears. 'I thank you and all the brave nurses I will meet tomorrow for what your survival has done for the Australian people. You are our heroes.'

Hanging up the phone, Nesta is embraced by Mrs Hinch. 'Let me walk you back to your hut.'

'I'd like that, it will give us a chance to say goodbye. Although I don't know how to say goodbye to you, Mrs Hinch, you have done so much for us, all of us, not just us nurses.'

'Nesta. Call me Gertrude. My name is Gertrude.'

The two women walk back to the nurses' hut arm in arm. Mrs Hinch steps inside to a sea of expectant faces.

'Ladies, it has been a privilege and an honour to know you. Godspeed.'

Nesta gives her one last hug.

'Bless you, Gertrude, you are one of a kind. I'll never forget you.'

'Nor I you, Sister Nesta James.'

No one attempts to sleep. There are meagre possessions to be packed, uniforms to be inspected and changed into and, of course, the excitement of finally 'going home'.

The camp lights pick out the huts in the dark, as the women gather in readiness for their final transport. As they step outside, into their last few moments in this humid jungle 'home', a thunderous sound of clapping erupts into the night. Cheers and whistles rend the air. Women and men line a path to where two trucks await, their engines running.

'How did you know?' one of the nurses asks.

Before anyone can respond, Nesta answers, 'Mrs Hinch!'

'You said my name, Sister James?' A smiling Mrs Hinch steps forwards. 'As much as you would probably prefer to disappear into the night, we could not let that happen. I may have mentioned you were leaving today, but they did the rest.' Mrs Hinch spreads her arms wide to embrace the population of the camp.

Mother Laurentia, Sister Catherina and Dr McDowell come forwards and hug each of the nurses.

'I've still got your Bible,' Betty tells Sister Catherina.

'You keep it.'

'I'll never forget you,' the doctor tells the nurses. 'We've suffered and lost, but we would have lost so many more without your dedication to your training.'

By the time the nurses reach the waiting trucks, after hugging and saying goodbye to so many women along the way, the sun is already peeking over the trees. Ena and John, supporting Norah, are last in line.

As the nurses approach, John extends his hand to Nesta. 'There is so much more for me to hear about you and what you have done for my wife, and all the women here. I want you to know I will be forever in your debt. My thanks are not enough, but they're all I've got right now. Please know they come from the bottom of my heart.'

Nesta nods, unable to say a word. She looks at Norah, who is also nodding, also unable to speak. Nesta reaches out and gently strokes her face, wiping away her tears.

'I'm going to say something, I have to,' Ena says. 'Sister James, Nesta, dear friend, I will spend the rest of my life telling everyone

I meet about the incredible Australian nurses I had the privilege and pleasure of knowing once upon a time in a land far away, and their dynamic pint-sized leader. You saved my life; you saved so many lives, and paid the ultimate price when you lost your own fellow nurses. We will find each other again.'

'I am no longer an only child; with you I have two sisters,' Nesta manages. 'You both have given so much to so many ... I'm so sorry. I'm finding it hard to speak. I love you both. Until we meet again.'

Fighting back her tears, Nesta allows herself to be helped on board a truck. They are escorted out of the camp to resounding cheers and calls of goodbye. And then they're driving down a narrow path into the jungle, and away.

Two days after the nurses leave the camp, Norah, Ena, June and John are told by Ah Fat they will be leaving too.

'For once, you are not the proverbial bad penny, Ah Fat,' Mrs Hinch tells the translator.

'Bad penny?'

'Bad penny, man. Do you not know it? And you such a fine translator. It's someone who always turns up with bad news.'

'But news is good,' Ah Fat insists. 'You are going home.'

'Oh, never mind,' Mrs Hinch says, with a smile. 'Today, not even you can ruin my mood.'

'Thank you, Inchi.'

Gathering their things, the women report, along with dozens of other sick and injured men and women, to be loaded onto trucks for the journey to Lahat. The remaining men and women, including all the Dutch nuns, come to see them off.

'I don't want to leave without you,' Norah tells Sister Catherina.

'It's all right, our turn will come shortly. Eventually, we will all leave this place,' Sister Catherina reassures her. 'What you have done to save the souls of so many will never be forgotten, I will make sure of that. You and Miss Dryburgh gave us hope when none existed, the two of you repaired our tortured minds, and gave our bodies the soulful nourishment we needed to wake up the next day.'

'Hmm? You repaired tortured minds?' John asks Norah, perplexed by the presence of the nun, dressed in her heavy habit.

'You must be John; I've heard a lot about you. I can't tell you how happy I am to meet you, even in this place.'

'You mean this godforsaken place, don't you, Sister?'

'Not words I would use; in fact, I would say God's presence was here in the form of your wife.'

'Please, Sister, we all did our bit,' says Norah. 'How can I ever forget the night we spent holding down the roof of our hut as a storm threatened to blow us all away? Seeing you up there, your habit flying in the wind, I thought you were a witch.'

'And yet you climbed up with me. What I remember is you laughing hysterically at the absurdity of our actions.'

'And I remember the language you used – words I never expected to hear from a nun.'

'Well, Norah, when pushed like we were that night, colourful language somehow seemed appropriate.'

'Will you tell me what it was my wife did, other than risk her life climbing onto a roof in a storm?' John persists.

Sister Catherina laughs. 'It was her gift of music, freely given, in our darkest moments that will be remembered by us all. I do not have the words, colourful or otherwise, to tell you the difference your wife made.'

'She's right, John,' says Ena. 'What Norah and Margaret did in creating choirs and orchestras was beyond what any of us could have imagined. I will never hear music again without thinking of this place and the people here, including you, dear sister. You will never be forgotten.'

'The trucks have arrived, it's time to go,' says the nun softly.

Norah, Ena and Catherina embrace. John gathers his strength, and gently picks up his wife in his arms. It isn't too difficult; she weighs practically nothing. Ena lifts June, who wraps her arms around her neck, snuggling into her chest, and together they board.

Mrs Hinch walks along the line of women, some hugging, some sharing brief memories of their time together. When she reaches Norah and Ena, she seems lost for words, perhaps for the first time.

'Why aren't you coming with us?' Ena asks.

'I leave when the last of us leaves, not before,' her friend tells her.

'I don't know what to say to you,' Norah says.

'Well, I have plenty I want to say to the two of you, but nothing that will truly reflect how I feel. We have laughed and cried, loved and lost, but we go on carrying the memories of those who don't journey with us. I will never forget you for as long as I live, and given I've managed to survive this, I'm planning on that being a long time.'

'You are truly one of a kind, Mrs Hinch,' Norah says.

'As are you and your sister. I don't think I mentioned it before, but my name is Gertrude. I was quite happy to be called Mrs Hinch, as pretentious as it sounded, because I've never liked my name, and I'm not a Gertie.' Mrs Hinch hugs Norah in John's arms as best she can, and then Ena, whose arms are full of June. 'Godspeed,' she says.

And then it's time to say goodbye to Audrey, who the sisters will meet again in England. Norah and Audrey silently embrace, each remembering their sessions over a firepit, carving the names of the dead into wooden crosses.

An open vehicle idles nearby and the remaining English men and women help each other into the truck bed. As they are hoisted on board, all the women turn to look at the camp, one last time, trying to understand how they survived, how they would recall their time. Or do they just want to forget? One thing they all know; they have been changed forever. Over three and a half years have passed. They have been tested, they have failed, they have succeeded.

Slowly, the truck moves off.

They have barely begun their journey when they hear the music.

'Help me sit up, John, help me,' Norah begs.

'Oh, my goodness! Norah, look!' Ena cries.

The truck driver brakes as the singing grows louder. It is Norah's music.

John and Ena gently position Norah so she can look out the back of the truck. John lifts her onto his lap for extra height as together they look at the row of nuns outside.

'What are they doing?' John asks.

The voices of the Dutch nuns, escorting the truck, escorting Norah, paying homage to the role she has played in their survival, soar in the familiar sound of 'Bolero', the much-loved – and even much-hated, due to its complexity – vocal rendition of Ravel's masterpiece. Unashamedly, Norah sobs.

'Is that what you taught them, Norah?' John asks, his voice trembling as the magnitude of what he is hearing hits him, the realisation that the woman who he holds in his arms is the recipient of this amazing tribute. 'It's Ravel . . . Ravel's "Bolero",' he stammers.

The truck slowly moves off again, and the final notes of 'Bolero' follow them away from captivity towards freedom.

'Oh, my darling, I have never loved you more than I do in this moment,' John whispers.

EPILOGUE

Final Performance

For two days, the nurses have sailed down the Australian coast-line, seeing for the first time in almost four years the country they left behind. They stand on deck as they enter the port of Fremantle, Perth. It has been quite a journey to get here. From Lahat, they were flown to Singapore as the sun set in a blaze of red light. Nesta had looked from the window as they flew low over the Banka Strait. She saw familiar beaches, palm trees and the lush foliage that once welcomed them, then became their prison. All the nurses had paused in their excited chatter when they saw the harbour now filled with Allied warships. When they reached Singapore, they were whisked away to hospital for full medical check-ups and from there they boarded this ship, for home.

Nesta moves amongst them now.

'Are you all right?' she asks each nurse in turn.

'No,' comes the answer, time and again.

'I'm here if you need me.'

Finding a quiet spot on the other side of the ship, Nesta watches the suburbs of Perth go by. Looking down at the waves, she remembers the last time she sailed into this port with Olive Paschke, later Matron Paschke. They were both excited, both eager to have this stopover in Perth.

'You should be here with me, Olive, here by my side as we sail home,' she screams into the wind, at the seagulls hovering around the ship. 'And you're not, and I don't think I can go home without you.' So many people lost to her. But not all, not her dearest friends who have made this long journey with her. Nesta pictures Dr Rick's face, smiling at her on those long night shifts. She wonders if she will ever see him again.

'Nesta, Nesta, we're docking. We're here!' Jean calls.

'Coming.' Nesta breaks out of her reverie. She takes a moment to dry her eyes, centre herself and paste a smile on her face. She hears the cheers from the wharf as the ship ties off.

Joining the others, seeing the thousands of people waving flags and flowers, they wait impatiently for the gangplank to be lowered. For the second time in a few weeks, the first person to greet them is Matron-in-Chief Colonel Sage.

'Welcome home, nurses. You left Australia to do your duty, you return, having achieved far beyond what could ever be reasonably expected of you, as heroes. I want to tell you what has happened here today. Earlier this morning, the local ABC radio station announced that you would be returning home and asked that if any locals had any spare flowers in their gardens, they might like to drop them off at the hospital you're about to be taken to.' Colonel Sage pauses, composing herself. 'There is not a flower left in any garden in the city of Perth. The line of men and women wanting to drop them off at the hospital extends for miles, every ward is full. I'm told they are even hanging flowers from the ceilings. It is a small gesture by so many who join us all in saying thank you for your service. Thank you for your duty to your friends and colleagues who have not come home with you. They will never be forgotten.'

Somebody says, 'Hear, hear.'

The nurses turn to see the premier of the state of Western Australia standing with the biggest bouquet of flowers.

'Mr Premier, may I introduce you to Sister Nesta James?'

The premier thrusts the flowers at Nesta.

'Welcome home,' he beams.

Back in Singapore, Norah, John, Ena and June are inseparable. The sisters are dozing one afternoon in deck chairs in the gardens of their hotel, while John watches a man approaching their small party. He is assisting an elderly woman with a stick.

'Oh, my God! Norah, Ena, wake up.'

'What is it?' Norah says, slowly opening her eyes. June, asleep in Ena's arms, awakes when her aunty sits bolt upright.

'No!' Ena shouts.

Walking slowly towards them is Ken, Ena's husband, with Margaret, the sisters' mother.

'Mama!' Norah shouts, as Ena jumps up to help Norah out of her chair.

Ken holds on tight to Margaret, who stumbles towards her daughters. He wants to run to Ena, but he can't let her go. The four collide, Norah gently sitting her mother in the grass, so they can embrace. They look into each other's tear-filled eyes. Ken and Ena are hugging, sobbing, laughing.

John takes a startled June in his arms and joins them. The little girl is introduced to Ken and becomes caught up in a family embrace. Slowly, they help each other to their feet and make their way back to the chairs under the tree. Only after they have settled down does Ena ask the question.

'Daddy?'

'I'm so sorry, my darlings,' Margaret says, fresh tears falling. 'He died a few days after we were moved to Changi. He was so sick, he would never have survived. I'm glad he went quickly.'

Ena and Norah now hold each other and weep, daughters grieving for a father they never had the chance to say goodbye to.

'You were all in the prisoner-of-war camp in Changi?' John asks.

'Yes, we were moved there a week or two after you left. There were thousands of us. I still don't know how we survived,' Ken replies.

'I know how *I* survived,' Margaret says.

'You're a strong woman,' John reassures her.

'That may be, but the only reason I'm not dead is because Ken wouldn't let me die. He sacrificed his rations, risked his life to trade with the locals, took the beatings when caught, and told me every day that we had to live long enough to see my girls again. Ena, your husband is the reason I am here.'

'You also saved me when I was sick,' Ken tells her. 'You found me food, water; we saved each other.'

'Don't listen to him, girls. Caring for him for a week does not compare to what he did for me for three and a half years.'

Norah and Ena exchange a look, a huge smile appearing on both their faces.

'What's so funny?' Ken asks.

'I think we shall enjoy sharing stories. Some are best left untold, however. But I think there's one we'll all cherish and that's the love of family,' Ena says.

* * *

It is only a day or two later a British officer, accompanied by a gaunt man in civilian clothing, approaches them in the gardens.

'Excuse me, are you Ena Murray?'

'I am; how can I help you?'

'This is Mr Bourhill, he's been in Changi, I'm sad to say, but we believe you have been caring for his daughter, June.'

On hearing her name, June stops eating and looks up at the two men, showing no recognition of either. Both Norah and Ena stand. June jumps up and hides behind Ena.

'I'm June's father,' the stranger says. 'I put her and her mother on the *Vyner Brooke* and I've been contacted by the Australian government to say my daughter survived and is with you. Is that her, hiding behind your backs?'

Ena gently pulls June forwards. He steps closer to the little girl, and then kneels in front of her. He is fighting to hold back his tears.

'June, June darling, it's Daddy.'

June clings to Ena's hand.

'You look so much like your mother. Do you not remember me, darling?'

'Where's Mummy?' she asks.

'Mummy . . . Mummy . . .' He can't speak.

'She's been through an awful lot, Mr Bourhill,' Ena tells him. 'She's terribly traumatised.'

'I know, I understand. June, do you remember your favourite toy? It was a cuddly puppy, you called him Mr Waggy and you used to wag his tail for him.'

'Mr Waggy? Where's Mr Waggy?' June asks, looking confused, hurt and scared all at once.

'You couldn't go to sleep without him. If you couldn't find him, we'd . . . we'd have to search the house until he was safe with you in bed.'

'Mr Waggy was on the boat, I've lost him.'

'That's OK, my darling. We can buy you another Mr Waggy when we get home.'

'Why don't we take a walk,' Ena suggests. 'Just the three of us.'

'That was a smart idea of Ena's to take them both off,' Margaret says, when they've gone.

'Ken, you have probably already realised how close Ena is to June. It's going to break her heart if she leaves, but if that is her father, that's what will happen,' Norah says.

'I know, I've tried not to think about it as I've watched the two of them together. I've grown very fond of her myself and started thinking she was going to be part of our family.'

A short while later, June runs back to them. 'I've found my daddy; he wants to take me home with him. Should I go, Aunty Norah?'

'Yes, my darling. You should go with your daddy, he loves you very much,' Norah tells her, biting her lip. This is a happy moment for the child, she shouldn't confuse her with her tears.

'Won't you and Aunty Ena miss me?'

'Oh, my darling girl, you have no idea how much we will miss you. Every single day, all day.'

'Could you come and live with me and my daddy?'

'No, but we will see you. We'll come and visit, and you can come and visit us. How does that sound?'

'Do you promise?'

'I promise.'

Norah and John have made the long journey to England and then Belfast, to Sally, who they now know is safe with John's family. Meeting them at the airport, John's sister then takes them to her

331

home to await Sally's return from school. She has been informed that the parents she had been told were dead have survived and are coming to see her.

Now Sally's parents are in the living room of John's sister's house, eagerly awaiting their daughter's return home from school.

Norah can barely contain herself. She paces the living room, sits down, gets up again and paces.

'Do you think she'll recognise us, John? Do you think she'll be happy to see us?' she asks over and over.

'My darling, we're her parents. Of course she will,' John reassures her. 'She might be a little confused, a little unsure of us, but you'll see. It will all come right. Will you sit down with me?'

Norah sits, but they both rise quickly to their feet when they hear the front door open.

'Hi, Mum, we're home,' an adolescent voice yells. A school bag can be heard hitting the floor.

'In here,' John's sister calls.

A gangly youth saunters into the room as Norah and John wait in silence for the girl whose footsteps they can hear. The boy looks at these gaunt strangers nodding a polite 'hello'.

When Sally enters, she pauses for a moment, staring at Norah and John. She slides over to her aunt and reaches for her hand. At twelve years old, she is taller, fuller in the face, but Norah's heart swells. She is still her little girl.

'Hello, Sally,' John and Norah say.

'Hello,' Sally replies, not making a move.

'Sally, this is your mother and father, they are safe. They're home, love,' her aunt says.

'It's all right, Sally, I know we must look like strangers to you,' says John. 'It's been a long time and I'm sure we've changed; you certainly have. What a beautiful young girl you are.'

'Sally,' Norah says. 'It's me, it's Mummy.'

Sally moves behind her aunt, peering out at the strangers who are threatening to upend her life here. She last saw them as a little girl; in a few months, she will be a teenager.

Norah takes a step closer and kneels in front of Sally.

'*Go to sleep, go to sleep, go to sleep, pretty baby, go to sleep, go to sleep, go to sleep, baby girl,*' Norah sings.

Slowly, Sally moves towards her, letting go of her aunt's hand. She takes another step. Norah sees recognition light up in her daughter's eyes. She spreads her arms, and Sally takes another step. When they finally embrace, Norah can feel her trembling. She holds her daughter away so she can look into her beautiful face. Sally's mouth curls around one word.

'*Mummy!*'

AUTHOR'S NOTE

Nesta was born Nesta Gwyneth Lewis James on 5 December 1904 in Carmarthen, Wales, the only child of David and Eveline James. Nesta and her parents migrated to Australia when she was nine years old, moving into the rural town of Shepparton in the state of Victoria. She trained at Shepparton Base Hospital, before moving to the Royal Melbourne Hospital in Melbourne. Seeking adventure, she worked as a nurse in a mine outside of Johannesburg, South Africa. On 7 January 1941, she enlisted in the Australian Army Nursing Service. Sent to Malaya with the 2/10th Australian General Hospital, she served as second in command to Matron Olive Paschke in February 1941. Captured on 15 February 1942, she was liberated on 11 September 1945. Nesta was adamant whenever interviewed about her term of imprisonment that she wasn't interred for three and a half years, it was three years, seven months. On her return home, she spent twelve months in hospital with ongoing medical conditions related to the tropical illnesses she contracted in Indonesia, and which plagued her for the rest of her life. In 1946, Nesta travelled to Tokyo to give evidence at war crimes trials being held there. She resigned from the army in 1946 and returned to her hometown of Shepparton to care for her mother. There she met and married Alexander Thomas Noy. Nesta died in 1984 at the age of seventy-nine in Melbourne. She is survived by second and third cousins.

Vivian Bullwinkel was born on 18 December 1915, in Kapunda, South Australia, the only daughter of George and Eva Bullwinkel. She had a brother named John. After training as a nurse at Broken Hill, NSW, she started nursing at Hamilton Base Hospital, Hamilton, Victoria, before moving to the Jessie McPherson Hospital in Melbourne. In 1941, Vivian attempted to enlist in the Royal Australian Air Force but was rejected for having flat feet. Signing up with the Australian Army Nursing Service, Vivian was attached to the 2/13th Australian General Hospital and sent to Malaya in September 1941. Vivian resigned from the army in 1947 after giving evidence of the massacre on Radji Beach at a war crimes trial. She went on to become Director of Nursing at the Fairfield Infectious Diseases Hospital in Melbourne. In 1977, she married Colonel Francis West Stratham. She dedicated herself to the nursing profession throughout her life, including raising funds for a nurses' memorial to be placed at Muntok on Banka Island, which was unveiled in 1992. Vivian died in July 2000, at the age of eighty-four.

Betty was born Agnes Betty Jeffrey on 14 May 1908. She was a nurse in the 2/10th Australian General Hospital along with Nesta. Betty joined forces with Vivian to open the Australian Nurses Memorial Centre in Melbourne in 1949. Having secretly kept a diary while imprisoned, Betty wrote her story in the book *White Coolies*. This book went on to inspire the film *Paradise Road.*

Norah was born Margaret Constance Norah Hope in 1905 to James and Margaret Hope in Singapore where her father was an engineer. Educated at boarding school in Aylesbury, England, she went on to the Royal Academy of Music in London, where she studied piano, violin and chamber music, performing with the Royal Academy of Music Orchestra under Sir Henry Wood. She married John Lawrence Chambers in 1930 in Malaya. Their only child, Sally, was born in 1933. As the Japanese invaded Malaya, the family made their way to Singapore, where they put Sally, aged eight, on a ship with along with Barbara, Norah's sister, and her children Jimmy and Tony. They lived in Perth, Western Australia for a period, before Barbara's husband Harry Sawyer, who had fled to Sri Lanka, arranged for them to travel to South Africa. Sally's paternal grandparents in Ireland learned she was saved and sent for her. In 1944, with an escort, Sally moved to Fintona, County Tyrone in Northern Ireland to live with John's family. After liberation and reconnecting with Sally in Ireland, Norah and John eventually moved to the island of Jersey, where Sally joined them after finishing her education in Ireland, and this is where Norah lived until her death in 1989. It is with deep sadness I write that Sally, this dear wonderful woman who I had the honour of meeting, talking and laughing with, died on 4 May 2023. Her son, Seán, keeps alive the memory of his mother, father, grandmother and grandfather.

Ena, younger sister of Norah, was born in 1909 and was married to Kenneth Scott Murray. Her role as 'mother' to her little shadow June is mentioned many times in testimonies and accounts by other internees, as is her practice of often being the first to volunteer to clean and empty overflowing latrines, one of the splendid people who did this filthy and nauseating task. She and Ken were repatriated from Singapore on the ship *Cilicia*, arriving in Liverpool on 27 November 1945. Eventually moving to Jersey, where she lived for thirty-seven years, she died in 1995.

Margaret Dryburgh was born in England, the eldest child of Reverend William and Elizabeth Dryburgh. She trained as a teacher, adding a nursing qualification before being posted as a missionary in 1919 in China. Several years later, she moved to Singapore, fleeing on 12 February on board the *Mata Hari*. Captured by the Japanese Navy, the captain surrendered his cargo, mostly women and children, a day later. Margaret kept hope alive in the camps through her plays and lyrics, but sadly died before the camps were liberated, at the age of fifty-five.

Audrey Owen was a New Zealander who was working for the YWCA in Singapore in 1942. Repatriated from Singapore by air on 14 October 1945 to Australia, she immediately returned home to New Zealand. Relocating to live in England, she remained friends with Norah and Ena for the rest of her life. When asked about her time in captivity, Audrey replied, 'I found myself there.'

Sister Catherina, one of only eleven survivors of the twenty-four teaching nuns who went with Mother Superior Laurentia into captivity, struggled with her vocation upon her release; however, after coming to terms with her liberation, she returned to the convent and to Java.

Mrs Hinch (Gertrude) was born in the United States (possibly Milwaukee) in 1890 or 1891, and was the first non-missionary expatriate principal of the Anglo-Chinese School in Singapore (1929–1946). Captured with her husband as they attempted to flee Singapore on the *Giang Bee*, she was interned from February 1942 until liberation in September 1945. Her husband was interned during this time at Changi prisoner-of-war camp in Singapore. Their daughter Kathleen, who had been repatriated to family in Milwaukee, was subsequently sent to boarding school in Toronto, Canada. Mrs Hinch and her husband returned to Singapore and reopened the Anglo-Chinese School in Singapore. They died in 1970, within a few months of each other.

Carrie 'Jean' Ashton was born in 1905 in Nairne, South Australia. After training as a nurse in Hobart, Tasmania, she enlisted in the Australian Army Nursing Service, and in 1941 went with the 13th Australian General Hospital to Malaya. She returned to Australia after the camps were liberated, and died in 2002 at the age of ninety-seven.

June was the only child of AG and Dorothy Bourhill. Her mother was listed as 'lost at sea' following the sinking of the *Vyner Brooke*. Her father was captured and held prisoner by the Japanese in Singapore. Reunited, they travelled back to Australia on board the Shaw, Savill and Albion liner *Tamoroa*, arriving in Perth on 11 October 1945. June's father brought her to England to visit Ena and Ken several times as a young adult. June returned as an adult, living in Ireland. She remained part of Ena and Ken's 'family' for the remainder of their lives and was a part of Ena's funeral service, Sally's son remembers.

Dr Jean McDowell was a medical officer in Selangor, Malaya. She was repatriated from Singapore on the ship *Cilicia* along with Norah, Ena and their families.

Captain Seki, camp commander, was sentenced to fifteen years' imprisonment for his brutal treatment of internees. His conviction was in part due to the evidence given at his trial by Nesta and Vivian.

Captain Orita Masaru of the 229th Regiment of the Imperial Japanese Army's 38th Division, who ordered the massacre on Banka Island, became a prisoner of war of the Soviet Union following Japan's surrender. After being held for three years, he was returned to Japan where he was charged with war crimes. On the eve of his trial, he committed suicide.

In advanced years and failing health, one of the nurses present when the brave four volunteered to go to the officers' club revealed the truth behind this incredible act of bravery. Confirming that all those present swore on a Bible never to reveal the names of the four, she did not break that vow. When making depositions and testimonies, in the case of Nesta and Vivian giving sworn evidence in Japan at the trial of senior Japanese officers, the nurses all held the line: no nurses were sexually abused. They all honoured the vow they made, taking those names to their graves. May they rest in peace.

The Japanese word for nurse is *kangofu*.

Seventy-six Dutch, British and Australian women died in Muntok and were buried by their friends in shallow graves dug by the internees under trees at the edge of the camp.

No postcards from the nurses were received in Australia.

Nesta had the Australian Government repay the loan from Mother Laurentia back to the Dutch Red Cross.

Lieutenant Jean Ashton, along with Captain Nesta James and Captain Vivian Bullwinkel were 'mentioned in dispatches'. This honour describes a member of the armed forces whose name appears in an official report, written by a superior officer and sent to high command, in which their gallant or meritorious action in the face of the enemy is described.

Major Jacobs made the comment: 'the morale of the women at the time of their liberation was much higher than that of the men in their camps. Perhaps the women were more adaptable or had greater inner resources than the men, because they seemed to withstand the rigours of imprisonment more stoically.'

The welcome home in Perth for the nurses was overwhelming. Within days, they were returned to their home states and told they were now free to get on with their lives. Family and friends were told by army psychologists not to ask the returned internees of their experience, to pretend their captivity never happened. For many of the nurses, coming home brought sadness and a sense of loneliness. Sleeping in a room on their own did not bring the sense of comfort dreamed of when sleeping side-by-side on a cold concrete floor. Nightmares and flashbacks haunted many, along with the ill health years of neglect and illness left them with.

The English female survivors travelled back to Britain on the same troopship as servicemen. Unlike the reception given to the returning men, there were no grand welcome-home celebrations; relatives and friends were told not to meet the ship when they docked. There was no press coverage acknowledging the bravery and resilience of a truly amazing band of sisters.

You will see in the following pages that I have listed the names of all the Australian nurses, not because their stories or their suffering was any greater than the other women from many countries, but because their names demand to be known. Here is a very brief list of other women who were a huge part of the story but whose experiences I have credited to others for the purpose of telling a streamlined story.

Mrs Brown and her daughter Shelagh	Alette, Antoinette and Helen Colijn
Mamie Colley	Cara Hall
Molly and Peggy Ismail	Doris and Phyllis Liddelow
Mary Jenkin	Dorothy MacCleod
Dorothy Moreton	Ruth Russell-Roberts
Elizabeth Simons	Margot Turner

I have not told this story so the women internees of the Japanese prisoner-of-war camps in Indonesia will be remembered. I have told this story so they will be known. How can you be remembered if you've never been heard of? Their stories should stand along-side those of all male prisoners of war, their suffering no less; their courage to care for their fellow sisters who perished and their own survival should be acknowledged and honoured.

Know now of them. Remember them.

As when writing any story based on historically known facts and participants, the biggest challenge is always: what to put in, what to leave out. This was a mammoth challenge for me. Each one of the more than five hundred women and children Nesta and Norah lived with, cried with, laughed with, sang with, said goodbye to, have a place in this story. In the end, it came down to the two families – Nesta's cousins in Cardiff, Wales, and Norah's daughter Sally and grandson Seán – who have generously shared their time, their memories, their keepsakes, who I have focused on. To those not mentioned and their families, please accept this telling of Nesta and Norah's story as telling the story of all others.

I am indebted to the efforts, past and continuing, of the Australian War Memorial in their archiving of manuscripts and testimonies of the Australian nurses. They have provided me with a wealth of information regarding the prisoners, both female and male, of the Imperial Japanese Forces in south-east Asia.

BIBLIOGRAPHY

Jeffrey, Betty, *White Coolies* (Angus & Robertson, 1954)

Manners, Norman, *Bullwinkel* (Hesperian Press, Victoria Park, 1999)

Shaw, Ian, *On Radji Beach* (Pan Macmillan Australia, 2010)

Warner, Lavinia & Sandilands John, *Women Beyond the Wire* (Arrow Books, 1982)

Members of the Australian Army Nurses Service who sailed on the *Vyner Brooke*, 12th February, 1942

Never made land, lost at sea

Sister Louvima Bates

Sister Ellenor Calnan

Sister Mary Clarke

Sister Millicent Dorsch

Sister Caroline Ennis

Sister Kit Kineslla

Sister Gladys McDonald

Matron Olive Paschke

Sister Jean Russell

Sister Marjorie Schuman

Sister Annie Trenerry

Sister Mona Wilton

Murdered on Banka Island

Sister Lainie Balfour-Ogilvy

Sister Alma Beard

Sister Ada Bridge

Sister Flo Casson

Sister Mary Cuthbertson

Matron Irene Drummond

Sister Dorothy Elmes

Sister Lorna Fairweather

Sister Peggy Farmaner

Sister Clare Halligan

Sister Nancy Harris

Sister Minnie Hodgson

Sister Nell Keats

Sister Jenny Kerr

Sister Ellie McGlade

Sister Kath Neuss

Sister Florence Salmon

Sister Jean Stewart

Sister Mona Tait

Sister Rosetta Wight

Sister Bessie Wilmott

Died in captivity

Sister Winnie Davis

Sister Dot Freeman

Sister Shirley Gardam

Sister Blanche Hempsted

Sister Gladys Hughes

Sister Pearl Mittelheuser

Sister Mina (Ray) Raymont

Sister Rene Singleton

Made it home

Sister Jean Ashton
Sister Jessie Blanch
Sister Vivian Bullwinkel
Sister Veronica Clancy
Sister Cecilia Delforce
Sister Jess Doyle
Sister Jean Greer
Sister Pat Gunther
Sister Mavis Hannah
Sister Iole Harper
Sister Nesta James
Sister Betty Jeffrey

Sister Pat Blake
Sister Violet McElnea
Sister Sylvia Muir
Sister Wilma Oram
Sister Chris Oxley
Sister Eileen Short
Sister Jessie Simons
Sister Valerie (Val) Smith
Sister Ada Syer
Sister Florence Trotter
Sister Joyce Tweddell
Sister Beryl Woodbridge

Thank you for your sacrifice, ladies. The world is a better place because of it.

AFTERWORD FROM KATHLEEN DAVIES AND BRENDA PEGRUM, NESTA'S RELATIVES

Nesta Gwyneth James was our father's cousin on his mother's side of the family. Nesta's father, David James, moved from Aberdare in South Wales and the family mining background and worked as an accountant. He married Eveline de Vere Lewis from Llansteffan, a village on the estuary of the River Tywi in Carmarthenshire, where Nesta, an only child, was born in 1904. The family emigrated to Australia when Nesta was a young girl and our father saw them off at the railway station, and then corresponded with Nesta for the next fifty years.

Nesta's Welsh background was important to her. In 1963, she and her husband visited Wales. They stayed in Aberdare with her father's family and spent two days with our father in Cardiff. Kathleen met her then, and what she remembers was just how very, very tiny Nesta was, while her husband was over six foot tall! Our father and Nesta spoke in Welsh.

Nesta worked as a nurse at the Royal Melbourne Hospital for eleven years. She enlisted in the Australian Army Nursing Service in 1941. Our father and two of his brothers had volunteered in

World War I, so he was supportive of Nesta's enlistment and anxiously followed her capture by the Japanese. Nesta's father died in 1942, but her mother's letter telling Nesta of his death was withheld by the Japanese so Nesta did not learn of his death until 1945. In 1955, Nesta then aged fifty-one, married Alexander Noy. They lived on a fruit farm in Shepparton, as Nesta's family had upon their migration to Australia.

Nesta and Alex were only married for nine years when Alex died, at which time Nesta moved to Melbourne, where our niece Debra lived, having migrated with her parents as a young girl. Debra remembers Nesta and her beloved Yorkshire terrier, Nikki, attending every Christmas lunch. Conversations never focused on Nesta's experiences as a POW. Deb says that maybe Nesta never discussed them, but as a teenager, she did not know the questions to ask. Debra often sang with Nesta while her mother was cooking the lunch and her father and brother were elsewhere.

Nesta died in 1984, aged seventy-nine. Debra remembers her mother saying she died from physical complications from her time as a POW. Brenda never met her, but recently she and her daughter Amanda listened to the oral interview the Australian War Memorial recorded with Nesta. They were impressed by Nesta's ability to recount so clearly her wartime experiences.

Kathleen Davies and Brenda Pegrum
Cardiff, Wales
September 2023

AFTERWORD FROM SEÁN CONWAY, NORAH'S GRANDSON

My grandmother Norah was born Margaret Constance Norah Hope in 1905 to James and Margaret Hope in Singapore, where her father was an engineer. She married John Lawrence Chambers, a civil engineer, in 1930 in Malaya. Their only child, my mother Sally, was born in 1933. The family lived in Malaya until the Japanese army swept down through the Pacific in 1941. They fled to Singapore and, with her husband John very ill in hospital and wanting to remain with him, in desperation, Norah and John placed Sally, aged eight, along with Norah's sister Barbara and sons Jimmy and Tony (Sally's cousins) on a ship bound for Australia. John and Norah were themselves forced to leave soon after as Singapore fell to the Japanese. They joined many desperate men and women on the *Vyner Brooke* merchant ship, which was bombed and sank off the coast of Indonesia. Norah and John survived and came ashore on an Indonesian island, only to be captured by Japanese soldiers. They were separated and spent the rest of the war in POW camps in Indonesia – Norah's story is reimagined in *Sisters under the Rising Sun*.

My mother, Sally, spent the war with her father's family in Ireland after travelling alone by ship when her aunt Barbara and cousins Jimmy and Tony were reunited with Barbara's husband Harry, Jimmy and Tony's father. Sally believed she was an orphan until some time after VJ day, because as prisoners of war, her parents were incommunicado in the camps. After being reunited with Norah and John at the end of the war, the family moved first to Glasgow, then in 1948 to London, before eventually settling in Jersey where Norah's sister Ena and brother-in-law Ken were living. Sally, working as ground hostess for BOAC, met my father Patrick, a flight engineer, at Heathrow airport when he was on a lay-over, and after a short time based in Sunningdale in Berkshire, they moved back to Sydney, where my father was based, working with Qantas. He then took a job with Middle East Airlines in Lebanon, where I was born. After a period in Ireland, we eventually moved to Jersey, joining my grandparents.

Norah was a hugely talented musician, who trained at the Royal Academy of Music. As Heather describes in her novel, she and Margaret Dryburgh created a 'voice orchestra' for the women in the Japanese POW camps as a way of keeping up morale. She wrote out musical scores from which the women sang, on salvaged pieces of paper, arranging the compositions for voice from memory. She kept the musical scores for the 'voice orchestra' she'd created in the camps throughout her life, and these scores were handed down to my mother Sally after Norah's death in 1989. I remember Norah as a wonderful grandmother who tried to teach me piano (before the guitar intervened) and I spent a lot of time with her and my grandfather John, who was less outgoing than my grandmother but had a tremendous sense of humour.

My mother Sally very sadly died in May this year. Till the end of her life, she remained bright, funny, loving and warm, and I couldn't have wished for a better mother, or father for that matter.

Seán Conway
Jersey
September 2023

Above: The Hope sisters together, L–R: Ena, Barbara and Norah in Malaya, c.1935.

Below: Norah Chambers (*née* Hope), Malaya, c. 1940.

Above: L–R: John Chambers (Norah's husband), James Hope (father of the Hope sisters) and Kenneth Murray (Ena's husband), in Malaya, c.1936.

Right: Norah and Sally in Malaya before the war changed everything, c.1939, when Sally was six or seven years old.

Left: Sally as a baby in Malaya, c. 1934, playing with her amah (nanny) while her father John watches on.

Above: Sally with her father John, safe and happy in Jersey, the war behind them, early 1950s.

Right: The surviving 24 nurses as they arrived in Singapore following liberation. Nesta is the first person on the left in the front row.

Left: The surviving 24 nurses on arrival back home in Australia. Nesta is buried beneath a huge bouquet fifth from the right in the second row. Vivian is second from right, on the second row.

Below: I could find very few photos of Nesta. This is one of her taken when she was back in uniform, c. 1945.

Above: Nesta and her husband Alexander Noy, c. 1963.

A handwritten score of Ravel's *Boléro*, arranged and transcribed from memory by Norah Chambers, to be sung by the women's voice orchestra.

A handwritten score of the Largo from the 'New World Symphony',
arranged and transcribed from memory by Norah Chambers, to be sung
by the women's voice orchestra.

Sumatra and the women's camps

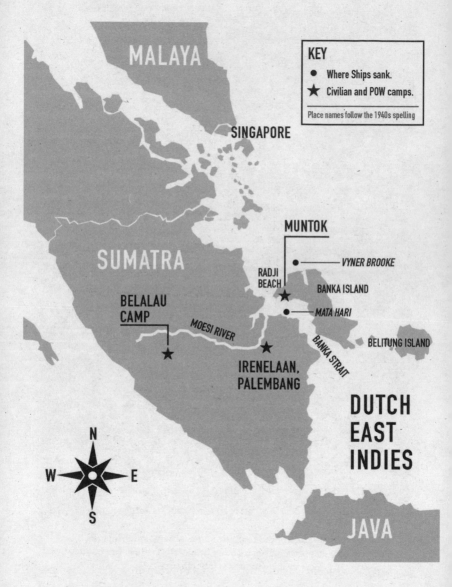

MALAYA

SINGAPORE

MUNTOK

KEY
● Where Ships sank.
★ Civilian and POW camps.

Place names follow the 1940s spelling

SUMATRA

RADJI BEACH

● — VYNER BROOKE

BANKA ISLAND

★

BELALAU CAMP

MOESI RIVER

● MATA HARI

BELITUNG ISLAND

BANKA STRAIT

★

IRENELAAN, PALEMBANG

DUTCH EAST INDIES

N
W   E
S

JAVA

ACKNOWLEDGEMENTS

'Have you heard the story of the Australian Nurses held as prisoners of war by the Japanese during World War II?' my dear friend and publisher Kate Parkin said to me several years ago. When I acknowledged my New Zealand education had not enlightened me, she suggested I take a look. In her words, 'there's a story that needs to be told to a new audience.' As always, Kate knew what she was talking about. With her support and encouragement, I went 'looking'. Kate, there are no words for the gratitude and love I have for you, not only pointing me in the direction of this story, but your friendship, along with that of your wonderful husband Bill Hamilton, means the world to me. You support me as a writer; you took care of me as I recovered from Covid far away from my family.

In the early days of my research, I mentioned to a past colleague of mine the story I was considering telling. She told me her cousin was one of those nurses; her name was Nesta James. Thanks go initially to our mutual friend Jan McGregor, who had invited us both to lunch, for the opportunity to catch up with you, Deb Davies, and get from you family documents, etc., to kick-start Nesta's story. Subsequently spending time with you and your cousins, Kathleen Davies and Brenda Pegrum in Cardiff, Wales, was overwhelming. Hearing your family history and Nesta's life in particular has been an incredible resource for me. I thank all three of you most sincerely.

Initially contemplating telling the story of the Aussie nurses, I became intrigued by the English woman also on the *Vyner Brooke*, Norah Chambers. Everything I read about Nesta included the incredible, talented, hard-working Norah. To tell the nurses' story and not have Norah, her sister Ena and best friends Margaret Dryburgh and Audrey Owens would have been to tell only half the story. Thanks to the talent of my researcher Katherine Back, we found Norah's daughter, Sally Conway, and grandson, Seán Conway, living on the island of Jersey. Spending time with Sally, hearing her stories of her parents and memories of being a young girl fleeing the Japanese, being separated from her mother and father, is a cherished memory. Thank you, Sally, from the bottom of my heart for being so warm and welcoming. Sitting with his mother, her incredible son, Seán, supported and prompted Sally when her memory wasn't sure, and subsequently provided us with the valuable documents and photos included herein. Forever in your debt, Seán, thank you.

She's my editor, publisher, dear *hoa* (friend), travelling companion, minder, manager, my wing-woman, Maverick: Margaret Stead. I apologise for coercing you into drinking shots of slivovitz when we visited Slovakia, but what you can do with that liquor in your chocolate brownies makes it worth it, surely? Thank you for coming to Jersey with me each time we visited Sally and Seán and to Cardiff to meet Deb and Nesta's family; thank you for taking my words and making this writer look good; but mostly thank you for your friendship. There are more adventures ahead for us.

Ruth Logan is a person everyone needs in their life, and so few will have. An extraordinary woman who came to Paris to 'nurse' me in a hotel while suffering from Covid, brought me food each day, joined me each evening at risk to her own health, to make sure I was OK, then brought me back to London when no longer positive. This is just one instance of Ruth going above and beyond her role as Rights Director at Bonnier Books. There is the little matter of also being the person who gets my books into the many countries outside of the UK so that readers in over forty-five languages can get to know Lale, Gita, Cilka, Cibi, Magda, Livi and now Nesta and Norah. She doesn't have the nickname 'Halo' for no reason. Thank you, dear friend.

She heads up the finest publishing house in the UK; she is available to me on call, a supporter of everything I write and want to write: her name is Perminder Mann, she is CEO of Bonnier Books UK, and I am so grateful that you continue to find time for me in your incredibly hectic and busy life, encouraging and supporting a huge stable of authors.

Assisting Ruth, of whom I know she sings their praises, are her rights team: Ilaria Tarasconi, Stella Giatrakou, Nick Ash, Holly Powell and Amy Smith, you are wonders. I appreciate more than words can say your efforts getting my words spread around the world.

Francesca Russell, Publicity Director; Clare Kelly, Publicity Manager; Elinor Fewster, Publicity Manager Zaffre – you who get me out into the world, into the presence of readers and publishers, I sincerely thank you. Good thing you know how much I love the incredible experiences you provide for me.

Blake Brooks, Head of Brand, Zaffre, you work tirelessly keeping me 'branded', keeping my website current and looking great. I would not exist on social media without you. Thank you so much to you and wonderful Holly Milnes for helping at all times of the day and night this tech-ignorant girl down under.

There is a team at Zaffre responsible for bringing *Sisters under the Rising Sun* to you readers and their talents need to be acknowledged: brilliant Team Editorial members Justine Taylor, Arzu Tahsin and Mia Farkasovska; Art Director Nick Stearn; Team Sales members Stuart Finglass, Mark Williams, Stacey Hamilton and Vincent Kelleher, Production Manager Alex May, to name but a few.

Sally Richardson and Jennifer Enderlin at St Martin's Press in the US, you took this story based on a scribbled one and a half pages of notes. Your faith and support in my ability to produce the story you hoped I would give you is so appreciated. Your continued encouragement for me to write the stories I want to tell means everything to me.

For the rest of the team at St Martin's Press, please accept my sincere thanks; I will acknowledge you individually in the US edition.

Last, but my no means least, there is a small team of incredible friends in Sydney who are always at the end of the phone for me, laugh and cry with me, led by the wonderful Juliet Rogers, Managing Director, Echo Publishing, her right hand and publicist Emily Banyard and the excellent Cherie Baird. Your talent and knowledge give readers in Australia and New Zealand access to me, put our books out there for them. My deepest love and thanks.

To the folks at Allen and Unwin Australia, thank you for the incredible role you play distributing my books throughout Australia and New Zealand.

She supported and worked with me on my first four books; she remains my dear friend, life coach, the one to make me laugh: she is Benny Agius. You are truly one of a kind; thank you for being in my life and making it that much better with your sense of humour, words of wisdom and sage advice.

You know what you mean to me. You know nothing I write means anything without you, without your unconditional support and love, my family. Ahren and Bronwyn, Jared and Bec, Dea and Evan and the five best reasons to get out of bed each day, Henry, Nathan, Jack, Rachel and Ashton the adorable.

HEATHER
MORRIS

If you would like to hear more from me, why not join the
Heather Morris Readers' Club?

I'll keep you up to date on all upcoming
projects, with early exclusives like extracts, videos and
behind-the-book details; as well as more on all my published
titles including real-life research, deleted scenes and
giveaways.

You can join anytime at
www.heathermorrisauthor.com/heathers-readers-club

Dear Reader,

Thank you so much for picking up *Sisters under the Rising Sun*. In my career as a writer, I've been so fortunate in being able to meet and talk to some amazing people. It's because of your loyalty, help and support as readers that I've been able to share the stories of Lale and Gita, of Cilka, of Cibi, Magda and Livia. Now, I'm just so honoured and humbled to have been able to tell this story which has been so overlooked by history – the story of Norah and Nesta and the amazing women and children who survived the brutal Japanese POW during World War II. I'd long wanted to tell this story, which I'd grown up hearing about – particularly the story of the Australian nurses who had volunteered to serve in the Pacific theatre of war, there to nurse Allied soldiers fighting the Japanese. Since my days working in the social work department of a busy hospital, I've been aware of the work nurses do – so often unsung – and I wanted to find a way, particularly in the wake of the pandemic, of honouring the service of these women.

In the early days of my research, I mentioned to a past colleague of mine, Deb Davies, the story I was considering telling. Deb put me in touch with her relatives, Kathleen Davies and Brenda Pegrum who live in Cardiff, Wales, and I was so moved by what they told me about their family, and about Nesta's life. What an incredible woman she was. Kathleen and Brenda brought Nesta to life: this Welsh Australian 'pocket dynamo', standing four feet 11 inches tall, who fought every day of the three years seven months she spent in captivity to survive, and to keep the women and children with her alive – and smiling. She was courageous, strong, tough, kind, loving and full of laughter. It's been a huge privilege learning about her and telling her story.

It is my enormous pleasure to share this heartbreaking, inspirational and uplifting story with you, my readers. If you would like more information about what I'm working on now, or about my earlier books, *The Tattooist of Auschwitz*, *Cilka's Journey*, *Three Sisters* and *Stories of Hope*, you can visit www.heathermorrisauthor.com/heathers-readers-club where you can join my readers' club. It only takes a few moments to sign up, there are no catches or costs, and new members will automatically receive an exclusive message from me. My publisher, Bonnier Books UK, will keep your data private and confidential and it will never be passed on to a third party. We won't spam you with loads of emails, just be in touch now and then with exciting news about my books, and you can unsubscribe any time you want. And if you would like to get involved in a wider conversation about my books, please review *Sisters under the Rising Sun* on Amazon, on GoodReads, on any other e-store, your own blog and socials, or talk about it with friends, family and reading groups. Sharing your thoughts helps other readers, and I always enjoy hearing what others experience from my writing.

Many thanks again for reading *Sisters under the Rising Sun*. I hope, if you haven't already, you might also like to read *The Tattooist of Auschwitz*, *Cilka's Journey*, *Three Sisters* and find out about the inspiration behind the books through a series of tales of the remarkable people I've meet, the incredible stories they've shared with me, and the lessons they hold for us all in *Stories of Hope*.

Love,
Heather

READING GROUP QUESTIONS

- Sisterhood is a prevailing theme throughout the book. Why is it so important? Do you think it helps the women survive in the camp?

- Why is music so important for the women in the camp? How does it help the women survive?

- Why do you think Mrs Hinch keeps her real name hidden for so long?

- In what ways does Nesta inspire and give hope to the other women in the camp? Why is this so important?

- How do Norah/Mrs Hinch put themselves at risk to help the other girls in the camp?

- How important is June's relationship with Ena and Nora, who act as her surrogate mothers? Is it more valuable/important than June's relationship with her own mother, who has died?

- How are the women in the camp able to prevail and keep hope in the face of so much misery?

- How far is Ah Fat complicit in the Japanese Soldiers and Captain Seki? Is he just doing his job?

- At the end of the novel, an Australian Soldier mentions the devastation caused by the atomic bomb in Hiroshima. Was the use of this atomic weapon justified? Was the loss of life fair if it resulted in the freedom of the nurses?

- Why do you think the local policemen and the Japanese army's treatment of the women of the camp differ so greatly?
- Nesta and the other nurses put their duty to serve the women in the camp ahead of their own welfare. Why do you think their service is so important to them?

The Auschwitz Trilogy

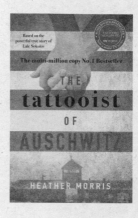

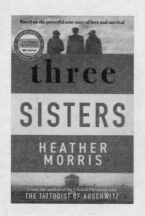

HEART-BREAKING

Tales of love, survival and strength amidst the horrors of Auschwitz

INSPIRATIONAL

The very best of humanity in the very worst of circumstances

UNFORGETTABLE

Their stories will stay with you long after you've turned the final pages

LIFE-AFFIRMING

Read the books of a century...
AVAILABLE NOW

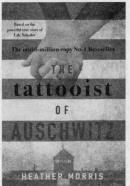

Read on for an extract from *The Tattooist of Auschwitz*

It has been raining for days, but this morning the sun threatens to shine a little light on the bleak Birkenau compound as Lale and Pepan prepare their work area. They have two tables, bottles of ink, plenty of needles.

'Get ready, Lale, here they come.'

Lale looks up and is stunned at the sight of dozens of young women being escorted their way. He knew there were girls in Auschwitz but not here, not in Birkenau, this hell of hells.

'Something a bit different today, Lale – they've moved some girls from Auschwitz to here and some of them need their numbers redone.'

'What?'

'Their numbers, they were made with a stamp that was inefficient. We need to do them properly. No time to admire them, Lale – just do your job.'

'I can't.'

'Do your job, Lale. Don't say a word to any of them. Don't do anything stupid.'

The row of young girls snakes back beyond his vision.

'I can't do this. Please, Pepan, we can't do this.'

'Yes, you can, Lale. You must. If you don't, someone else will, and my saving you will have been for nothing. Just do the job, Lale.' Pepan holds Lale's stare. Dread settles deep in Lale's bones. Pepan is right. He either follows the rules or risks death.

Lale starts 'the job'. He tries not to look up. He reaches out to take the piece of paper being handed to him. He must transfer the numbers onto the girl who holds it. There is already a number there, but it has faded. He pushes the needle into her left arm, making a 4, trying to be gentle. Blood oozes. But the needle hasn't gone deep enough and he has to trace the number again. She doesn't flinch at the pain Lale knows he's inflicting. *They've been warned – say nothing, do nothing.* He wipes away the blood and rubs green ink into the wound.

'Hurry up!' Pepan whispers.

Lale is taking too long. Tattooing the arms of men is one thing. Defiling the bodies of young girls is horrifying. Glancing up, Lale sees a man in a white coat slowly walking up the row of girls. Every now and then the man stops to inspect the face and body of a terrified young woman. Eventually he reaches Lale. While Lale holds the arm of the girl in front of him as gently as he can, the man takes her face in his hand and turns it roughly this way and that. Lale looks up into the frightened eyes. Her lips move in readiness to speak. He squeezes her arm tightly to stop her. She looks at him and he mouths, '*Shh.*' The man in the white coat releases her face and walks away.

'Well done,' he whispers as he sets about tattooing the remaining three digits – 5 6 2. When he has finished, he holds on to her arm for a moment longer than necessary, looking again into her eyes. He forces a small smile. She returns a smaller one. Her eyes, however, dance before him. Looking into them, his heart seems simultaneously to stop and begin beating for the first time, pounding, threatening to burst out of his chest. He looks down at the ground and it sways beneath him. Another piece of paper is thrust at him.

'Hurry up, Lale!' Pepan whispers urgently.

When he looks up again she is gone.

Several weeks later Lale reports for work as usual. His table and equipment are already laid out and he looks around anxiously for Pepan. Lots of men are heading his way. He is startled by the approach of Oberscharführer Houstek, accompanied by a young SS officer. Lale bows his head and remembers Pepan's words: 'Do not underestimate him.'

'You will be working alone today,' Houstek mumbles.

As Houstek turns to walk away, Lale asks quietly, 'Where is Pepan?'

Houstek stops, turns and glares back at him. Lale's heart skips a beat.

'You are the Tätowierer now.' Houstek turns to the SS officer. 'And you are responsible for him.'

As Houstek walks away, the SS officer puts his rifle to his shoulder and points it at Lale. Lale returns his stare, looking into the black eyes of a scrawny kid wearing a cruel smirk. Eventually Lale drops his gaze. *Pepan, you said this job might help save my life. But what has happened to you?*

'It seems my fate is in your hands,' snarls the officer. 'What do you think about that?'

'I'll try not to let you down.'

'Try? You'll do better than try. You *will not* let me down.'

'Yes, sir.'

'What block are you in?'

'Number seven.'

'When you're finished here, I'll show you to your room in one of the new blocks. You'll stay there from now on.'

'I'm happy in my block, sir.'

'Don't be stupid. You'll need protection now that you're the Tätowierer. You now work for the Political Wing of the SS – shit, maybe *I* should be scared of you.' There is the smirk again.

Having survived this round of questioning, Lale pushes his luck.

'The process will go much faster, you know, if I have an assistant.'

The SS officer takes a step closer to Lale, looking him up and down with contempt.

'What?'

'If you get someone to help me, the process will go faster and your boss will be happy.'

As if instructed by Houstek, the officer turns away and walks down the line of young men waiting to be numbered, all of whom, bar one, have their heads bowed. Lale fears for the one staring back at the officer and is surprised when he is dragged by the arm and marched up to Lale.

'Your assistant. Do his number first.'

Lale takes the piece of paper from the young man and quickly tattoos his arm.

'What's your name?' he asks.

'Leon.'

'Leon, I am Lale, the Tätowierer,' he says, his voice firm like Pepan's. 'Now, stand beside me and watch what I'm doing. Starting tomorrow, you will work for me as my assistant. It might just save your life.'

Auschwitz-Birkenau Concentration Camp,
February 1945

Cilka has been sitting in the block, as close as she can get to the one stove that provides heat. She knows she has already drawn attention. The other able-bodied women, her friends included, were forcibly marched out of the camp by the SS weeks ago. The remaining prisoners are skeletal, diseased, or they are children. And then there is Cilka. They were all meant to be shot, but in their haste to get away themselves, the Nazis abandoned them all to fate.

The soldiers have been joined by other officials – counter-intelligence agents, Cilka has heard, though she's not sure what that means – to manage a situation the average soldier has no training for. The Soviet agency is tasked with keeping law and order, particularly as it relates to any threat to the Soviet State. Their role, she's been told by the soldiers, is to question every prisoner to determine their status as it relates to their imprisonment, in particular if they collaborated or worked with the Nazis. The retreating German Army are considered enemies of the State of the Soviet Union and anyone who could be connected to them is, by default, an enemy of the Soviet Union.

A soldier enters the block. 'Come with me,' he says, pointing to Cilka. At the same time, a hand clutches her right arm, dragging her to her feet. Several weeks have passed and seeing others being taken away to be questioned has become part of the routine of the block. To Cilka it is just 'her turn'. She is eighteen years old and she just has to hope they can see that she had no choice but to do what she did in order to survive. No choice, other than death. She can only hope that she will soon be able to return to her home in Czechoslovakia, find a way forward.

As she's taken into the building the Soviet Army are using as their headquarters, Cilka attempts a smile at the four men who sit across the room from her. They are here to punish her evil captors, not her. This is a good time; there will be no more loss. Her smile is not returned. She notices their uniforms are slightly different to those of the soldiers outside. Blue epaulettes sit on top of their shoulders, their hats, placed on the table in front of them, have the same shade of blue ribbon with a red stripe.

One of them does eventually smile at her and speaks in a gentle voice.

'Would you tell us your name?'

'Cecilia Klein.'

'Where are you from, Cecilia? Your country and town.'

'I'm from Bardejov in Czechoslovakia.'

'What is the date of your birth?'

'The seventeenth of March, 1926.'

'How long have you been here?'

'I came here on the twenty-third of April in 1942, just after I turned sixteen.'

The agent pauses, studies her.

'That was a long time ago.'

'An eternity in here.'

'What have you been doing here since April 1942?'

'Staying alive.'

'Yes, but how did you do that?' He tilts his head at her. 'You look like you haven't starved.'

Cilka doesn't answer, but her hand goes to her hair, which she hacked off herself weeks ago, after her friends were marched from the camp.

'Did you work?'

'I worked at staying alive.'

The four men exchange looks. One of them picks up a piece of paper and pretends to read it before speaking.

'We have a report on you, Cecilia Klein. It says that you in fact stayed alive by prostituting yourself to the enemy.'

Cilka says nothing, swallows hard, looks from one man to the next, trying to fathom what they are saying, what they expect her to say in return.

Another speaks. 'It's a simple question. Did you fuck the Nazis?'

'They were my enemy. I was a prisoner here.'

'But did you fuck the Nazis? We're told you did.'

'Like many others here, I was forced to do whatever I was told by those who imprisoned me.'

The first agent stands. 'Cecilia Klein, we will be sending you to Kraków and then determining your fate from there.' He refuses, now, to look at her.

'No,' Cilka says, standing. This can't be happening. 'You can't do this to me! I am a prisoner here.'

One of the men who hasn't spoken before quietly asks, 'Do you speak German?'

'Yes, some. I've been in here three years.'

'And you speak many other languages, we have heard, and yet you are Czechoslovakian.'

Cilka doesn't protest, frowning, not understanding the significance. She had been taught languages at school, picked others up by being in here.

The men all exchange looks.

'Speaking other languages would have us believe you are a spy, here to report back to whoever will buy your information. This will be investigated in Kraków.'

'You can expect a long sentence of hard labour,' the original officer says.

It takes Cilka a moment to react, and then she is grabbed by the arm by the soldier who brought her into the room, dragged away, screaming her innocence.

'I was forced, I was raped! No! Please.'

But the soldiers do not react; they do not seem to hear. They are moving on to the next person.

Montelupich Prison, Kraków, July 1945

Cilka crouches in the corner of a damp, stinking cell. She struggles to register time passing. Days, weeks, months. She does not make conversation with the women around her. Anyone overheard speaking by the guards is taken out and brought back with bruises and torn clothing. Stay quiet, stay small, she tells herself, until you know what is happening, and what the right things are to say or do. She has torn off a section of her dress to tie around her nose and mouth in an attempt to minimise the stench of human waste, damp and decay.

One day, they take her out of the cell. Faint from hunger and exhausted by the effort of vigilance, the figures of the guards and the wall and floors all seem immaterial, as in a dream. She stands in line behind other prisoners in a corridor, slowly moving towards a door. She can lean, momentarily, against a warm, dry wall. They keep the corridors heated, for the guards, but not the cells themselves. And though the weather outside must be mild by now, the prison seems to trap cold from the night and hold on to it through the whole next day.

When it is Cilka's turn, she enters a room where an officer sits behind a desk, his face bathed in greenish light from a single lamp. The officers by the door indicate she should go over to the desk.

The officer looks down at his piece of paper.

'Cecilia Klein?'

She glances around. She is alone in the room with three burly men. 'Yes?'

He looks down again and reads from the paper. 'You are convicted of working with the enemy, as a prostitute and additionally as a spy. You are sentenced to fifteen years' hard labour.' He signs the piece of paper. 'You sign this to say you have understood.'

Cilka has understood all of the officer's words. He has been speaking in German, rather than Russian. Is it a trick, then? she thinks. She feels the eyes of the men at the door. She knows she has to do something. It seems she has no choice but to do the only thing in front of her.

He flips the piece of paper and points to a dotted line. The letters above it are in Cyrillic – Russian script. Again, as she has experienced over and over in her young life, she finds herself with two choices: one, the narrow path opening up in front of her; the other, death.

The officer hands her the pen, and then looks towards the door, bored, waiting for the next person in line – just doing his job.

With a shaking hand, Cilka signs the piece of paper.

It is only when she's taken from the prison and pushed onto a truck that she realises winter has gone, spring never existed, and it is summer. While the warmth of the sun is a balm to her chilled body, her still-alive body, the glare of it hurts her eyes. Before she has a chance to adjust, the truck slams to a stop. There, in front of her, is another train carriage, on a cattle train painted red.